"*It's Elementary* ....y ...y..................... With the intrigue and drama of *Big Little Lies* and the warmth and humor of *Abbott Elementary*, Elise Bryant's first foray into the genre is a delight. A perfect next read for anyone looking for a charming cast, clever writing, and a hint of romance alongside their whodunit."

—Emily Henry, *New York Times* bestselling author of *Funny Story*

"Sassy and spirited, Elise Bryant's *It's Elementary* is the perfect puzzle to unravel under the covers. This cozy mystery isn't just about finding out who did it—it's about finding yourself along the way."

—Christina Lauren, *New York Times* bestselling author of *The True Love Experiment*

"A delightful mash-up of PTA wars, adorable children, a hot school psychologist, and the eminently winning Mavis Miller. . . . In Bryant's fiction, just as in the real world, the smallest conflicts can cause the most damage."

—*The New York Times*

"Mavis's first-person-present narration evinces a razor-sharp wit, complementing the clever, twist-riddled plot of YA author Bryant's effervescent adult debut. Myriad mysteries and an enchanting will-they-or-won't-they romance work in tandem to maintain tension throughout, while boldly drawn characters help spotlight issues such as racism, gentrification, and the devaluation of female labor. . . . A smart, funny novel that's certain to make a splash." —*Kirkus Reviews* (starred review)

THE GAME
IS AFOOT

ELISE
BRYANT

BERKLEY
New York

BERKLEY
An imprint of Penguin Random House LLC
1745 Broadway, New York, NY 10019
penguinrandomhouse.com

Book design by George Towne

Library of Congress Cataloging-in-Publication Data

Names: Bryant, Elise (Elise M.), author.
Title: The game is afoot / Elise Bryant.
Description: First edition. | New York: Berkley, 2025.
Identifiers: LCCN 2024049561 (print) | LCCN 2024049562 (ebook) |
ISBN 9780593640807 (trade paperback) | ISBN 9780593640814 (ebook)
Subjects: LCGFT: Detective and mystery fiction. | Humorous fiction. |
Romance fiction. | Novels.
Classification: LCC PS3602.R9474 G36 2025 (print) |
LCC PS3602.R9474 (ebook) | DDC 813/.6—dc23/eng/20241021
LC record available at https://lccn.loc.gov/2024049561
LC ebook record available at https://lccn.loc.gov/2024049562

First Edition: July 2025

Printed in the United States of America
1st Printing

The authorized representative in the EU for product safety and compliance is
Penguin Random House Ireland, Morrison Chambers, 32 Nassau Street,
Dublin D02 YH68, Ireland, https://eu-contact.penguin.ie.

For my therapist

THE GAME IS AFOOT

ONE

PEARL AND I STARE AT OUR REFLECTIONS IN THE SMUDGED, toothpaste-splattered bathroom mirror that I really should clean one of these days.

"You've got this."

"I've got this."

"You are beautiful and wonderful and special."

"I am beautiful and wonderful and special."

"You can do hard things!"

"I can do hard things!"

"Or you can at least do, um . . . medium things. I'm pretty sure you can do those."

"Excuse me?"

"I'm just being realistic, Mommy. No offense."

My jaw drops and my eyes go wide. "Pearl!"

But she just smirks, arms crossed over her unicorn-printed sweatshirt, all *I said what I said*. I try to give her a look right back, because I'm the one who taught her everything she knows about looks, but it's almost immediately undermined by a laugh that bubbles up all on its own. This isn't the pep talk *I* would have given myself, but maybe it's the one I deserve.

"I can do medium things," I repeat finally, and Pearl nods in approval. She leans closer to the mirror, her eyebrows furrowing into a fierce stare.

"You are going to get a raise."

"I am going to get a raise."

"And if that Rose lady doesn't give you the raise, then you're going to stomp on her foot and run out the door because she's a meanie-head and you don't work for meanie-heads!"

I shoot her a side-eye at that, and she smiles her sweet one-dimpled smile, like she said I should hold my boss Rose's hand and go skipping under a rainbow in a field of flowers.

"I don't know about all that, Pearl."

She lets out a long, weary sigh that would be right at home at a Sunday service and gently pats my shoulder. "You just have to believe in yourself, Mommy."

She says it with the confidence of an *almost*-eight-year-old—her birthday is in a little over a week. It's the same confidence that gave her the audacity to clear her throat and correct the urgent care doctor last month when he called her seven and *not* almost eight. And then, after he prescribed her antibiotics for her ear infection and asked us if we had any more questions, her only one was whether or not he updated her chart with almost eight, *not* seven, so he wouldn't make the same mistake again.

That kinda confidence.

I wish I could bottle up that confidence and spray myself down, like a middle schooler who just discovered Axe body spray, before my annual performance review with Rose today. It's not my first time around the performance review block. I started working at Project Window, a teen mentoring nonprofit, just a few months after Pearl was born, so my time there is *almost* eight, too. And I've done this whole song and dance so many times that I could recite Rose's long, gushing love bomb of a speech about how I'm indispensable to the organization and how they're so lucky to have me. I could probably time it down to the millisecond when her eyes will start welling with tears, to emphasize that her gratitude is *so* authentic, *so* real, that it just overwhelms her with emotion. (Even though she must have those things on lease, with how quickly she trots them out and then puts them back away.) I could also call the exact moment when those same eyes, suddenly dry, will begin to drift to the door behind me as I'm making my case for a promotion, searching for any excuse to hit the emergency eject button and launch herself right on out of this conversation.

And I already know what Rose's excuses will be, because I hear them in the middle of the night when I'm staring at the ceiling and questioning all my life choices. "I would pay you a million dollars if I could, but that's the nonprofit life!" And: "Knowing you're changing the world is its own kind of compensation, isn't it?"

So, yeah. I shouldn't be nervous, because I know exactly what's coming for me today. But I'm hoping to switch it up this year—with bathroom mirror pep talks from my almost-eight-year-old and a sense of unending possibility that's seeming more and more delusional as 9:00 a.m. approaches.

God, maybe I *should* just stomp on Rose's foot and be done with it.

I can tell Pearl is thinking the same thing. She squints her dark brown eyes at the mirror, wiggly fingers pressed into a steeple. But before she can further tempt me into choosing violence, there's a clatter of something falling down in the living room, and then the clicking of our puppy's nails across the hardwood floor. That's the most notice Polly, our Shar-Pei–pit bull mix, will give us when someone's at the door. She's the worst guard dog. She only barks at old people and babies. Well, except for one other time, which was the *most* inconvenient time . . .

"Mavis? Pearl? Y'all all right in there?" Yeah, definitely not an old person or a baby.

Pearl's face quickly transforms from seeking vengeance to unbridled joy as she leaps off the step stool and sprints out of the bathroom.

"Daddy!"

I follow after her with considerably less joy. My thoughts have transformed from *Am I wasting my life away at a job that's never going to see my true worth?* to *Why is this man just letting himself into our house?* He has a key, but that key is for emergencies. And taking Pearl to school on his regularly scheduled morning when we're not even late—hell, we're *early*, thanks to this new routine I've got us on—that's not an emergency.

But I fix my face into something neutral because it's still so new for Pearl, seeing us interact with each other almost every day, and *I'm* not going to be the reason why there's tension.

"We're fine, Corey!" I call as I grab my blazer off my bed. "Just a little startled with the front door opening like that. No warning from the doorbell . . . or even one knock."

Okay, well, I'm not immune to just a pinch of petty. It's basically my right after years of solo parenting while he got to travel the world, putting his work first.

As I turn the corner, though, slipping on a couple of gold bangles, my eyes lock on that one-dimpled smile, identical to Pearl's. Polly runs around him in circles like this is the best day of her life and Pearl has launched herself onto his side, her striped-socked feet dangling off the ground, but Corey's flashing that smile right at me, his eyebrow playfully arched.

"Now imagine how startled you'd be if it wasn't me but some axe murderer off the street walking on in here."

"Axe murderer?" Pearl asks, an edge of worry in her voice. Which makes sense—axe murderers aren't some far-off scare when only a few months ago, your friends' mom locked you in a room to escape kidnapping and assault charges.

I arch my eyebrow right back at him and let out a long, weary sigh to rival Pearl's for good measure. But when he holds up his hands in apology, my cheeks instantly burn with embarrassment.

In one hand is a brown wicker basket with shiny lemons and something green peeking over the top—probably the latest bounty from his new apartment complex's community garden. But it's what's in his other hand that makes me want to dig a hole right here in the floor and fling myself into oblivion. It's my keys, with a black fob for my Prius and a keychain Pearl made me for Christmas that says "Mom of the Year" in sparkly beads. I swear the words are taunting me as they dangle back and forth from Corey's fingers.

"Did you know your keys were in the door?" he asks, reaching out to hand them to me.

"Uh, yeah. Of course." I mumble as I snatch them back. "I was just . . . getting them ready to go."

"Getting your keys . . . ready to go?" He flashes another infuriating dimple that makes me want to ban all dimples even though Pearl's is up there on my list of things that make life worth living.

"Yeah, Mommy is so silly! She does that all the time." Pearl's feet are back on the ground, and she starts digging around in Corey's basket. "She's always like, where are my keys? I can't find my keys! And then me and Papa have to find them in the door, and then we're late to school. But it's okay because Ms. Lilliam in the office likes her now. Hey, this smells good!" She holds up a big bunch of fresh mint, smiling wide, and I take back what I said about her dimple. All dimples are out to get me apparently.

Corey laughs, high and hearty, and I roll my eyes at both of them. For the record, I have a *lot* of things in my hands when I'm walking in at the end of the day—my bag and my laptop and this giant water bottle because we're all supposed to care about drinking water now—so sometimes I just don't have the physical capability to also get my keys. It's not my fault my hands are small. And anyway, our neighborhood is safe—Ms. Joyce across the street would come hollering from her perch at the window and probably try to take down the intruder herself if anyone *actually* tried to break in.

"Plus, she is already thinking about a lot," Pearl continues, and I almost pump my fist and shout out "Yeah!" But I'm trying to look like a responsible, non-petty adult. "She's asking for a raise today, and also she might have to fight that lady Rose."

"Oh yeah?" Corey says. "Rose trying to square up?"

"*No one* will be fighting." I slip on my flats by the front door so we can move this morning along before Pearl tells her father how I let her have ice cream for dinner last weekend. Or what word I muttered when that Kia Sorento cut me off on the 405.

Corey, thankfully, gets the message. "Is it okay if I leave my car here while we walk?"

Pearl crosses her arms and looks him up and down, like *They really just let everyone parent these days, don't they?* At least with him back in Beachwood full-time, someone other than me is getting that look regularly.

"Are you sure we have time for that?" she asks, and Corey throws his head back in another raspy chuckle. "It's less than a mile, my Pearl girl. And school doesn't start for another thirty minutes."

Pearl looks to me to confirm this, and I nod, begrudgingly. We haven't ever walked, me and Pearl, but technically, in so-perfect-they-are-basically-unrealistic conditions, it's possible. Even with my new routine, though, our mornings are never that perfect.

"It's a good way to start your day, with fresh air and sunshine," Corey says. "My therapist recommended it, and it's a lot easier than everything else he has me doing, that's for sure. Here, you gotta smell these, too, baby girl. I picked them for y'all this morning."

He pulls a lemon out of the basket and scratches the rind, holding it up to Pearl's nose. They both breathe in deeply, eyelids fluttering closed. It's such a quiet, special daddy-daughter moment that I'm tempted to snap a picture with my phone, but my mind is still stuck on the whole "my therapist" part. I mean, it's not the first time he's brought the guy up. He talks about therapy now like it's no big deal. Which, I know, I *know*—it isn't. But he didn't grow up thinking that, just like me. You only went to therapy if there was something really wrong with you. If you were working a steady job, doing what you needed to do—you didn't need *therapy*. And if you did, you certainly didn't talk about it.

But ever since he put his touring career on hold and moved back to Beachwood to be here for Pearl, Corey all of a sudden is someone who casually talks about therapy and starts his day with sunshine and stops to smell the lemons. I know he's not doing the work he wants to do—he's had to transition to mostly studio drumming instead of playing live music like he's always loved. But still, he just seems so—so . . . *content* all the time. Like he's got that elusive *balance* thing figured out.

And I'm . . . I don't know. Jealous?

Because how is he so good at that?!

That was my plan last year, after everything went so bonkers and I ended up getting sucked into the dark, dangerous world of the PTA and becoming an amateur detective for a few weeks. I was going to rest. I was going to take care of myself, or "practice self-care" as all the woo-woo books and Instagram posts refer to it. I was burned out and had no choice.

And don't get me wrong, I've tried! I've perused the afore-mentioned woo-woo books and Instagram posts. I bought green juice. I didn't know it would go bad so fast and had to throw it out, but I *bought* it. And I got a ten-day streak on my meditation app last month. I may have fallen asleep a few of those days and let Tanya keep talking over my snores, but see? Rest!

It's all just . . . a little harder than I thought. Which is really a scam if you think about it. Why is taking care of yourself so much *labor*?

I tried to put on my oxygen mask first, but turns out the strap was all twisted and maybe I should try and gobble a few pretzels first because who knows if they'll even be serving food later with all these airline budget cuts?

Anyway, it'll all be better once I finally, finally get this pro-motion. I've had to focus on that, had to put my head down and work, because with Corey here and present as a co-parent, *not* doing that would just be wasteful. Once I get it, though, I can stop putting so much of my mental energy toward daily existen-tial crises and have more time to do . . . *whatever* it is I need to do so my heart doesn't beat so fast all the time. And yes, that goalpost for when I can finally rest is constantly moving, but this time, *for real* this time, once I hit it, I will garden and walk and actually do something just for myself like paint my nails or get my eyebrows done because these things are out of control, and not in the cute Gen Z way, but in the way that'll have Gen Z making Bigfoot truther videos on TikTok. I will finally be able to breathe. Because why is it so hard to breathe?!

"Um, Mommy? You're in the red zone," Pearl says, sticking her face close to mine. I can see the eye boogers I missed when I washed her face. "Jack says when you're in the red zone, you should squeeze a squishy ball or do a calming dance or drink a glass of water."

"I have been drinking *so* much water. I'm not convinced humans are supposed to drink this much water. Like, is this a conspiracy between the water bottle companies and . . . I don't know—Big Water? Making us drink all this water?"

"Big Water?" Corey laughs.

"Also, you're supposed to take deep breaths. Jack says to take deep belly breaths to get yourself back in the green zone." Pearl demonstrates this, eyes wide to make sure I'm paying attention, but instead of getting closer to the green zone, I just move even farther in the red. Crimson. Maroon. Because after learning about these zones at school as part of the new social-emotional education initiative, Pearl's been diagnosing my colors constantly. When we were on our third chapter of Percy Jackson before bedtime and I was dozing off (blue). When I caught her trying to lure a squirrel in the back door because he looked lonely (yellow). And let me tell you, when you're trying to stop your daughter from potentially contracting rabies, it's real annoying to be told what color you are (red). The school psychologist didn't seem to take that into consideration when he was enlisting the whole second grade into his color zone police force.

"Remember, you're supposed to call him Mr. Cohen, baby girl."

"I know, but it's soooo hard to call him Mr. Cohen when he's at our house all the time, and I *can* call him Jack then. Also, he doesn't even care, I don't think, because he barely even says anything when I call him Jack at school. And he thinks you should take deep breaths, too."

Yeah, that school psychologist spreading the annoying color gospel is also my boyfriend of a few months. And it's a good thing he's cute (and incredibly kind and supportive and in possession of green reading glasses that make my stomach do somersaults when he puts them on) because what do you mean *he thinks I should take deep breaths, too*?

My eyes dart to Corey because that's another thing that's new. Not Corey and I being divorced—that was finalized a long time ago—but him being around when I'm dating someone else. Me dating at all, actually.

But he's kneeling on the ground, his face hidden from me, as he scratches behind Polly's ears.

"I need to give you some love, don't I, Polly Olly Oxen Free? Because you've been waiting so patiently, haven't you, girl?"

She wags her tail and squirms her whole body in appreciation, and Pearl drops down, too, to kiss the top of her head.

"Ewww, ewwww! What's that? My knee is wet!"

"Whoops, it looks like she peed a little. I guess she was excited to see me. You got a change of clothes, Pearl girl?"

Something tells me I'm about to experience the whole damn rainbow of zones by the end of this day.

TWO

I'M IN THE PUCE ZONE WHEN I GO TO PICK UP PEARL FROM her after-school theater class.

Or whatever color is uglier than puce.

Dark mustard.

Beige.

Because Rose went off script in my performance review.

I was prepared for the tears. I was prepared for the love bombing and gaslighting—or *fawning for five minutes over my clearance blazer from Old Navy* and *taking just a moment to look at things through another lens*. I was prepared for her to blame Project Window's shoestring budget, even though they somehow found the funds to hire a middle manager last fall.

What I wasn't prepared for was her bringing up my reward money.

God, even hours later, sitting in my car instead of across from Rose and her rancid-smelling mason jar of kombucha, my stomach is still churning with rage and regret.

"I'm so glad you got all that money from that principal at Pearl's school, Mavis. It's so hard to live this nonprofit life at times. You know that *none* of us are paid what we deserve. But I mean, how fortunate that you were set up like that! That you don't have to worry!"

I should have explained I still have plenty to worry about. I should have told her that, actually, my finances outside of my salary are none of her business, thank you very much. What *is* your business is the labor that I've given this company for almost eight years, which you've exploited as you sit high up on the perch of your moral high ground, trusting that the importance of our mission will keep me in line. And hey, if you want to talk about how *none* of us are paid what we deserve, then okay, yeah, let's talk about your Tesla and your Goop meal delivery and what salary you're bringing home to deserve all that.

But instead I sat there blinking at her like I was a robot who just got rebooted, my default code-switching, nice-accommodating-Black-person programming taking over.

"I *so* wish we were able to give you a salary increase this year, and Nelson here can vouch for just how much we tried to make it work." Her eyes flicked to Nelson, the aforementioned middle manager, who at least had the decency to look sheepish when he showed up for my performance review, less than five months with Project Window under his belt. "But I truly believe that everything works out the way it's supposed to, and how wonderful that you got that cushion. The universe always provides!" Rose clutched her vaguely ethnic printed scarf around her shoulders and smiled. "And from what I've heard, it provided you with a *lot*!" She did an infuriating little shimmy as she cooed that last word.

Nelson's eyes went wide before wincing, and that's all the confirmation I needed that he's the one who told Rose about the reward money. It makes sense, with how his wife, the school librarian, was wrapped up in the whole sordid drama. I wanted to grab him by the collar of his Death Star–printed button-down and demand an explanation, but again, nonconfrontational, professional robot Mavis was running the show. So I just—*beep boop*—thanked her for her time and stood up to leave.

"And if you *are* looking for any extra ways to practice your leadership skills, I am still searching for someone to run our upcoming series of DEIB courageous conversations. It starts next week because, yay, it's almost February! Happy Black History Month! Your voice and perspective are so valuable to us, Mavis. And there's a *fifty-dollar* stipend!"

That made my are-you-fucking-kidding-me operating system come right back online, which means I had mere seconds before my bitch face loaded, too.

"I think I have the binder with the curriculum here if you're interested." She spun around in her leather chair, digging in the messy cabinet behind her desk. "Oh, wait, actually, it's *two* binders. How fun!"

Her face was excited, like this was an ideal ending to the performance review I'd been anticipating for weeks, like this great opportunity was a consolation prize I should be grateful for. The veins on my knuckles pop out as my grip tightens on the steering wheel now.

Bile yellow. Rust. Goose poop green.

I wonder if Pearl's learned about *those* zones yet.

I jerk the key in the ignition and turn off the car, replacing the blasting Beyoncé with the equally loud rushing of blood in my ears—so loud, I don't even hear the slam of my car door. As I stomp across the grass toward the front gate of Knoll Elementary, my thoughts spiral and swell.

This was supposed to be the goalpost, the finish line. After many disappointments and epiphanies that fizzled out into false starts—like when Nelson swooped in and got the promotion I wanted last September—I was going to make this last push, get everything settled and squared away with work, and then finally have the breathing room to switch my focus to myself. To "practice self-care." To have space to dream beyond survival and what Pearl and I need right now and instead think more about what I want. What makes me happy.

Well, so much for that.

So what do I do now? Do I quit? I feel like I've been asking myself that same question forever now. And I know the answer. I *know* what I need to do. But then why can't I be brave and trust that there's something better out there for me?

I thought "all that money" might be what I needed to finally tell Rose and Project Window peace out, too. That it was the *last* goalpost I needed to reach. But turns out that "cushion" is a lot smaller than I thought and losing its fluffiness *rapidly*. Jack and I split the twenty thousand dollars of reward money from the Smiths 70-30. (He insisted, and I obliged because I *am* the one who found Principal Smith locked up in that wine room and confronted my new-mom-friend-slash-covert-kidnapper, Corinne.) But, like, half of that was gone with taxes. And then there's all the activities I signed Pearl up for because what else is that money for if not to give her everything all the other kids have? Just because I'm trying to do less in my life doesn't mean Pearl should have less than them. After the tuition and uniform for the bougie club soccer program run by an ex-pro player, and the annual registration fee and *another* uniform for Clover Scouts, and then this after-school theater program at Knoll, and all the deposits for summer day camps which are due in *December* for some reason . . . well, *I'm* not having Gwyneth deliver me chia pudding and braised lentils every day, that's for sure.

And oh my god, what the hell is DEI-*B* anyway? How did I miss that they're just slipping a *B* in there now? When did that happen, and what does it stand for? Black person approved? Or no, more likely: bullshit.

"Yoo-hoo!"

The greeting startles me, but doesn't make me feel like I got struck by lightning, which is progress. Trisha Holbrook's sharp dark brown bob glints in the afternoon sun, and I can feel the heat of her fiery blue stare even from across the street.

Exactly one hundred feet across the street.

She's the reason Pearl is even in this theater program. I mean, my girl definitely has a flair for the dramatic, but she's not one of those kids who came out of the womb belting "Seasons of Love." Anabella—her best friend and Trisha's kid—signed up for the class, taught by Knoll's music teacher, Mr. Forest. And Pearl is down for anything that gets her extra time with Anabella (especially because I'm always dodging playdate requests or anything else that means I also have to have extra time with Trisha). I have my suspicions that Anabella doesn't have some deep passion for theater, either, because I've heard that child singing along to the *Frozen* soundtrack in my back seat and she's definitely no Idina Menzel. But knowing Trisha, this is probably all part of the master plan to get Anabella into Stanford that she's been working toward since they cut the umbilical cord—and before *that* even.

"The auditorium is that way." Trisha scowls as she points behind me.

"Oh, I know!" I call back, not stopping. It's best if we keep our interactions quick and cordial.

"Well, you don't look like you *know*," Trisha snaps. "Because you just walked past the front gate, and *everyone* knows the fastest way to the auditorium is through the front gate, not the side gate."

I pause, realizing that she's right. I was too busy replaying my meeting with Rose and spiraling over everything I should have said to pay attention to less important things, like where I'm walking. But I'm not about to admit that to her.

"I was . . . taking the long way."

She scoffs and rolls her eyes, which seems like an overreaction to the fact that I'm walking a few extra steps, but it's probably because I'm the reason she's waiting for Anabella across the street instead of walking into campus and up to the auditorium steps herself. Well, no—*she's* the reason the school has banned her from the premises and taken out a restraining order to enforce the ban. Because *she's* the one who stole thousands of dollars' worth of books just because they might have had—oh, the horror!—diversity in them. But I doubt she sees it that way.

"Have a good one, Trisha!" I make my voice sound extra cheerful and wave at her like I'm on a float as I stroll around the corner and walk in whatever gate I want. I don't turn around, but I can visualize the ripple of angry wrinkles that are probably erupting on her forehead, and it makes me giggle.

"I take it the meeting went well then?"

Jack's familiar citrus and pine scent and the soft touch of his hand on my elbow are almost enough to hold off the frown pulling on my lips. He's wearing the green floral button-down I got him for Hanukkah, the one that matches his eyes, and beaming his crinkly-faced smile that always makes me smile, too. But as I shake my head, answering his question, I can feel my face crumple.

"Oh Mavis, I'm so sorry." He threads his fingers through mine at our side, squeezing my palm. And there's comfort in the simplicity of that. He doesn't tell me that I deserved what I was asking for, doesn't ask what my next steps are. It's unspoken that I don't need that right now, that I'm already a storm of all those questions inside. And man, I really feel like shit, but that's a glimmer of a lining to these clouds. With everything going wrong, and another finish line moved just out of reach again, I have this one thing I know is right.

Jack's eyes flick around us, checking to make sure the coast is clear, and then he wraps me in a tight hug, pressing a quick kiss to my neck.

"I'm going to quit." If I say it out loud, it holds me accountable. Then hopefully I won't put it off for another few months . . . or almost eight years.

"If that's what feels right to you, then I support you." He pulls back, moving his hands to my waist.

"Not yet. I need to write up a new résumé first, and get my references figured out, because who knows what kinda mess Rose will say. And I don't think I even know my LinkedIn password anymore, but I gotta get back on there, maybe tonight, and see who is hiring. Because I can't quit until I have something else lined up, you know, and . . . and—did you tell Pearl I should take deep breaths?"

He was nodding along with my, admittedly, frantically expanding to-do list, but that makes him pause, a guilty grin that really has no business being so charming appearing on his face.

"I didn't . . . *not* tell her that." I laugh and punch his shoulder. "But in my defense, it was more in the spirit of *all* parents taking deep breaths. If that's what they need. Not specifically in reference to your need."

"So you *do* think I have a need then?"

"I mean, don't we all require oxygen at the end of the day?" He shrugs. "And wait, did she tell you about the impression she did of your breathing? Because I really feel like I'm being unfairly sold out here. She had the class laughing straight through my one-two-three-eyes-on-me with what I think is, for the record, an *extremely* exaggerated impression of that huffing thing you do."

"What do you mean, that huffing thing I do!"

He puts his palms up. "Hey, that's all I can tell you. What happens in Making Friends With Big Feelings class stays in Making Friends With Big Feelings class."

"Did you intend for that to sound so cult-y? Because it's leaning more Children of God than Daniel Tiger. Am I about to be interviewed for a podcast?"

"That reminds me, did I tell you that your dad texted me last night about being a guest on his?"

"Oh no. What—"

A baby lets out a loud squawk next to us, followed by a long squeal of displeasure. And while I need to get more information about why my sixty-something father is soliciting guests for his *Law & Order* recap podcast, like, as soon as possible, this is a good reminder that I'm in public at my kid's school, not just giggling with my boyfriend—as much as I want to be.

"Hello, Mavis! Mr. Cohen! How are you both?" The bearer of the baby is Florence Michaelson—mother to Axel, a boy in Pearl's second-grade class. She's wearing a gauzy beige dress with Birkenstock Boston clogs, and her white-blond hair is tucked under a wide-brimmed felt hat. Her daughter is strapped to her chest in one of those fabric wraps that I was always scared to try with Pearl because she was so big and I was sure she would slip right out. And *this* baby is definitely too big to be in one. Though, I forget how old she is because Florence said something ridiculous like 19.564 months, and I had to use all my mental power not to roll my eyes into the back of my head, so I didn't actually retain the information.

"Doing well, Mrs. Michaelson." Jack's hands quickly drop from my waist, and Florence's dark, laminated brows raise.

"Oh, you don't have to do that for me. I just love you two together. We all do!" She reaches forward to squeeze Jack's arm, and her 19.564-month-old daughter smacks her in displeasure. "I also want to thank you for the good work you're doing in the Making Friends With Big Feelings classes. Axel helped us all reach the green zone yesterday, and it made him feel so empowered. I told all of my followers about it last night on my Live, and now they all wish they had a Mr. Cohen at their schools, too. Truly, you're a gift to Knoll."

"I'm happy to hear that. Thank you," Jack says, stepping back to subtly remove himself from her grip. "I need to head to my office now, but I'll see you both later. I hope the kids had fun with Mr. Forest!"

As he waves goodbye, he makes eye contact with me, communicating all the things he can't say with his fangirl here. *We'll figure this out. I'm here for you.* I mouth *cult* at him and smile in delight at the little snort that escapes when he's trying to hold in his laugh.

"He is just so wonderful, isn't he? How lucky you are."

I mumble something that isn't exactly identifiable words, but it seems to appease Florence, who smiles beatifically.

"I'm so anxious to hear how this first day went, aren't you?"

"Yeah. This is Pearl's first time doing something like this." I point toward the auditorium, where a crowd of parents are starting to gather.

"Axel, too. He's extremely selective about who he reveals his full self to, but he's always had music in his soul. He sings us the most beautiful songs before bedtime each night. And he's all self-taught! So now I feel like it's my job as his mama to help him channel his talents and truly connect with others."

The baby reaches up and smacks Florence again. I wonder if she's already getting exhausted, too, after 19.564 months of this bullshit.

Florence is . . . nice. Fine. There's nothing bad I can really say about her without sounding like an asshole myself. She's just so . . . stiff. And smiley. It's like she's constantly aware that every moment is a possible thumbnail photo for the perpetual day-in-the-life video that is her existence. And that's not an exaggeration. She's one of those moms who's documented every second of her kids' lives on Instagram, with saccharine captions like "Making memories!" and "So lucky to be their mama"—and has gained quite a lot of followers doing it. Even now, I can see her fingers twitching as she clutches her phone at her side, getting ready to capture content.

"Yes, um, I hope Pearl also . . . connects."

Florence clutches her hands to her heart, flashing me a look she'd probably pair with a long post about sharing this journey called life with other mamas.

God, I wish I convinced my friends Jasmine and Dyvia to sign their kids up for this theater class, too, because I'm already starting to sweat thinking about the long weeks ahead of me dodging this small talk. Maybe I could just wait in my car until thirty seconds before dismissal and then sprint out, grab Pearl, and go. If I wear sunglasses, they can't catch my eye . . .

Florence reaches forward and squeezes my arm. So I guess that's not just a thing she does to Jack, the gift to Knoll. "Oh, and I wanted to check in with you. Do you need any guidance for snack tomorrow? I know it's your first time."

Florence is also the team mom for that club soccer program I signed Pearl up for—even though Axel is way more interested in picking the tiny white flowers that grow on the field than kicking the ball. Her team mom duties, from what I can tell, seem to consist of sending out surveys about team colors and then choosing what she wanted all along (aquamarine) and policing the snacks families bring each Saturday to make sure they're sugar-, dairy-, gluten-, and fun-free.

"No, I think we're good. Corey is going to take care of it, actually." She winces slightly, and I rush to add, "He knows all about Axel's food sensitivities. And to make sure everything's organic and has GMO . . . or, um, no GMO. Whatever the good one is!"

I'm actually not sure he knows all this. Because the extent of our conversation was: "I'll get the snacks." "Okay, cool." But he's probably not shopping until tonight anyway.

The baby in the carrier turns her head around to look at me, like she just realized I was there. "No. No, no!"

Man, I thought we were on the same side here, baby.

"Oh, she's being silly, Marigold. Don't worry," Florence says, stroking Marigold's fuzzy blond head. She smiles at me again—this one would probably accompany a #realtalk caption about the witching hour or wine o'clock. "And I'm so happy to hear this, Mavis, because Hank said he saw Corey at Target buying Capri-Suns and I just knew that couldn't be right."

Damn Corey, being all balanced and on top of everything. But also *why* is this lady's husband spying on Corey in Target like he's some undercover cop doing a sugary drink bust, and *why* did she bring it up to me as a test?

"Make sure he remembers the enrichment bags, too!" Florence chirps. I want to correct her and call them goody bags, if only to see the same horrified face she made last time I called them that, when she was passing out hers and I realized this is apparently an expectation at every single children's soccer game now. Because that's what they are, *goody bags*, even if the junk inside that will inevitably end up cluttering my house is fair trade or made of wood or whatever. But it's probably for the best that the auditorium door creaks open and kids begin to file out.

Pearl runs down the steps and I pull her into a hug. She smells like sweat and tempera paint and peanut butter.

"How was it, baby girl?"

"Fine." She shrugs, and then shoots a glance at Anabella that looks anything but fine. I'm surprised they didn't walk out together—they're usually joined at the hip—but Anabella's long ponytail is already swishing to the front to meet her mom one hundred feet from the school gate. I'm definitely going to need to push more once we're home.

"So, what do you want for dinner?" I ask as we stroll toward my car. "Papa's working on his podcast with Bert, so it's just us. We can order a pizza? Or I can make that lemon pasta again that you liked so much last week."

She wrinkles her nose. I guess she *didn't* like the lemon pasta.

"You told me we could drive through McDonald's on the way to the Clover Scouts meeting and that I could get a hot fudge sundae if I promised not to spill it on my uniform, and I promise! Did you bring my uniform?"

I did not bring her uniform. I didn't even remember that she *had* a Clover Scouts meeting, and now I'm mentally rearranging my whole night . . .

But maybe this is just what I need, actually. There are no dishes with a Happy Meal, and after I drop her off, I can go home and log into LinkedIn, start applying to jobs.

Or no. No! I'm going to self-care. Right now. No more excuses. Because as frustrating as my failed performance review was, maybe it was a wake-up call to stop pushing the goalpost and do what's best for me when I need it, not in some distant, ideal future.

I'm going to take control of my life and stop giving the power

over to people like Rose! I'm going to do one of those yoga videos on YouTube, the ones with the lady and her dog, and not get
winded and turn it off halfway through! I'm going to—

"And also, don't forget you signed up to volunteer."

I'm going to scarf down a cheeseburger in the car and volunteer at the Clover Scouts meeting.

THREE

"SHIT!"

I drop the lavender vest and pull my finger to my mouth, hoping I can stave off the pain. Ironing these badges to the girls' vests seemed like the perfect volunteer shift—no small talk with other parents, no leading an activity and having to pretend it's just peachy when these other people's kids talk over me. But I've already burned my hands three times, and I'm barely halfway through this stack of cloverleaf-shaped badges the girls have earned this month.

"You should watch out. You're already on Claudia's bad side."

The woman who's appeared across the table from me looks like a *Rosemary's Baby*–era Mia Farrow, with a strawberry blonde pixie cut and big doe eyes. So much for the no small talk, but . . .

"Is that the lady in the Clover Scouts Mom T-shirt? The blonde? Because she *has* been giving me the stink eye, right?"

I've felt her glare on the back of my neck since I plugged in the iron. And after a few quick glances to rule out if I was just being oversensitive (which is probably the reason for all the burns), my mind hopped to the natural question that arises when I can't make sense of nonsensical behavior: Is it because I'm Black? There's also a new question joining that one lately, though: Is she a Trisha Truther who's got beef with me because I unseated her queen from the PTA president throne? Either way, I'm just glad I've got confirmation someone else is seeing this. Even if it means more small talk.

"She has. And it's because she always does the badges in odd-number months. Ruth does the even ones. It's been an unspoken thing since the troop formed. *Everyone* knows."

I feel my skin prickle with annoyance. And a little bit of embarrassment . . . which I then feel *even more* embarrassed to be experiencing. I'm not gonna let this lady, *the mother of the Antichrist*, chastise me.

"Well, I was just trying to help," I say with a huff, reorganizing the stack of badges, which don't need reorganizing. I swear in her email the troop leader, Christine, said to sign up for whatever slots we wanted. "Why didn't she say something instead of mad-dogging me? I'm not some, like, badge enthusiast. I would give this to her willingly."

"Because this way she gets to be a victim, and some people feel most comfortable remaining there." Her wide-eyed expression is transformed by a smirk and a raised eyebrow. And I realize: she thinks this is as ridiculous as I do. So, I'll stop thinking of her as Satan's mom, I guess.

As if on cue, Claudia sighs so loudly, I can hear her clear across the room, over the sounds of the girls happily decorating butterfly habitats. "Well, I guess I'll head out then! If I'm not needed! I cleared the whole evening, so I really have no idea what I'll get up to instead!"

Across from me, the woman with a perfectly normal daughter, I'm sure, not a demon at all, nods her head toward Claudia, like *See, I told you.*

I cover up my laugh. "Again, I'd *willingly* take a whole evening to myself. Should I chase after her and beg for forgiveness?" I gesture at the iron, my new nemesis. "It might save me a few more burns."

"Ah, they gave you this old thing instead of the new mini iron they bought just for badges with our cookie money last year."

"So I'm being hazed by the Clover Scouts moms?"

She shrugs. "Pretty much." And then her nose wrinkles with a grin, and I'm hit with a flash of recognition. She looks *so* familiar. I guess it's probably from one of the other meetings when I just dropped Pearl off and dashed.

"Have we met already? I'm Mavis."

"No, I don't think so. My husband's been doing a lot of the drop-off and volunteering. This is my first meeting back after . . . a little break." Her eyes flicker with something heavy, but it's replaced by a bright smile in a blink. "I'm Bethany. Nice to meet you."

She points to a girl sitting at the same table as Pearl with purple glasses and chestnut waves. "That's my daughter, Dakota. She's in third grade at Knoll."

There, that's where I know her from then. We've definitely sat in the auditorium for the same holiday pageant or passed each other at the book fair. She probably knows all about how I unmasked Trisha and found the missing Principal Smith . . .

"She just transferred this semester from Willmore, the private school on the west side? It's been a hard transition, but already knowing so many of her Clover Scouts friends there has really helped her. Now, who's your daughter?"

I'm relieved that she wasn't here for all the drama last fall and this isn't another attempt from a Knoll parent to get me to spill the details. It's almost enough to ease the itchy feeling in the back of my brain. But it's fine. It'll come to me later.

I point. "That's Pearl. She joined the troop in November."

"Oh, what a good name. So precious." Her fingers rise to her lips and she tilts her head like something has just occurred to her. "Hmm. Have you tried pearl powder? It's in the wellness dust I sprinkle on my smoothies every morning. Very effective."

Her dulcet tone is similar to Florence's from earlier, eerily calm even while being slapped in the face by a whole-ass toddler. Bethany's not dressed in that Florence crunchy mama uniform of gauze and Birkenstocks, but I *do* see the telltale Lululemon logo. That's just as much of a warning sign of this type. But before I can make a run for it, she lets out a throaty giggle.

Okay, no, she's *funny*. I think I like her.

Maybe this is a chance for a do-over. Yeah, my last attempt at trying to make a mom friend ended with me getting locked in a bedroom and playing Guess Who? for hours (which wasn't the worst part of the evening, technically, but it felt like it). But I've got to stay open to the possibility again, because things *were* fun with Corinne before they got a little kidnap-y. I'm sure that's what a therapist would say—if I had time to go to a therapist.

"Are you happy in your job?"

Okay, whoa—what? Did I miss a few jumps in this conversation? Because somehow this lady is now reading my mind?

Bethany holds her hands up and laughs again. "Sorry. You're probably thinking 'Hey girl. Hold your horses there!' Just . . . I hope it's not too forward of me to say, but you have that look, of someone who had a hard day at work and is already dreading going back on Monday."

I don't really know what to say to that because it's kind of like when someone tells you that you look tired or asks if you're okay, unprompted. Like, is Bethany calling me ugly? Does she not see I have a hot iron in my hands?

I grab a vest off the stack and press the iron onto another badge so I'm reminded of its intended use.

"I just mean . . . you seem like you could use some self-care—a *life* centered on self-care."

"Thank you, but I'm good. Really."

I'm not, but she doesn't need to know all that. Maybe that pearl dust smoothie comment wasn't a joke after all. She *does* look like someone who could list all the seven whole grains by name.

"Okay, I know I'm being so annoying and I promise I'll zip it in a second, but it's that whole idea of an airplane going down, and the oxygen masks drop. Moms *never* put theirs on first." That makes my hands pause, and the iron lets out a puff of steam that billows between us, making everything look hazy. *Is* this lady in my brain? Because I was just thinking this earlier today . . . and really every day since the fall. I know I need to put that damn thing on before I go putting on everyone else's, but how? And why is it so hard?

"It's what we've been programmed to do," she continues, as if I spoke that all aloud. And lord, maybe I did with how this day is going. "We never give ourselves what we need because good mothers, good women, are selfless. Their joy comes from the needs of others being met." She sighs and shakes her head. "But you can't keep pouring and pouring *and pouring* if your cup is empty. You have to acknowledge what is happening or everyone around you is going to die of thirst. If you get a small tear in your favorite T-shirt, does it help the thing to ignore it? If you keep living life as normal, it's only going to get bigger and bigger, until the shirt is destroyed and unwearable, and your only option is to throw it in the rag pile. No, you have to mend the tear as soon as possible to save that shirt. To *go on*."

Well, that was . . . a whole lotta metaphors. But she's not wrong. And I was telling myself that I need to stop pushing the goalpost and commit to taking care of myself now. She's a little preachy, yeah, especially because we just met. We don't know each other like that. *But* maybe the universe decided preachy and obvious is what I need because I've been ignoring all the other signs. So it dropped her in my lap and got right to business—like, here you go, tired ol' rag! Get it together already!

"I did have the worst day at work," I'm confessing before I can talk myself out of it. "I'm pretty sure I'm going to quit my job—really this time, instead of just saying I'm going to. And then I forgot about Clover Scouts and ate a McDonald's Happy Meal, which my stomach is currently protesting. And then I came here and stole goddamn Claudia's job, even though I'd rather be home doing that lady with the dog's yoga, or really just *watching* that lady with the dog's yoga and drinking a beer."

To her credit, Bethany doesn't make a face at my overshare or, like, back away slowly. Instead she starts nodding emphatically, her whole body joining in the movement.

"I know what I need to do, but I don't know how to make the time, you know?" I laugh, shaking my head. "Self-care is a full-time job."

I was joking, mostly. Being a doctor, like my friend Jasmine, is a full-time job. Teaching middle school, driving an ambulance, cleaning houses . . . *Not* meditating and pretending you like the taste of green juice. But Bethany's eyes widen with sincerity, and her nodding is now only a step away from jogging in place.

"Yes. Yes, you get it. I could just tell. This is actually my area of expertise. I'm a certified self-care coach."

A self-care . . . coach? I didn't realize that was a thing. And certified where exactly? She leans forward slightly, unblinking, as if she wants me to fall right into her wide-eyed gaze. And oh. I know that look. It's the same look Ruth from the PTA gives when she's trying to hawk her essential oils. Or the one Corey's auntie Bernice makes when she's making yet another Mary Kay pitch, desperate to get her leased pink Cadillac. What kinda car would a self-care coach be trying to earn? A teal Subaru?

"Don't worry. I'm not trying to sell you a bunch of overpriced crap that'll just sit in a pile for months and clutter up your house."

I feel my whole body unclench. It's fine. I'm safe. She's just a nice fellow mom worried about my well-being, trying to be my friend.

"It's really more of a lifestyle."

Oh no.

"Me and my team of self-care specialists help our clients develop their own custom self-care rituals through my variety of digital products and in-person self-care seminars. Is that something you'd be interested in? I'd love to share my newest course with you. It's called The Care and Keeping of U—and it's totally free! No obligation! I think you'd really get a lot from it."

Oh no, oh no, *oh no*!

I almost fell for it! But this lady isn't trying to be my friend. This was all an MLM pitch. And I walked right into it, like a mouse strolling into a trap, grateful the humans put out a little charcuterie board for them. God, my judgment is seriously out of whack. First a kidnapper, then a girlboss.

"*The Care and Keeping of You* . . . isn't that the American Girl book about puberty?"

I'm not sure why that's the first thing out of my mouth instead of a definitive "hell no." Must be the nice, accommodating

Black person programming from this morning still hanging around.

"That's *you*. Like *Y-O-U*. This is *U*. Just the letter."

She blinks at me as she smiles brightly, as if that was my only hurdle.

"Um, thanks for the offer, but I'm not really interested in pyramid schemes." I start moving my hands at double time, burns be damned, because I gotta get out of here now.

"Oh, girl, it's not one of those! Those are illegal! And anyway, my compensation plan isn't even shaped like a pyramid. It's more of a—a . . . well, I'm not a geometrist!" She laughs, batting at the air.

"Well, whatever shape it is—"

"I wouldn't even say it was a shape! It's more of a . . . tree." I blink at her, and she takes advantage of the silence to keep going. "And you don't have to worry—this is nothing like those other MLMs. I know exactly what you're thinking of. But we are *not* about the hustle." She holds up her hands in a cross in front of her, like she's warding off a demon. "Balanced With Bethany is about the rest."

Balanced With Bethany? Is this your idea of a joke, universe? Because I don't care what I said I wanted, I need this gift removed from my lap instantly. I am perfectly content being a rag!

"Let's get you in for a personalized self-care consultation and then we'll just see what happens from there," Bethany coos, like this is already a done deal. "I'm in talks to develop a Balanced With Bethany supplement line that will be exclusive to self-care consultants and their clients, so it's really the best time to get in on the ground floor."

I keep my head down, speedily affixing another badge like I'm on some badge-ironing game show. "Yeah, I don't—"

"I know it's scary to take that first step, but that's why you just have to leap. And like you said, you're ready for a change in your career."

Why the hell did I tell her that?

"You can start your own business on your own terms."

Yeah, I'm pretty sure it's *your* business, lady, because you're the one on the top of the pyramid—excuse me, *tree*.

"My self-care consultants see growth almost immediately, especially when they bring in their own self-care consultants downstream from them."

"Down . . . line?" My stack of badges is almost done.

"No, downstream! I think that imagery better reflects the way we really *flow* into each other at Balanced With Bethany. And you know, Mavis, you can really open up a whole new market for us because you bring in a demographic we haven't reached yet."

I put the iron down. "Oh yeah? What do you mean by that?"

I think I know what she means by that.

"Well, I mean . . ." She smiles, tucking a short strand behind her ear. "Madam C. J. Walker started the first MLM."

My eyebrow nearly reaches my hairline. "Now, who brought her into it?" I shake my head. "No, actually, never mind. I don't need to hear any more of . . . *that*." I hold up the stack of finished (or at least, close enough to finished) vests. "I'm gonna pass these back out to the girls."

"Listen, I'm not trying to be pushy." I can tell by the slightly manic edge to her smile that she knows this is her last shot. "I just really feel like it's my duty in this life, my *calling*, to help others when I see they're in need. When they're stuck in that pattern of victimhood." She looks to the door where Claudia left, and I see the beginning of our conversation in a whole new light. This has *all* been a pitch.

"I was just like you," she continues. "I found myself in a really tough spot. And I have full confidence that dedicating myself to practicing self-care is what turned the tide and led me to the life I am supposed to lead."

I don't roll my eyes. But it takes everything in me not to roll my eyes. Like, I'm pretty sure I popped a blood vessel or pulled a muscle not rolling my eyes. Because whatever kind of self-care she's shilling is definitely not the kind I need.

I mean, I'm not sure what it is I need, because almost all of it makes me roll my eyes like this: the oils, the meditation lady who talks like Bane from Batman after sucking on some helium, the sound baths that seem to entail just lying there and pretending you like the way a gong sounds. Except for the yoga lady with the cute dog. I like her. I think she could be my white-lady best friend. I wish I was with her right now.

"Just consider it," Bethany says softly, pressing her business card across the table.

Balanced With Bethany is written in loopy teal script (so, I would have been right about the Subaru), and under her website and socials, it reads, *Guiding you on your self-care journey with the I LUV ME method!*

I am not going to consider it.

LATER, I'VE SECURED PEARL AND HER BUTTERFLY HABITAT (which really ended up being more of a gaudy butterfly McMansion) in the back seat, and I'm trying to figure out if it's considered littering to toss this business card on the lawn. The back says it's 100 percent recycled paper, so it'll just . . . absorb into the grass, right? Recycled is the same as biodegradable . . . I think.

"You should steer clear, Mavis." The urgent voice makes me jump, and the business card falls from my hand onto the asphalt.

I squint in the darkness to see Ruth, the PTA mom and essential oils girlboss, gesturing to me from across the street. Her waving hand is at her hip, as if she's trying to be discreet, and she's illuminated only by the dim, eerie overhead light in her car. Her daughter, Ryleigh, is in the back seat, already deep into a video on her tablet.

"Um . . . excuse me? Did Trisha send you as one of her goons, because she already tried to intimidate me this afternoon, and it's not—"

"Shhh!" Her eyes dart back and forth, looking out for . . . I don't know. Trisha hiding in the bushes? And then she scampers across the street, apparently determining the coast is clear.

I shoot an uneasy glance at Pearl through the window, and all that's missing is the popcorn—she's riveted.

"Not Trisha," Ruth says, arriving in a cloud of patchouli. "*Bethany*. Don't let her try and trap you. Her whole 'self-care business'"—she makes air quotes—"is shady. It didn't go the way she says it did."

"What didn't go . . ." I stop myself because I don't care. I'm not trying to be involved in any drama with these moms. Especially Ruth, who I'm pretty sure gets her entire life force from the parents' Facebook group and gossip at the school gate. "It doesn't even matter, because I told her I'm not interested."

"Good. You have terrible judgment, Mavis, but you actually made the right call there."

"Ooooh-kay, well, good night, Ru—"

"I don't care what she says," she spits out, twisting open a roller bottle that has somehow appeared in her hands. "Bethany's self-care method had nothing to do with her cancer going into remission."

I put my hand on the door handle, ready to flee. But that stops me. "What? Cancer?"

"She had stage four breast cancer. She didn't tell you?" Ruth fixes me with a skeptical look as she aggressively rolls oil on both of her wrists. "She tells everyone. That's her whole sales pitch—and it's not right!"

Bethany had cancer? I replay our entire interaction in my head and some of the comments she made have new meaning—the "little break," the "tough spot." Even her desperation to sell me on her coaching takes on a new meaning if she's only recently in remission. It was probably hard to stay in the traditional workforce when going through an illness so huge and life altering, and maybe this venture brought her a sense of purpose, something to hold on to.

And her daughter, Dakota. My chest gets tight thinking of her. I wasn't even two when my mom died due to the exact same kind of cancer. I still feel the pain of that loss now, but I can't imagine how scary it must have been for her to be old enough to know what's going on, to have to prepare to say goodbye. What a blessing it is for her mom to even *be* at the Clover Scouts meeting. Yeah, it was annoying that she was trying to recruit me for her MLM, but . . . god, I *was* kind of an asshole. I mean, I don't want anything to do with the I LUV ME method, that hasn't changed . . . I just maybe shouldn't have judged her so quickly.

"She never told me her self-care method cured her cancer," I say to Ruth, who's now rolling her concoction on the back of her neck.

Bethany didn't tell me that . . . did she? No, she definitely didn't. I'd remember that.

"Good, because self-care didn't cure her cancer."

"Glad you cleared that up. Now, I really—"

"The essential oils did."

"Oh my GOD, Ruth!"

She throws her hands up. "I know you're close-minded to

natural health solutions." She says that with the same tone as *I know you like to feed Pearl trash off the floor* or *I know you like to set forest fires for fun.* "But I need to set the record straight. She may have left Agape Essentials to start her own thing—totally screwing over her upline, I might add—but that doesn't mean she gets to tell these fairy tales around town."

"Oh, I get it. You're mad she left the—the . . . oil pyramid you recruited her to? So now you don't make any more money off of her?"

"I'm disappointed she abandoned the *thriving essential oils business* I helped her to build from the ground up. But that's not why I'm—"

"Ruth, okay, enough. I'm not interested in hearing any more."

All these alternative lifestyles (extreme self-care, essential oils . . . whatever Florence has going on) feel like grown-ups playing pretend, like how we used to make potions out of grass and flowers and rainwater in the backyard as kids. Which is fine, I guess, if you're having fun. Other women can do what they want. But being caught in the middle of some MLM turf war between a cancer survivor and a PTA soldier, when I just want to shut this whole day off and try again tomorrow, is decidedly not fun.

Ruth looks like she's gearing up for another round of Bethany bashing, but inside my car, Pearl knocks on the window and taps the imaginary watch on her wrist.

"It's close to my bedtime!"

Saved by the almost-eight-year-old. I'm going to let her have a second dessert tonight.

"Okay, well, I better—"

"Just one more thing. We actually have an exclusive special going on at Agape right now for brand-new consultants. So many people think it's not their thing, but Mavis, I really think you have the potential to open up a whole new market for—"

I speedily slip into my car, barely cracking open the door, like I'm fleeing from the zombie apocalypse. It's only as I'm driving away that I realize I left the recycled paper, probably biodegradable, business card abandoned on the street.

Hello Troop 1207 Moms!

We had such a fun meeting learning about the migratory patterns of monarch butterflies and building our beautiful butterfly habitats! Thank you to Claudia, Suzanne, and Ruth for the donations to our butterfly homes! The mini diffusers were ADORABLE 😊

Cookie season is fast approaching! I hope you're as excited as I am!! Please take a moment to complete the survey for our parent cookie meeting if you haven't already. Of course, like all things in Clover Scouts, this venture will be entirely girl-led, and they will determine our troop selling goals and plans for our earnings at our cookie kick-off meeting next month! But we find it's extremely helpful to come to a consensus between moms at this pre-kick-off meeting so we can guide them in the right direction!!

And I have just a few friendly reminders for you:

1. Claire is SO GENEROUS to allow us to use her BEAUTIFUL home, and we want to make sure that we're showing her our gratitude and respect AT ALL TIMES! Thank you in advance for keeping her lawn and her neighborhood litter free!!

2. We appreciate your volunteer work SO MUCH!! We really have THE BEST moms in Troop 1207! 😺 We know it can be difficult to decide where your talents would be most useful, especially if you're new to Clover Scouts, so please reach out if you need help deciding what to volunteer for—or what your husband should do if he's on babysitting duty for the night, LOL! We want to make sure you're given a job where you can be the most successful, so everyone gets a chance to shine 😄

(And please make sure to select at least two volunteer slots on our Sign-Up Genius if you haven't already. Many hands make light work!!)

   Note: If your Insect Helper badge wasn't secured properly, please feel free to bring it to my house this week, and I can help you fix it! I am very busy prepping for cookie season and making costumes for the 4th grade choir concert, but I can always make time for something this important!!

Warmly,
Christine Fountaine
Troop 1207 Leader
Room Mom for Ms. Laguna's Class
Proud Mom of Austin, Harlow, and Olive

floplusbabies2

Hey mamas! 👋 🌼

Can I just be vulnerable with you for a second? This mama life is hard work!!

I truly believe that each of our littles has a unique gift to share with the world, and it's our job to foster those gifts and help to share them with the world! But what do you do when the other adults in their lives, the ones you entrust with their fragile spirits, don't treasure those gifts? 🥺

I've shared on here before what a wonderful school psychologist we have at Axel's school, but unfortunately not every staff member shares his loving-kindness and commitment to recognizing all that Axel has to offer the world. How do I keep my little's light shining when others are just determined to blow it out? Comment a 🤍 below if you can relate!

Anyway, that's what's been heavy on my heart today! Thank you for letting me share—I don't know what I'd do without my circle of mamas ✨ I love you all to the moon and back!!

FOUR

AT 8:42 A.M., BRADY PARK IS ALREADY SO CROWDED THAT we have to park three blocks over, and even then I have to make some risky moves to squeeze my Prius between two minivans.

The place has the energy of Coachella . . . or at least what I think Coachella is like. I don't willingly go places that will require me to use a porta-potty and/or stand for more than ten minutes. But there are devoted fans staking out their spots, an electric anticipation of what's to come, and cheers already filling the air even though the first game of the morning doesn't start until nine thirty. The crowd is a lot shorter, I guess, seeing as most of them haven't yet hit puberty, and instead of a sea of sponsored Revolve clothing, there are soccer uniforms in a rainbow of colors. Still, this is the Coachella of extracurricular activities, and I'm expected to brave it bright and early every Saturday morning.

"Is that your seventh cup of coffee or your . . . infinity-eth?" Pearl asks as we walk across the big field. She's teetering to the right under the weight of her gear bag, which she insisted on carrying herself.

"It's only my third, baby girl."

She raises her eyebrows. "That still seems like too much to me."

Two toddlers in orange jerseys and matching hair bows kick their ball our way, and I just barely dodge getting knocked in the head. *Seems like not enough right now.*

"That's why you couldn't get off the can this morning," my dad says, hoisting our two lawn chairs farther up on his shoulders. "You're messing up your stomach with all that caffeine. One a day, that's all you need! My alarm got me up at five thirty a.m. every day for forty years, and that's all I ever needed! Otherwise you get all . . ." He makes a very helpful swirling motion around his stomach, then flicks his fingers behind him, in case I was uncertain what he meant.

"I'm sorry, can we *not* talk about my bowel movements? Also, you're the reason I couldn't sleep last night and needed all this coffee. You woke up Polly, coming home all late."

"Bowel movements, bowel movements," Pearl repeats, trying it out in her mouth. "That sounds funny!"

"Hey now, Bert coordinated a guest for us to interview last minute. We had to work with her schedule if we wanted her on the show," he explains. "And anyway, that dog may run your life, but she doesn't run mine."

He says that as if I don't see him passing her scraps off his plate every night, insisting she needs just a little taste.

"Oh yeah, Jack mentioned that you asked him to be a guest, too. Since when are you having guests on your podcast? And anyway, Jack doesn't even watch *Law and Order* unless I put it on."

"Well, our focus is shifting slightly—"

"Bowel movements. Bow-wel mooooove-ments."

"What's a bowel movement?" Langston, one of Pearl's

friends, falls in line with us. He's wearing an aquamarine jersey that matches hers.

Pearl shrugs. "I don't know, but my mom has them."

"It's a poop, little man," Jasmine, Langston's mom and my best friend, explains with a loud laugh, and her husband, Leon, joins in. "And what's going on with yours, Mavis? Did you have a weird one? Do you need some advice?"

"Oh my god, no! Can we all stop talking about this?" I mean, I can't be *too* indignant, because I do go to Jasmine for medical advice often. She's an ob-gyn and her husband is a nurse, so between the two of them, I'm usually covered. But not for this. And not so loud in the middle of Brady Park. My bowel movements are *fine*.

"Okay, girl. Suit yourself." She pulls me into a tight hug, filling my nose with her comforting scent of cocoa butter lotion and floral perfume. She's wearing a sweatshirt with *Go Sports!* embroidered on the front and eyeshadow to match the team's jerseys. "Just text me, and I'll help you out," she adds in a whisper. "But please, no pictures."

I groan and play-shove her away, and her eyes dance with mischief.

"Coach Cole said this is going to be a tough one, Elijah," Leon says, clapping my dad's shoulder. "There's an eight-year-old on the other team that looks like he's thirteen, and I hear he keeps diving. Always at the end of the second half, too."

My dad sucks his teeth. "Well, we gotta watch that ref then. Make sure he calls a foul. And has Cole checked that birth certificate?"

They always launch into this soccer strategy talk as soon as they see each other. Leon's the one who suggested we enroll Pearl in the league, and my dad was measuring her feet for cleats before I could even give a definite answer. I could ask what the hell *diving* has to do with soccer when there's no water nearby, but then I'd get a whole lesson on soccer fundamentals followed by a play-by-play through the whole game. And it's just not that serious for me—or Pearl. The most strategy she employs during these games is making sure she's on the bench at the same time as Axel so they can pick flowers for crowns together.

"Hey Jack! Hey Derek!" Jasmine calls, waving to where Jack is sitting with his brother. She turns to me. "Oh, he's so cute, getting here early and saving spots. Do you ask him to do that, or does he keep doing it on his own?"

"He does it on his own."

She puts the back of her hand to her forehead and feigns fainting, and my skin warms like the sun just came out. Jack asked for a copy of Pearl's game schedule, and the next time I was at his place, I saw it up on the refrigerator, right under the lunch menu for Derek's day program. It's still new between us, only a few months now of officially dating, but moves like that make me start dreaming of . . . well, a lot longer.

Jack jumps up, runs to meet us, and quickly slides one of the chairs from my dad's shoulder.

"Hey." He kisses my cheek, scratching me with his salt-and-pepper stubble, and takes my only cargo, my giant water bottle. No more moving the goalpost: *Self-care starts today!* And drinking water is, like, level one of self-care.

"I'm glad you're here," he continues as we follow him back to the side of the field, where he's laid out a blanket and a sweatshirt next to his and Derek's chairs. "There's been a lady hovering behind me, asking if I really need all that space. She went to the restroom, but I think I was maybe two minutes away from her taking me out."

"Who was it?" I ask, looking around. Florence has already

claimed her space, right next to Derek, complete with a lace-covered folding table, leather butterfly chairs, camera tripod, and the quilted team banner that she made herself. She's the only one who cares enough about her placement on the sidelines to fight over it—the rest of the parents from our team are just standing around and chatting while their kids chase each other across the field.

"Her daughter was wearing purple, and I'm pretty sure the Purple Platypuses don't even play until eleven fifteen."

"Is it *platypuses* or *platypi*?" Pearl swoops in between us, throwing her bag to the grass. "Because *platypuses* doesn't sound right."

"*Platypuses*," Derek answers, not looking up from the book of game show trivia he has on his lap. "Because *platypus* does not have Latin roots."

Pearl nods, satisfied. "That makes sense." And she runs off with Langston to join the other Aquamarine Alligators in their game of tag.

"That *is* right!" The slow and overly cheerful voice makes me tense immediately. A lot of people speak that way to Derek because of his Down syndrome, and it's quickly becoming one of the things I hate most in the world.

"Yeah, he knows," I say sharply and turn around, ready to give this lady my best stank face. But it's quickly replaced with a look of horror.

"Heyyyyy girrrrrl!" Bethany—self-care coach and girlboss Bethany—puts her arms out wide to pull me into a hug, and I just let it happen for some reason. "What a fun surprise!"

I catch a raised eyebrow from Jack, and I can feel Jasmine's glare, too, asking *Who is this?* I flash them both wide eyes back. *I'll tell you later.*

"Dakota isn't playing until the next round," Bethany continues, much faster than the way she spoke to Derek, of course. "But I like to get here early and get the best spot!"

So *she's* the one trying to start something with Jack over our saved spots? But as she gestures to her daughter in a purple jersey, huddling with some other girls around an iPad, I remember what I learned last night and hold in my eye roll. *Don't be an asshole, Mavis!*

"I'm so glad I ran into you, because I just couldn't get our conversation out of my mind all night. I know you were hesitant, but have you given any more thought to—"

"Oh, what's that, Dad?" I turn around and pretend to catch my dad's eye, even though he's muttering to himself as he tries to unfold our chairs. "Sorry, I need to help him with that. But so good to see you! Have fun today, Dakota!"

I'm not going to be an asshole, but that doesn't mean I want to give Bethany a chance to pitch me again in the name of Madam C. J. Walker. Because then, despite my best intentions, my asshole-ness might just jump right out!

My dad jerks the chair open before I can even pretend to aid him, and there's a loud clang as it knocks over my giant metal water bottle.

"That thing is as big as a baby, Mavis," he says, shaking his head. "No one needs that much water."

"We're supposed to get thirty-two ounces a day!" Never mind that I was just thinking the same thing yesterday.

"So you *did* get a chance to check out my I LUV ME method," Bethany says, settling her chairs not even a foot behind us, as if someone else is going to try and swoop in after we leave. "The *I* stands for Imbibe those ounces! And really, you should try and get at least sixty-four!"

I blink at her, at a loss for words because 1) I didn't realize I

LUV ME was a goddamn acrostic poem, and 2) am I going to have to keep swerving this lady's pyramid—excuse me, *tree*—scheme for the whole morning?, and finally 3) sixty-four ounces? How is that even possible??

Luckily, Jasmine sees I need an assist and loops her arm through mine, pulling me farther down the field. "Sorry, I need to borrow her for a second."

Jack sits down next to Derek, a knowing smile pulling at his lips. I'm leaving him right in the line of fire, but I think he should be safe. He's not part of Bethany's target demographic.

"Are you wafting some pheromone or something that makes you attract the most annoying women?" Jasmine mimes fanning my armpits. "What is going on?"

I fill Jasmine in on last night's Clover Scouts meeting—Bethany's "business" opportunity and Ruth's whispered warnings in the dark. Her head is falling back in laughter before I've even finished.

"I can't decide if little miss *Ruthie* warning you about her makes this lady a hero or an even worse villain than Ruth?"

"But like Ruth said, she had cancer. And stage four! Coming back from that, the recovery . . . it could make you do some weird things. My mom didn't get the chance to—"

My voice cracks, and Jasmine puts her arm around my shoulders, pulling me in close. I don't have to finish that sentence for her.

"And I feel for her," Jasmine murmurs, rubbing soothing circles on my back. "No mom—no *person*—should have to go through that. But you can be a cancer survivor *and* be a pushy MLM evangelist. One doesn't cross the other out. Especially if she's claiming some miracle cancer cure to shill her online courses."

"For the record, she never actually said that to me. And Ruth claims her oils are what really cured her cancer, so, like . . . consider the source."

"But the I love me method?" Jasmine wrinkles her nose like she smells something funky.

"And *LUV* is spelled with a *U*," I mumble.

Jasmine's face folds into a grimace. "Yeah, *annoying*. There's something they just love about you."

As if summoned, Florence waves to us from behind her iPhone as she slowly pans it across the field, gathering content. I can already picture what it'll look like in her Instagram stories, with a filter to make the sky even bluer and a "Happy Saturday!" GIF.

She's going to have to put some music over it, though, to block out Axel's quickly escalating tantrum.

"I don't want to wear it!" Axel crosses his arms over his white tank top and stomps one of his cleat-clad feet as his dad, Hank, shakes the team jersey in front of him. "No! No, no!"

Hank looks . . . exactly like who you'd expect to be married to Florence. He's wearing jeans cuffed over expensive-looking boots, with a beige Henley shirt and leather bracelets tied to his wrist. His longish brown hair is tucked under a wide-brimmed hat that I'm not convinced isn't the same one Florence was wearing yesterday. Even with the shadow it casts over his scraggly-bearded face, though, I can still see the twitch of his jaw and the bulging vein in his neck.

"Just put the dang thing on already, Axel."

"But—but . . . it doesn't feeeeel like an aquamarine day!"

"It doesn't matter how you feel. Now, it's time to get your head in the game, son, so you can win this thing."

Florence quickly cuts her content session short and dashes between them. She drops to a knee in front of Axel, cupping his face in her hands. The 19.564-month-old in her precarious-looking wrap turns to eye Axel like, *What is your problem, man?*

"I hear you and I see you, my boy. You get to decide what you put on your body. That's so valid."

Hank mutters something and rubs his hand down his face, and Florence waves him away.

"I'm wondering, what—" Marigold slaps Florence, and she quickly takes her out of the carrier, putting her down on the grass. "What do you think is leading to such big feelings about aquamarine this morning?"

I can't hear Axel's response because he's drowned out by Marigold's shrieking cries as Hank throws his hands up in a little adult tantrum of his own and stalks away.

Hank and Florence both seem to have the same end goal. It's unquestioned, an inarguable fact for them, that Axel is a gift to the world—but what they want to ensure is that everyone *knows* he's the best. They go about it in very different ways, though. Florence seems determined to gentle parent that kid right to the presidency, and she has a tight-gripped control on his narrative through her momfluencer account in the meantime. But Hank's approach is much more WWE than gentle, like he's going to piledrive square-peg Axel through the round hole of what *his* definition of the best is.

Like, with this soccer team. Axel is much more invested in constructing his spring/summer collection of daisy chain jewelry. (He gave me a bracelet last week—the craftsmanship was impressive!) But Hank's convinced he's the next . . . well, some famous soccer star that I would name if I actually knew famous soccer stars. Whenever Coach Cole puts Axel on the bench—which, for the record, Axel seems to love as much as Pearl does—Hank is at his side in seconds, arms crossed high at his chest, as he demands an explanation. And it's even worse when Axel is on the field, because then Hank starts pacing with his hands at his hips, yelling out plays like he's the one in charge, getting increasingly agitated as Coach Cole then proceeds to ignore all of those plays. Last week, I swear he was gonna sucker punch Coach Cole in the middle of the end-of-game parent tunnel before Florence expertly pulled him away. I'm getting sweaty already thinking about what's coming today if the tension is starting this early over a *jersey*.

"What's her username?" Jasmine whispers, motioning to Florence. She appears to be singing Axel a song to get the jersey on while Marigold screams at the sky. "I gotta see how she spins this."

"It's like . . . Flo and babies? No, Flo plus babies two." As if I haven't hate-scrolled her account more times than I could count.

"What kind of Rumpelstiltskin-ass name is that?"

I snort out a laugh, and she quickly joins in, but our cackles are tempered by Coach Cole himself striding up to the field.

"Good morning, Ms. Miller, Dr. Hammonds," he says with a salute. "It's a great day to play the greatest game in the world!"

He pulls down his wraparound sunglasses from the top of his buzzed head and jogs the rest of the way to the quilted Aquamarine Alligators banner, taking a swig from the energy drink that seems permanently connected to his hand.

"Let's go, Alligators! Huddle up!" he shouts, clapping three times. "Axel, wipe your face and get your jersey on! Let's go!" Then he lets out a loud, piercing whistle with his fingers as if he's showing off to the metal one hanging around his neck. That seems to do the trick with Axel—he's shrugging the thing over his head while Florence looks on in shock. And even my feet start moving all on their own to follow Coach Cole's directions, but Jasmine gently tugs my elbow, holding me back.

"I meant to text you. How did your performance review go yesterday?"

I shake my head. "I don't want to talk about it."

Her eyebrows press together in concern, and I can tell that she wants to say more. But with our touchy past conversations over this same subject, she doesn't push it. "Okay."

In the seconds it takes us to reach the group, the kids are already in a perfect circle, with Coach Cole pacing around them as they stretch to reach their toes. I can't even get Pearl to put her dirty plate in the sink half the time, but here she is, following this guy's every command—and with a smile on her face!

Like I said, soccer is so not my thing, but apparently it's *a lot* of families' things—and Coach Cole has this market on lock. Apparently he's a former pro player—though where he played and why he's not doing that anymore instead of coaching players who might still need their grapes cut into halves is a mystery to me. But he must be some big deal, with the way he's built this kids' soccer empire in the past year. What was just a fall sport has now taken over Brady Park for Saturday morning games and weekday practices year-round. There's a mile-long waiting list Jasmine told me people are trying to get on with their first positive pregnancy test to even have a *chance* of forking over hundreds for a spot on the toddler league.

Honestly, though, the way some of these moms—and dads— watch him from the sidelines, their eyes locked on his muscular, tanned thighs in those breezy navy shorts he wears instead of the goal that their little Penelope just made . . . I don't think they care where he used to play pro soccer either.

"Hey, my man!" Coach Cole jogs over to where Leon is standing and daps him up.

"How's it going, brother?"

Leon is the reason Pearl not only jumped the waiting list, but made it onto the most coveted team, the only one in the league that Cole coaches himself—parent volunteers run the rest of the teams, which I'm sure Hank wishes Axel was on so he could have full control of his budding professional career. Before he transitioned into pediatrics, Leon was a nurse at the orthopedic center Cole frequented, and they became fast friends during his weekly visits. It was no question that Langston would be on his team, and I'm pretty sure Jasmine planted the seed that Pearl should join, too, just so she could have me to gossip with on the sidelines.

"What are your thoughts on this ref?" Leon asks, and my dad quickly jumps up from his chair, his knees popping, to complete their huddle.

"He's fair, he's fair," Coach Cole says, finishing off his energy drink with another big gulp. He pulls out a new can from the pocket of his shorts. "And I already gave him the heads-up on the diving, though we're starting to see it with a lot of players. The kids see it on TV and want to try it, too."

"And you checked his birth certificate?" Leon gestures across the field to the Blue Badgers. "Because that eight-year-old's got a thicker mustache than me!"

"Yeah, it was legit," Cole confirms with a sigh.

My dad leans in. "You're sure it wasn't doctored?"

I roll my eyes at Jasmine as I sit down in our chairs next to Jack, avoiding eye contact with Bethany. "I swear my dad's about to call his private investigator buddy to get a background check on this poor kid."

"I caught Leon looking up his parents on Facebook last night, like he could confirm his date of birth that way. They need to chill." Jasmine laughs and rolls her eyes, too. "And what number energy drink is that man on? I swear he's going to have a heart attack one of these days."

Jack pats my leg, and when I look at him questioningly, he tilts his head back to the men. Coach Cole is looking right at us, his eyebrows, with two notches shaved into each side, lowered over narrowed blue eyes.

Whoops. I turn to Jasmine, hiding my burning cheeks, and she presses her lips tightly together.

Florence jumps in front of us before I can decide if we should apologize.

"You're still bringing the snack, right, Mavis?" she asks, and then looks around dramatically, her hands hooded over her eyes. "I don't see Corey yet?"

The game doesn't start for twenty more minutes, lady, so why don't you chill the fuck out? That's what I want to say. But instead I just smile. "He'll be here."

"Actually, there he is, right there," Jack says, and I follow his gaze to see Corey walking up. He has on a cool camp shirt with a bright, abstract print, black shorts, and Ray-Ban Wayfarers, with his neon chair strapped to his back. And yep, there's the snack in his arms, so you can settle down, Florence. Except . . .

I jump up and speed-walk to meet him.

"You got Capri-Sun."

"Yep," he confirms with a dimpled smile, but it quickly falters. "Okay, but why are you saying that like I bought them beer . . . ?"

"Did you read Florence's guidelines?" Did I send them? I'm pretty sure I sent them. If only all these stupid extracurriculars would send things to both parents, instead of just assuming the mom is the default.

"It's one hundred percent juice! And I got orange slices and Goldfish, too. The rainbow ones Pearl likes." Defensiveness is quickly creeping into his breezy tone. "Why are you making that face like these are not normal soccer game snacks?"

"I'm not making a face." I am totally making a face. "But it's just—there are . . . expectations. Like, last week, Florence and

Hank brought charcuterie boxes for snack. Do you remember that?"

"Char-whaterie? Wait—you mean the Lunchables they passed out? Well, if you had told me you wanted those, I coulda thrown them in the cart at Target instead."

"They weren't Lunchables. Hank cured the prosciutto himself." He announced it like a million times, to make sure everyone knew. "And each kid's number was carved out of sharp cheddar from that organic farm in Irvine, plus the dried figs . . ."

I trail off in the face of Corey's *really?* look because okay, they were basically Lunchables. Just *bougie* Lunchables.

"Why does it matter? The kids will love these—*our* kid will love these. And isn't that the point?" He holds up the box of individually packaged rainbow Goldfish, and I wince, remembering Florence's thoughts on food dyes.

I sigh. "Did you bring the enrichment bags?"

He sighs right back. "Yes, I did. Even though I think goody bags at every game is ridiculous."

And he's not even wrong. I think they're stupid, too. But it's like that damn elf last month. Corey got one for his place, because Pearl was very concerned she wouldn't also be surveilled for Santa there. Except he just had it sitting in different places, like appearing on the refrigerator the next day was enough. I *want* that to be enough. I think giving us a whole 'nother part-time job in December is ridiculous when our plates are already so full. We have no choice but to be more creative than that, though, when these other parents have the things building zip lines and writing poetry or painting the *Mona Lisa* with candy canes. You gotta do the same or Pearl is going to question why her elf hates her and then that's only a short jaunt to why she doesn't deserve love.

"Are these up to standard?" Corey asks, holding open a bag with bubbles and a plastic fidget toy.

I don't even have to be the bad guy, though, because super-villain Florence has caught up to me. "Oh. Cute."

Her tone makes it clear that she means *cute* like some other four-letter words. Last week, she brought nontoxic, made-in-the-USA wooden cup and ball toss toys, and the week before that Franklin's parents passed out a set of mini bilingual books.

"Let me set this up for you." Her face is puckered with barely concealed distaste as she takes the Target bags from him. She turns on her heel toward the lace-covered snack table, and we follow behind her like two scolded children.

As we reach our group, Corey leans down to hug my dad before he can stand up. "Good morning, Pops."

"Here, let me make you some space." Jack doesn't give Corey a chance to protest, moving his chair back so there's room right on the sideline, next to me.

"Hey, thanks, man." Corey speaks just to the right of Jack's face, and Jack stares at his chair with great focus, like the thing is going to wrestle itself from his grasp. I don't know if they've looked straight into each other's eyes more than a handful of times these past few months of coexisting—though they're *very* polite about it. And as I try to avoid possibly awkward eye contact with either of them, I notice Jack's only able to move because Bethany is gone. Which is strange, since she was all up in our business before. Why would she give up her coveted spot so easily? But I'm not complaining.

Leon shakes Corey's hand and slaps his back, and Jasmine jumps up to greet him, too.

"Better you than us, Corey, to be up for snack parent on the third game. I was telling Leon, we need to show up with those cigarette candies we used to get from the ice cream truck when we were kids—you remember those things? Just to dare her to say something. Fight the power!"

I know she's trying to distract from any weirdness, and I love her for it.

Corey waves her away, though. "Nah, Mavis is right. I should have followed the guidelines. You just gotta play the game sometimes if it's what's best for your kid."

Wait, what? I'm . . . right? Corey and I have so many years of fighting between us that it feels almost as natural as breathing sometimes. But this is new. There's been a lot of new lately. It makes me feel . . . well, I'm not sure. My stomach is doing something strange.

"Um, thanks."

I sit down and grab my water bottle, sucking down what feels like all thirty-two of these ounces. Hopefully that'll take care of that.

FIVE

HERE'S HOW THESE GAMES GO: THE KIDS ALL RUN TOWARD one side of the field and half of the parents clap and cheer, "Good hustle!" while the other half yells, "Defense!" And then the kids chase the ball to the *other* side of the field and half of the parents yell, "Hold it!" while the other half cheers, "Get out there!" Followed by a goal that results in either Taylor Swift concert–level screaming or groans like they all simultaneously took a jagged, rusty dagger to the gut.

I guess I could investigate the details of what's going on a little more—because the way Coach Cole hugs his clipboard and shouts out directions, pounding can after can of energy drink, it's clear there might actually be some method to this. But I mean, Pearl's highlights of this morning's game seem to be the special edition flavor of Gatorade my dad brought her as a special treat and the white butterfly that landed on Axel's finger at halftime. So I think we're both content in our soccer ignorance.

The person who's not so content is Hank. When Axel ran off

the field before the ref blew his whistle to chase the aforementioned butterfly, Coach Cole shook his head and chuckled. "He's
just in his own little world, isn't he?"

Hank stepped up to him so closely the brim on his stupid hat
nearly touched Cole's forehead and growled, "What did you say
about my kid?"

Coach Cole smiled with his hands up in surrender. "I just
meant he's doing his own thing. Didn't mean anything by it. It's
sweet."

Which I think was a very kind response considering Axel
tripped over the ball on his way out, sending it right into the
Aquamarine Alligators' goal—and even *I* know that's a gut-
stabbing, groan-worthy offense. But Hank's neck vein looked
about ready to pop like an overfilled balloon as he muttered
something about "bad plays." But that's all part of how these
games usually go, too.

What *doesn't* usually happen is a giant mower pulling up to
the edge of the field with two minutes left on the clock.

Before we can even process what's happening, it's chaos. The
parents' cheers quickly turn to cries of confusion, and soon
they're all drowned out by the roaring engine of the machine.
Grass cuttings shoot out in its wake, covering everyone nearby
in a hazy layer of green. The Blue Badgers' goal blows over,
nearly taking their pigtailed goalie with it. But the guy sitting
on top, controlling the thing, doesn't make any moves to stop.
He's wearing giant headphones over the top of his ratty baseball
hat and a tan jumpsuit that looks like a uniform. So, he works
for the park, probably, and isn't some, like, kids' soccer protes-
tor? But he doesn't seem bothered by the fact that he's interrupting the game. In fact, I think he might actually be . . . smiling?

"Oh, come on!" Coach Cole throws his empty can to the
ground and runs after the mower, just as it makes a sharp turn

and nearly takes out the Pink Penguins' neon banner the next field over.

"What the hell is going on?"

"Who is that jerk?"

"No, you stay right there, Donovan! Defense!"

"Oh no! Axel's allergies! Hold on, my sweet boy—it's going to be okay!"

That last one is Florence, clutching the sides of her face like some white lady version of Edvard Munch's *The Scream*. She dives toward her giant leather backpack, probably digging for some natural remedy she blended herself.

Coach Cole stalks toward the interruption, and as the man sees him, he stops moving but keeps the engine running. His eyes are covered by dark sunglasses, but it seems like his gaze is locked on Cole in a challenge. He straightens his posture, sitting taller on his throne on top of the mower. His chest is broad and his body is braced, as if he's ready for a fight.

Corey leans in, raising his voice to be heard over the mechanical roar. "Does anyone have the scoop here? 'Cause I feel like this is more than just a mix-up in the park maintenance schedule."

Jasmine closes her eyes and shakes her head, like *Whew, chile*, jutting a thumb out at Leon.

"That's Dom Dwyer, the facilities manager here at Brady Park. He's got some beef with Cole. Well, clearly."

"*Beef* means *fight*," Derek adds.

"Mm-hmm, and these men are too big to be fighting like this at a children's soccer game." Jasmine nods her head toward the scene unfolding. Coach Cole appears to be screaming, though his words are muffled by the mower, and Dom is gesturing toward his headphones with a look of mock concern on his face— basically the adult version of *nah nah nah boo boo*.

"Well, for the record," Leon continues, "Cole has done everything by the book. When he decided to expand the league year-round, he checked with Beachwood's director of Parks and Recreation first, to make sure it was even a possibility to use Brady on Saturdays through the winter. It's not *his* fault Dom didn't reserve the fields through the official channels. Cole tells me he had no idea Dom used the park for his capture the flag rec league in January and February."

"Let me get this straight. *This*"—I gesture toward Coach Cole, who is now stomping his foot like Axel did earlier as Dom revs his engine in a show of dominance—"is all because Cole stole the fields from him? And now Dom can't teach kids how to play capture the flag?"

"I think the capture the flag is for adults, actually," Jack says, and Leon nods. "Derek and I drove past once, last year. It looked pretty intense."

"You know, Bert told me about that!" my dad says, snapping his fingers. "He played one season right after he retired, but when he came home with a split lip and dislocated shoulder, Vera made him quit. Couldn't even go to the awards banquet."

"Okay, my bad. So this is all because Coach Cole is stopping Dom from playing extreme capture the flag? Why can't he just move to, like, Sundays?"

Dad's eyes go wide. "Sunday is seniors Tai Chi. They are *very* territorial."

Leon nods, his eyes also wide in . . . fear? And now I have so many questions about these seniors, but Leon continues, "Dom's had an informal agreement for a long time, I think, but Coach Cole was willing to pay a huge rental fee. He could afford it because, well—" He holds his hands out toward the six fields of kids that'll stay packed until the late afternoon. "Anyway, Dom lost the park, had to pause his league indefinitely. It's gotten pretty contentious, from what he's told me."

It *looks* pretty contentious. Coach Cole is standing as close to the mower as he can without losing a toe, jabbing an angry finger in the air, while Dom leans back, arm over the back of his seat, legs wide. Even with no words, it's clear what *that* signifies: dominance.

Suddenly Coach Cole whips around and is stalking back. As he makes his way to the center of the field, he's red-faced, with his fists tight at his sides. He pulls the metal whistle around his neck to his mouth and blows. It sounds like defeat.

"I'm sorry, folks," he yells, struggling to be heard over Dom's mower, which is now moving toward the toddler field. "We're going to have to cut this game short because of, uh—a miscommunication with the parks department. We're tied, so we're going to call it a draw." He looks to the ref, who nods in confirmation.

Some kids groan, but most of them are already eyeing the snacks on the sidelines. Pearl is bouncing excitedly with her Gatorade on the bench like they just won the World Series . . . or whatever it is they play in soccer. It's mostly the parents acting like Coach Cole announced that soccer as a sport is canceled for the rest of eternity. Hank is shaking his head in disappointment like he somehow expected this from Cole, like he has been betrayed *personally*.

We do the mandatory lineup of high fives. The kids mumble, "Good game, good game, good game." And as a mob of concerned parents circles Coach Cole, the kids run back to the sidelines to get their food and goody bags. Florence passes out Corey's offerings with a look of apology and mild disgust in her eyes, but the Aquamarine Alligators are delighted with their red

dye 40 Goldfish and ocean-destroying-plastic fidget spinners—
which just makes Florence's face twist even more.

"Good game, my Pearl girl," Corey says, picking her up and
twirling her around.

I pat her back. "Yeah! You really, um . . . hustled!"

"Yeah, yeah," Pearl says, waving that away. We both know I
have no idea what "hustling" actually entails. She points toward
Dom and the mower, the next field over. "That thing is cool. Do
you think he'd let me ride on it?"

"Baby girl," I say, arching an eyebrow to communicate the
rest: *be serious*.

Out of the corner of my eye, I see Coach Cole walking back
to the sidelines, leaving a crowd of angry parents huddling behind him like they're plotting the next Ides of March. Cole
picks up one of his energy drinks that he abandoned before, but
when he shakes the can, he sees that it's empty. His whole body
seems to deflate in sadness—even those thighs.

"What if—what if I asked really nicely?" Pearl asks, bringing
me back. "And said *please*?"

"Um," I say, and Pearl jumps up in excitement as if that was
a *Hell yes!*

"Thank you, Mommy! I'm going to tell my friends!" And
she's off before I can get another word in. Corey and I lock eyes
and laugh. I remember one of her preschool parent conferences,
before everything was officially over between us. We talked
about how stubborn she could be, never trying new foods, never
putting on the pants I picked out, never sleeping in her own bed
if she decided it wasn't a sleeping-in-her-own-bed night. It was
exhausting. That was *something* Corey and I could agree on, at
least. *Let's reframe that as something positive*, her teacher insisted,
though. *She's persistent. That's a quality that will serve her really
well as an adult.* And afterward in the car, before we surely got

into another fight, we just sat there and marveled in silence for a moment over our *persistent* little girl. I wonder if he's thinking about that now, too.

There's a creak behind me as Jack folds up my chair, and it pulls me out of my memories. Behind him, disappointed-looking Purple Platypuses are crowding together, probably wondering if they're going to get to play. I don't see Dakota—or Bethany, thankfully. Maybe they already gave up and went home.

Cole paces past us, ignoring the searching looks of the Platypuses, sucking down a Capri-Sun like it's a beer at the end of a long day. I snort-laugh at the sight of Florence eyeing him as if him choosing the Capri-Sun is a personal attack on her.

"Good job with the snacks," I tell Corey, and he smiles. "Oh yeah?"

Pearl is back in between us, and she's dragging Langston with her. "Okay, Langston, we're going to ask the guy if we can take a ride. My mom said it's okay."

"Oh, did she?" Jasmine asks with a smirk.

"I don't think it mattered what I said." I lean down and put my hands on Pearl's shoulders, preparing myself for the battle that's going to be getting her out of this park without hopping on that mower for a joyride. But before I can begin to present my case, loud gasps erupt around us.

"Oh my god!"

"Cole? Cole!"

I turn just in time to see Coach Cole stagger and then fall over. His head smacks the field with a loud thud.

"Someone call nine-one-one!"

I'm struggling to process what's happening, what I'm looking at. Because he was just standing there, completely fine. But now he's clutching his chest, fingers curled into claws. His rapid breaths are quickly descending into a crackling wheeze that makes my own chest ache. And there's vomit on the ground next to him, the same neon yellow as his countless energy drinks.

Jasmine and Leon rush to his side to help.

I should, too. Or, no. I shouldn't. Because I am not a nurse or a doctor and I would just be in the way. But I should do *something*. I should call the police, the ambulance. I should help push back the kids who are creeping closer, trying to see. I should help them calm down.

But that would require being calm myself. And I am anything but calm right now.

My vision swims and my chest tightens even more. I can't catch my breath, like my throat is one of those stupid paper straws collapsing with a single drop of liquid, which totally defeats the purpose of a straw, but we're all just supposed to pretend like we like them because of the turtles, and I shouldn't even be thinking this because I'm supposed to care about the environment—I *do* care about the environment—but also I shouldn't be thinking about this because there is an emergency happening right in front of me, right now, and why am I still standing here? Why am I thinking about fucking paper straws? My racing heart is like a frantic drumbeat and as it thunders in my ears, its message rings clearer, drowning every other stupid thought out, until it's all I hear and think and understand. Run, run, *run*!

So I listen. I do the only thing that makes sense. I pick up Pearl and run.

SIX

"DO YOU WANT TO TALK ABOUT WHAT HAPPENED?"

Pearl and I made it safely to my car, her giggling the whole way like it was a silly game. But she sobered quickly when she saw the not-so-silly faces of Papa, Corey, and Jack, who chased after us.

Later the worst was confirmed through a short, whispered call with Jasmine. Coach Cole was dead, the cause unknown for now, but it sure looked like a heart attack. He didn't even make it to the hospital.

And dealing with that—explaining the unthinkable to Pearl, holding her tight when her little body shook with sobs, answering all her unanswerable questions—took up so much of the weekend that I didn't even have time to process my own feelings. How I reacted, running away with Pearl instead of . . . doing anything rational.

But now it's late Sunday night, I'm out on the back patio while Dad and Pearl snore away inside, and of course my school psychologist boyfriend is going to give me my very own personal session of Making Friends With Big Feelings. If only he didn't look so cute doing it, and then I could be a lot more annoyed.

He reaches between us, where our two metal chairs meet, and threads his fingers through mine. His hand is a warm anchor in the cool night air.

"You mean how I threw Pearl over my shoulders like a sack of potatoes and did a Flo-Jo to my Prius?" I avoid his eyes because then maybe I can get away with keeping this light.

"It was quite the athletic feat."

"Well, *athletic* is a stretch. I think I'm gonna need to mainline ibuprofen as punishment for the foreseeable future."

"Mm-hmm."

"Do you think they'll give me a frequent-buyer discount already? I swear me and my dad must be responsible for, like, at least a twelfth of their annual sales."

He squeezes my hand and brings it to his cheek. He knows what I'm doing.

"When did my body start hurting this much? I used to be in shape. Or, I mean . . . vaguely, um, capable. Not *unhealthy*."

"Mavis," he murmurs. I sigh, finally meeting his gaze. His green eyes are curved into half-moons as they gently search mine. He kisses my fingers, communicating without words that he'll be patient, but, like, maybe we don't have to pretend that I ever could have easily carried an almost-eight-year-old any distance. And that's really all I need to take a swing at the wall I had to put up for Pearl.

"I feel like I'm losing it," I admit in a whisper. "Or no—that I've already . . . lost it."

My voice cracks, and he curls in closer to me.

"For the record, I don't think you've lost it," he says, breath soft on my cheek. He brushes a quick kiss to the side of my lips.

"But feeling like that . . . it would be understandable considering all that you've been through, babe."

"I've—I've always been able to keep it moving, keep it going, no matter the stress." The wall had a tiny break, and now it's crumbling. Tears well in my eyes faster than I can blink them away. "I've *known* I need to slow down. And like . . . take a beat and take care of myself, and it's even felt dire at times. But—but it's never actually *been* dire. That's why I've been able to just reschedule taking care of myself for so long. And keep pushing the finish line, you know? But now it feels like I've finally pushed it too far. Because I was really acting crazy, wasn't I? And I'm just—just . . . so *tired*. It's like my brain shut down yesterday and my body took over. It felt like I wasn't in control, and I'm *always* in control."

"You are very capable," he says, wiping my cheek. "And that's a good thing. But it can also be a bad thing."

"How can that be a bad thing?" I sniff. "*Very capable* is a good thing by, like, definition. You're really gonna take that away from me? Now, in my hour of need?"

I grin at him through the tears and snot, and he smiles back. "Because you are also human, Mavis, and no matter how capable you are at pushing it down, trauma still does things to the body."

I roll my eyes at him, and he laughs. Because he knows that's veering a little too close to the woo-woo for my taste. But he also pulls me close and rests his chin on my head as he rubs my back, because he knows that I need a beat to take it in, too.

Trauma in my body? Is that why I felt like I was frozen—why I *still* feel like I'm frozen, even though *I* wasn't in any real danger yesterday? It's lessened since then, sure, but my chest is still tight, my heart racing out of nowhere. And my mind keeps replaying that moment over and over again, like a broken video trapped in an ancient VCR, of Coach Cole hitting the ground. I can't get it to stop.

"The crack of his skull, the—the thud of his body . . . I can't stop the sick show in my head. And my body feels stuck in the fight-or-flight of that moment. Does that make sense?"

"Of course it makes sense." Jack sighs, kissing the top of my head.

"And then . . . I feel guilty for even feeling like this? Because this is *not* about me. A man died yesterday. Like, who cares how *my* body feels?"

More tears fall, and I let them. It feels safe, doing this in Jack's arms. It feels like I can finally let go.

"I know we've talked about it before, but with all this, well . . . have you given any more thought to trying out therapy?"

That makes my whole body brace again. I jerk up from his chest, trying to hit him with a snarky side-eye, but my face ends up giving more "Dawson crying meme."

"You think I'm that bad?"

"No, you don't have to be *bad* to need therapy. It's just helpful to talk feelings through, get them out."

And yeah, yeah, I *know* that, like intellectually. Or whatever. But it feels like he's telling me I should talk to someone else. Like, *This is serious. You need a real professional.* And he *is* one, so then what does that mean?

He must be able to read this all over my face because he quickly adds, "I go to therapy. Well, not at the moment, but I have gone to therapy."

"When?" I should probably know the answer to that already. I feel a pang of guilt, adding up all the time we spend talking about my problems.

"Off and on in high school, especially after my dad left. And later, when I took over care of Derek from my mom."

"So the big moments, then?"

"Yes, big moments, but not just those. I swear I spent at least three months of therapy when I was sixteen exclusively complaining about my bacne. And whether there was any hope that it would go away."

I snort out a laugh, despite all the other feelings storming, and he smiles proudly. It is very cute.

"And, well, last fall," he continues, "I had some check-in sessions with my therapist, Jamie—that's his name."

What's left unspoken is that last fall *was* a big moment for me. My life has been *a series* of big moments since then . . . since even farther back, if I'm being honest with myself.

And if I keep up this whole honesty thing, I know what this is. Anxiety. Panic attacks. This isn't the first time Jack and I have talked about it. I can even admit the anxiety's probably always been there—in the way I run through every wonderful and terrible possibility for Pearl's future at night when I should be sleeping, in the way I constantly think about how the other moms see me. Corinne just made it much harder to throw a blanket on it and pretend it wasn't there. But putting an official diagnosis on these feelings, admitting they're enough of a problem to *seek professional help* . . . it's just another thing I want to keep putting off.

Because that life strategy has been going *so* well for me.

"I've actually been thinking of scheduling another check-in with Jamie soon."

"For help coping with your girlfriend who won't go to therapy?" I smile, eager to make it easy, light, but his face stays serious.

"I don't want to push you, Mavis. I just 1—" He stops, leaving that consonant—and what might have come after it—hanging in the air. Even in the dark, I can see that his face is flushed.

"I only want what's best for you," he says, finally.

I nod, and run my hand through his hair, and then along his

cheek. He leans into my touch. "So . . . does this mean I made friends with my big feelings?"

He smiles but doesn't give me the low, rumbly laugh I'm craving, or throw in a diagnosis of what color zone I'm in.

"Just think about it, Mavis," he says, planting a kiss on my temple.

AND I'M STILL THINKING ABOUT IT MONDAY MORNING.

All of it.

Therapy, and if that L-word was the L-word I thought it was and maybe hoped it was, and how I feel about that and what I would say back if he actually said it out loud and why the hell didn't he say it out loud, and has he been conspiring with Corey or something to push this therapy agenda, and how are they both so goddamn *balanced* and what does it mean about *me* that I attract these balanced men, *not that I'm attracting Corey*, and oh my god, Coach Cole, I can't stop seeing his head hit the ground, and I wonder if his family knows what the cause was yet, and does he even have family nearby, should I organize something, and is my child scarred for life because of what she saw, am *I* scarred for life, and is the trauma in my body also responsible for the crop of zits on my chin that seem like they've decided to just take out a mortgage?

It's like an alarm bell has been rung and now my body is living in the reverberation, trapped in this pulsating, overwhelming beat. And it's all rushing together as it plays on repeat, so it sounds more like:

Therapy-L-word-therapy-balance-Coach-Cole-scarred-for-life-trauma-zits-with-a-mortgage

Therapy-L-word-therapy-balance-Coach-Cole-scarred-for-life-trauma-zits-with-a-mortgage

So when Pearl shoves a Post-it right up to my eyeballs, I almost fall off the kitchen stool because that beat is blocking out everything, including approaching footsteps.

"What does this mean?"

I blink, trying to process why my daughter is holding up a Post-it with *shit* written in glittery orange gel pen.

"Pearl!" I say, snatching the thing from her. "That's a bad word."

She crosses her arms and juts out her hip. "*You* said it on Saturday when you ran me to the car. I wrote it down so I wouldn't forget."

"I said that?" But even as I'm responding, I *know* I said that. I can sorta even hear myself saying that, if I push through the hazy cloud of panic that's still surrounding Saturday morning in my memory. But if I *admit* I said that, Pearl will probably share it with her whole class in today's morning announcements.

"Yeah. Well, you said, 'Shit shit shit shit shit—'"

"Don't say that!" My finger flies up to her tiny, innocent mouth that shouldn't be spewing out expletives. The FBI agent in my phone is probably listening in horror and typing up reports to the appropriate authorities.

"You said it," she repeats, tilting her head to the side and raising her eyebrows in a challenge she knows she's going to win.

I sigh, conceding. "I did say it."

"What does it even mean?"

I sigh again. "Poop."

Her brown eyes light up in delight, and I can tell by the mischievous smile pulling at her lips that she's already come up with five ways to use it in a sentence.

"But it's still a bad word! And if you say it to Mrs. Tennison, you're going to get in trouble."

"Even if I tell her you taught me it?"

Lord.

"Even if you tell her I taught you." *Please don't tell her I taught you.* "Sometimes grown-ups say words when they're really upset that they shouldn't say. And that's what I did."

She looks down and sucks in her bottom lip, sadness knocking her over like a rogue wave at the beach. "You were upset because . . . because Coach Cole died?"

Her voice sounds small, unsure—like she's trying out a new language. We've already talked about what happened—it feels like *all* we talked about this weekend. But I understand her need to keep confirming, to keep making sure this is all real, because I can hardly believe it myself.

"Because Coach Cole died," I say, and her bottom lip immediately sticks out, the first warning sign before the tears fall.

"Come here, baby girl." I pull her into my lap, stroking the braids on her head. My wall is back up. I relaid all the bricks last night after Jack left. It may be shaking slightly with *Therapy-L-word-therapy-balance-Coach-Cole-scarred-for-life-trauma-zits-with-a-mortgage-FBI-agent.* But I need to stay steady and strong for her.

"It isn't fair," she whispers.

"It isn't."

"And I feel . . . sad. And mad. But mostly sad."

"And it's okay to feel everything right now."

Even as I say it, I hear the irony in how I make myself live the opposite—especially right now with my wall up.

"I didn't want him to die."

"I didn't either. I'm so sorry, Pearl."

"And he's—he's not going to be here for my *birthday!*"

Her whole body deflates at that. And I resist my first instinct to tell her that he wasn't going to be here anyway. We just have a small family dinner planned for her celebration next weekend. But I can see how she's trying to work this out, to trace how this unraveling spool of loss, of grief, will extend beyond the pain of right now into her future.

"He's not. And I know that's really hard to think about."

I rock her as we sit in it together, letting the minutes on the clock tick by, even as I know we're creeping closer to the late bell. And then when her breath finally does slow, when I've rubbed her back in the exact right soothing pattern, her face crumples again at the realization that those feelings are still there, regardless. It's the same face she made when I accidentally let Polly out and we couldn't find her for the worst twenty minutes. Or when Corey left on his last big tour before he took this indefinite pause. Sad and mad, but mostly sad.

So that gets added to the beat, too, after I finally drop Pearl off at Knoll's side gate, and now it's:

Therapy-L-word-therapy-balance-Coach-Cole-scarred-for-life-trauma-zits-with-a-mortgage-FBI-agent-sad-and-mad-and-sad

My footsteps seem to hit the pavement in time with each word, as if it's choreographed, as if it's my own heartbeat.

Therapy-L-word-therapy-balance-Coach-Cole-scarred-for-life-trauma-zits-with-a-mortgage-FBI-agent-sad-and-mad-and—

"How are you holding up? It's so sad what happened!"

I jump, and Bethany grins as if I'm doing a bit.

"And what was that about the FBI?"

"Oh, nothing, I just need—" To get out of your presence right now because I'm this close to losing it, and apparently have no control of the words coming out of my mouth.

Which is what I think, but apparently my face reads more as, I just need a hug. Because that's what Bethany does, pulling me into one so tight that I have no choice but to sit there and take it, even as she caresses my back and murmurs, "There, there. I'm here."

When she releases me, I have to engage every muscle in my

face to keep it cute, and it gets even harder when I take in what she's wearing: a beanie with a pom-pom, puffer jacket, thick scarf, and tall plum-colored Ugg boots. Lady, it's January, but it's not *January*. The thing that finally breaks my composure, though, is the pointed, deep green crystal in her left hand, which she's gripping just as tightly as she did me, rubbing her thumb in a continuous circle on its side. I blink furiously to keep away the side-eye.

But again, she drastically misreads my face. Or maybe the thing is on the fritz.

"Oh, Mavis. Please let it out—I'm here." She tries to hug me again, but I bob and weave to avoid it. "In times like these, I've found that I really need to lean in *even more* to the self-care that I know works for me. You have to protect yourself as you maneuver this grief. We don't even have to talk about the business side yet if you just want to try out my 30-Day Oxygen Mask Challenge. But who knows, maybe this is the universe showing you that this is your moment . . ."

Wait. Is she *really* trying to use Coach Cole's death to sell me on her stupid MLM again? That is bonkers, even for a girlboss. But if what Ruth said is true . . .

"And if you do decide to take that first brave step, you don't have to put anything down yet, just—"

"Bethany, do you think your I LUV ME method can—" My voice catches. It feels icky to even say out loud. "Can . . . cure cancer?"

Her glossy, nude lips drop open into a perfect O, and her hand flies to her chest. "No. I would *never* say that!"

My whole body floods with relief. She's annoying. And pushy. But at least she's not *the worst*.

"But I do believe the body and mind are connected and when you show that you care for one, it gives the other the will to keep fighting. And my I LUV ME method encompasses all that I learned through my journey, the exact combination of brain and body care I did to bring about the healing of my whole self. That's why I'm so humbled and grateful that I *did* walk that road, so I can share it with women walking their own paths and help them find the peace and *protection* they need to live *healthy*, happy, and well-balanced lives."

Okay, so, scratch that, she *is* the worst.

"That's bullshit, Bethany. And you know it."

"Mom! You said it *again*?" For some reason—probably because I forgot to say my prayers one night or forward a bad luck chain email—Pearl has appeared at my side, hands on her hips like, *I can't take you anywhere.*

"Why are you out here? I sent you through the gate." I glance behind her at the gate for confirmation, and Mrs. Nelson at least tries to look like she wasn't just using us as her morning entertainment.

"You didn't give me my backpack." She nods to my side, and I realize I do still have her sparkly rainbow backpack in my hand. My nails have left deep curves in my palms with the effort.

"Sorry, baby girl," I say, quickly sliding it over her arms.

"That's okay." She gives me a look that lets me know *We're going to talk about this later, missy*, and then skips back through the gate. Mrs. Nelson smiles and waves.

"You really should consider joining us, Mavis."

I sigh. Apparently my foul language was enough to get me in trouble with Pearl, but not enough to scare Bethany away.

"I am not interested."

"I used to be just like you. Flustered in the morning, barely able to get myself together, didn't do my hair or brush my teeth—"

"I brushed my—" *No. Mavis, you are not about to tell this lady you brushed your teeth.* "I need to go to work."

"And see, imagine how much your days would open up if you took the leap to work for yourself. The flexibility you'd have. I'd love for you to talk to one of my self-care consultants, Pamela. She was just promoted to the Ultimate Wellness Goddess rank with fifty consultants in her downstream. Maybe we could hop on a call—"

"Oh my god, I said NO!"

I know immediately I was too loud, and it's quickly confirmed by the startled look of Mrs. Nelson, the moms huddled in front of the kindergarten gate staring my way, and Francine the crossing guard already whispering behind her hand to her gossip buddy.

Because I just screamed at a cancer survivor in front of the school.

I'm for sure going to be the villain of the day on the Knoll Elementary Parents Facebook group. A blond lady in black athleisure wear and chunky Hoka sneakers—Della, I think her name is—is already furiously typing something one-handed as she sucks down coffee from her holographic Starbucks tumbler.

Bethany cowers back like *I'm* the predator, like she hasn't been harassing me for days now. Like she didn't just say in woo-woo speak that the self-care method she's selling to tired moms cured her cancer!

But I shouldn't even be surprised. Angry Black woman beats out pushy MLM girlboss always.

So I don't even try to smooth this over. I turn and speed-walk to my car, and now the beat is:

Therapy-L-word-therapy-balance-Coach-Cole-scarred-for-life-trauma-zits-with-a-mortgage-FBI-agent-sad-and-mad-and-sad-angry-Black-woman

It gets louder and louder in my ears as I drive to work, park, and walk in. It hits rock concert levels when I see that everyone is already gathering in the conference room, Ruth in the front with two giant binders on display in front of her. The same two binders she offered me on Friday. And when I check and see the meeting invitation on my phone, sent out sometime this weekend when I was either holding my crying kid or crying myself, it reaches the decibels of that one volcano I read about whose eruption was so loud it traveled around the world multiple times and killed people on the spot.

That doesn't seem like such a bad fate right now. Like, please, take me from this mortal plane, too, loud volcano. I mean, not really, of course. Of course! God, I'm worse than Bethany, joking about death when I just witnessed a death. What is wrong with me??

But also, I can't even think straight because:

Therapy-L-word-therapy-balance-Coach-Cole-scarred-for-life-trauma-zits-with-a-mortgage-FBI-agent-sad-and-mad-and-sad-angry-Black-woman-DEIB

Therapy-L-word-therapy-balance-Coach-Cole-scarred-for-life-trauma-zits-with-a-mortgage-FBI-agent-sad-and-mad-and-sad-angry-Black-woman-DEIB

I sit between Nelson and Sally, who's eating the last bites of her brussels sprouts omelette from a Tupperware, and try to take deep breaths to quiet down the thundering in my ears. I just need to reboot the professional robot Mavis software, keep it cute, and then I can hide in my office for the rest of the day and get my real work done. I need to avoid any meaningful eye contact and "opportunities" for me to speak for the entirety of all Black people for an hour. I can do this.

"Welcome to our first of several DEIB courageous conversations," Rose begins. Her voice is ostentatious and her arms spread wide, like she's presiding over the grand opening of a grocery store or performing slam poetry. Or both at the same time. "If you weren't already aware, DEIB stands for diversity, equity, inclusion—and belonging. I'm going to repeat that again because it's so important. The *most* important, in my opinion. *Belonging.* Because here at Project Window, we want to make sure our BIPOC employees feel seen and heard and belonging—" She coughs. "Excuse me, like they belong."

This is the same woman who was walking around saying "bisexual people of color" with her whole chest just a year ago before I quietly informed her what it actually meant, but okay. At least I know what the *B* stands for now. Though I'm still not convinced it isn't . . . that bad word I'm not supposed to even think anymore.

"So after a lot of listening and learning, we chose this curriculum, which Nelson and I will be tag-teaming, because we know we need to"—she pauses to refer to one of the binders in front of her—"do the work. We all are going to do the work and be agents of change together."

My god, was this written by, like, social justice ChatGPT? How much did they pay for this bull— This . . . stuff? They have no money to give me the raise I've been working toward, but they can pay probably thousands for a curriculum of courageous conversations to make me feel like I belong? And I'll be forced to sit here and smile and pretend like all the microaggressions that are surely coming are okay as we do this Diversity 101 just to make them feel good. Because if I *don't* it'll be something that's brought up at my next performance evaluation as something I need to work on, as that one last hurdle before my next promotion. And that cycle will just continue on forever and ever with no progress, no money to be found in the budget, because I'm doomed to be trapped here forever.

Therapy-L-word-therapy-balance-Coach-Cole-scarred-for-life-trauma-zits-with-a-mortgage-FBI-agent-sad-and-mad-and-sad-angry-Black-woman-DEIB-trapped-forever

Rose squints down at her binder again. "Before we begin, I want to recognize the different cultural holidays we are near. Martin Luther King Jr. Day, of course, and . . . um . . ." She pauses and stares at the ceiling, as if the answer is there. Finally, she snaps her fingers. "Oh! And Chinese New Year! No, um, *Lunar* New Year." Her eyes return to the safety of the binder. "We celebrate them today and every day."

My eyebrow shoots up all on its own, a glitch in my programming. It would have been real nice to celebrate MLK Day on the *actual* day last week, with a paid day off. Corey got to take Pearl to play mini golf while I was stuck here, fielding Rose's email requests to convert Word docs into PDFs for the billionth time.

Therapy-L-word-therapy-balance-Coach-Cole-scarred-for-life-trauma-zits-with-a-mortgage-FBI-agent-sad-and-mad-and-sad-angry-Black-woman-DEIB-trapped-forever-I-want-to-quit

"It's also very important for us to acknowledge that we are currently on insert name of tribe—oops!" Her blond, curly head flies up, and she mimes wiping sweat off her brow. "I saw this. I *know* I did. Maybe in the index?" She flips forward in the binder, holding up a finger. "Give me just a moment."

Therapy-L-word-therapy-balance-Coach-Cole-scarred-for-life-trauma-zits-with-a-mortgage-FBI-agent-sad-and-mad-and-sad-angry-Black-woman-DEIB-trapped-forever-I-quit-I-quit-I-quit

". . . think that's how you say it—Mavis?"

I realize I'm standing up. How long have I been standing up?

"Mavis?" Rose repeats, eyes narrowed in concern. "Did you just say . . . *I quit*?"

Did I just say that? I wanted to say that. I've *dreamed* about saying that forever. Seriously, it shows up on the dream roster at least two nights a week. But did I really, finally say those words out loud?

Next to me, Nelson lets out what sounds like a comically fake sneeze, and Rose looks grateful for the chance to move on.

"Bless you!" she chirps, flipping back to the front of her massive binder. "Now, let's begin with module one of fourteen: Words Matter. And, you know, this one was really interesting for me because there are even more words than I realized that we need to be careful with now. Like, for example—"

"I quit!"

Knoll Elementary Parents Facebook Group

Della Lively

What problem does Mavis have NOW? I saw her yelling at a new Knoll parent this morning—not to mention cursing? I know she helped out the school in September, but I don't think that gives her a free pass to act however she wants.

Trisha Holbrook

I mean, we all know she has a flair for the dramatic 🙄

Charlie Lee

Oh I hope it's not the new mom I just met! She's had a really tough but inspiring journey and I want her to feel welcomed!

Ruth Gentry

I'm not taking Mavis's side here because she unfairly attacked me the other night too 😔 But that's Bethany Bowman and well . . . let's just say she's definitely not some innocent victim. Please DM me if she's approached you about joining her team because I have a much more lucrative and legitimate business opportunity. Don't forget—clary sage is still 50% off for new Agape Essentials members in the month of January!

Florence Michaelson

I'm confused??? Mavis is starting a new team? I'm already the Team Mom for the Aquamarine Alligators, and she really should have checked in with me first. This is hurtful 😔

Dyvia Mehta

No. We are not doing this. Please refer to the social media usage policy that I sent out at the beginning of my term as PTA president. There are sections on gossip and MLM solicitation if you need a refresher.

Trisha Holbrook
INTERIM president

balancedwithbethany

Some people are just not ready.

We live in a culture that's addicted to the hustle, and so many find their value in the busyness, their sense of self in the struggle.

So when they see another way, they lash out! What else can they do with that building resentment, when they see others living the authentic, balanced life they wish they had? The only other alternative is really committing to introspection and breaking down the limiting beliefs they have for themselves. And that's hard 😦

But listen, Balanced With Bethany family, I'm not judging! Many of you know my story and my truth: I used to be that way, too. What my self-care journey has taught me, though, is that if you don't slow down and do it on your own, well, life will knock you right over and make you take care of yourself! And that can look like a stage four breast cancer diagnosis after a routine mammogram. (Visit the link in my bio to read what I did next! 🔼)

I don't wish my journey on anyone. But I am so humbled and grateful that I did walk that road, so I can recognize women on the same path and help them find the peace and protection they need to live healthy, happy, and well-balanced lives . . . when they're ready.

Some people are just not ready . . . but are you?

Comment "READY" below, and I'll send you a link to my 30-Day Oxygen Mask Challenge so you can start today!

SEVEN

AFTER I SAY THOSE WORDS, THE INCESSANT, MADDENING beat is instantly replaced by an eerie silence. I hear nothing as I scramble from the conference room, grab the picture of Pearl dressed as Tiana off my desk, and take off to my car. I have no idea if Rose or Nelson or anyone else calls after me. Maybe they're as shocked as I am by what I just said, what I just *did*. But it's like that moment immediately after an explosion when your ears are too stunned to take in any more sound. There's only endless quiet.

Which feels appropriate, because oh my god oh my god I just blew up my life.

My body goes into autopilot as I drive home, or at least I hope it does because it's like I blink and then I'm pulling up to the curb with no memory, at least, of any major traffic violations along the way. My chest and shoulders loosen slightly with the realization that it's still midmorning, so I won't have to face Pearl just yet. I still have hours until pickup to get it together. Corey's supposed to get her anyway, so really I have until dinnertime to figure out how I'm going to explain that I quit my job of almost eight years with no backup plan . . . to everyone else and also to myself. Dinnertime, yeah, that feels *totally* possible. I may have to dodge my dad, but didn't he say last night he had another interview for his podcast? That's another thing I need to figure out, what the hell is going on with this podcast. But not right now. Right now I'm going to face-plant into my bed and put on some *Housewives* and remind myself that my life is bad but not *that* bad.

That immediate game plan goes out the window, though, when I step out of the car and see Corey standing on our path. His arms are full with a toolbox, a plastic Home Depot bag, and a canvas tote, and he looks just as surprised as I am.

"What are you doing here?" I ask him before he has a chance to ask me the same question.

"Well, good morning to you, too." He pauses to look meaningfully at the picture frame tucked under my arm, tilts his head so I know he saw it and is letting it go . . . for now, then continues, "I'm here to help Ms. Joyce with a project." He gestures to my neighbor's house across the street, and I see her front curtains twitch, as if in response. "But I thought I would install a chain on y'all's front door first since I'm already here."

I narrow my eyes, and he adds quickly, "I texted your dad this morning to make sure it was okay."

"Did *he* ask you to do that?"

"No, but I just want to make sure y'all are safe. Because, you know . . . on Friday."

A flash of annoyance burns in my chest, but it's almost immediately extinguished because it isn't the *worst* idea. Not that I leave my keys in the door every night, but when I do . . .

Still, "I could do that myself."

"I know you can," he says, voice dripping with syrupy patience that makes me feel immediately guilty for being the difficult one. "But you have a lot going on. I just wanted to help."

He just wanted to help. That's been his excuse for all the things he's been doing to annoy me lately. Because it implies that we *need* help, and we don't. We're fine—*have been* fine.

I mean, I get that it might not look that way to the outside world when I'm leaving our front door open to burglars and pulling in sweaty and exhausted to the late bell. But I have my own way of doing things, and I don't need some new, more efficient way. Because the new, more efficient way implies that my way is wrong, and *that* triggers my instinct to take off my earrings and fight someone. A particular someone.

Like this fucking laundry app he loaded on my phone. I have this totally normal habit of forgetting to move the loads to the dryer, which sometimes—rarely—leads to me having to wash the clothes again, and of course Pearl, my sweet little narc, informed him of this. Tell me why a few days later, I started getting notifications on my phone saying, "Damp laundry has been sitting in the washer for ten minutes." When they first popped up, I was confused, like, *Is my washer texting me?* And he was so proud to show me what he set up to help me remember. I swear my whole body burst into flames, and the inferno only grew when those notifications started stacking on my home screen, taunting me: "Damp laundry has been sitting in the washer for thirty minutes, one hour . . . ten days."

But this is how Corey showed love when we were married. My gas tank was always full, the trash cans were always brought to the curb. He's not doing anything wrong. It's nice. Which makes me feel like an asshole for complaining now . . . and then. I didn't have the words to explain back then that I needed something else from him, something *different*. And now apparently I just make snotty faces and comments while he tiptoes around me, waiting to see which step is going to trip the alarm today.

"How is Pearl doing?" he asks, and I soften with the reminder of our common love, the reason I have to get it together and keep the peace.

"She cried again this morning. It was . . . hard. It doesn't make any sense to her, this happening, and it's hard to help her through it because death *doesn't* make sense. It's not fair."

"Is that why you're home? Are you picking her up early? I can tell Ms. Joyce that I need to reschedule for another day, if you want some backup."

That douses the flames in my chest even more, because it would be a relief to have someone there, to not have to always be the lead, the person with all the answers. But then a rogue spark ignites another fiery blaze because he can *decide* when to give this, when I haven't had a choice for years. God, I wish I could just snap my fingers and be grown and permanently on the high road. I'm trying.

Thankfully, before I have to answer, Polly's muffled barks sound from the front window. And because she only barks at old people and babies, I don't have to even turn to know who's approaching right now.

"Mmm-mmm chile, you better get in line! I reserved Corey's services last week."

Ms. Joyce steps in between us. She's wearing a floral-printed caftan with a matching scarf tied around her fro. Her voice is like honey, but her stern face and the hand on her hip show she means business.

I hold my hands up. "Don't worry, you can have him, Ms. Joyce!" I lean down to give her a hug and a kiss on the cheek, and she pats my shoulder, satisfied.

"What kind of project do you got for him? He's real good at scrubbing stains out of grout, or—cleaning hair out of shower drains. Yeah, he *really* likes to do that."

I flutter my eyelashes and smirk at Corey, but Ms. Joyce

doesn't even seem to notice, because she's beaming at Corey, too, like he's her knight in shining armor.

"He is installing my brand-new security and surveillance system. I bought the whole package, the doorbell thing and the cameras and the panic button—they threw that in for free." She lets out a long sigh and shakes her head slowly. "You know I had no choice with your little friend next door and her Ring-Ring, Bling-Bling, whatever that nonsense is called."

It sounds like Ms. Joyce's system is a lot more intense than Mackenzie's Ring camera "nonsense," but I know I can't say that.

Instead, I remind her, "Mackenzie is not my little friend." Even though I know there's no hope in denying it, because I wave hello to Mackenzie when I see her and maintain a neutral, neighborly relationship. In Ms. Joyce's eyes, that means I'm fraternizing with the enemy.

Not that Mackenzie Skinner, Ms. Joyce's next-door neighbor, has really even *done* anything to be considered the enemy. Her life seems to consist of jogging around the neighborhood in neon exercise clothes, as far as I can tell. But she's part of the new crop of people moving into a quickly changing Beachwood, and she once asked Ms. Joyce if there was an HOA for our neighborhood she could join. Then she installed her Ring doorbell and a couple of cameras, and Ms. Joyce took it as a grenade being thrown over the fence.

"I need her to know that I'm watching her," Ms. Joyce says, throwing a deadly look over her shoulder at Mackenzie's heavily remodeled black-and-white modern farmhouse.

"You're really going to encourage this?" I ask Corey, and he shrugs like he has no other choice.

"I mean, I coooooould just do it myself." Ms. Joyce purses her lips and taps her chin. "The ladder *is* in the back of the garage, but it shouldn't take me but an hour to get it out. And I'll take it slow because of my hip replacement, but I'm sure if I bust it again, they'll give me a discount on the next one."

Corey makes a face like, *Case in point*, and okay, so maybe he didn't have a choice.

"Now, Corey," Ms. Joyce continues, making it clear that the discount hip replacement was never really an option. "I was perusing the manual that came in the box. It says the whole system needs to connect to the Wi-Fi. Do I need the password for that? Because I haven't known that doggone thing since the man came to set it up. It was—something like . . . argle-bargle-nine-one-one? But that doesn't work so I've just been hooking up to Mackenzie and Todd's internet when my phone isn't moving fast enough on the *New York Times* Connections game. You think we could hook this up to their Wi-Fi, too? This *is* their fault, after all, and they *really* should be a little more careful, anyway. Their wedding anniversary was just too easy for me to guess."

I can tell from Corey's tight cheeks that he's holding in his laughter, but he keeps it locked down. "Let me talk to Mavis real fast, Ms. Joyce, and then I'm ready to get to work."

She looks like she's about to protest, but then he holds out the canvas tote. "Oh, I forgot—here. I brought you some greens and key limes from my garden."

"Okay." She beams at him again, charmed. "But make it snappy, because Tamron Hall is on at one, and she's having that Common on. He seems like such a nice boy, doesn't he?"

She shuffles back to her house, riffling through the tote bag along the way. Corey waits until her door is firmly shut before he asks what he's been waiting to.

"So . . . do you want to tell me why you have that picture from your desk at work under your arm?"

"No. Not particularly."

He raises his eyebrows, clearly prepared to wait me out. I

press my lips together tightly and raise my eyebrows right back so he knows he's going to be waiting a long-ass time. There's no way I'm telling him right now I quit my job; I haven't even processed it yet myself.

The charged silence is cut through by the squeaking of brakes, and we both turn to see a gray sedan pull up to the curb. A moment later, a woman steps out of the driver side. She looks like she's in her early forties, maybe older. Her dark hair is pulled back into a severe low bun, and she's wearing a pin-striped blouse and black slacks, with a slight bulge under her jacket on the left side. I immediately know she's a cop. My body tenses, and I involuntarily take two steps back.

"Hello, Officer." Corey flashes her a one-dimpled smile, but I can tell he's just as nervous as me by the way his left hand is curled, the thumb slowly circling the pinkie.

A guy gets out of the passenger side, and my eyes zero in on the same bulge under his jacket, thinking how easily things could shift . . .

That's why it takes me a couple extra beats to place him.

"Hey, I know you."

"Good morning, Ms. Miller."

The male officer has close-cropped, shiny black hair and light brown skin. He looks around my age, but his gray suit and tie hang on him awkwardly, like a boy dressing up for eighth-grade promotion. He was wearing a uniform, not a suit, the last time I saw him, when he busted down the bedroom door in the Ackermans' house and freed me and Pearl. He asked the first questions at the scene, too, before the detectives took over and brought me to the station.

"Officer De La Rosa."

"Detective De La Rosa now, actually," he says, and I see a flicker of the proud smile he probably gave his parents, announcing this promotion. But then his eyes jump to the woman next to him, who is clearly not amused, and his voice drops an octave. "This is—"

"Detective Berry," she cuts him off. "And are you Corey Harding? Pearl Harding's father?"

Corey nods, his smile still in place while his thumb speeds up its rotation. "Yes, ma'am."

"Apologies for not calling ahead, but we found this address in your daughter's soccer registration and thought it would be best to just head over. We have a few questions about Saturday."

Saturday? Why would they want to talk to *us* about Saturday? And why would detectives be involved in the first place, unless something . . . illegal happened?

But no. That's just the anxiety taking over. What happened Saturday was tragic, not *criminal.* And anyway, there's definitely no reason for Corey and me to stress. I'm probably just extra jumpy because Officer—excuse me, *Detective* De La Rosa is here, and it's bringing up everything that happened with Principal Smith and Corinne. And see, *that's* why I don't need therapy, because I can recognize all that on my own!

"Would it be okay with you if we talked inside?" Detective Berry asks, nodding toward the door.

Out of the corner of my eye, I catch Ms. Joyce's front curtain flickering in protest. Corey's going to have a lot of questions to answer while he's installing that security system.

"Um, sure. Of course." I hold out my hands and then lead the way. When I open the door, Polly is there waiting for us. She doesn't bark because we haven't brought her an old lady or baby threat, but she jumps on Corey.

"Hey, Polly," he says quietly, scratching behind her eyes and gently moving her out of the way. Just Polly, not some silly nickname like "Polly with the good hair" . . . so he's for sure nervous.

"Mavis, what is this?"

At first I think my dad is referring to the cops I just let in, but then I see the *Shit* Post-it in his hand. Corey's eyes widen in recognition at the sparkly orange handwriting, but hopefully whatever these detectives have to say will quickly make both of them forget that.

"Oh, hello." My dad tucks the Post-it in his pocket and puts out his hand. "Elijah Miller."

"Dad, this is Detective De La Rosa and Detective Berry."

Detective Berry expertly takes out her badge and De La Rosa hurries to do the same. It's clear she's the one in charge.

"We're gathering information regarding the death of Cole Robinson. We understand you were there."

"Yes, it's so sad what happened. We saw when he first fell, and our friends Jasmine and Leon went with him to the hospital. Have you talked to them already?" Detective Berry furrows her brow at me, and I guess I should have known she's not the type who wants to be told how to do her job.

"Did they determine what the cause was yet?" I rush to fill the awkward silence. "Obviously I'm not a medical expert, but the guy *did* drink a lot of energy drinks, and I read an article— I think it was in the *LA Times*? Or actually, maybe on that doctors show on ABC? Anyway, I heard they can cause heart attacks, right? That's why they don't let kids buy them anymore?"

I didn't think Detective Berry's eyebrows could drop any lower, but look at that, they sure can. Shit. I did it again.

"Mr. Robinson didn't die of a heart attack," Detective De La Rosa says finally, eyeing his partner to see if this is the right move. "We're currently investigating this as a homicide, Ms. Miller."

Shock hits me like a blast of cold air, sending goose bumps

up my arms. Corey's mouth drops open and my dad cocks his head to the side, like he must have heard wrong.

"A homicide?"

It doesn't make any sense. Someone killed Coach Cole? And if someone did . . . why would the detectives want to talk to *us*? We didn't see anything, and we definitely didn't *do* anything.

Unless . . .

Maybe they want to talk to me as a . . . oh, I don't know, local expert? It did make the news, me finding Principal Smith, and Detective De La Rosa took my first statement, so he knows how good I am at remembering details. Maybe someone, Jasmine probably, mentioned that I was there Saturday, and they just want my take on things, to see what I noticed. That's a lot of pressure, but . . . what *else* do I have going on now?

"Here. Why don't you come sit down?"

I lead them to the living room, and we settle in our seats— my dad in the armchair, the detectives on the big couch, and Corey and me on the love seat. Polly twirls to look at everyone, wagging her tail furiously like it's a party.

Sweat begins to gather at the back of my neck. What can I tell them? Did anything stand out on Saturday? There has to be something. I don't want to let them down, but also it's a hell of a lot easier to remember important details when you *know* something bad is happening to you—like, you know, when your mom friend pulls a knife on you.

"As we were saying," Detective Berry says, pulling a small notebook out of her shirt pocket. "We have reason to believe that Cole Robinson did not die of natural causes. And—"

"Okay, so I can tell you everything I remember, but outside of the thing with the guy on the mower—Dom? I think his name was Dom?—well, it was a pretty normal day. Except when he fell. That definitely wasn't normal. But I don't know if I saw anything suspicious. I know I helped you guys out last year, but, um, maybe that was kind of a fluke? I'm not really a detect—"

Detective Berry holds up a palm, and all the words vacate my mouth like magic. "Ms. Miller, thank you for your willingness to . . . assist. But we've already received several witness statements about the morning leading up to Mr. Robinson's death." She turns her whole body toward Corey, her knees pointing at him like a neon arrow. "We actually wanted to speak to you, Mr. Harding, because from our understanding, you brought the snacks."

"The . . . snacks?" Corey blinks at them, trying to catch up. "Yes. Yes, I did."

"What did you bring?"

"Goldfish, Capri-Suns, orange slices—the usual. Detectives, I'm sorry, but I'm confused. What does this have to do with Coach Cole?"

I'm confused, too. Why does it matter what snacks Corey brought? Did Florence sic them on him? Like, *Excuse me, Officers, while you're investigating this murder* (oh my god, *murder*, I want to throw up), *can you also look into this case of inorganic snacks?*

"The reason we're interested in where the snacks came from is because the park's Green Team, led by a . . ." She flips to another page in her notes. ". . . Angela Hart? Well, they found an empty Capri-Sun pouch when they did their weekly cleanup later that day, and Ms. Hart brought it into the station."

"A Capri-Sun pouch? Why would she bring that in? Did *she* send you here?"

Corey brushes his hand against my knee, just barely, but the message is clear. *Settle down.* Which is easy for him because *he* didn't have to deal with Angela and her little SoSo Hart last year.

"She brought it in because she noticed a suspicious residue on the edge of the straw hole. And she was right to do so. Because of the unknown cause of Mr. Robinson's death, we tested the Capri-Sun pouch and found traces of sodium nitrite residue."

"Can you say that again? And a little louder? And slower?"

He's not—is he? Oh my god, *he is.*

My dad is holding out the fancy microphone he bought for his podcast, the bright red timer on his phone's recording app speeding forward. I try to communicate with wide eyes that this is beyond not okay, but he purposefully avoids looking back, like Pearl when she's hoping I'll forget bath time another night.

"Sodium ni—" Detective De La Rosa starts, but Detective Berry shoots him a stern glare that makes him clamp his lips shut.

"Did he even drink a Capri-Sun?" I ask. "He always drank those energy drinks in the cans. Did you test *those?*"

I get the answer in the form of my own stern glare from Detective Berry. *None of your business.*

"Sodium nitrite," my dad continues. "Isn't that used in gardening? That odorless, tasteless substance that can dissolve in liquid?"

Detective Berry leans forward and squints at Dad, her lips pressed flat.

"He knows that because he watches a lot of *Dateline*," I rush to explain. "Not because he goes around poisoning people!"

Detective Berry's face stays deliberately the same, but De La Rosa's mouth drops open. And yeah, I guess maybe that wasn't the most convincing thing I could say.

"My dad has never poisoned anyone," I say firmly. "None of us have."

"That's an interesting method for homicide, but how would they get it in the pouch undetected? And what did the toxicology report come back with? I need to do my research, but that would need to be a significant amount, to kill a man of that size so quickly. Unless . . . it's been happening for a while. Did you test the cups at his house?"

"Sir, we cannot give you any more information, and I'm really going to have to ask you to put that microphone away."

"I will in just a moment. But first, what do we know about his family? And who—"

"Detectives," Corey says calmly. My first instinct was to tackle my dad to the ground and, I don't know, swallow that goddamn microphone. But sure, that works, too. "I'd be happy to show you the receipts for everything I brought. And as far as I know, the kids drank them with no issues, but we can give you the numbers of all the families so you can call around and check. We'll help in any way we can."

Again, Corey is smiling, polished, but his thumb continues its circle and there's a tightness to his jaw.

"That would be great," Detective De La Rosa says. Detective Berry opens her mouth to ask something else, but Polly starts barking. There's a knock at the door, and Ms. Joyce is walking in before any of us can even stand up.

"Corey, those greens you brought me are top notch. I already have them simmering on the stove with a ham hock. And these limes." She holds one up. "You said they were key limes? Because they look mighty big for that. What kinda fertilizer are you using—oh, Officers! What a nice surprise!"

It's no surprise at all. She wants to know what's going on already, not wait a moment longer for Corey's secondhand story.

"Are you here about the reports I made about my neighbor? Because I took your colleague's advice and I'm installing my own cameras. I'm keeping them on my side of the fence because he was right, that *may* be against the law, but I couldn't find the specific code, so . . ."

She keeps talking, as if the detectives showed up on her doorstep for a social visit, but her voice fades away as I struggle to process everything we just learned.

Coach Cole was killed by drinking a poisoned Capri-Sun? It doesn't sound real . . . but these detectives sitting here in our living room, asking questions—*that* feels very real.

Who would do that? And why?

Do the detectives really think we could have anything to do with it? My dad or Corey poisoning Coach Cole, hurting *anyone*—the very idea is ridiculous.

But as I follow Detective Berry's narrowed gaze to the lime in Ms. Joyce's hand—the lime grown in Corey's garden, when apparently a substance used for gardening was put in Coach Cole's drink to murder him—I get a sinking feeling in my stomach that she may not think that's as ridiculous as I do.

EIGHT

AS THE DETECTIVES ASK THEIR QUESTIONS, MY MIND IS spinning with a million of its own.

Who sent them Corey's way? Did they insinuate that he could be involved, or did the detectives do an Olympic-level high jump to that impossible conclusion all on their own? Who would want Coach Cole dead anyway? Enough to poison a fucking Capri-Sun pouch? And has Angela Hart switched her focus to litter and recycling or whatever, now, since the whole DEI, I-care-about-Black-people thing didn't work out for her? Does she wear her pink pussy hat while she's picking up old Capri-Sun pouches?

But after Detective Berry closes her notebook and Detective De La Rosa thanks us for our time and we get Ms. Joyce back to her house with the assurance that there's still plenty of time before Tamron Hall—only one question falls out of my mouth.

"The hell was that, Dad?"

His lip curls up and one of his eyebrows drops dangerously low, a look with a very clear meaning: *Who do you think you're talking to?* It's a look that works just as well at thirty-two as it did at twelve.

"I just mean—like—" I start to stammer. "Why were you—you recording, instead of stepping in as—as an . . . I don't know—defense attorney? You know, the job you did for forty years?"

Okay, so some snark creeped back in there, and his eyebrow sinks even lower to let me know he picked up on it.

"Who needed a defense attorney?" Corey asks before my dad can explain himself.

I reel my head back. "You!"

"Me?!"

Dad sticks his microphone into Corey's scrunched-up face. "And how does that make you feel?"

"Oh my *god*, what is this, Dad?" I twirl my hand at his phone and mic. "Are you . . . is this for your *podcast*? How could this possibly be useful for your *Law and Order* recaps? You could have gotten Corey in real trouble with them."

"Again, what kinda trouble do you think I'm in, Mavis?"

"Well, our focus has shifted, just slightly," my dad says, scratching the back of his neck, suspiciously avoiding eye contact. "But it's the same genre, really."

"What does that mean?" I know my tone is veering into snotty teen territory once again, but now he's looking more guilty than offended.

"Have you heard of true crime podcasts? Oh, well, yeah, I guess you have, because I told you about them."

And because they're the most popular thing on the planet. But what does—*oh no.*

"There was that *Mommy Murders* one I was listening to, the one about the message board. And then their follow-ups on that shady kids' gym and the preschool playgroup singer . . . the things she did with that ukulele when she was off duty." He shudders and then shakes his head. "Really stellar reporting there. Anyway, Bert and I decided to try our hand at one. We're thinking maybe we can even do a live show in a few months, once we build our fan base up."

"Dad, you *cannot*. Corey's legal troubles are not—"

"My legal troubles! Now, hold on there. They didn't say anything about—"

"And wait—you were interviewing someone Friday night, weren't you? Who was that? You didn't know this would happen. *Right? You didn't know this would happen?*" I've upgraded from snotty teenager to slightly hysterical.

"Well, that was Mrs. Nelson," Dad says, as if that makes sense.

"Mrs. Nelson?!" My voice comes out shrill, close to that pitch only dogs can hear. Corey cringes. "What does *she* have to do with this, Dad?"

"I told you. Me and Bert are doing a true crime podcast. And the best ones come from people who are close to the crime. Like how Veronica was cousins with the lady who sold that girl her ukulele." He shudders again. "So we were going to focus on Principal Smith's kidnapping and how Corinne fooled us all. But *this*—this is better. I can't wait to tell Bert. We'll get in from the beginning, track what's happening *while* it's happening. This is going to blow the *Mommy Murders* right out of the water."

"Dad, are you kidding me? You cannot do that. First of all, those true crime podcasts are so exploitative—"

"Exploitative!" He lets out a loud grunt of disagreement. He starts making a show of looking around, his right hand cupped over his wide eyes.

After it's clear he's not about to stop anytime soon, I begrudgingly ask, "What are you looking for?"

"Oh, me? I'm looking for the daughter who watched a *Dateline* marathon with me a couple weeks ago? She didn't seem to think *that* was exploitative."

"That's different." Is it different? Or does it just feel different because my personal experiences aren't being mined for a story? I can tell from Dad's smug face that he knows he's got me, so I throw in some fighting words. "Plus, you're no Keith Morrison."

Corey lets out something that's either a gasp or a choked laugh. My dad sucks his teeth and bats me away.

I know it's a cheap shot, and he's going to bring it up probably once a month for the rest of my existence, but I also know I need to stop this. Like, twelve people listen to their *Law & Order* recap podcast, most of those their former lawyer buddies, but this? This might actually have a tiny chance of getting some attention. And we don't need that. First, because it's wrong to capitalize on Corinne's desperate actions, on Coach Cole's tragic death—whatever his focus is. But also? It's . . . *embarrassing.* I feel like I'm back in ninth grade and my dad's pulled up right to the front of the school, blasting Gladys Knight & the Pips and dancing in his front seat. Can't he just, like, take up golf or get really into researching World War II—you know, a normal old-man hobby?

"What about Corey?" I continue, clinging to the one thing that might make him reconsider. "This isn't just entertainment to Corey. He's a suspect for *murder.*"

Corey puts his palms up. "I need you to stop saying that, Mavis. I'm not a suspect."

"Ummm, you're a suspect."

"I'm *not* a suspect," he repeats, looking at me like I'm crazy. "I didn't do anything, and they know that now."

"Then why were you doing this?" I twiddle my thumb around my pinkie, in an exaggerated imitation of his nervous tic.

"Because I am a Black man being interviewed by the police. Did you expect me to be calm? But we good now." He waves his hand as if this was all just a gnat flying by his face, a mild annoyance. Then a smirk appears on his lips—one I know all too well from arguments past. "And if we're asking questions, I have one. Why are you home? In the middle of the day?"

I roll my eyes at him. Sure, my dad is trying to make Corey the Adnan Syed to his Sara Koenig, but let's bring this back to me.

"Yeah, why are you home?" Dad asks, raising his microphone again.

"Put the mic away, Dad," I say through my teeth, but he only lowers it slightly, hoping I don't notice. I don't want to do this right now—or, like, ever. But it also seems like I don't really have a choice. Maybe it's better to rip off the Band-Aid . . .

"I took a half day?"

Who am I kidding? I never rip off the Band-Aid. I take those suckers off one stinging millimeter at a time.

Corey purses his lips and tilts his head to the side like, *Try again.* And I can already see the gears moving behind my dad's narrowed dark brown eyes. I need to start talking fast before one of them says the Q-word.

"I left early because . . . well. I'm . . . taking a sabbatical."

Yeah, that's it. A sabbatical. A sabbatical sounds much more mature and grown than quitting without a backup plan when I have a child to support and a quickly dwindling savings account.

"Was this planned?"

None of your business . . . is what I want to say. But again, mature and grown.

"Not quite, but don't even worry. I'm looking for something, and I already have a lot of leads. I'm sure I'll find a place that appreciates me in no time, probably next week."

I take a deep breath before I meet my dad's eyes, steadying myself to see the inevitable worry, maybe even disappointment there. But he speaks before I can gather the courage.

"Good."

"*Good?*"

I nearly fall over.

He nods confidently. "Yes, good. You've been there for almost eight years. You've been an exceptional, loyal employee. You deserve to be compensated to reflect that."

It's not the response I expected from my hardworking, never-quit-a-job-in-his-life father. It's . . . overwhelming. My throat immediately feels scratchy and tight, and I have to blink away pesky tears in the corners of my eyes. "Thank you, Dad. I thought you might be . . . upset with me."

"Nah, I trust you, Mavis. You know what's best for you and Pearl." He squeezes my shoulder, and I feel my heart squeeze in tandem. If my dad approves . . . maybe this was the right choice after all. Maybe this will all be okay.

"Now, Corey, I'm not about to make the mistake of getting in between you and Ms. Joyce, but why don't you stop by after you're finished and we'll get down some tape of your initial reaction?"

What is *not* gonna be okay, apparently, is this true crime podcast my dad is stubbornly moving full speed ahead on, but that'll just have to be a battle for another day because, whew! I'm tired.

"Sounds good, Elijah."

Corey's too respectful of Dad to disagree, even though I can tell he wants to, and anyway, my dad's already walking down the hallway, like he didn't really need confirmation. Before he turns the corner, I hear him mutter to himself, "Bert is about to lose his mind."

And so am I.

I awkwardly turn back to Corey, expecting him to leave, too, before Ms. Joyce sends up an emergency flare. But he just keeps standing there . . . not leaving.

"So . . ." I try.

"Are you okay?"

The question takes me off guard, but then I soften a little. He just cares about me as a co-parent—as a friend. I need to stop looking for a fight and be nicer to him. If only for Pearl.

I open my mouth to reassure him, to thank him, but he's faster than me. "With money, I mean. Are you gonna be okay with money?"

And . . . all the softness is gone. I'm spiked and steely and sharp.

"Do you think I'm so irresponsible? Do you think I would do this if I had no money?" Which, yes, I didn't put much thought into this decision. I just rage-quit when Rose was about to start listing all the words she can't say anymore like the harbinger of the HR apocalypse. But he doesn't know that!

"I'm fine. I've *been* fine! You already pay your share, so you *don't* need to worry about mine. You don't need to worry about me at all."

"I was just trying—"

I shoot him a look that makes the rest of that sentence die in his throat. And I also maybe growl a little.

"Okay. Okay, okay. I got you. I'm sorry." He looks like he wants to say more, make another excuse, but then thinks better of it. "I'm gonna go help Ms. Joyce now. And I can do the chain on the door after . . ."

I'm already shaking my head. "Just leave it here, and I'll do it myself."

He sighs but takes the chain and a pack of screws out of his Home Depot bag.

"All right. See you later, Mavis."

SO, I HAVE EVERY INTENTION OF IMMEDIATELY LOGGING onto LinkedIn and searching for job postings.

Honestly.

I do.

But then I try every one of my passwords, and none of them work, even the real obscure one I only use for my IRS login. And then I can't get the password reset email to go through, no matter how many times I try, and *then* I'm somehow locked out of my account. So, I switch over to ZipRecruiter, because I heard an ad for it on a podcast (don't worry which one), but my vision starts to blur in boredom with every "Program Manager" and "Project Director" position I scroll past, and before I know it I'm over on Google, typing "Coach Cole" and "murder" in the search bar.

It's really just to look out for Corey. The father of my child. Because I'm a good person.

My curiosity is second to that—a very distant second.

Nothing relevant comes up with that first search, so I change "Coach Cole" to "Cole Robinson" and "murder" to "death," and that brings up an article from the *Beachwood Breeze*, a local online news site, from yesterday afternoon. Skimming the article, I see that it doesn't seem to have many more details than I had at the same time. It says he "collapsed on the field" and the "cause is unknown." But I guess that makes sense. We would have heard sooner, before the police arrived, if it were described as a murder in the *Beachwood Breeze*. Ms. Joyce would've been banging on our door with a printout, courtesy of Mackenzie Skinner's Wi-Fi connection. At the end, though, a familiar name does catch my eye.

Aquamarine Alligators team mom and online parenting expert Florence Michaelson describes the immediate aftermath of the beloved coach's medical emergency. "Marigold, my 22-month-old, was inconsolable, and Axel clutched his own chest, almost like Coach Cole's pain was his own. He tried to run to him . . . to be a helper like we've raised him to be. It was a moment that will leave a mark on my littles' hearts, and mine as their mama. We have a lot of healing to do as a family—and as a community."

God, leave it up to Florence to find a way to make this man's death about her and her precious, sensitive child.

I don't remember Axel, or her, doing anything after Coach Cole fell to the ground. It was Jasmine and Leon who rushed to his side—not that *I* should be talking. That reminds me, though—I should text Jasmine and see if they've been visited by the detectives yet. I have to believe, for my own peace of mind, that Corey wasn't their only stop.

But first let me see if I can find out anything more about Coach Cole. Because the question that keeps lingering in my head is *Why?* Why would someone want to do this to him? Something so obviously premeditated and conniving? Who was this guy, anyway?

So I take away "death" from the search bar, leaving just "Cole Robinson," and . . . there's not much there at all. I scroll past a lot of *other* Cole Robinsons—a Realtor in Oklahoma and a *Bachelorette* contestant sent home at the first rose ceremony. There's another article in the *Beachwood Breeze* about this Cole Robinson's expanded soccer program, and a personal website with links to registration for this season, plus some workout boot camps he apparently runs on weekday mornings. But no mentions of him in sports articles, no Wikipedia page . . . which doesn't make sense if he was such a big soccer player. Maybe it was overseas?

Hmm . . . okay. That's something I need to follow up with Leon about.

I say a little prayer that the FBI guy assigned to me is on his lunch break, and then type "sodium nitrite" into Google. Pictures of a yellowish-white substance in a tiny glass jar pop up, along with formulas that give me panicky flashbacks to tenth-grade chemistry. I barely passed that class with a 70 percent, and even then I'm pretty sure Ms. Collier was just taking pity on me.

I scan and see that it's tasteless and odorless—so my dad was right there, even if he *should* have kept that to himself. Combing through a few more pages of results, I learn that it's used for preserving meat and fish and as an antidote for cyanide poisoning. And there are even some articles about a disturbing new wave of it being used in suicides, and how it reduces a person's ability to breathe. I feel sick, remembering how he clutched his chest, the disturbing sound of his quick, wheezing gasps for air. But could Coach Cole have done this to himself? No . . . the detectives must have ruled that out, right? God, I wish I had asked more questions, gotten more information, but the shock of it all was just too overwhelming.

The one thing I *don't* see, though, is anything about gardening. Could Dad have gotten *that* wrong? I really hope so, because I don't think I was just being paranoid. Detective Berry was looking at that lime from Corey's garden weirdly . . .

I type "sodium nitrite" and "gardening" and a lot comes up . . . but wait. This says "sodium nitrate." Are they different? I toggle back and forth, looking at the formulas, the descriptions, but my eyes start to cross. It seems like they're . . . basically the same thing? Or one breaks down into the other? One site calls them cousins . . . Chemicals can be cousins??

God, I'm bad at this. Ms. Collier definitely did some incredibly kind math to get me to that 70 percent. I *must* have remembered it wrong, and they said nitrate, not nitrite, because I know for sure they didn't contradict what Dad said about gardening. I'll ask him later, just to double-check . . . or maybe not. I'm not trying to be on his podcast.

I let out an involuntary groan. Another thing I need to worry about. *Later.*

So . . . sodium nitrate then. It's used as a fertilizer, it looks like? Mostly for organic farms?

Why would someone have that on hand? And I feel like there are a lot of other, more convenient poisons that could be used . . . not that I spend a lot of time thinking about poisons. It just doesn't make sense—unless the murderer is someone familiar with sodium nitrate because they use it often . . .

I don't think Corey uses whatever this stuff is in his little apartment complex community garden. If he did, he would have said that, at least to me and Dad. So who else was around that works with plants?

Well, there *is* Dom Dwyer, the facilities manager who wielded that lawn mower like a weapon in his battle with Coach Cole. A quick search confirms that sodium nitrate isn't used on grass . . . but there are lots of other plants used in the landscaping at Brady Park, too?

He *clearly* hated Coach Cole. But why would he be so obvious about it if he was just going to poison him? And he didn't come anywhere near the Capri-Suns, as far as I remember—he was too busy making the toddlers on the next field sneeze and cry. He could have sent someone, though? And maybe the big fight was to throw off suspicion?

Hold on, I need to write this all down. It'll all float right out of my brain by tomorrow otherwise—like my Social Security number and Pearl's first word and everything else important.

I grab the first thing with paper I see, which is the gratitude journal I bought myself last month in one of many recommitments to self-care and never actually got around to using. I turn to the first page, cross out the *What I'm Grateful For . . .* heading and write *Suspects* instead.

1. Dom Dwyer

. . . and that's all I've got. Is that really all I've got?? There has to be someone else who's a possibility.

A crazed fan, maybe?

I mean, no one *looked* like a crazed fan, outside of the moms fawning over his thighs. But they definitely didn't want him dead. And from his online presence, it doesn't seem like he was really big enough to have some stalker coming for him.

There's also . . . Hank?

He didn't make a secret of how much he hated Cole. But is being pissed about your kid not getting enough play time a motive for *murder*? Would someone really kill over *that*?

Still, stealing the field from an adult capture the flag league isn't much more of a reason either . . .

2. Hank Michaelson

Okay, now, who else?
Trisha?

Her name flashes in my mind like a reflex. Could it have been Trisha? Was Trisha even at the park?

No. But. I wouldn't be *surprised* if she was involved somehow. That woman is pure evil.

3. *Trisha Holbrook*

Clearly I'm stuck.

There's one person I know it'll help to talk this through with, though. Because we've done this before: solved a mystery no one asked us to with absolutely no relevant experience or resources, just nosiness and *the audacity*. So I pick up my phone and text him.

> So, turns out Coach Cole didn't have
> a heart attack. He was murdered.

In a few minutes, Jack's response comes in. **What??**
And then, **Can you step out for a minute so we can talk?**
Oh yeah, because it's working hours, when my phone is usually on do not disturb. Except I no longer *have* working hours.

> Right. I also quit my job?

My phone buzzes almost immediately.

"You quit your job? Mavis, what happened?"

I quickly fill him in on the DEIB courageous conversation from hell and how after years of keeping it together, my professional Mavis software short-circuited and I just couldn't do it anymore. Couldn't keep going and pretending everything was fine when Rose made it so clear for the billionth time last week that there was no promotion, no pay raise, on the horizon, or ever. And so I said "screw it" to the sunk cost fallacy, threw away almost eight years of hard work and building my reputation, and walked out without looking back.

When I'm done unloading, it's almost silent—the only sound is me catching my breath. And I feel a wave of worry over what must be going through Jack's head. Does he think I was stupid? Immature? I did exactly what you're *not* supposed to do, after months and months when I *could* have researched other positions, asked for letters of rec, given a proper notice . . .

Finally, he speaks. "Good."

"Good?!"

Did he and my dad coordinate how to play this or something?

"Yes, good," he repeats. "Now you have time and space to find something that really makes you happy. A company that appreciates all you have to offer. That treats you with the dignity and respect you know that you deserve."

"Why do I feel like you're about to break out into 'The Greatest Love of All'?"

He lets out a low chuckle, but his voice remains sincere. "And you can finally get some rest, like you're always saying you want to do."

"Yeah!"

"Which is definitely what you're doing right now, and *not* writing out a list of suspects."

I glance guiltily at my repurposed gratitude journal.

"Yeah?"

He sighs, but I can hear the smile behind it. "Okay, tell me what you've got then. Is Trisha on there?"

". . . Yeah."

He laughs, long and loud. "Trisha wasn't even *there*, Mavis. I think we gotta let her off the hook for this one."

"Fine," I grumble, begrudgingly crossing her off. I quickly fill him in on what we learned from Detectives Berry and De La Rosa today, how it's being ruled a homicide, the traces of sodium *nitrate* found on the Capri-Sun pouch, and the unsettling feeling I got from Detective Berry when Ms. Joyce talked up Corey's homegrown produce. I give him my best *Chemistry for Dummies* summary of sodium nitrate and its uses with plants, and I tell him all of my thoughts on Dom Dwyer and Hank Michaelson as suspects. Their motives sound even weaker when I say them out loud, though.

"But still, it's more than *Corey*," I insist. "There's just no way at all he could have done that. Sourcing some obscure chemical, funneling it into a Capri-Sun pouch—and what? Resealing it? It's laughable. Corey did even worse than *me* in chemistry—he had to retake it the summer before senior year! I wonder if we could get his transcript to show the detectives?"

"We *could*. But also, regardless of his chemistry grade, there would be no reason for Corey—"

"Yeah. Yeah! There's no motive! Corey just met Coach Cole. And they were . . . normal with each other. Acquaintances. What's their theory here? That he did this *for funsies*?!"

Okay, so I *do* yell that, but it's just a minor yell. Like an ahhh-look-at-that-spider yell, not an a-car-just-ran-over-my-grandma yell. There's no reason for the, in my opinion, very judgy throat clearing I hear on his end.

"I'm just . . . going to throw this out there. Don't get annoyed with me." Those words instantly summon all the annoyance in my being. "Do you think maybe you're . . . trying to find a distraction? From how you're feeling, and what happened at your job?"

"Of course not! This could be so dangerous for Corey if it goes the wrong way. I have to protect him. He's—family."

Never mind that I was just kind of an asshole to Corey over . . . god, I barely even remember now. I still *care* about him and that's the *main* reason I'm looking into this. If it's a distraction, too—well, that's just an added bonus.

"You're right. I get that. And I'm going to help you in any way I can. I just don't want you to lose sight of taking care of yourself, especially now that you have this time to make it a priority." There's a pause, and I wonder if he's thinking about bringing up therapy again. If he does, there may be an a-car-just-ran-over-my-grandma yell in our very near future.

"You know I think you can do anything. If there's anyone who can figure this out it's you . . . but it's also okay to let the detectives do their job, too. Take a nap, watch some *Bachelor*—that's on again, right?"

"The new guy has the personality of the crusty old sponge you find under the sink when you first move into a new apartment," I say, stubbornly ignoring all the rest of Jack's, okay, fairly good points.

"But you're still gonna watch it."

"Definitely."

"So I'm not going to tell you not to do this because I know you will anyway—"

"And you would be correct."

He laughs, and it feels like sunshine on my skin after being stuck in office air-conditioning all day. "But just . . . take it easy, don't let it take over your life like last time."

I want to remind him that if it *hadn't* taken over my life last time, then Principal Smith might not have been found until it was too late. I wouldn't have the extra money in my savings account that makes this unexpected unemployment less terrifying. *We* wouldn't have found this relationship.

But I'm also sitting on my bed in the middle of a completely free weekday, and I'm choosing to spend it writing down suspects in a gratitude journal I bought in the name of self-care. A gratitude journal that I couldn't even make myself do *one* page of when its only purpose was to help me.

He's not wrong that when given the chance, I will put everything in the world before myself.

Still, my time is my own again, and I get to decide how to spend it—*he* just said that. I finally have the space to do what makes me feel good. And I *do* feel good right now, especially compared to this morning. Instead of overwhelmed and exhausted, I feel . . . useful. Present. *Balanced.*

It's like the messy desk in my brain was cleared off, and I have control over what gets put back on there. Pearl. Jack. A slow, intentional job search. A possible murder investigation. There's lots more room for it all with Project Window's sprawling, infuriating piles swept right into the trash.

I hear the rustling of his hand over the receiver and the murmur of children's voices. "Sorry, one of my small groups is here. I have to go."

"It's okay. And I hear you, I promise. But I'm all good. I feel better than ever, actually."

Hi Mavis,

I really hope that you'll reconsider your decision today. Can we hop on a call or a Microsoft Teams meeting to discuss? I'll hold off on locking your accounts until I hear back from you!

If it's about the DEIB meeting . . . I wasn't actually going to say the words, only the first letters. Just so you know. And I really think it would have been so much better if you had delivered it like we had originally planned. If you do decide to come back, I can double the stipend!

Anxiously awaiting your reply!!

Warm Regards,
Rose

PS: I've attached a Word document that I need to convert into a PDF . . . can you help me with this for old times' sake (haha 😊)? I tried to do it the way you showed me, but I just can't get the hang of it. Maybe you can send screenshots with directions if you're really not coming back? Nelson says he doesn't know how to do it either.

———

Rose Johannes
Executive Director
Project Window

Please consider the environment before printing this email.

Mavis,

I knew it was going to be a shit show, Rose delivering a diversity training, and I should have stepped in and shut the thing down as soon as she tried and failed to do that land acknowledgment. But I guess that doesn't help you now, does it? I'm sorry, I don't know why I'm even sending this. I think I feel like this is all my fault? You really deserved my job. I wouldn't have applied if I knew they were passing over someone as qualified as you to hire me. I would quit if it meant you would get it but . . . we both know it doesn't work that way. Also, Rebecca filed the divorce papers last week, so I really need the money. I hope you understand. I know you'll land somewhere great in no time.

Sincerely,
Nelson
——

Nelson Nelson
Program Director
Project Window
"Do. Or do not. There is no try."—Yoda

NINE

"HEY, MOMMY. I HAVE A NEW MYSTERY FOR YOU TO INVEStigate."

Pearl and I are walking to school—well, I'm walking and she's scootering—because this is something we have time to do now that I'm unemployed. It felt peaceful, the first peeks of sunshine on my face, the cool morning air that hasn't had a chance to turn too warm yet and remind me I need to be worried about climate change. My heartbeat—which, it turns out, has a setting other than thunderous—has slowed even more, and my breath was smooth and normally paced. I was just thinking, *Wow, I could get used to this.* Is this how those enlightened white ladies—the YouTube yoga lady with the dog, Tanya from the meditation app, even *Bethany* . . . is this how they feel all the time?

But now I'm ready to switch right back to unenlightened Mavis again because *how does she know?* Corey and I agreed that we wouldn't tell her anything about the police visit, and he doesn't know that I've decided to look into this myself. Did she overhear my dad working on his stupid podcast? He always forgets to plug his headphones in.

God, Pearl has been through so much these past months, and this is just further evidence that I wasn't doing a good job of protecting her. How much I've been dropping the ball . . .

"It's the mystery," she continues, "of why Mr. Forest gave Anabella the lead in *Annie* when she can't even sing! She sounds like . . . like—permission to say that bad word you taught me?"

"Permission *not* granted."

Intense relief (mixed with amusement and slight horror at this child's *audacity*) makes my voice come out all strangled.

"Well, she sounds bad, and I think there's something suspicious going on. Because . . . someone *else* should have been Annie. And it makes me feel like I'm—I'm in *the red zone!*"

That much is clear from the tight grip she has on her scooter's pink handlebars and how she is furiously pumping her leg. I also can probably guess who she thinks should have been cast as Annie instead.

"Watch out!" I warn as she almost takes out an Australian cattle dog being walked the other way. I wave an apology at its pajama-wearing owner.

"No, Anabella needs to watch out!" Pearl snaps. "Because someone is going to do something about this, and that someone is *you*, Mommy!"

"Oh my god. Where did you come from?" I ask, because what do I even say to that.

Pearl throws me a side-eye over her shoulder. "Your belly!"

I laugh, and she scoots faster, throwing her head back as she breaks into song. Each note is louder, more dramatic than the last, as if Mr. Forest is walking with us and this is her moment to prove just how wrong he was.

"Wem-blee! Wem-bleeeeeeeee!"

She takes one hand off her handlebars to hold up her pointer finger like Mariah Carey and just barely dodges a woman pushing her kindergartener in a stroller. I jog to keep up with her, and as sweat drips down my back, I start to regret this whole walking-to-school business.

"Wem-bleeeeee-eeeee-EEEEEE-eeeeeeeeeeeee!"

"Is that one of the songs from *Annie*, baby?" I ask once she reaches the corner and has to stop.

"Oh, no. I heard Daddy say that on the phone. Wem-blee. It sounded funny."

Wem-blee? Now, why does that sound so familiar?

But then I get a flash of another phone call of Corey's I overheard, years ago. His agent calling to tell him he'd been chosen for a big pop star's band on the international leg of her tour. The first stop: Wembley, a huge stadium outside London. He was so excited to play there for the first time that he didn't notice how upset I was about him leaving, again.

There's only one reason Corey would be talking to someone about Wembley. Because he got another offer, another opportunity he can't pass up—another reason to leave.

I shouldn't even be surprised, but I am. He made a promise—not just to me this time, but *to Pearl*. How can he go back on that so easily? After only a few months . . . Pearl was just getting used to him being here. I was, too.

I'm all flustered, as worry and anger and sadness swirl in my chest, but luckily Pearl doesn't seem to notice. She's scooting ahead and has moved on from her *Annie* beef to *another* beef she has with Mrs. Tennison, who apparently still owes them a pizza party for good behavior, which she promised a whole month ago.

"—and she didn't even care when I reminded her that my birthday is on Sunday and that would be the perfect occasion for a pizza par— Ahhhh! Ew! Eeeeeewwwww!"

Her scrunched-up face—and the smell—quickly give away what she rolled her scooter through on the sidewalk. But her disgust seems to be rapidly shifting to excitement.

"Permission to say that bad word you taught me?!"

"No. The answer is still no."

WHEN I GET HOME, SWEATY AND SORE FROM HUNCHING over to roll Pearl's scooter the whole way back, I almost text Corey.

You gotta lot of nerve butting into my business—not to mention getting our daughter's hopes up!—when you're apparently plotting your getaway after NOT EVEN THREE MONTHS!

But after doing a few laps around the house while Polly excitedly scampers around my feet, and doing some deep cleansing breaths that really sound more like attempts to breathe fire—I decide *no*. This is my time. I get to decide how to spend it. I get to control how I feel. I'm not going to interrupt this new calm—this enlightenment—for him, or anybody.

I am going to rest. I am going to self-care!

I have a whole day ahead of me, just *for me*.

So I'm doing it for real. Right now.

Well . . . first I do a load of laundry because I get another one of those goddamn alerts on my phone that I can't figure out how to stop. And *then* I do a load of dishes just to work off the rage I feel about *him* putting that stupid app on my phone in the first place and acting like he cares so much *when he's leaving*! (Also, the whole house smells like the salmon I made for dinner last night, so I don't really have a choice.)

But then I get back on track and do one of those YouTube yoga videos. Polly doesn't get the message that she's supposed to act like the sweet, compliant dog in the video and keeps flopping on my head during child's pose. Still, it's very relaxing. My heartbeat goes back to that slow, steady rhythm.

When that's done, I try and make an appointment to finally get my eyebrows done today because those suckers continue to rival Eugene Levy's. But Vicky, my eyebrow lady, doesn't have anything available on her online booking system, and I have to send her a message begging for something this year. It's okay, though. I have time! This is my restful, balanced life now. I don't have to fit it all into one day.

So *then* I decide to meditate because I never have time to and now I have nothing but time, but turns out it's hard to sit in quiet contentment when my brain is occupied with how I'm going to pick a fight with my ex-husband and the murder investigation I've started to outline in my gratitude journal because I was trying to *help* my ex-husband, and also, hmmmm, I wonder if the detectives have talked to Dom Dwyer yet because *surely* people have already informed them of his behavior on Saturday, too, so they *must* know that he's a way more likely suspect than Corey . . . and then the meditation is over. But again, it's okay. I don't have to be an expert meditator right away. Tanya says it's a practice, and the most important part is showing up. And I showed up!

I drink what feels like at least half of my giant water bottle and check the clock over the stove. It must be almost time to pick up Pearl at this point. But wow, no . . . it's somehow only ten. That can't be right. I check my phone, though, and okay. Yeah. I guess it is. There are . . . a lot of hours until pickup. But hey, that means I'm self-caring efficiently. I'm already, like, really good at this. And I'm also not thinking about Corey or his betrayal at all, so I need to keep it up.

Hmmm . . . what else, what else . . .

Those wellness ladies seem to really like crystals. Or maybe

I could look into that senior Tai Chi my dad was talking about? Oh, wait, exercise! Exercise is self-care! I don't need Bethany's MLM course to teach me that. I can walk. Or run! Even better.

I rummage in my drawers for exercise clothes. I don't have the Lululemon wardrobe of most of the moms at Knoll, or even the Old Navy dupes, because I don't exercise enough to have a specific outfit for it . . . or exercise at all. I find some black leggings under a stack of old T-shirts I've received for free over the years and then apparently vowed to hold on to forever. The bottom is a little worn out, but I hold them up to the sunshine streaming in the window. Not . . . *totally* see-through. They'll do. I pair them with the longest of those free T-shirts, just in case—a black one with **Beachwood Credit Union Has My Back** printed in Comic Sans on the back (very clever), which I'm pretty sure they included in a bag with a branded pen and mini sewing kit when I signed up for my first debit card. And then I add the fancy belt bag Jasmine gave me as a birthday gift in November—which I haven't worn yet, because as far as I can tell it's just a fanny pack that has been rebranded and are we really out here wearing fanny packs now? But I *do* need somewhere to put my stuff.

I look at the finished product in the mirror. I resemble a woman who regularly runs . . . a woman who regularly walks. A woman who is capable of walking if she absolutely has to and there is no convenient tram available.

I take a selfie as proof to text Jack. **Going for a run! Woo! Self-care!**

And then I guess . . . I actually have to do this? Yes, I'm going to do this.

I shut the door on a betrayed-looking Polly and then start walking—briskly—up our street and the next, to the crosswalk on Maple, and over to the neighborhood surrounding Brady

Park, where I do a few laps around the track. I even break into a little jog at one point, and then immediately regret it when my lungs decide to be all dramatic and act like they don't work anymore, and then I just walk again.

And it feels good. Eventually I get into a rhythm where my lungs calm down and breathe in fresh air and my limbs warm up and start moving like they've done this before. And my mind clears of all thoughts except *Isn't this nice, that I can feel this good, that I can do what I've always wished I had time to do.* And *that's* what I'm thinking when all of a sudden I'm standing in front of the storage shed on the edge of Brady Park, across from the now-empty playground and the basketball courts.

I squint at the typed sign on the door, protected with clear packaging tape: *Office of the Facilities Manager.* I didn't even *know* Dom Dwyer had an office. It was my subconscious that brought me here, if anything. Probably just coincidence, most likely. That's *definitely* not the reason I wore all black.

I was exercising. Self-caring! But now that I'm here—well, how can I not take a quick peek? It's just . . . multitasking. And it made me feel so good yesterday, poking around at the puzzle, using my brain for something useful and interesting. It'll probably help me relax even more right now if I find some answers. Like, I don't know, a giant bottle of sodium nitrate sitting on his desk? Perfect. I can tell the detectives, clear Corey's name, and then take a nap! It's a win-win for everyone. Except, well . . . Dom.

I do a quick scan around the park. There are two guys playing on the basketball courts, but they're too busy to pay attention to me. And I don't see Dom anywhere. There's a speck on the far, far side of the park, near the duck pond, that *may* be him on his mower, but I would hear him coming on that thing. What harm would it be to just take a look around?

I twist the doorknob before I can talk myself out of it.

Locked. Damn it. Of course it's not going to be that easy. I wish I had acquired some more useful skills in my thirty-two years on this earth, like lock-picking or kicking a door open like they do on TV shows—but if you need me to convert a Word doc to a PDF, I'm your girl!

What about that credit card thing they *also* always do on TV shows? Does that actually work? It looks so simple (and like it doesn't require as much core strength). I might as well try . . .

I grab my wallet out of my fanny pack—excuse me, belt bag—and flip through my cards. Which one can I afford to lose if this goes horribly wrong and the thing snaps in half? My Project Window employee ID card sticks out at the top like it's volunteering as tribute. I'm not going to use *that* one again, especially after that email Rose sent me last night.

After a quick study of a wikiHow article and three failed attempts, the lock makes a satisfying click. I'm in! I do a little shoulder shimmy and, *okay*, something resembling the sprinkler because, oh my god, I did it! But then I remember that this is technically illegal and I swiftly shut the door behind me so I don't get caught.

The sign on the door may say *Office*, but the decor in this place definitely leans more shed-chic. There's a Weedwacker leaning next to the door, with two large jugs of gasoline seemingly supporting it. Two of the walls are covered with shelves loaded with supplies, interrupted only by two dingy windows that cast the tiny room in an amber light. The only thing that hints at an "office" is a metal desk in the corner with a brown folding chair pulled up to it. It's covered with messy stacks of papers.

Since it looks like I'm not going to get lucky with a dartboard that has Coach Cole's face on it or a signed note titled "This is How I Killed My Nemesis Cole and Why," I start searching the room for clues. There's a big bottle of Roundup on one of the sagging shelves. I remember a *Dateline* episode about some woman slipping that in her husband's morning coffee for a few months. On one of the wall hooks holding up the tools, I see some particularly sharp garden shears. You could slice an artery with those. And I almost trip over a giant blue jug of graffiti remover and nearly take myself out. Dom could've conveniently left that next to Cole during one of his paces next to the field— or just knocked him over the head with it.

But, of course, none of those are the actual murder weapon I'm looking for. I don't see sodium nitrate anywhere . . . but I guess he would have to be pretty careless to just leave it around?

I head over to his desk, holding out hope for a printed receipt from ChemicalsForYou.com. I sift through some invoices, a repair to the park bathrooms. Nothing useful. Underneath is a blue file folder, stuffed with more papers. The first is an official-looking form that reads: **Appeal of the Beachwood City Council's Decision.**

The form is filled in with scratchy handwriting. **Dominic Dwyer** is listed after **Complainant**, and under **Reasons for Appeal**, he wrote: *I believe that Cole Robinson (formerly Cole Dabrowski) of Coach Cole's Soccer Stars has been dishonest with the council, and in light of this, Brady Park's weekend schedule should be reviewed again. Please see attached documents.*

Cole Dabrowski? I flip to the documents. There's Coach Cole on the front page of West Virginia University's student paper—much younger, but unmistakably him. He even has the same notches shaved into his eyebrows. Below his picture is an account of a physical fight he got into with the ref. The next page is another fight, this time with an opposing player, and after that, an article about how he lost his athletic scholarship.

Okay, so Cole had a temper, clearly. And he changed his name? What happens if I google "Cole Dabrowski" instead?

I quickly pull out my phone and . . . there we go. Here are all the hits I expected to find the first time I searched him up. Cole Dabrowski *was* a professional soccer—or football—player. But after he left West Virginia University, he seems to have played only one season on a team in Iceland before a knee injury took him out. So, not exactly the big-shot career I thought he had.

Suddenly, I'm aware of the sound of the mower buzzing. Was that always there? It's kind of like white noise . . . but no. I know I didn't hear it when I first walked in here. Still, it sounds pretty far away—I remember from Saturday, how loud it is when it's close. So I think I have a couple more minutes to look through Dom's file.

The next page makes me gasp.

It's a mug shot. It's definitely Coach Cole, much closer to his current age . . . or the age he *was*. Except his eyes are bloodshot and he's missing the charming smile he always had at the ready for the parents.

I frantically flip to the next page, and there's a long rap sheet. Public intoxication, disturbing the peace. Many of these look like they line up with his college years, but there are some later, too, probably after he returned from Iceland. And next is what looks like a police report? How did Dom even get this?

Incident Type: Domestic Dispute

Address of Occurrence: 9856 Sumac Ave., Riverside, CA 92202

So, he lived in Riverside. That's not too far from here, depending on the traffic. The 22 to the 55 to the 91. I keep reading.

On April 17, 2018, officers arrived at the residence of Cole and Irene Dabrowski in response to a noise disturbance complaint. When police approached the house, Mrs. Dabrowski ran from the front door and shouted, "The only crime that happened here is that disgusting woman willingly sucking his crusty-ass toes. A crime against humanity!" Mr. Dabrowski emerged after her. We observed redness on the right side of his face under his eye, possibly from altercation.

And then, a little farther down . . .

After speaking with both parties and a cooling-off period, Mr. Dabrowski asked us to leave. He was counseled regarding his options but stated repeatedly that nothing occurred and he did not feel as if he was in danger. He also asked us to add to the record that his toes are not crusty.

Whoa. Coach Cole was kinda . . . a fuckup. Not that I'm trying to speak ill of the dead! But . . . is there another way to say it? Being a fuckup isn't a reason to get killed, though. It seems like he really just messed up his own life. Well, except for his wife—who is probably his *ex*-wife at this point. I never saw him wearing a ring. But would she kill him over infidelity from that many years ago? She got violent, clearly, but still, that motive feels pretty weak. Dom's motive does, too, honestly, especially after finding all this. Why would he poison Cole if he was appealing the city council's decision and still had a chance for his capture the flag league? Was he just, like, hedging all his bets? It seems extreme. *All of this* seems too extreme for my current list of suspects.

The buzz of the mower cuts through my thoughts. Yeah,

that's definitely getting louder. And closer. I need to get out of here before I'm caught.

I can't just leave all this behind, though. I need to show Jack—I need to show the detectives! Do they know all of this about Cole's background? Detective Berry would probably hang up on me before I got a word out, but I feel like Detective De La Rosa might be receptive, at least.

My hands shake as I fumble with the folder. I can't just take it, because then Dom will know for sure someone has been here. And if he does have something to do with this, I don't want him on guard. My heart pounds. The panic builds, tightening my chest. Damn, I made it, what—twenty-four hours? A normal heart rate was nice while it lasted.

I don't—ugh—maybe I can stick it—*No, Mavis, there is absolutely no reason for you to stick these papers in the back of your already stretched-out leggings. You have a camera, for god's sake.*

The blood rushing in my ears is thunderous as I take a few photos, but the hum of the mower is almost drowning it out. It must be right on the other side of the shed. I don't have any more time.

I do my best to put the folder back where it was and then sprint out of the shed . . . right into a mob.

TEN

INSTEAD OF PITCHFORKS, THE MOB IS WIELDING WATER bottles in limited edition colors.

They're all women, late twenties to middle age, with balayage hair in swinging ponytails and expensive sneakers. And they're all wearing black athleisure. The expensive kind. Their clothes don't have stretched-out, slightly sheer bottoms or advertisements for the local credit union.

And slowly, as I come down from the fear of being discovered by Dom, I realize I know some of them. There are a couple of moms I recognize from drop-off and PTA meetings at Knoll, plus Christine, the Clover Scouts troop leader and queen of passive-aggressive emails, and Claudia, whose badge-ironing job I stole. She's *still* scowling at me, so I guess she hasn't let that total betrayal go yet. In sharp contrast, my neighbor Mackenzie Skinner is right next to her, waving and smiling. I almost don't recognize her at first because I don't think I've ever seen her wearing anything other than spandex in various shades of neon.

"Mavis! Oh my god! Hi!"

I wave back. Hopefully Ms. Joyce isn't hiding in the bushes, adding this to her long list of evidence that Mackenzie is my little friend.

Someone who was kneeling down, tying her shoe, suddenly jerks up. It's Bethany. My stomach drops, and from the way her eyes narrow, it's clear she's not happy to see me either. But then her face quickly morphs into a practiced smile.

"Hey girl! What are you doing here?"

I don't know if it's embarrassment over yesterday morning's scene or fear that I'm about to be pitched again, but I get the overwhelming urge to run away. Except Dom's mower has pulled into view, and I'm only going to call attention to myself if I take off now. So I step into the mob and try to look like I belong. I've got the outfit down, at least.

"Oh, yay! Are you going to join us?" Mackenzie says, clapping her hands in excitement.

I nod, accepting my fate. "Yes. Um. Totally!"

"Are you sure, Mavis? I didn't think this was your thing." With her weird, plastic smile still firmly in place, Bethany looks me up and down with suspicion. She turns to the group. "This isn't really her thing."

"Oh, this is my thing!" I insist. "This is, like, more my thing than . . . anything."

I have no fucking idea what exactly it is I'm claiming as my thing, but out of the corner of my eye, I see Dom shutting off his mower and looking at us with interest. I adjust my position so my face is out of his view.

"Are you sure? I know you're busy." She swivels to look at all the women again. "She's *busy*."

The way she says it, I know it means more than just the *Merriam-Webster* dictionary definition to this group. Claudia wrinkles her nose in confirmation, and I feel a flash of annoyance bordering on anger. This feels like middle school shit.

I mean, I get it. Bethany's probably pissed at me about yesterday, and okay, I shouldn't have yelled at her. But also, she should have taken no for an answer the first time instead of pushing it to that point.

I need to fit in with this group, though. At least until Dom is gone. I sneak another quick glance and see that he's pulling his keys from his belt loop to unlock his shed/office door. Did I remember to lock it? God, I hope I put everything back where it was.

"I'm actually on a, um . . . *sabbatical* from work, so I'd love to join. Really."

Bethany looks unconvinced, which is a sharp turn from the relentless saleswoman yesterday, but Mackenzie loops her arm through mine. Yeah, if Ms. Joyce hears about this, it's going to set me back like six months of me-and-Mackenzie-are-not-friends protests.

"Well, we're going to set up over there." Bethany points to an open area in the park. "Everyone's welcome."

She manages to say that in the *least* welcoming tone, but no one else seems to notice it as they smile and follow her, picking up on whatever conversations I interrupted. I try to look back at Dom again, but Mackenzie pulls me in closer and tugs me along.

"I think this will be good for you," she says, her voice bubbly and bright. "Ms. Joyce told me that you knew Cole, too, and that's why the police were at your house yesterday. This will be *such* a good way to deal with those feelings and find closure, you know? I'm so glad you ran into us."

Wait, Ms. Joyce and her were talking? And about *me*? Why is Ms. Joyce allowed to make small talk with her nemesis but I can't even wave hello across the street?

But I ask the most pressing question.

"What does Cole have to do with this?"

"Oh, Cole ran our Tuesday morning exercise boot camp! It's part of the Balanced With Bethany program. Exercise is the *E* in her I LUV ME method!"

"He did? And—*you're* in her downline?"

"Downstream," she corrects me with a seriousness that does not match the silliness of that term at all. "And yes, I love it! I was one of the first to join Bethany. *Before* she got sick."

Her eyes well up. I wonder if she believes the bullshit, that Bethany's personal brand of self-care cured her cancer.

"So I've seen, firsthand, the miracles this method can work. It's been *so* inspiring."

Yep, and there we go. I take back everything I said about yelling at Bethany. She deserved that. She deserved *more*.

"I'm so humbled and grateful that I get to work with her to help women live healthy, happy, and well-balanced lives. And my business just keeps growing and growing! I'm going to hit the Absolute Wellness Guru rank next month!"

Her phrasing feels familiar, but that's probably because it's lifted straight from the handbook. And Absolute Wellness Guru—is that lower or higher than Ultimate Wellness Goddess? How much does Bethany get off each of them?

But as much as I want to snark, I need to bring it back to the most confusing thing here. "So . . . Bethany—she knows Cole?"

I guess it would make sense, because her daughter was enrolled in his soccer program. But there are hundreds of kids in his program . . .

"Yeah! Oh yeah, they've collaborated for *years* now. He's helped her develop a lot of her exercise curriculum in the method, and they're partnering together on a new Balanced With Bethany supplement line. It's so exciting! Well, uh . . . partnered, I guess." She fixes her face into an exaggerated frown and mimes a tear falling down her cheek. "But from what I've heard, they were mostly done before he, well . . . *you know*." Her face lights up, sadness over. "Actually, it would be a great time to join us and build your own business. You could get in at the ground floor, because Balanced With Bethany is just going to skyrocket from here! If you're interested, we can hop on a call later—"

"Okay but what does *this* have to do with Cole? Whatever you guys are doing right now?"

I have a lot of other questions swirling in my mind. *Bethany and Cole knew each other? They were in business together? Why didn't she mention that yesterday? And what about the game on Saturday—did they even say hi to each other that day?*

Also, *Why does everyone keep trying to pitch me? Do I look like an easy mark?*

First, I need to know what I've just signed up for, though, because there's an electric energy, an almost rabid enthusiasm, in the air—reminiscent of a Christian youth group or the crowd that waits outside of T.J.Maxx before it opens. What the hell does this have to do with the guy who just died on a soccer field three days ago? The guy the cops think was *murdered*?

"Oh, this is a memorial exercise boot camp. To honor Cole."

I try to keep my face in neutral. I'm probably going to have to ice it later from the strain.

"What exactly is a . . . memorial . . . boot camp?"

"Well, we're wearing black," she says slowly, holding her hands out to the other women, who have stopped walking and are already organizing into perfect, evenly spaced lines.

"Yes. I gathered that."

"And we're going to work out together, like we did with him every Tuesday morning. You know, burpees and squat jacks and *lots* of suicides—because those were his favorites." My eyes go wide, but she's oblivious to my horror, apparently, and just keeps making it worse. "He always said to push past your comfort. If you feel like you're dying then you're doing it ri—"

I see the exact moment it finally clicks for her because her eyes widen, just like mine, and her cheeks turn a shade of pink that matches the sports bra and leggings sets she normally wears.

"It's what he would have wanted," she adds, defensiveness creeping into her tone.

Bethany appears in between us, her face now a mask of concern.

"You still can leave if you want to, Mavis. It's going to be really intense, and we understand if you're not really : . . operating at this level."

Irritation burns in my chest. Why is she being like this? So . . . bitchy. This can't just be because I yelled at her yesterday, can it? I mean, here I am, ready to be sucked into one of her MLM activities, like she wanted. You'd think she'd be pulling up the lifetime contract on her phone, ready to lock me down as her newest downstream.

There has to be some other reason . . . is there something she doesn't want me to know? She *did* keep it from me that she and Cole knew each other well. And it wasn't just that it didn't come up—it was purposeful. Because she was trying to use Cole's death to scam me into her MLM just yesterday. It would have *helped* her cause if she brought up their personal relationship and her own grief, but instead she lied by omission . . .

"I *said*, I'll do it." I raise my eyebrow in challenge, and she mirrors me.

Sure, I'm still winded from the mere brisk walk over to the park, but something's not right with this, with *Bethany*. I need to see if I can find anything else out.

Mackenzie squeezes my hand encouragingly, like we've been besties for years and not just vaguely friendly neighbors, and then she walks to the front of the group, facing everyone. She clutches her hands under her chin as she smiles beatifically at her audience

"I'm humbled and honored to take the lead this morning. As we all know, Bethany and Cole were so, *so* close. And she wanted to be up here—you know she did! But I wanted to give her an opportunity to be fully present today as she's navigating this very intense grief journey."

So close? Very intense grief?

I'm sure of it now, they *didn't* greet each other or talk Saturday morning. She was right behind Jack—I would have noticed. And actually . . . she disappeared after making such a big deal of saving that spot. Was that before Cole showed up, or after? I don't remember, but if they're such close friends and longtime business partners, wouldn't she have at least said hi when he first walked up?

A few spots down from me, Bethany wipes a tear from her cheek. But is it real?

I follow her gaze to the phone she has set up on a tripod behind Mackenzie to record this event. It's probably for content to recruit even more "self-care consultants," make even more money. No, she can't be *too* devastated.

I look at her again to see if this performance is fooling anyone, but she's good. There are more tears streaming down her face as Claudia pulls her into a hug and another woman rubs her back with—is that a crystal? Yeah, it's a crystal. Oh my lord. As Bethany tucks her short hair behind her ears and accepts condolences, I get another overwhelming feeling that I know her from somewhere else, before she targeted me at that Clover Scouts meeting. But where? I still can't place her.

"All right, Balanced With Bethany family!" I turn back to the front and Mackenzie is now jogging in place. "Are you ready to sweat out the grief?!"

She's smiling joyfully, *exuberantly*, like this is a tampon commercial and not . . . a memorial exercise boot camp. But I guess I don't really have other memorial exercise boot camps to compare this to.

No one else looks horrified. They're smiling and jogging in place, too. So I push away the feeling that Bethany's phone footage is also going to be used in a future HBO cult documentary and let the herd mentality take over. I also start jogging—and not even to run home to Polly and no-commercial episodes of *The Bachelor* waiting for me on Hulu.

"Looking good! Now we're going to start with a light warm-up!" Mackenzie presses her hands together in the middle and starts lunging from side to side. "And we're going to pray that Cole has found peace! Hold that pose! And pray, and pray!"

I hold in the eye roll that wants to unleash and follow the motion. It definitely doesn't feel like a warm-up to me. My hips and thighs already feel like they're on fire, but I can do this. I'm fine.

"Okay, now, heels to glutes! Heels out!" She starts doing this weird kicking back and then front thing, like an agitated donkey, and everyone switches flawlessly, as if this was previously choreographed. "Heels to glutes! Heels out! And we're going to kick away those sad feelings because *we know* he's found peace! Woo!"

I try to copy her and nearly face-plant. Is this still a warm-up?

Just when I think I've got the hang of it, Mackenzie starts swinging her arms widely around. "Breathe, you got this! Cole's spirit is here with us! We got this!" She drops forward, slamming the grass with her palms. "And now, turn to touch! Turn to touch!" She alternates each hand reaching up. "Reach for Cole! Can you feel his spirit?! I can feel it! Woo!"

This is so ridiculous, and normally I wouldn't be able to hold in my laughter. But laughing is impossible because my lungs are on fire and there are sharp pains in my sides and my knees and my butt and other places I can't even identify because they've just transitioned to numb. Also, I'm pretty sure I've sweated out all of the water I've consumed from that stupid, giant water bottle in the past month.

"Okay! Woo! Now let's rest for five seconds and then we're going to get started!"

I let out a cry for help. But Christine must mistake it as overwhelming excitement for exercising or an outpouring of grief because she pulls me into a hopping hug and tries to hold my hand while we do the first round of jumping jacks for joy that we even knew Cole.

MY PLAN IS TO STAY UNTIL THE END OF THE MEMORIAL EXercise boot camp and make small talk with the women to see what I can find out about Cole and Bethany's relationship. But that plan goes out the window after I learn what a burpee is and briefly lose consciousness during my fifth attempt at one.

Bethany was right. I am not on this level.

So, after checking to make sure Dom is long gone, I make my escape, mumbling some excuse that involves the oven and Polly and maybe the dentist? I'm not really sure . . . I haven't fully regained sentience or feeling in my extremities.

As I'm hobbling home, though—sweaty and sore and desperately wishing that I had my giant water bottle in this rare moment when I actually *need* a giant water bottle—I realize there's someone I should talk to. Right now.

I pull my phone out of my belt bag (which I guess *is* very convenient when my shoulder feels like it's still in danger of falling off) and call the Beachwood Police Department. After I'm put through to a few different people, he finally gets on the line.

"Off—" He clears his throat. "*Detective* De La Rosa."

"Hi! Detective De La Rosa! I have something important to tell you!"

"Who is this? And do you need . . . medical attention?"

Okay, rude. I'm not breathing *that* heavily. But anyway—"It's Mavis Miller! And yes, I just worked out for the first time in, well, I think my whole life, but listen! I learned something about Coach Cole. Or should I say—Cole *Dabrowski!*"

There's no immediate gasp like I expect, which is disappointing. Maybe he just needs a beat to catch up.

"Dabrowski!" I repeat, helpfully.

I wait for excitement, profuse thanks, maybe even an offer to make me an honorary member of the department, seeing as I've helped them out *twice* now.

Instead, he sighs.

"Yes, Ms. Miller. We learned that when we reached out to Cole's ex-wife on Sunday. She was his emergency contact."

Why didn't they mention that when they showed up at our house?

"Oh you mean, *Irene?*" He doesn't audibly marvel at the fact that I know this, but I'm pretty sure I can feel it. "They have . . . well, *had* a pretty contentious relationship. A history of public intoxication, domestic disputes—"

He cuts me off. "Yes, she told us."

Okay, he doesn't want to waste time. And I agree. Let's get down to our next steps.

"So do you think she had something to do with it? Have you brought her in for formal questioning?"

I hear an intake of breath, like he's about to say something, but then there's rustling and the sound of footsteps. A door closes.

"Listen, Ms. Miller, I appreciate you trying to help us. Really, I do." His voice sounds softer, kinder. And there's something else there . . . "I know what happened last fall must have been very traumatic." My body cringes at the word. Pity—that's what else is there. "Maybe *that's* why you feel called to interfere in this investigation. But I am not at liberty to discuss this case, especially with your ex-husband's involvement."

"You can't think—Corey had *nothing* to do with this!"

"I don't think he did, either, but . . ." He grunts in frustration. "I can't talk to you any more about this, Ms. Miller. Please trust us to do our jobs here. I am confident we will find out what happened to Cole."

"What about Bethany Bowman? Have you looked into her at all?" I'm talking too fast, but I need to give him this information. I know there's something strange going on with her. "That's whose exercise class I just left, and she knew Cole *really* well, but she didn't even say hi to him that day. She just disappeared. And I know that sounds like she's not involved, but—"

"Sorry, I need to go."

"Okay, I get it. But can you just hear me out with this one thing?"

A click, and then the dial tone, is my answer.

balancedwithbethany

Today we honored a cherished member of the Balanced With Bethany family. It's so hard to say goodbye to someone who was so passionate about the I LUV ME method and this journey we're on together, but we found peace in knowing he would have been proud of the way we took care of our bodies and showed love to ourselves this morning! 💪 🤍

Comment "PEACE" below if you want to show yourself some love next Tuesday!

Comments

naturallysteph

You are so inspiring!! After everything you've been through, you give back so much to others! 🤍 ✨

knollgreenteam

PEACE

wanderingroseessentials

I'm so sorry for your loss Bethany!

thee.charlie.lee

PEACE

mb5512

Bethany, I just need to tell you how much you've helped me on my own cancer journey. Every day, I'm showing myself that I LUV ME, so my body knows to keep fighting. And I know good news is coming for me at my next scan 🙏 Thank you for everything you do for us!

honeyfamilyfarm

Is that woman in the back okay? The one with the credit union shirt?

balancedwithbethany

@honeyfamilyfarm It definitely wasn't easy for her but

she showed up for herself! What a beautiful reminder that the Balanced With Bethany program is inclusive and welcoming to people of all levels!

cottageivystyle
PEACE

ELEVEN

"YOU ALL RIGHT, MAVES?"

I made it as far as the front door before collapsing in the en-tryway, to Polly's delight. She lay down right next to me and has been snoring her Hickory Smoked Chicken–flavored dog-food breath in my face for . . . well, I don't know how long it's been. But I'm not sure my body would move even if I told it to.

"Do you know there's a hole in the back of your leggings?" my dad continues with his interrogation. "Did you leave the house like that?"

Yes, I left the house in questionable leggings. But I *also* broke into Dom's shed and discovered the truth about Cole's career and sordid past and then stumbled upon another suspect in his murder who may not even be on the detectives' radar yet!

I can't actually tell him all that, though. Because then it'll end up on his podcast, and if Detective De La Rosa doesn't al-ready think I'm a joke now, he *definitely* will when my theories show up on a *Law & Order*-recap-turned-true-crime podcast with twelve listeners on an especially good week.

"Is something wrong with you and Corey?"

That makes me shoot up, and Polly narrows her sleepy eyes at me in disapproval.

"No! Why would you think that?"

I mean, he might be leaving us again. And I'm sad I'm going to have to figure out how to explain that to Pearl. And I'm pissed that he's even put me in this position, that he can't even have an adult conversation with me about it. But, like, what about me lying facedown on the floor gives that away?

"I feel like I'm getting flashbacks to high school. You used to do the same thing whenever the two of you had a fight." Dad laughs and runs his hand over his mostly gray hair. "You remember that one time he missed your birthday because of a show in Sacramento? You spent most of that weekend right there."

I was turning sixteen and only wanted to celebrate with him, but his band got invited to open for another band at a club/pizza restaurant six hours away, and he said he couldn't pass up the opportunity. I guess it's a good reminder that it's always been this way with Corey and his music, so why am I expecting anything to change? What's the saying? Fool me once, shame on you, fool me 2,076 times . . . wow, what a fucking idiot.

"Corey and I are fine. I just attempted to exercise."

"Ohhhhh! Well, that explains it." Dad's walking away to his room before I can even decide if I should be offended. "You should stretch next time."

"I did stretch!" I call after him, but he just laughs in response.

As I lie back down on the cool floor, I can feel my body tense, thinking about Corey and the argument I know is coming, but I try to push it out of my mind. I'll deal with that . . . later. When I'm not already achy and exhausted (because okay, yeah, I didn't stretch) and I have the energy to think up the exact-right combination of words to cut through to the bone, to hurt him the way this is going to hurt me and Pearl.

But almost as soon as I lock away his stupid one-dimpled smile, it's replaced with the image of Cole's head hitting the field and the sounds that filled my brain before the panic swallowed up all of my senses—the heavy thud of his body, the gasps of the crowd. And my heart starts to race just like it did that day, which feels even worse than my anger at Corey.

Take deep breaths, I remind myself. In through my nose, out through my mouth, like Jack taught me.

And it helps . . . but barely. God, am I just going to be like this forever? Polly sighs loudly in my ear, as if to say, *Girl, I don't know.*

I felt so good yesterday when I was starting to investigate this, forming my theories. It made me feel better than meditating did, that's for sure. Maybe that's because getting some closure here would help? Finding out who did this, I mean, and understanding the why behind this traumatic thing that I witnessed. If I knew *that* for sure, maybe then my body and brain could move on. Maybe that would help with everything I'm still carrying about Corinne, too, because it wouldn't be someone I know and trust this time.

And there is also therapy. I know, *I know.* Jack is sure that's the answer for this panic, the trauma in my body, but also it's my choice. I'm my boss now. I get to control my time and decide what's best for me. So maybe solving this mystery is what I choose? And that would be way more ideal than therapy because solving a mystery doesn't require health insurance and now mine will be ending soon . . .

Fuck, I need to read that email about COBRA and make sure we're still in network for Pearl's pediatrician and I can't believe I was so irresponsible to even put us in this situation and I wouldn't have to worry like this if *Corey*—no. *No.* Not right now. Right now: suspects.

Yes, breathe in suspects, breathe out all thoughts of my ex-husband, my job, and my place in the world.

So, suspects.

There's still Dom. He cares enough about his adult recreational capture the flag league to destroy Cole's reputation and business . . . but enough to murder him? I'm still not convinced. He seemed to be doing this by the book. Except when he drove his mower through the children's soccer games . . .

And then there's Hank, though I still think offing Cole would be a big leap to take just because Cole didn't think Axel was a soccer star. It's more likely Hank would try to get him fired. But I should look into him more. If these past few months have taught me anything, it's that people do crazy things for their kids.

And Trisha . . . no, wait. I crossed Trisha off.

So that just leaves Bethany. There is something there. I'm convinced of it.

She didn't want me to know that she had a relationship with Cole. And she may have left on purpose when she saw him on Saturday. Was she avoiding him? Or did she just not want to be at the scene of the crime when shit went down? He also runs this boot camp for her program, and then there's the supplement business Mackenzie mentioned. How financially entangled are they? And how much money are we talking here? Those gummy vitamins that Kardashian sells cost more than I spend on an entire outfit—were Bethany and Cole on the cusp of raking in some big bucks? Did Bethany want to get rid of him so she'd have a bigger share?

I do a quick scan of my body. My breathing has slowed. My

heart has stopped trying to burst out of my chest. I feel . . . better. Yes, better.

But I also feel . . . powerless. I feel like a *nuisance*.

Detective De La Rosa couldn't get off the phone with me fast enough, and what progress can I make if they're not on my side?

I need to get some more evidence. Something he can't just brush off. I need to show him how useful, how indispensable, I can be.

But I check my phone—it's almost time for pickup. Man, I really have been lying here for a while . . . There's nothing I can realistically do about any of this now, and I know my mind is going to go right back to where it was before.

Except. There is *another* mystery. And it's an easy one—I can probably wrap it up this afternoon. It'll be like when you add "fold the towels" to your to-do list, even though you're already on the last washcloth, just so you can check it off. Instant gratification. A little dose of protection from existential dread.

And, even better for my self-esteem, which is currently languishing in the gutter, it'll get me some Cool Mom points with Pearl, too.

THE SIGN ON THE DOOR READS PARENTS PLEASE KEEP OUT in large, typed letters. And then underneath it, added in loopy handwriting: *and allow your children the freedom to explore the arts and express themselves without pressure to please!*

I went around the back of the auditorium partly to avoid the crowd of parents already waiting out front and engaging in the dreaded small talk and partly to see if I could slip into the *Annie* rehearsal covertly. But apparently I'm not the first person to try it.

I mean, that sign doesn't really apply to me, though. I'm not here as a stage parent. I'm a concerned citizen—a freelance investigator! Just here to make sure everything is aboveboard with casting and the mystery assigned to me by my client (i.e., my almost-eight-year-old daughter). Really, I am acting in the spirit of the sign and *encouraging* her to express herself, if you think about it.

I look around to make sure no one is watching, in case their interpretation of the sign differs from my own, and turn the knob. It's not even locked. Which means I don't have to use a credit card for another round of B and E. This is just E—and that's totally legal. Of course, that's not gonna stop me from playing it up for Pearl later and milking every ounce of the Cool Mom cred I'll deserve after this.

Slowly, I pull the door open, wincing as the hinges creak. The sound feels ear-piercing, even over the tinkle of piano playing and kids chatting, so I freeze and wait to see if I'm going to be caught by the stage-mom police Mr. Forest hired to guard the door. But no, the piano continues uninterrupted. I recognize the song from that *Annie* adaptation that had the cute girl with the afro. "Maybe," I think it's called. It must be concealing any noise I'm making back here, but still, I softly close the door, pausing just before the latch, and then tiptoe into the room.

I'm behind the large burgundy curtain on the stage in the auditorium. I've always been on the other side of it, for kindergarten holiday pageants and contentious PTA meetings. And I feel a little thrill as I look around—my second secret lair of the day. Except this one has a lot less stuff that could be used for murder. There's a case of La Croix (probably leftover from Trisha's reign), plus a tangled pile of extension cords and a wide red dust mop—very anticlimactic. I guess that's what you want in an elementary school auditorium, though.

"Okay, orphans, stage right!"

I jump at Mr. Forest's voice and trip over two backpacks, steadying myself right before I fall on my face. One is covered in spikes like Bowser's shell, and the other looks like the knapsack a Depression-era kid would use when running away (and probably cost more than my car payment). The orphans follow Mr. Forest's directions, and their clattering footsteps hide any sounds I made, thankfully. Pearl is one of them. She was cast as Tessie—a grave mistake, a miscarriage of justice on Mr. Forest's part, in her opinion. I'm about to figure out just how dramatic my kid is.

"The *other* stage right!" Mr. Forest clarifies, and there's another stampede of orphans on the other side of the curtain. He keeps playing the piano lightly. "Annie and Molly, you're downstage. Good. Yes. And now we're going to run through that again. Anabella, are you ready?"

He pauses, waiting for her response, and then begins to play more enthusiastically.

At first, I think Anabella has frozen, which would be an answer to Pearl's mystery, but a pretty sad one. Maybe the girl just has a little stage fright (and my girl is just being an asshole). But then I hear it.

"She's sitting playing piano, he's sitting paying a bill—"

It's a monotone, breathy whisper, like someone gave Billie Eilish a couple of sedatives. I creep closer to the curtain and risk a peek through the folds, to confirm that this strange sound is really coming from Anabella. And yep, there she is—and she's doing a strange body roll dance move to accompany it.

Is this some . . . experimental version of Annie? Like is Annie a TikTok girlie who sings in cursive instead of a scrappy, curly-headed orphan?

But I maneuver slightly so I can see the orphans' faces, and they look just as confused as me. Well, except for Pearl, who is glaring at Anabella as if her eyeballs are a magnifying glass and Anabella is an unlucky ant.

The piano abruptly stops. "Um, yes. Good." Mr. Forest's voice is slow, slightly strangled, as if he's trying to pluck out the right words from a squirming mass of wrong ones. "Let's do that once more. With . . . feeling?"

Anabella looks Mr. Forest up and down, like he's the one who screwed up that last take, then nods. A groan from the audience, where the non-orphans are sitting, catches my attention, but when I try and find the source, I realize I'm right in their line of view. I jump back again before I'm caught—because being discovered hiding in the auditorium curtains would definitely hurt rather than help my Cool Mom cred.

So I can't see Anabella when she starts singing again, but I can hear her. Everyone in the city of Beachwood can probably hear her. She's taken Mr. Forest's "with feeling" note to heart, and now instead of Billie Eilish, she's Fergie—if she drank a few Trenta Frappuccinos and decided to give that National Anthem one more shot.

Mr. Forest's hands hit a sharp note on the keys. "Okay, okay maybe . . . with a little . . . *less* feeling?" He looks pained at the thought. "Actually, look at the time. Your parents are probably waiting. Why don't we stop here and pick this up next rehearsal? Please practice! *Please.* And don't forget your backpacks if they're backstage! Jonah, I *cannot* let you in after hours again!"

He's talking fast, clearly ready to get the hell out of here, and the orphans and the kids in the audience were already up and moving as soon as he said to stop. Their chatter and exiting footsteps echo in the room, and I'm picturing what Pearl's face is going to look like when I'm not immediately out there to greet her, so that's why it takes me an extra beat to process what he's said. Backpacks. Like the backpacks I tripped over sneaking around here. The ones I'm currently standing just a few feet from.

Axel and another boy leap onto the stage and dash toward the curtain. Just in time, I spin around and wrap myself up in one of the folds like a mummy, hiding myself from view.

"It's not fair! I wanted to be Annie." I hear Axel stomp his foot and can picture the same face he made on the soccer field when it didn't feel like an aquamarine day.

"You can't be Annie. You're a boy!"

"My mom said I could be any part I wanted! And I would be a better Annie than Anabella. But now I'm just the stupid Star-To-Be."

There's a giggle and a snotty "*Oh*-kay" followed by a rustling. Then one set of footsteps takes off back across the stage, quickly followed by another. I can hear the big double doors at the front of the auditorium slam behind them.

They're gone. Here's my chance. I need to get out right now—so I don't get caught, but also because Pearl *still* brings up that one day I was two minutes late to get her in kindergarten with burning fury in her eyes.

I take two silent steps toward the door. Then another few. I'm almost there, and then—

"I need a fucking Tylenol."

Mr. Forest suddenly appears through the curtain, his leather satchel hanging from his stooped shoulders and a defeated expression on his face like he's rethinking all of his life choices.

I jump and knock over the tall dry mop. It loudly clatters to the ground.

Mr. Forest's eyes go wide in surprise, and then . . . fear? He holds his hands up, as if in defense.

"Ms. Miller, listen, if it's about the casting, I am not talking to any parents about this. The parts are final and every child was given the role where they have the best chance to shine. If you have a problem—"

"No, it's not about that." I put my palms up, too, talking fast. "It's about, um—"

Now I just need to figure out what it *is* about. Because something tells me *solving the mystery of why you cast Anabella as Annie to make Pearl think I'm cool and distract myself from another mystery and also all of MY life choices* isn't going to fly.

"Yes?"

"I wanted to talk to you about something else."

He raises an eyebrow, like *Get on with it.*

"Um, well, it's almost Pearl's birthday. It's Sunday."

Out of all the things I could have said, why did *that* come out? But I guess it's probably because she's been reminding me it's almost her birthday for months now . . . it's imprinted on all of my cells at this point.

"You're backstage during our closed rehearsal to tell me about Pearl's birthday?" He narrows his eyes at me and then begins shaking his head. "Ms. Miller, I'm not sure what's going on here, but I think I'll have to speak with Principal Smith—"

"No, um, I mean—do you want to . . . *come?*"

He frowns, confused. But at least now he's not still talking about snitching to Principal Smith. "You want me to come to Pearl's birthday?"

"Um, yes! Yes I do! To play. Music. For the kids. At the party. We need some entertainment."

My mouth has gone rogue. Because what do you mean *party*? And *entertainment*? All we have planned is a small family dinner, in large part because I *didn't* want to be in charge of organizing shit like this. I still have flashbacks to her first birthday, where I had a total breakdown over the color of her smash cake. There are so many other believable things I could have said that didn't involve conjuring a birthday party out of thin air!

But Mr. Forest's face immediately softens and then bursts into a brilliant, all-teeth smile. "Sure! It's a little last minute, but I do love sharing the joy of music with my students." He starts moving toward the door. "Just email me the details. And then I can send you my invoice, too. I'd need the deposit by tonight, of course, to lock in the date."

He's digging in his bag for that Tylenol as he walks away, so he misses my stank face at the word "deposit."

So . . . I guess I'm hosting a birthday party.

I walk out into the late-afternoon sun in a daze, trying to reckon with that fact. A fucking birthday party. In days. Children at my house. All because I was sneaking around to see if Anabella deserved her role in a goddamn elementary school musical.

Man, Future Pearl better not be one of those adults posting videos online about how their parents screwed them up, because I have *tried*, clearly.

As I round the corner, I'm hit by a loud, wailing sob. My body goes tense immediately, and I search for Pearl, but it's not my kid. There's a boy sitting on the ground with a red face and cheeks covered in tears. I'm pretty sure he's the same kid I saw with Axel just a few minutes ago, and yes, there's that spiked Bowser shell, cast off next to him. His mom crouches next to him, alternating between rubbing his back and glaring at Florence over her shoulder.

Florence doesn't seem to notice, though, because her eyes are locked on Axel as she kneels in front of him. She balances expertly on arched feet, even with Marigold in her carrier.

"How you're feeling right now is valid, my sweet boy. And

you don't have to apologize if that's not your truth. I know it hurt your arm, too, when you bumped into him."

As soon as she mentions his arm, Axel reaches up to clutch it. His face is stormy as he stares at the ground.

I spot Pearl on the other side of them, crossing her arms with her own stormy expression, and I give them all a wide berth. I'm not trying to be involved in *that*.

"Hey baby girl. I'm—"

She cuts me off before I can apologize. "You're late."

"Well, actually I was early, but I was . . ." I can't exactly finish that with *spying on your best friend—and you were right, she's terrible!* At least not in front of an audience of judgy parents. So instead, I go with bribery. "Do you want to go get boba?"

She nods once to let me know that'll do . . . for now. But Florence blocks our escape.

"Hi Mavis! I'm so glad I caught you!" Axel is curled into her side, pouting, and Marigold sucks on her thumb, dozing. "I wanted you to know that when Detective Berry asked me about the snacks I had no idea that it would cause trouble for Corey—"

I make a weird, guttural noise that startles even me, but I need her to stop immediately. Corey and I decided not to tell Pearl anything because we don't want her to worry, and I'm not about to have Florence ruin that for us.

Marigold starts to cry. I woke her up. But Florence continues, "Did they have him go in, too? To rule out his fingerprints—"

Pearl tilts her head to the side in curiosity.

"I really think it's just a formality—"

"Pearl's having a birthday party on Sunday!" I shout over her. "Does Axel want to come?"

"I am?"

"Um . . . you are. Surprise!"

It sounds flimsy, even to me, but Pearl's whole face lights up, and she starts clapping. "I always wanted a surprise party! Oh, thank you, thank you, thank you! I'm sorry I was calling you that bad word in my mind for being late!"

"Excuse me?

"*This* Sunday?" Florence asks, her voice dripping with judgment, as Marigold continues to cry and slap her face.

"It's kind of a last-minute thing. It'll just be a few friends and some pizza and cake. Mr. Forest is going to sing with them." I'm only figuring out the plans myself as they leave my lips. "It's totally okay if you can't make it." Please don't make it.

"That *is* late notice, but I'm sure we can make it work."

Axel stomps and growls, "I want a birthday party with Mr. Forest!"

Florence drops down next to him again as Marigold cries, "No, no, no!"

"It's okay to feel jealous, my sweet boy. That's a natural, normal feeling."

"Sorry, we need to run. Lots of planning to do!" I grab Pearl's arm and get out of there before Florence tries to talk me into respecting Axel's valid feelings and making this a joint thing.

"A party! Mommy, I'm so excited! I didn't even know that I *wanted* a party until you said I was *having* a party, and now we have so, so much to do!"

I thought Mr. Forest would be long gone by now, but he's across the street, exactly one hundred feet from the school.

"Did you hire a clown? And what about a shaved ice machine? And we need, need, need a tattoo artist!"

Anabella is tucked away in the back seat of their minivan, but Trisha is still here, too, towering over Mr. Forest. Her jaw is clenched and a cascade of wrinkles has erupted on her tight forehead as she speaks to him. Her voice is quiet, but I feel the heat from her blue-flame eyes from here.

"Emory had a tattoo artist at her birthday party!"

Trisha jabs a finger into his chest, snarling something that makes Mr. Forest flinch even more.

"The tattoos weren't permanent, because she used air? Or I don't know, something? Have you looked into that?"

Mr. Forest clutches his bag and sprints to his Kia like he's being chased by a predator. Only the predator is getting into her minivan, smiling smugly. Maybe this wasn't just a quick mystery I could wrap up in an afternoon to make my kid think I was cool. Maybe there's actually something here.

"Mom! Mom!" Pearl tugs my arm. "Did you hear me? Are we gonna get tattoos?"

My eyes snap back down to her.

"What?"

TWELVE

"AND THEN RUTH SAID ANY ELECTION WE HAD WOULDN'T even be fair because everyone is going to vote for me, as if that makes any sense. And then Felicia, as a *solution*, suggested making everyone bring their IDs to vote, so we can be sure they're registered PTA members and not just my friends. As if I have some seedy underbelly of non–PTA members conspiring for me. Not to mention the implications of . . . Mavis? Is something wrong?"

I jerk my head up and see that Dyvia's face is creased in concern.

"What—no. I'm fine."

"Are you sure?" She raises a skeptical eyebrow. "Because you just glued Claudette Colvin's picture on the Constance Baker Motley poster."

"Shit." My cheeks warm, and I carefully pick at the edges of the picture, trying to remove it without destroying the whole display. When did Elmer's get so strong? And god, I hope I haven't made any other mistakes.

We've been prepping the pictures and information for these

Black History Month bulletin boards all morning, and this is a project I'm so excited about. We're highlighting lesser-known figures so kids can learn about them as they walk through the hallways to class. It's one of the many things me and Dyvia's DEI team has planned for this month, and because of my new open schedule I actually get to work on the projects in the daylight instead of late at night after Pearl goes to sleep. It's just, I took on something *else* with my new open schedule, and it's quickly occupying a significant amount of my brain space . . .

"Is it this last-minute birthday party?" Of course she gets it right in one, but I try to keep my face neutral, to not give it away. "We can go, by the way. Rohan is really excited for the airbrush tattoos."

I booked that airbrush lady last night. Luckily she had a cancellation, though I'm pretty sure she charged me extra. And Pearl narrowed down a theme, after lots of back-and-forth with my dad over dinner: rainbow unicorns . . . and also Shrek? My Amazon cart looks real crazy right now.

"The party is going to be great. Everything is coming together."

"Your sabbatical then?" A small smile tugs on her lips, letting me know what she thinks of that term, and I know it sounded pretty flimsy when it came out of my mouth. But I had to tell her *something* since I usually can't meet during the workday.

"Come on, out with it already. I can tell something's bugging you." She gives me the no-bullshit look I've come to appreciate in our friendship (especially because I gave her *so much* bullshit when we first met) and then follows it up with a playful smirk. "You're very transparent."

I don't think anything's *bugging* me necessarily. I already feel better than I did when I was working at Project Window. *So* much better. And I finally have time to do all the things I've wanted to do. Show up for Pearl—through this bonkers rainbow-unicorn-Shrek-airbrush-tattoo party and volunteering with the PTA. Take care of myself. Investigate a murder.

But . . . "Okay, fine. I think I'm just struggling with . . . not feeling like I'm doing enough? My whole days are open now, and it . . . feels wrong. I'm not rushing. I'm not busy. And, I don't know. I'm not used to it."

Dyvia's nose wrinkles. "You've been writing and cutting and gluing for hours. How is that not doing enough? And even if you weren't, what's wrong with taking a break? You can afford it?"

I nod. "Yes."

I did the math in between submitting my résumé for jobs I'm not sure I even want, and we'll be good for longer than I thought. Months, not weeks.

"Then you don't need to throw the term *sabbatical* on it to make it acceptable. You're taking a break from work. I think that's great. I think you're gonna *feel* great."

I know what she's saying is true . . . technically. People take breaks all the time. But there's something else there, something more complicated that I'm still trying to figure out. Because I feel it so deeply in my bones that, yes, people take breaks—but not my people. Maybe if I try and explain that out loud, it'll make more sense?

"I don't know . . . I mean, I know rest is good. I know self-care is, like, a *thing*. But it seems like it's only okay for these white ladies to rest and self-care. And for me—for us? Don't get me wrong. I did it—I'm *doing* it! It just feels kinda . . . lazy?" Yeah, I'm not sure if this is making any sense, but Dyvia is biting the side of her lip, thinking it over instead of reporting me to the POC police, so I keep going. "Like, my ancestors." I wave a hand over the famous, or should-be-famous, Black faces in front of us.

"*Your* ancestors. They worked so hard to prove that we could do anything, and I'm going to waste my little time on this earth meditating? Napping?" I grab a cutout of Ketanji Brown Jackson off the table and hold it up like it's exhibit A. "I should be breaking down barriers! I should be on the Supreme Court!"

Dyvia is nodding. "I totally understand what you're saying, but my therapist . . . oh my *god*, Mavis! Did you just roll your eyes at me?"

I freeze. "No."

Her mouth falls open in shock mixed with silent laughter. "You rolled your eyes at me. I saw it!"

"Okay, I did. I did! But I mean—does *everyone* have a therapist now? Did I miss the memo?" I feel like I did as a kid when everyone switched to MTV instead of the Disney Channel, seemingly overnight, and I was still trying to talk about *That's So Raven* like an oblivious, uncultured baby.

"Everyone *should* have a therapist," Dyvia says, rolling her eyes right back at me. "But anyway, what I was going to say is: My therapist told me that ascribing our worth to our productivity is really toxic. Because we're inherently worthy as we are. If you want to be on the Supreme Court because it makes you happy, fine! Good! But your value is the same if you're doing that, or if you're . . . I don't know, lying in bed eating bonbons."

"Or watching *The Bachelor*?"

"Personally, I prefer *Love Is Blind*. But yes," she confirms. "My therapist says it's actually capitalism and white supremacy—"

I hold up my hand. "Your therapist gets down like that?"

Dyvia laughs. "Yes. She says it's actually capitalism and white supremacy that drive us to prove our worth through our labor, and we can choose to remove ourselves from that system. Because freedom can also look like *not* having your worth tied to your work."

I fall back in the tiny plastic chair I've been perched on all morning and nearly topple it over. "Damn."

"Yes, I had a similar reaction." Her brow furrows and she chews on her lip again, like she's considering something, and then I see her face smooth with a decision. "I used to feel guilty about being a stay-at-home mom, that's why I started seeing her. I felt like I—wasn't as strong? Or as smart as the other moms, because I didn't also work outside the home? But she's helped me a lot with those feelings. And she helped me realize I'm doing plenty of labor, with the kids and here." She gestures to our project in front of her, and it's just one of many, I know, that she has going on as the current PTA president. "Knoll—and pretty much all successful schools—rely on full-time parent volunteering to make up for the lack of resources provided by the district."

"I know that's right." I used to judge moms like Dyvia for being so present at the school. Hell, I'll be honest, I used to judge *Dyvia*. I was kind of an asshole. But I've since realized how much they contribute and how it benefits all kids—well, when they use their powers for good instead of evil, like Trisha.

"Also, even if I was lying in bed eating bonbons, then I would still be a good person, too."

"The best person." I reach forward across the table and squeeze her hand. "Thank you, Dyvia. Now, do you accept HMO insurance, or . . . ?"

She swats my hand back playfully. "You still need to get a professional! But in the meantime, I need you to google the Nap Ministry—"

"Oh, Dyvia, I was hoping I'd find you here!" Mrs. Tennison glides into the PTA workroom (where, for the record, Dyvia can be found every day). Mrs. Tennison is in her early fifties, with dyed-black hair and shrewd, dark eyes that can lock in on the exact moment a seven-year-old pulls a contraband container of slime from their backpack and give a silent, but effective, warning to put it away. She's wearing a denim overall dress and a primary-color-striped shirt, like the patron saint of all elementary school teachers. She doesn't have Pearl, or any of the other kids in her class, trailing after her, so it must be recess.

"Can you help me with something?" she asks, clutching her wooden-beaded lanyard. And then she launches into her plea before Dyvia can even nod. "I'm just having the hardest time finding a new room mom. As you know, I no longer have one because of mine . . . being banned from the premises. And well, I really need some help planning the class pizza party, grading the spelling tests, doing stuff like this." She gestures to our project. "It'll be Valentine's Day in just over two weeks, and I don't have any hearts cut out to put around the room."

"That must be so difficult. I'm so sorry!" Dyvia says, hand to her chest like she can really feel Mrs. Tennison's pain. This is why she's so good at this job. "Have you emailed the parents?"

"None of them have responded," she says tightly, and it feels like a spotlight just hit me. I am one of those parents.

"Now I know Trisha was quite . . . passionate and made some . . . unconventional choices." That's one way to put it, lady. And it's clear in her long pause, as she wrings her hands, what she's leaving unspoken: that *I'm* the one who brought light to those *unconventional choices*. "But," she finally continues, "she *did* cut out a mean heart. And she would *always* volunteer to drive to Costco for the cheaper pizza!"

Mrs. Tennison frowns, and the spotlight gets brighter, nearly blinding me. I feel a drop of sweat roll down my back from the heat of its focus.

And I know exactly what to say to make that frown shift into a smile. To make her happy with me—and, most importantly, Pearl.

"Mrs. Tennison—" Dyvia starts, but I cut her off.

"I can do it."

There's a clattering as Dyvia accidentally knocks the markers off the table, and I steadily avoid her glare.

"Great!" Mrs. Tennison claps her hands. "I'll go get the construction paper now. I trust you have a good pair of scissors—I just need two hundred or so cut out. And can you add some positive, encouraging messages on a few of them? Like conversation hearts? You can send me your rough ideas, if you need feedback. Oh! And I also need a new George Washington costume for the Presidents' Day skit we do next month. The last one . . . well, it was a particularly bad flu season. Do you sew?"

She's out the door before I can confirm or deny.

I sigh, returning to the poster in front of me. "Okay, so is Claudette Colvin going in the fifth-grade hallway or the fourth? You know what, I might have to reprint this picture."

Dyvia is silent, so I'm forced to look at her, even though I already know what's waiting for me there: bemusement and an exasperated delight, with just a dash of horror.

"Mavis, did you really just take on *another* responsibility when we were talking about unapologetically doing less, like . . . five seconds ago?"

"Yeah, yeah. I'm a work in progress." I pose with my face in my hands, beaming my most ridiculous grin at her until she's forced to laugh. "But wait, can we go back to how Ruth and Felicia are trying to Jim Crow–ify the PTA? Because I feel like I didn't give that the attention it deserves."

I END UP TAKING A NAP IN THE AFTERNOON, DYVIA'S OR-ders, but it's restless and sweaty and filled with hazy, panicked dreams about Cole's body hitting the field. So I don't feel like

I've taken a nap at all when I finally head back to Knoll to pick up Pearl.

I start to wonder if I'm *still* dreaming, though, when I see Corey at the front gate, a few steps back from the usual crowd of moms, with his arms crossed and sunglasses on. *Why is he here?*

He tilts his head to the side when he sees me, probably thinking the same question.

"It's Wednesday," he says when I reach him.

"Okay . . ." Annoyance flares immediately because I *am* aware of the day of the week. Most of the time.

"And I always pick up Pearl on Wednesdays because you stay later to do that mentor training." He sucks his teeth, realization hitting. "Except not anymore because . . . your sabbatical."

We both look at each other, deciding whether to make it a thing, but he shrugs before I can give in to my petty instincts. "She'll be really happy to see both of us."

I smile, imagining her smile. "She will."

"I'm almost done with the goody bags, by the way. And all the candy's organic—I double-checked." His dimple makes an appearance. "Even found these little Shrek figurines at that tiny party store down on Orizaba? He has three of those—what are they even? Horns? Tentacles? But I don't think they'll notice."

"Thank you for doing that." A wave of tenderness takes me by surprise because he didn't even question it when I told him about this last-minute party. He just asked for half of my to-do list. It was nice to have someone I could lean on without guilt, because I know he wants to make Pearl happy just as much as I do.

"I was thinking about getting her a keyboard and microphone set for my present, since she's been so into singing lately. That good with you?"

"Yeah, I think she'll like that."

"I'm trying not to get too excited and scare her off, but I can't help it. You know I've always wanted her to get into music." He grins. "I've got a buddy who gives lessons at his studio over on Olive, by the Trader Joe's. Maybe she'd be into that after *Annie* wraps?"

And just as quickly, I remember what he's keeping from me, how the ground is about to fall out from all this, and I feel stupid.

I want to yell. I want to press a finger into his chest and ream him out for putting me in this position. For trusting I'm going to pick up the pieces, take her to these lessons, when he goes and follows his dreams again. And what about my dreams, huh? When do *I* get a chance to figure those out?

"Um, so, actually . . ."

"I'm the new class mom."

And now I sound just as stupid as I feel, but I can't let him say whatever he was about to say. Because what if it's *that*? And what if I lose it? No, it's not the time, surrounded by all of these eyes. I'm being talked about on that Facebook group enough.

"Cool?" He looks confused, but quickly covers it with a nod. "Cool. Is that what you . . . wanted?"

No, of course not. "Yes."

I check my phone. There's still a few more minutes left before the bell rings. God, how can it be so awkward with someone I've known longer than almost anyone?

"Hey y'all!" Leon walks up to us, still wearing his scrubs, and I nearly jump into his arms in gratitude.

"How did the fingerprinting go, man?" he asks, clapping Corey's shoulder. "They treat you good?"

That hits me like a punch to the gut. "Fingerprinting?" I ask, twisting to look at Corey. "They brought you in for fingerprinting and you didn't think to mention that?!"

He glances at the audience around us, and I'm annoyed. But mostly because he's right. We don't need a scene. I was *just* worrying about that.

"It was just to rule me out, I think," Corey says, modeling the quieter tone he wants me to use. And again, I'm hit by fierce annoyance followed by begrudging understanding. "It seemed like they expected my fingerprints to be on it, honestly, because I brought the snack? But I told them I didn't take it out of the package myself. And I saw Florence when I was leaving, so it looks like they brought her in, too, to eliminate hers." That's probably what Florence was trying to talk to me about yesterday before I threw out a party invitation to distract her.

"I'm sure there were probably *a lot* to eliminate, the way those kids attack that snack table," he continues. "And I don't know, they must not have found anything to worry about because they haven't called me again."

Leon shakes his head. "It seems like they really are casting a wide net and just bringing in everybody. Don't make no sense to me. They took Irene's fingerprints, too."

"Irene? His ex-wife?"

"Yeah," Leon confirms, but then he stops and scratches his cheek. "Wait, how do you know her?"

I can't exactly say it's because I found a domestic dispute police report in the Brady Park facility manager's shed/office after breaking in. Honestly, it's probably better Detective De La Rosa wrote me off before questioning the source of my information more.

"I, um . . . don't. I just heard he had an ex-wife named Irene."

Corey shoots a skeptical side-eye my way, but thankfully, that seems to be enough for Leon, and he keeps talking.

"Yeah, I called her later that afternoon, when . . . he was gone." His voice catches and he clears his throat. Because Cole was more than just his kid's coach, I remember. This was Leon's friend. "I knew she would want to be here. As soon as possible. And then the hospital called her anyway because she was listed as his emergency contact."

"His emergency contact? I thought it was contentious?"

"Contentious? No." Again, he scratches his cheek. "Where did you hear that?"

"I don't know. I just . . . assumed? Because she's his ex?"

Now Corey's eyes are narrowed in my direction. I can feel them burning my cheek. I really need to be quiet.

"Sorry, go on."

"They *did* have some bad years, especially when Cole was still drinking. I don't think he was a great husband. But they were good friends. She's the one who actually pushed for additional toxicology reports, before that Green Team lady even found the Capri-Sun pouch. She kept telling 'em how healthy he is—don't matter how many of those energy drinks he pounded per day."

"Wait, so they found the sodium nitrate on the toxicology report? Because from what I understand, it's not something that would show up? And even then they have to examine the muscle tissue to see if it has a brown discoloration . . ."

I trail off, taking in how Corey and Leon are both rapidly blinking at me.

"I mean . . . I heard." From my best friend, Google.

Corey raises his eyebrows, making his skepticism clear. "You seem to be *hearing* a lot of things."

"Sodium nitrate? Nah, that doesn't sound right. It was something that started with a T. Tetri . . . ?" Leon snaps his fingers, as if that'll help it come to him. "Sorry, I'm just coming off a twelve-hour. I can't remember the exact name, but I know it starts with a *T*."

That must just be a mistake in his sleep-deprived brain, though, because I know it was sodium nitrate. Or at least sodium . . . something. The one used on plants! Maybe there's an even *more* technical science term or whatever, that starts with a *T*? But I've gotten to, like, page ten on Google, where the deep cuts are, and I didn't see anything like that.

"So, they found something that started with a *T*," I say, trying to sound totally casual and like I have an average, normal level of interest. "But then how do they know Irene didn't have something to do with it?"

I haven't fully considered it before, but it makes total sense. An ex with a long-standing grudge over . . . whatever Cole was doing with his crusty toes—*infidelity*. Leon may think they were good, but who knows how accurate his read on that is. And this is who it always ends up being on *Dateline*. Maybe this case is actually straightforward. Easy.

But Leon is vigorously shaking his head, and I can almost hear a phantom Keith Morrison slyly say with his drawn-out vowels, "Easy? Nothing is ever easy."

"Nah, she's good people. Her and Cole didn't work, but she wanted the best for him. Like, she waited to finalize the divorce so he could stay on her insurance and get a surgery he needed done on his knee."

"And she asked them to do a toxicology report," Corey adds, eyes flaring in a subtle warning. I pretend I don't see it. And honestly, he has a lot of nerve—I'm trying to help *him* here.

"On Saturday, she was at the Cabazon outlets. You know, way out by Palm Springs? She manages the Adidas store."

"Okay, so she says, but—"

"It's been verified."

It's clear from his clipped tone that he's done with this

conversation, and I feel a flicker of embarrassment. I'm being insensitive. This was his friend, who died unexpectedly just days ago. It's more than just a whodunit for him.

But I push that feeling down because I have to ask one more question. That can't hurt any more. I *need* to know this.

"What do you know about Beth—"

The dismissal bell cuts me off, and almost instantly there is a mass of kids running toward us. Leon gives a quick wave before starting his search for Langston, probably glad to get away.

"Is that what I thought it was, Mavis?" Corey asks, leaning in close, and I want to swat him away. First, because he sounds so judgy, but also because he smells like the same warm and spicy cologne he's worn since high school. "You were mad at your dad for—"

"How am I ever supposed to know what you're thinking?" I shoot right back, injecting venom into my words, because how dare he? He's keeping just as many secrets as me.

Pearl walks out then, and her eyes light up like we brought Shrek and a rainbow unicorn here to greet her. We both plaster on our happy-family faces and keep pretending that nothing is wrong.

Hello Aquamarine Alligators family,

I hope you'll forgive how long it's taken me to reach out. I know you and your littles have come to rely on me as a leader in our soccer community, and I'm just crushed that I couldn't show up for you. As many of you know, our Axel is an empath and feels everything so strongly, so it's been an overwhelming, life-encompassing task to help him weather this tremendous grief and loss. I'm sure you've been doing the same with your littles on some level.

We will unfortunately have to cancel Thursday night's practice, but I didn't want to do the same for our scheduled game on Saturday. It's so important to keep up a routine and sense of normalcy to help our littles regulate their feelings and process this on their own unique, developmentally appropriate timelines. So I've reached out to the team mom of the Purple Platypuses, and we've organized a game for Saturday morning at 10:00am on Field B in Brady Park. This will be an "unofficial" game, as the league is currently on a hiatus and all coaches have technically been let go. But I hope we can all come together anyway to bring our littles this joy!

(And please correct me if I'm wrong, but I think our wonderful school psychologist, Mr. Cohen, will be present at this game, as he has been in the past. Maybe he can lead us all in a quick discussion in recovering from trauma?)

All my love,
Florence

THIRTEEN

"IT'S SUCH A SHAME THAT JACK COULDN'T MAKE IT! IS HE feeling ill?"

It's Saturday morning, and Corey and I had the great fortune to be pulling into parking spots at the same time—right next to Florence and her family. So now we're walking into the unofficial, just for our littles' joy, game together.

"Yeah, no. He's fine! He had some work to catch up on."

More like he didn't want to be volunteered to lead a counseling session for kids on his day off, so he opted to sit this one out. We have plans to see each other tonight instead.

"What a great guy!" Florence coos. "He works so hard!"

Even though we're not touching, I can feel Corey stiffen on the other side of Pearl—it's that invisible tether between us that has never seemed to go away, no matter how far apart we get. I want to squeeze his arm, to comfort him because I know it's not easy hearing how these parents go on about Jack sometimes. But then I remember that I'm still mad at him.

"Um, Mommy?" Pearl has stopped in her tracks. "I thought we were playing soccer."

"What do you mean? We are." But as I follow her gaze, I can see where the confusion is. On Field B—on all the fields, actually—there are adult men racing across the grass, dodging and diving, yelling and grunting. All of them are wearing T-shirts in either lime green or pastel peach, representing two teams. I see a guy in green with linebacker shoulders tackle someone on the far end as he tries to get to something surrounded by orange traffic cones. On the other side, a man in peach falls to his knees and slaps the grass in fury while another whoops over his head, signaling in a wave of reinforcements.

They're playing capture the flag.

Axel throws his bag of gear down. "Why are they on our field? This was not the plan!"

"We're supposed to have these fields until the end of the season." Hank runs his hands over his face, which has quickly turned stormy. "I'm gonna go talk to these guys. This isn't right."

"I don't think that's the best idea, bro," Corey says, as one of the men in peach picks up a buff opposing player who nears their flag and tosses him like a paper ball.

Hank flinches and takes two steps back, probably imagining what they could do to him. Yeah, we don't need to start a fight we're definitely going to lose over an *unofficial, just for our littles' joy* soccer game. I wonder why Dom didn't bring these guys instead of his mower on Saturday. It would have been just as effective.

And oh—there's Dom, right there in the middle, wearing a black-and-white-striped referee polo, surveying his adult recreational capture the flag kingdom. He seems to see me right when I notice him, and his whole body freezes. First he narrows his eyes in confusion, and I'm probably doing the same because why is he staring at me like that? He doesn't know who I am, and I slipped away into the workout group before he got there on Tuesday . . . right? But as the chaos of his game continues around him, his face shifts into what looks like recognition and then an expression that's unmistakable: anger.

"Maybe we should go to the park instead," I say, quickly turning my back to him. "The kids just want to spend time together, right? So that might be better for them anyway. Just playing without the pressure of competition."

"I don't know . . ." Florence frowns, looking back at the game. She *would* stroll right into guaranteed danger if it meant securing what was rightfully Axel's. She could probably get at least a week's worth of posts out of it.

"Wow, look at the way the light is hitting that swing set? Isn't it beautiful? It would look *so good* in pictures." Florence's eyes brighten in delight as she looks to the playground on the far end of Brady Park, visions of Instagram Stories and Reels in her head. I've got her.

"I'll text Jasmine." I start taking large steps even farther from the field and Dom's suspicious glare, giving everyone no choice but to follow me. Pearl is already bouncing with excitement over skipping soccer.

"Who else is coming, Florence?" I ask. "Can you tell them?"

She lets out a long sigh and shakes her head. "Not a lot of people confirmed. One of the moms was even mad about my email? Can you believe that?"

Yes, I can definitely believe that. And if we didn't even have enough kids coming today to play a game, then why did she have us show up? Corey's smirk lets me know he's thinking the same.

"Oh look, there's Bethany! She's the Purple Platypuses' team mom. Let me go tell her about the change of plans." Florence plucks a squirming Marigold out of her carrier and hands her to Hank before trotting over to Bethany and her daughter in a purple jersey. I should have made that connection sooner. Of course she was going to be here. Maybe this is my chance to do some more poking around, ask some subtle questions. *What was Cole's share in your supplement business, and how much more do you stand to earn now that he died?* Okay, a little more subtle than that.

"Come on, Axel! Race you to the slide!" Pearl takes off and Axel stomps after her, pouting at the ground. I'm probably going to get a talking-to from Florence later about how unexpected competition hurts Axel's heart.

Corey, maybe anticipating the same thing, jogs after them so Pearl doesn't—god forbid!—try and play tag. And I'm left to walk alone with Hank and Marigold, who seems to be able to toddle along just fine on her own, even in the long white lace sack dress they have her in. Hank is wearing rolled-up tan jeans and a professionally distressed linen button-down with a wide-brimmed straw hat and Birkenstocks. They look like they're coming from a photo shoot at one of those magazines for white millennials who only wear neutrals and have homesteads, not going to a Saturday morning soccer game.

"They found my prints, too."

"What? I didn't—" I *was* just thinking I should find a casual way to bring up the investigation to one of my few, if unlikely, suspects, but did he read my mind?

He chuckles softly. "Flo told me that she saw Corey there, and—I wanted to make sure that you weren't worrying. They're just following protocol with all this."

"I know," I sigh. "But I'll feel better once they move on from him, like . . . officially."

And if they're looking in Hank's direction, taking his fingerprints, maybe that'll happen sooner rather than later. Except, *wait.* A chill rushes over my skin despite the sunny February morning, my body moving ahead of my thoughts. He said they *found* his fingerprints, not that they were taking them. Why would Hank's fingerprints be on that Capri-Sun pouch?

I'm not doing a great job of hiding my feelings, as usual, because he rushes to explain. "I offered to come in after Flo did, just to eliminate my prints. Because, you know, I always help her with snack."

"Oh yeah?" I say, studying Marigold's blond head so I don't have to look at his face.

I don't remember Hank helping with snack at games, but I *guess* it could have happened this one time. He could be like so many dads, bringing up that one example of basic parenting forever to prove that they're such an enlightened, equal partner. But it could be something else, too. He has a motive. He hated Cole. This unlikely suspect may be looking a little more likely . . .

"Did they interview you, too?" You'd think I would be better at the subtle thing at this point.

"I told him we weren't each other's biggest fans, if that's what you're asking," he says, defensiveness making his voice rougher. "Doesn't mean I was happy to see him go down like that, though. He didn't recognize Axel's potential, and that pissed me off, yeah, but it's not like I'd wish *death* on someone because of that. Also, we don't know if it was even murder—"

"Bethany's going to sit this one out!" Florence steps into place in between us. "She says she's having a tough day—you know about her health journey, right, Mavis? She says she wants to listen to her body's cues and conserve her energy so she can be her best self at Pearl's party tomorrow."

I blink at her, trying to determine if there's even an ounce of self-awareness in between the woo-woo Instagram caption-speak, and still processing everything Hank just said. But also because I'm caught on the last part.

"Pearl's party? Bethany is . . . coming to Pearl's birthday party?

"She said you invited Pearl's whole Clover Scouts troop! How kind of you!" She smiles and then winces dramatically. "But I understand with these very, *very* last-minute things—you want to make sure *someone* is there. I'm so glad it worked out for Axel's schedule!"

I ignore the passive-aggression and replay all of my late-night party planning sessions since Tuesday. Did I really send that evite to the whole troop instead of just Christine? I need to check the RSVPs—did I even add an RSVP option? I might need to order a bigger cake.

And Bethany in my house? If she's capable of what I think she might be . . . is that safe? But no, she wouldn't try anything with all those people there. And this'll be a good chance to keep my eye on her, see if I can figure anything else out about her relationship with Cole, any possible motive. I have a whole day to brainstorm some *actually* subtle questions.

We reach the edge of the sand surrounding the playground, and Florence scoops up Marigold. "I'm going to take her on the swings!"

Good. Maybe I can ask Hank more about his experience at the station, with a lighter touch this time. They found his fingerprints . . . and who else's? Are they going to bring the kids in next? Is this whole investigation of theirs really hinging on a Capri-Sun pouch?

Florence holds her right hand out in a half rectangle and mimes the clicking of a shutter. "And maybe some extra video content? I need more B-roll," she mumbles. Hank nods, clearly knowing this job well, and they walk over to the swings together, as Marigold chants, "No swing! No swing!"

Langston dashes past me, a blur of aquamarine and brown skin, and then a second later, I hear: "Tetrahydrozoline!"

"Baby, that's a weird-ass greeting," Jasmine says, whacking Leon's shoulder.

"Sorry, just—I couldn't remember the word when I was talking to Mavis yesterday. When she asked what they found in Cole's toxicology report."

"Oh, she asked you that, did she?"

Jasmine purses her lips at me, and then turns back to Leon. They have a whole little conversation in jaw twitches, squinted eyes, and slight nods—the way that couples who've been together forever can do. And then they both look at me with the same expression, and I can read what they've decided: *Mavis is playing detective again, and we're just gonna go with it.*

"Tetrahydrozoline," Leon repeats. "It's Visine. Someone must have put it in that Capri-Sun?"

"Visine? Visine can kill someone? But you can buy it at CVS?"

"I remember seeing this before! In some Facebook post . . . or maybe it was that *Snapped* show?" Jasmine chimes in. "Some lady was putting it in her husband's coffee, and he didn't know because it's tasteless! For a while, before it got him, it just gave him some bad diarrhea."

"Yeah, and it mimics a lot of natural illnesses, so it wouldn't come up on most screenings, even in very large doses. They only caught it because Irene pushed for the more exhaustive tests."

"But that doesn't make any sense." I can feel my heart speeding up in frustration. "The detectives *told* us there was a powder residue when they came to talk to Corey on Monday."

I rack my brain, playing out that afternoon. I *know* I'm remembering at least that part right.

"Sodium nitrate. That's what they said. It's used as a fertilizer."

Leon strokes his jaw, considering this. "Was it on the grass or something? And it just happened to transfer?"

"No," I answer confidently. "It's not used on grass."

Jasmine lets out a long whistle. "So *two* poisons, then? Someone really wanted to make sure he . . . you know."

Is that what this means? Or did Leon just get something wrong? But as I look at his pained face, I know he would take care to get this right. Cole was his friend.

"And *that* is what doesn't make any sense. He was a good guy, Jas." Jasmine leans into him, slipping her arm around his waist. "I just can't understand how this happened to him . . . Who would do this?"

They hold each other, having another one of their silent conversations, and I look away to give them their privacy.

Who *would* do this? Two poisons to make sure he dies. That's a lot of planning, a lot of effort . . . so there has to be a lot of bad blood. Something flickers at the edges of my mind, like a gnat in the corner of my eye that disappears every time I turn my head. I've seen all three of my suspects this morning, yet I don't feel like I'm any closer to a solution. Is Hank's motive enough to justify killing Cole with two poisons? And what about Bethany? I don't even really understand her motive fully yet. Then there's Dom . . .

My eyes find his shed, where there are some shiny new additions: a chain across the top of the door frame and a massive, ID-card-proof padlock.

"JUST SAY IT."

"What?"

"I know you want to say it. You keep looking at me."

Jack leans over the pile of cut-up construction paper spread out on the living room floor in between us and kisses me. "I keep looking at you because I think you're beautiful."

"I know what you're doing. You're trying to distract me from the fact that *you've* been so distracted instead of just saying what I know you want to say. And it's not going to work. I won't be distracted." But then I kiss him back, immediately losing all of my credibility.

"I have no idea what you're talking about," he murmurs on my lips.

I pull back and grab a pillow off the couch, putting it in between us as a buffer.

"When you repress your thoughts, it can lead to physical consequences in your actual throat. Did you know that? Like sores. Or tumors. And . . . and—throat disease."

His smile is bracketed by two perfect parentheses.

"I'm sure the TikTok you learned that from was accurate."

I scoff. "Uh, it was actually a Reddit post *referencing* a TikTok."

"Oh, so it was peer reviewed?" He arches an eyebrow, trying to hold in his laughter, but then falls right into it with me.

"Actually, you know," he says a few minutes later, after we've gone back to our respective cutting projects—red hearts for him and green Shrek silhouettes for me. I can tell he's trying to be low-key, with purposefully relaxed shoulders and a totally chill tone. "What you're saying, about my throat . . . it does sound a lot like what I was telling you, about trauma in the body. How do you think you're . . . dealing with that?"

I throw my scissors down, giggling again. "See! I knew you wanted to say it!"

He grins and puts his hands up, guilty. "I'm *not* going to bring up therapy again, don't worry. It's just . . . I've been meaning to check in with you about how all the resting is going. And here we are on this Saturday night—a day of rest, one might say—working on elaborate party decorations." He waves to the felt Shrek headbands with the glue gun strings still hanging from them and the cake topper I made out of clay tonight after Pearl insisted she needed one with Shrek riding a rainbow unicorn. "Not to mention the whole murder investigation you've got going on, which I've also been meaning to check in about."

"I've barely been investigating," I say, as my eyes flick to the gratitude journal I was adding some more notes to before he arrived.

"Mr. Forest told me he caught you creeping around backstage. Does that have something to do with Coach Cole?"

"Mr. Forest told you that? I *paid* his deposit."

"Wait—you hired Mr. Forest for this so he wouldn't tell anyone he saw you?"

"Anyway, that didn't have anything to do with Cole. That was the other mystery," I rush to add, before he can put together that this *whole party* is happening so Mr. Forest wouldn't tell anyone he saw me. I really should get a discount . . .

"You have *two* mysteries now?" His face is a little bit exasperation, a little bit awe.

I quickly fill him in on Anabella getting the role of Annie, even though she sounds like Billie Eilish meets Fergie but bad, and the interaction I saw between Mr. Forest and Trisha after school on Tuesday. "I don't know what, but I know she's doing . . . something to him. We've got to watch them tomorrow."

"And—I'm just trying to follow—this is all so . . . Pearl can be Annie?"

"I mean, I just wanted her to think that I was cool, but if she does get the part that would be an added bonus. Her voice *is* pretty good."

Jack throws his head back in laughter and I feel proud, even though it may just be because exasperation inched into the lead.

He reaches over and threads his fingers through mine, pulling my hand onto his lap. "Listen, I love how you love your kid." There's that word again. So his tongue and lips and whatever else—the uvula?—are able to form it. It's not, like, a mechanical problem. "And I'm here to help you always. I'm just saying, I'm pretty sure Pearl would think you were just as cool if you didn't investigate the mystery of why her friend is Annie and cut out hundreds of hearts for her party decorations." He nods toward the substantial pile he's finished in the past hour.

"Well, those hearts aren't for the party."

"What? Why do you have me doing this then?"

"Because Mrs. Tennison asked me to cut out two hundred of them. I have to go hang them all up during recess, so the kids will think the Valentine's Day fairy came or something. Do you think you can add some positive messages to some of them? She sent me a list of approved ones."

"That's a lot of work for her to expect from you. Why would she ask you to do that?"

"Because I'm the new class mom." I mumble it into my hand, but I can tell from the way his jaw drops that he heard me.

"Mavis—*what?*"

"She was complaining about how she doesn't have one. Because of *me*—because I got Trisha ousted. And I knew that she wanted me to offer, so I didn't really have a choice. Plus, it's going to make her really love Pearl."

I see him gearing up to go all psychologist on me—nodding thoughtfully, one finger pressed into his cheek—so I beat him to the analysis.

"It's just one more thing. And I have all this free time, so why wouldn't I give it to Pearl? What kind of mom would I be if I didn't?"

"Still a great one." He reaches up to cradle my face. "It's okay for your time to just be yours."

I feel a flash of irritation. My cheeks flush and I pull away. "That's easy for you to say because you're not a parent. You don't *understand*."

I know that's not completely fair. He has a lot of caregiver responsibilities with Derek. But it doesn't seem to weigh on him the same way it does me. Nothing I give will ever be enough because Pearl deserves even more. And if *I*, the person who loves her more than anyone, am not giving her everything, then what hope do I have that the world will even give her a fraction? That everyone else will value her and treasure her because they see just how valued and treasured she already is?

I don't say all of this to Jack because I don't even know how to put it into words. It feels like both nonsense and the most sacred truth, and speaking it aloud is wrong either way.

"I just want what's best for you."

"Then trust I know what's best for myself." The words come out harsh and hot. I immediately want to take them back, but they hang in the air like smoke from an extinguished flame. I don't even think I'm mad at Jack, necessarily, it's just that I'm mad that he keeps trying to help me, mad that I constantly *need* to be helped.

His lips part, and I know he's about to apologize. And I *know* that's going to make me feel even worse. So I talk first. "If you say I'm in the red zone right now, I'm going to kick you in the balls."

"I definitely wasn't about to diagnose you with a color." He holds his palms up, and a sly smile creeps in. "Though that is certainly something someone in the red zone would say."

I laugh and lean into him, luxuriating in the broken tension.

He kisses the top of my head. "I'm sorry if I've been overbearing. I *know* you know what's best for you. I'm sorry for telling you what you should do with your own time," he says.

"Don't say sorry! I'm sorry!"

"I'm still learning how to show up for you. And I l—" There's that damn consonant again. I watch his Adam's apple bob as he swallows. "—care for you. So much. I won't always say what's right, but I'm trying my best. I hope you know that."

He lifts my chin and presses his lips to mine.

"I know. I do."

Do I even want him to say it yet? Because what would I say back? Love—is that what I'm feeling for this man who lets me be messy and grumpy and all over the place, and yet still looks at me like I'm exactly who he wants?

I deepen our kiss, parting his lips, intertwining my fingers behind his neck. And his hands drift around my waist, up my shirt, pulling me closer. I curl my knee over him, settling myself in his lap, and soon my lips hum with his frustrated sigh.

Because it's unspoken but understood that we can't go much farther when my dad is snoring in his room at the back of the house, and Pearl's asleep, too, on just the other side of the kitchen. We have to plan in advance for that. I groan in frustration, too. I'm thirty-two years old and feel like a horny teenager.

He kisses both of my cheeks, my forehead, the side of my neck. "I should probably go."

I feel the familiar aching tug in my belly. I don't want him to go. But I know it's for the best.

He stands up and readjusts his jeans. "Do you want me to take this paper home, finish these hearts?"

"That's the sexiest thing you've ever said."

Later, after I've cooled down and made a batch of flying unicorns to hang from the ceiling with yarn and soothed a stirring

Pearl, that same buzzing-gnat feeling from this morning at the park comes back, and I still my mind to chase it.

It's Hank. What did he say again? Before Florence interrupted us?

Also, we don't know if it was even murder.

Yes, that's it. What did he mean by that? Was he trying to hint at . . . suicide?

I did see some articles about sodium nitrate being used for suicide . . . but why would Hank bring that up to me? Was he trying to cover for himself? Or did he google the same things I did?

I move the Shrek headbands aside and shuffle around some papers on the coffee table, looking for a pen. I need to write all this down so I don't forget it in the morning. But my gratitude journal is almost full, and I hate flipping the pages back and forth, anyway. I need to see it all laid out, everything I've learned so far. I need to see if there are connections I'm missing.

I grab some Shrek silhouettes and a few of the hearts Jack left behind and get to work.

FOURTEEN

"IS THIS . . . A MURDER BOARD?"

My eyes slowly flutter open and my dad's tall, lanky frame, standing over me, comes into focus. I must have fallen asleep on the living room couch last night, instead of making it to my bedroom. And my neck and back and hips and . . . well, *everything* is very mad about it.

Dad's whole face is pinched in confusion as he studies something over the fireplace. I wipe away the gunk on my lids and lashes and start to take in flashes of red and green. Now, what is that?

"A murder board? What's a murder board?" Pearl calls from the kitchen, and I can hear the rustling of her coming to find out, Polly right there with her.

"Happy birthday, baby girl!" I call. "Uh, stay there! I'm going to make you your birthday pan—"

"Whoa!"

I sit up, a string of drool trailing from my cheek, and see what she sees: hearts and Shrek silhouettes taped up on the wall, with the rainbow yarn I used to hang the flying unicorns strung between them. And there are words written on the hearts and Shreks in my scratchy late-night handwriting that, okay, looks a little serial killer-y in the morning light.

Hank. Bethany. Dom.

Irene?

And other snatches of words related to the investigation:

Visine, sodium nitrate, capri sun, sucking toes.

In all caps, drifting into Shrek's horns, tentacles—whatever:

WHAT DOES BETHANY'S CANCER HAVE TO DO WITH THIS? and HANK NEVER HELPS! and WHY DOES DETECTIVE BERRY HATE ME?

It looks . . . insane.

"No offense, Mommy," Pearl says delicately. "But this wasn't really my vision for the decorations."

I hop up off the couch and my whole body screams in protest. "I know! I was just . . . experimenting. I'm gonna take it down."

"Hold on. Wait a minute." Dad is snapping pictures of my accidental murder board with his phone, but he's also somehow turned on his flashlight in the process, so hopefully they don't turn out.

"You've made some good progress here, Maves," he says as I rip a couple of Shreks down—carefully, so I can look at them later. "But this one right here I have a question about—hey, *hey!*"

"Okay, this is boring! I'm ready for my birthday pancakes now! I want eight because I'm eight!"

THE DOORBELL RINGS, AND PEARL SQUEALS, HOPPING OFF my bed to run and answer it.

"Wait, you need to put lotion on," I say, barely grabbing her arm in time.

"No one will see my legs!" She swishes the long rainbow dress that has been laid out on the chair in her room since Tuesday, proving her point.

"But *I* will know you're ashy."

She wrinkles her nose to let me know how much she cares about that and then wiggles free and takes off toward the door. And as soon as she opens it, squealing even louder when she sees Christine's daughter Harlow, it's like the day catapults forward in flashes and marvels and moments, until it's all over and I don't know how that happened but I know I feel both exhausted and overwhelmed with joy.

It's the same what-is-time way I felt during the biggest days of my life: both graduations, our courthouse wedding, Pearl's screaming entrance into the world. But the smaller days, too: an unexpected trip to Disneyland as a family because Corey's friend could sign us in, a walk around the duck pond in the park when Pearl was two, drippy ice cream cones at sunset on the pier.

It's like there's so much good all at once, my mind can only process a little bit of it at a time. So then I'm rushing to catch up when the day is over, cataloguing everything I don't want to forget.

After everyone's gone and the house is as cleaned up as it's going to get tonight and I'm lying in bed with Pearl curled up next to me, her face still a mess of chocolate frosting and glitter—that's what I do.

There's the truly impressive victory dance Dyvia did when she beat all the kids at pin the whatever on Shrek, beginning with the robot and ending with the worm.

And the glittery rainbow horn Jack got painted on his forehead after Pearl sat in the chair of the airbrush tattoo lady—who she specifically requested, for the record—and immediately got cold feet. She got a matching one right after, and they looked so cute, I didn't have the heart to tell Jack they last for twenty-four to seventy-two hours.

Mr. Forest led the kids in a rousing rendition of "I'm a Believer," and when the girls took turns grabbing the mic, Pearl outshined Anabella by far. Silent satisfaction warmed me up like a cup of hot cocoa. Not at a seven-year-old's embarrassment, of course—I'm not a monster!—but at Trisha's seething rage.

There was also Jasmine pretending to give my dad an exclusive interview, with the big boom mic and headset he acquired god knows when. And the way his face squinted up as he slowly realized she wasn't giving him new details about the case, but the plot of *The Bodyguard*, so he laughed and swatted her away with "Man, forget you!"

I want to remember the jolt of pure bliss that hit Pearl as she opened up each present. Never mind that she conveniently forgot our plan was to open them up after everyone left. That deep dimple, her eyes big and sparkling like a Disney woodland creature, as she screamed with the utmost sincerity, "Walkie-talkies! This is what I've always wanted!" Even though I'm completely sure she's never mentioned walkie-talkies in her life. If that bliss could be bottled up and sold as an antidepressant, I swear—wars could end, the world would heal.

And my favorite moment came at the end of the party, as Pearl leaned over her wonky Shrek-rainbow-donkey cake because the lady at the grocery store bakery was (understandably) confused. She had her eyes squeezed tight, taking her time to think of her perfect wish, and I looked over her head at Corey. Our eyes met in the warm glow of her candles, and it was like everything ugly and hard and hidden between us disappeared, at least for now, because look at this beautiful girl we made together.

"This is the best day of my life," Pearl whispered. Then she blew out her candles and everyone cheered.

AND THEN THERE'S THE NOT-SO-GOOD PARTS THAT I'M also cataloguing tonight.

Bethany cornered me right after I finished dishing out Costco pizza and was just about to sit down with my own slice.

"I talked to your dad about your mom," she said, leaning in too close and caressing my arm. She smelled like patchouli and whatever that grass is they have behind the counter in smoothie shops. Her eyes were wet as if she'd just been crying. "It came up naturally. I was asking him what made you so defensive and suspicious of human connection, and of course it's the mother wound. I don't know why I didn't recognize it before. I'm so sorry, Mavis. Maybe that's why we got off on the wrong foot. I trigger thoughts of that deep loss in your journey."

I froze, teetering between which *Real Housewives* play I should employ, glass-smashing or table-flipping, and she used that as an opportunity to make it much worse.

"What do you think she would want for you? You know what I think? I think she would want you to have peace in your life." She pressed her lips together, and one single tear broke free, trailing down her cheek. "And that's why I want to invite you to my self-care party on Wednesday. No pressure for anything more and free of charge! Like the boot camp class you . . . hopped on into this week. I know you may think it isn't your thing, but I just feel so called to offer this to you. I think it'll bring you so much peace and healing."

I looked around, seeing who was about to witness some glass-smashing *and* table-flipping (plus maybe some metaphorical wig-tugging, too), and that's when I noticed my dad. Smiling. Holding two thumbs up.

"Your dad agreed that some self-care would be *really* beneficial for you."

"Um. He did?"

And that was enough of a confirmation (or maybe she saw the spirit of Shereé shining through in my eyes) because she wiped her tears and was up in a second.

"I'll send you the Paperless Post! Can't wait!"

I walked over to my dad, and he winked. "You're welcome, Veronica."

"Why would you volunteer me for that scam party? And who is Veronica?"

"You are, and I'm Keith. Have you seen *Veronica Mars*? Bert let me borrow his season one box set." He shrugged. "I saw her name on your murder board and figured this would be the perfect opportunity for you to get some of those questions answered. And then tell me, so I can put it on my show."

He brushed off both his shoulders. "Keith Mars and Keith Morrison." And then he strutted away, as if he didn't just commit me to an evening in my own personal hell.

That would've been plenty bad enough for one afternoon. But later, when I was stealing a moment to catch my breath as Corey led the attack on the unicorn piñata, Derek waved to me from behind the kitchen door that leads into the laundry room, one finger to his lips.

"I know exactly what that was, Alexander, and it was not fucking cute. You think you can cross me? You think this is a game?"

I recognized the venomous whisper immediately. Trisha. But who was Alexander? And why was she talking to him like that?

"I will fucking destroy you. I will set fire to your sad little life and dance on the motherfucking ashes."

My eyes worriedly shot to Derek. Should he be hearing this?

But his face was alight with the laughter he was holding in. He scooted slightly, making room for me to see in the slight opening of the door hinge. And there was Mr. Forest in his sweater vest, with the ukulele he brought to play clutched to his chest as a shield. Trisha is only an inch or two taller than him, but it may as well be ten feet with the way he was cowering.

"Mrs. Holbrook, I was just giving another child a chance to shine at their own birthday party. Not everything is about Anabella—"

"And that is where you're wrong. We had a deal here, and because you've now attempted to *sabotage* the deal, you are going to give me something else. Anabella says there's another solo she wants. In that "N.Y.C." song. She says there's a star in it, and Anabella is supposed to be the *only* star."

"Anabella already *has* a part in that song. And she has more solos than any other child—"

"Because that is what she deserves. Now you're going to give her this solo, whatever it is. And if you don't, then everyone is going to know what happened that Memorial Day weekend in Downey. Am I clear?"

And there it was: confirmation that Trisha is still running the show at Knoll. Even with her title stripped, even with her crimes exposed, her fingers still have a tight grip on the strings of everything, making sure her kids get more than anyone else. I should have felt victorious—here's proof, a clear solution to my *other* mystery. But honestly it was more . . . depressing. Defeating.

"And just like I told Mr. Reed, I'm sure you don't want—"

I accidentally bumped the door, making a loud creak, and Trisha's whole body tensed. "Who's there?"

I was ready to give us up because this is my house and she

had no business acting like she owned the place, let alone using it as her evil lair to threaten elementary school music teachers.

But Derek patted my shoulder, signaling for me to stay, and stepped out into the open.

"Hiiiiiii." Trisha's voice immediately jumped, like, ten octaves.

"Can I tell you some facts I know about my favorite game shows?"

"Gaaaaaame shows?" she repeated, slipping into that familiar too-slow, too-loud speech. "Yeeeeeesssss. I would looooove that."

And actually, you know what, I take it back—what I said about this all being not so good. The little thumbs-up Derek did behind his back before I tiptoed away unseen was very good. The most good.

FIFTEEN

I'M SITTING IN THE LIVING ROOM TAKING JACK-APPROVED deep, steadying breaths to prepare for a meeting I don't want to have but know I *need* to have, when I realize that someone is in my house.

"It's always my fault, isn't it?"

Whatever progress I've made toward clarity and calmness is immediately gone at the sound of the male voice breaking through the silence.

"Dad?" I try, rising slowly to my feet, even though I know that's not right. My dad's voice is lower, older. And my dad is out with Bert, doing something with his podcast that I refused to humor him by listening to him describe. But maybe he left his TV on? The voice does sound a little choppy, muffled.

"You act like you . . . no wrong."

"Hello?"

That didn't sound like it was coming from my dad's room, and if his TV was on this whole time, then I would have noticed it sooner, right? The way he keeps his volume set, the *Law & Order* "dun-dun" nearly shakes the walls.

No, I think it was coming from the side of the house. Pearl's room?

I need to go check it out, but I can't just stroll in there unarmed. I'm not about to be like one of those silly girls in horror movies who investigate with only their jumbo boobs as a shield. And my deflated A-cups aren't going to provide much protection from a psycho stabber.

I quickly look around at my options. Pearl has spread out all her presents from her party yesterday across the living room floor so she could survey her bounty all at once. There's gotta be something here I can use as a weapon. My eyes catch on the keyboard Corey got her—that could probably knock someone out. But I grab the much lighter badminton racket instead—I could fight someone off with this. Or wait—I dash over to a sleeping Polly and slide a neon-orange plastic bow out from underneath her, part of the archery set Pearl also declared was "just what I've always wanted!" Polly lifts her lids just barely and glares at me like I'm the villain here, waking her up from her nap. Never mind the *intruder*! God, I really do have to take care of everything around here.

I decide on the racket and the bow, plus a few of the suction cup arrows—better to be safe than sorry—and then start to silently, slowly creep toward Pearl's door. I don't hear any movement, any voices, just a quiet buzzing sound. Did he leave? Did I imagine this?

"I'm just asking for some collaborative, clear, emotion-focused communication using 'I' statements. That's all."

Okay, now, that was a different person. Definitely coming from Pearl's room. What the fuck? Are *two* people here? Was I really so into my breaths that two people got into my house? I would be proud of my meditating ability if I wasn't outnumbered and possibly about to be murdered. And oh my god, what am I *doing*? I should've run out the front door and called the police instead of trying to fight with a dinky racket and plastic archery set, as if that is going to do anything. I guess I'm not much better than those horror movie girls.

"You always make it about what I'm doing wrong." There's the man again. "You don't like my communication. You don't like the way I load the dishwasher."

"Well, that's because you put my jade plates on the bottom rack, but, ugh, that's not—*I* just want us to work together instead of against each other."

Wait. I know that voice. And actually . . . the first one, too. Why the hell are *they* in my house?

In a burst of indignation, I jump into the doorway, brandishing my toys/weapons. "Arghhhhh!"

And . . .

. . . there's no one there.

How was I hearing their voices if they're not here? Florence and Hank are weird, but they're not hide-under-Pearl's-bed weird . . . right?

I get down onto the ground to check just in case, and that's when Polly finally comes running in, jumping on my back with her tail wagging. The *worst* guard dog.

"*I* am tired of being the bad guy!" Hank shouts, and I jerk up. Where is that coming from? It's so loud, so close. But I'm the only one in this room.

"*I* feel like I can never please you. *I* helped out on Saturday, just like you're always saying you want me to do more! *I* listened! But that's just forgotten now, huh?" I search around the floor, looking for the source of Hank's voice. "*I* don't like how you question my intentions, but *I* can never question yours."

There's a flash of red light, pulsating with his passive-aggressive words. It's the pair of walkie-talkies on the ground, abandoned next to the polka-dot pajamas Pearl didn't put in her hamper. That's where Florence and Hank's argument is broadcasting from—but how?

"My intentions? My intentions are *pure*," Florence shouts, making the screen on one walkie-talkie light up red again. "I'm always doing what's best for our children—our family! That is my guiding light!"

"Oh, is that what you tell yourself? You're forgetting I'm not one of your Instagram followers! I know you."

"I can't help it if other people don't see it that way, but *you* should, Hank."

I feel a little flutter, a *thrill*, at seeing behind the perfect family front. Is this about that tone-deaf email she sent, the one that most of the team parents are still mad about, or the sun-flare swinging pictures she posted along with a caption about the back-and-forth nature of grief? (Along with a code to try the children's therapy app that sponsors her, of course.) Does Hank actually call her on this shit?

I guess I feel a little guilty snooping on their private conversation, too. But it's not like I sought this out!

Still, I grab the walkie-talkies off the ground, looking for the off buttons. They both have *CHNL* and then a number on the front. One says *06*, and the other, the one that's been lighting up and broadcasting their voices, says *18*. I push a button on the top of that one, but instead of going dark, the walkie-talkie emits a blaring beep.

Their bickering immediately stops.

"What was that?" Hank asks.

There's a rustling and then: "It's this monitor. It's always been a little glitchy. Peaceful Baby offered to send me their deluxe video one for just twelve stories, two reels, and three posts—but I don't know if we should upgrade. Video uses 5G, right? And who knows what that could do to Marigold? The *waves*."

A monitor? *Oh*—a baby monitor! That must be the radio signal that this thing is picking up. I really need to read the manual for these walkie-talkies before Pearl plays with them any more, because I don't want anyone hearing what goes on in *our* house.

"Do we even need the thing anymore? She's almost two, Flo."

"She is *not*. And we cannot just *leave* her in here unattended."

"She's unattended in front of *Bluey* right now."

Bluey? This is the same lady who told me her kids don't have any screen time because of its harmful effects on emotional and social development—even *more* scary than 5G waves. I wonder what else I'll find out Florence is lying about if I keep listening . . .

Okay, no, I need to turn this off now, before it becomes my new favorite show.

I find the right off button this time—turns out it's next to whatever that beeping button was—and then put the walkie-talkies under Pearl's bed, so she hopefully won't play with them again until I can figure out how to get them to work the way they're supposed to.

I check my phone—no time for any more deep breathing before my meeting. But honestly, seeing another side of perfect-parent Florence might have brought me all the clarity and calmness that I need.

"SO WHAT BRINGS YOU HERE TODAY, MS. MILLER? MS. LIL-liam said you informed her that it was urgent."

I've only been sitting in Principal Smith's office for less than a minute, and I can already tell that he wants me to leave. His dark, deep-set eyes drift to his computer screen, and he clicks his mouse a couple of times, as if to show how busy he is, that I should feel *lucky* he made the time.

I open up the Project Window file folder in my mind and get that professional-Mavis software running, because I'm clearly going to need it.

"I wanted to bring your attention to an unfortunate situation between Mr. Forest and Trisha Holbrook. On two occasions, I saw her approach him in a threatening manner, and this is concerning because, as you may know, Trisha's daughter was cast as Annie in Mr. Forest's after-school program."

"Let me stop you right there, Ms. Miller." Principal Smith threads his fingers on his desk and leans forward. His thick mustache lifts in a patronizing smile. "Listen, you're not the first mother who's come to me upset about her child not getting the part they preferred in this performance. And I understand how disappointing that can feel, but I'll tell you what I told her: something like this builds resilience in both the child *and* parent."

I shake my head. "No. No, this is not about Pearl. *At all.* It's about Trisha continuing to manipulate and—"

He cuts me off with a loud sigh. "I can hear that you're frustrated, but it's my policy to not get involved with interpersonal issues between parents."

"But it's *not* an interpersonal issue. She's blackmailing a staff member."

"Blackmail?" He flashes me that patronizing smile again and I imagine ripping that mustache right off. "That seems like it might be a slight exaggeration."

I take a deep breath, keeping my mask in place and my tone in check. Because I know being the angry one here isn't going to help anything.

"She told him she would tell everyone about some weekend in Downey—if he didn't not only cast Annabelle as Annie, but give her some other kid's solo, too."

There's a flicker of interest in his eyes, but he blinks it away and holds his palms up. "All after-school staff are hired as independent contractors by the district, so it's really not my place to tell them how to run their program."

"But Mr. Forest is a teacher here during the school day. And it's happening at *your* school. The one you're supposed to lead." Even as I'm saying it, I know it won't make any difference, as he's clearly committed to not hearing me. But I can't just say *nothing*. "I'm not the only person who heard her. If you don't believe me, you can talk to—"

"That's not necessary." His fingers tap the desk, and his face is tight with a look of finality. "I know you helped me last fall and I am forever grateful . . . that is why I *paid* you the fee my wife promised." He raises his eyebrows at me, as if he's waiting for something. A thank-you of my own? Well, he's going to be waiting a long time then—I earned that money. Who knows what would have happened to him if I hadn't figured it all out? Finally, he relents. "What I'm trying to make sure you understand here is . . . I no longer owe you a debt, Ms. Miller. I'm not going to be used in some vendetta against Ms. Holbrook."

I feel my stank face break through. "What—I'm not—I just want you to do what's right."

"Right is relative." He shrugs. "Isn't that what you think about your friend Corinne? That's why you told the police I . . . bothered her. As if that was an excuse for her assault on me."

Oh. There it is. I told the police everything Corinne told me that night—*of course* I did. So this man is mad at me, trying to *punish* me, for that honesty?

Right now, with his narrowed eyes, his lips in a thin, smug

line, I can almost see him through Corinne's eyes that night, when he propositioned her, grabbed her arm. It doesn't fully excuse what she did, but it's not like he was some innocent victim either. And *he* didn't face any consequences for his actions— well, except for a couple of weeks tied up in a wine room. But nothing from the cops. He's here doing his job as normal, so I don't know why he's holding a grudge against me.

"You know," he continues, "if you know anything about where she is, it's your duty to report—"

"I don't."

He flashes me a smile so phony it looks painful. "Well, then maybe you should turn your sleuthing skills there, Ms. Miller, instead of the elementary school production of *Annie*."

He nods, and his eyes flick to the door behind me and then back to his screen, sending his message loud and clear. *We're done here.*

So I mumble a "Thank you for your time" that's as phony as his stupid smile and walk out. But as soon as I click the door shut, all of the not-calm, not-centered feelings that were swelling inside of me shoot out like I've sprung a leak. I do this weird grunty snarl thing, and okay, maybe stomp—but just once.

Ms. Lilliam looks me up and down from her perch behind the front desk, a cup of cinnamon coffee steaming in front of her. "I've dealt with enough temper tantrums today if you want to take whatever this is outside."

But then a small grin appears, the one I've been seeing more and more from Ms. Lilliam ever since she decided she doesn't hate me and will even occasionally tolerate my presence. Her eyes dart to Principal Smith's closed door, then she leans in and whispers, "But I get it. I wish he was missing again. Mm-hmm, I had things running *a lot* more smoothly around here when he was."

Good afternoon Mavis,

When you are able, can you provide me with an ETA on the George Washington costume? I saw you were on campus today and thought you might be here to deliver it, but it appears I was wrong. Usually we would have begun dress rehearsals by now, but I can be flexible.

Did I mention we also require a new wig? I felt it might be implied because it is part of the full costume, but I'll make it more clear here, just in case.

Can't wait to see what you've created!

Thank you,
Mrs. Alene Tennison

Hello Troop 1207 Moms!

Thank you to those of you who have already filled out our parent cookie meeting survey! Friendly reminder to please take a moment to complete the survey if you haven't already. I need your responses to make important decisions before our pre-cookie-kick-off parent meeting next week and the girls' cookie kick-off meeting the following week! There are a lot of moving parts during cookie season, so please help me make this our best year yet!!

Also, Dakota's mom Bethany has graciously invited all of us to her self-care party Wednesday night! How fun!! Her business, Balanced With Bethany, focuses on supporting and empowering all women to take care of themselves, and it has a nonprofit division. So it could be a great option for the philanthropy portion of our cookie funds! Hope to see you there!!

Warmly,
Christine Fountaine
Troop 1207 Leader
Room Mom for Ms. Laguna's Class
Proud Mom of Austin, Harlow, and Olive

SIXTEEN

"SO IS THIS LIKE HERBALIFE?" JASMINE ASKS AS WE WALK down the sidewalk, searching for the address on Bethany's evite for her self-care party. We're on the west side of Beachwood, closer to the ocean, where the home prices are so high they'll make your jaw drop—or at least mine did when I scoped them out on Zillow before we left. Because it's by the beach, though, we had to circle the neighborhood five hundred times looking for parking, and even then we're blocks away.

"Yeah, but Herbalife meets . . . Gwyneth?" I roll my eyes. "This lady teaches people how to take care of themselves. As if that's some special skill. As if meditating and exercising and sleeping enough hours at night is going to fix all your problems. And who even has the time to do all of that anyway? It's bullshit."

Jasmine stops, looks me up and down, and then keeps walking. "Hmmm."

"Why *hmmm*? What's *hmmm*?"

"Just . . . hmmm." She shrugs and smirks. "Sounds like maybe you're a little jealous of ole girl. Because, I don't know, she so easily takes what you feel too guilty to give yourself."

I brought Jasmine along with me on this mission because Jack's been so weird about all of this. Even though he was my partner in (investigating) crime last fall, it feels like every conversation about this current investigation could trigger some deep talk about my feelings and my trauma and how I'm using this to deflect all that—and that kind of defeats the purpose of the whole deflecting thing. *Not that I'm deflecting.*

I assumed Jasmine would keep it easy and light, but *clearly* I misjudged that.

"Um, excuse me, ma'am," I say, dodging some roses peeking out from behind a white picket fence. "For your information, I've been doing a *great* job of taking care of myself lately! And why are you talking to me like a therapist? Oh my god—do *you* go to therapy, too?"

Am I the only one left?

She smiles and loops her arm through mine. "No."

"Whew, okay! Because I feel like everyone—"

"I *was* bingeing that French lady therapist podcast this week, though, and"—she shrugs again—"I don't know, sounds like it could be right."

She giggles and I bump her with my hip. "There's no deeper meaning here. I'm just going to this thing to look for evidence and see if she's involved in what happened with Cole."

"How likely do you think it is . . . that she hurt him?" Jasmine asks, her face suddenly serious.

"She's my number one suspect. I mean, there's the facilities guy at the park, Dom. And I even considered Hank Michaelson, too." Jasmine's dark brown eyes widen at that. "But I don't think it's either of them."

The only real clue I had to go on with Hank is the strangeness of him saying he helped with snacks that morning, which I don't remember. But after hearing him bring it up *again* to

Florence through the baby monitor over a week later, well, I'm thinking that probably was the one time he did help. And now he wants a Dad of the Year trophy for it, or at least a commemorative medal.

"Bethany, though—things just keep adding up with her," I continue, lowering my voice as we get closer to the corner where the house is supposed to be. "Do you remember how she disappeared that morning? Right before he fell?" Jasmine nods, though it looks like she's just humoring me. "Well, they were friends. Business partners. So how does that make sense? And it's possible she would actually benefit financially from his death, because they were creating these supplements together, and now he's not here to get his share. *And* remember what Ruth told me about her? Well, I confirmed it. She *does* say her program cured her cancer. She's using that to scam even more women into giving her money."

Jasmine's silent, and her brow is furrowed in . . . something. I'm not sure. I can't read her.

"Is this—are you . . . you're not mad at me, right? I mean, you and Leon knew I was trying to figure this out."

"Yeah, we know."

"Does Leon not want me to, then? Because I know this is his friend, and I don't want to be insensitive to that. I could—I *will* . . . stop."

She cocks her head to the side, narrowing her eyes, and this time the message is much more clear. *Girl, neither of us believes that.*

"I'm just trying to get this straight." Her face is still wrinkled, stern, but I see the flicker of a grin pulling on her lips. "We're using this rare moment away from our precious children to go to this self-care party—*not* so you can actually *care* for your *self*. But so you can prove that the self-care lady is a scammer and maybe a murderer?"

"I did make that clear when I invited you. And investigating . . . it helps me relax." She arches an eyebrow in response, and I smile guiltily and let out a long sigh. "I know I'm a mess." The Shrek murder board incident maybe made that just a teensy bit clear.

"I didn't say that."

"Well, you didn't have to, because I know it. I am aware!" I laugh, but it comes out sounding more like a sob, which just highlights further what a mess I am. Probably sensing that I'm right on the edge of making this even more like an episode of her French lady therapist podcast, Jasmine leans into me, murmuring into my hair, "Oh, come here, girl."

We stop on the grass of someone's beautiful, expensive lawn because keeping it cute *and* walking is a lot to ask of my body all at once. "I—I feel like I've been a mess for a long time. Like, I've learned the lessons and I'm still here, with a cloud of flies and dust around me like that . . . stinky *Peanuts* character. Do you know what I mean? And god, I'm sorry, I've been dumping my feelings on everyone lately. It's probably so annoying."

"Well, first of all, I love you, so dump away." She holds out her hands like, *Gimme*. "And second of all, you talking about Pigpen?"

"Yes, Pigpen! See how easily you named him? Because I *am* him."

She laughs and shakes her head, but then looks me right in the eye. "There's messiness in the rebuilding, Mavis. And you've had to rebuild a lot in your life these past few years. With Corey. With your job."

Okay, move over, French lady, maybe Jasmine should have her *own* podcast.

I sigh. "Yeah, I know."

"It's like when they knock down an old, decrepit house on one of those HGTV shows—"

"You think my life was decrepit?"

She purses her lips. "*You* said it."

"Did I?"

"Anyway, the bones are good, but most of it has got to go in order to make something beautiful. And, whew, that little redhead sure can design! Did you see the episode where she—"

"Um, can we get back to me?"

I take back what I said about the podcast.

"I *guess.*" Jasmine scoffs and playfully bats my shoulder. "What I'm trying to say is, it looks real bad. It looks like they'll never get it together and there's usually some drama with her contractor because he's always—"

I give her a look, and she smiles, continuing. "But it's all necessary to get to the final product. And I know you're on your way to making something beautiful for you, even if it looks a little rough to others sometimes."

Her words make me feel lighter and warm, like I'm floating in a pool on a July afternoon. I'm so lucky to have a friend like Jasmine, who will be honest with me, who will see the beauty in my mess—who will go with me to a scammy self-care party in order to investigate a murder no one actually asked me to investigate.

I squeeze her tight and then smirk. "So you're saying . . . I'm being gentrified?"

"Girl, whatever!" she shouts, smiling wide. "That was my one heartfelt moment of the month. I hit my quota! I hope you enjoyed it!"

We both lose ourselves in cackles, only stopping when a woman in a Lilly Pulitzer shift dress and a denim jacket draped over her shoulders walks past us with concerned eyes, giving us a wide berth. I follow her with my gaze as she approaches a large white Craftsman house on the corner. It has a lot size double the ones on either side and a wraparound porch that looks more Southern than Southern California—definitely on the upper end of that Zillow range. A giant pastel balloon arch sways in the salty evening breeze.

"I think that's it."

"We about to be the only Black people here, aren't we?" Jasmine asks.

"Yep." I grab her hand and squeeze it. "Have I told you lately how much I appreciate you? How you're my best and truest friend?"

"Yeah, yeah, yeah."

We can hear laughter and high-pitched chatter drifting from the windows as we walk up. There's a ceramic pot of bright pink azaleas on each step and a matching wreath on the glossy black door. And that door swings open as soon as we step on the *Welcome to Our Happy Home!* mat, as if we tripped a wire or something.

"Hello! Thanks for coming!" coos a woman with wavy blond hair and sharp clavicles. Stacks of wooden bangles clonk together as she extends her arms out wide, and she's wearing a long batik-printed caftan that's either from a pier-side gift shop or Johnny Was—but I can pretty confidently guess which one. "Are you some of Bethany's Clover Scouts friends?"

I flinch at the term *friend*, which she must take as a denial. "One of her True Living Med Spa friends then? Or one of our new consultants moving over from Agape Essentials?" She doesn't wait for me to confirm or deny. "Don't you just love how she brings everyone together? I'm Pamela, by the way, your host for tonight. I'm a Balanced With Bethany Ultimate Wellness Goddess!" She does pause at that, but I'm not sure if it's for

applause or for us to introduce ourselves. When we give her neither, though, her eyes light up in understanding. "Oh! You must
be doing Bethany's self-guided silent retreat. I've done it myself
five times. Very fulfilling!"

Jasmine and I glance at each other and come to a quick consensus. *Yeah, let's go with that.*

"Come, come," Pamela continues, guiding us in. "She's about
to get started, so you're just in time!" She shakes her fists next to
her face like an excited kid about to get cake at a party.

We walk through what in our neighborhood would be called
an entry and what in this neighborhood could only be referred
to as a *foyer*. It's fancy, grand—and it only gets grander as we
walk past the double staircase with its intricately carved banister
into the living room. Even that doesn't feel like the right word
for it, though, because my dad's entire house could fit into just
this room. The *luxuriating* room, maybe. The *lounge and complain about taxes and how difficult it's been to get permits for the
Scrooge McDuck money pool you're trying to build* room.

"And here's my humble abode!" Pamela declares, because of
course she does. "Go ahead and get yourself settled. There's a
rosé bar over there, and some cupcakes, too, if you're feeling a
little naughty tonight."

I'm glad I've fully committed to this whole self-guided silent
retreat thing, because otherwise I might start making involuntary hurling sounds.

Pamela flits away, and Jasmine and I take in what we've gotten ourselves into. We *are* the only Black people here, and two
of only a few people of color. Which isn't a surprise, considering
Bethany brought up Madam C. J. Walker and how I could
"open up a whole new market" for her when she first tried to
pitch me. The ladies mingle next to eight, maybe more, round
white tables set up in the back of the room—each one is

decorated with dried flower arrangements in the same pastel colors as the balloons outside. Rows of chairs fill up the middle of the space, and on the other side of the room is a Balanced With Bethany step-and-repeat hanging from a metal frame. Women are posing for photos in front of it now, but it's probably where Bethany will do . . . whatever she does at a self-care party. Hopefully it won't take too long. Where is she, anyway?

"Here you go," Jasmine says, sticking a name tag on my shirt. It reads *Kim*, and hers says *Moesha*.

"We're here undercover," she explains. "They don't need to know our true identities. Oh hey, there's your suspect."

I follow her nod to Bethany, surrounded by a circle of adoring fans. She's wearing cuffed white pants and a T-shirt with her logo on it, her short hair slicked back to let her big doe eyes shine. As if she heard Jasmine, too, she does a double-take, but the surprise, maybe even slight alarm, quickly shifts to her signature smile. Is that because she knows I'm onto her and doesn't want me on her trail? Or probably more likely: my prickly, less-than-enthusiastic reception to her invitation made her think I wouldn't actually show. That's good. I want to catch her as off guard as possible, so I can get *something* out of her tonight.

"Mavis! Hi!"

Mackenzie Skinner waves to us from the chairs, where everyone is starting to grab their spots to get the best view of Bethany. Mackenzie signals to the two spots next to her in the third row, and when I look to Jasmine she shrugs and nods.

"I'm so happy to see you here. I wasn't sure after last week in the park because you . . ."

"Because I almost passed out?" I offer, and Mackenzie blushes. "No, yeah—I'm really, um . . . intrigued at what Bethany has going here." I ignore Jasmine's snort next to me.

"She's totally transformed my life," Mackenzie says, with

complete sincerity. I glance at the alleged life-transformer, who is making her way to the front of the room. "I was a little lost when we first moved to Beachwood. Todd travels so much, you know, and I was really trying to figure out what my purpose is, what *I* was supposed to be doing." Well, that's a very privileged question to even be considering, I think, holding back an eye roll. But then I realize that tears are gathering in the corners of her eyes as she twirls her blond ponytail. No matter what my judgy ass thinks, this is serious to her. "Bethany helped me to realize that my first job is to take care of myself. I need to do that well before I can really think about any *other* job."

Smile and nod, Mavis. You are undercover. You are not yourself right now. "Uh-huh."

"Mavis! I was wondering if that was you." Christine, Pearl's troop leader, turns around from the row in front of us, saving me from myself. "I was hoping a lot of the Clover Scouts moms would be here. Bethany made such a great proposal to me and Claudia." Next to her, Claudia fixes me with a stank eye because she's apparently never getting over those fucking badges. Jasmine leans into my view, raising her eyebrow in questioning, but my mind is still stuck on "proposal." Proposal for what? I know Christine sent out an email yesterday, but I clicked out of it after reading the first passive-aggressive line.

Murmurs of excitement begin to build, though, and Christine turns around before I can ask.

"Well, I wasn't planning on crying tonight!" Bethany shouts, immediately commanding everyone's attention. Is that . . . her greeting? And wait—*is* she crying? I swear her eyes were dry a second ago, but yes, oh my god—they really *are* welling up. She wipes away a single perfect teardrop after it's made it halfway down her cheek, and I see a couple phones raise to capture it. Is everyone here about to cry? Are they gonna expect me to? Because I don't know if my undercover skills extend that far . . .

"It's just so *heartening* and *life-affirming* to see so many women in front of me, passionate about their own self-care journeys. And I'm so, *so* overwhelmed with joy and gratitude that I get to talk to you about the *M* in my I LUV ME method tonight." Applause overtakes the room, and she clutches her hands to her chest, mouthing *Thank you.*

"As many of you know, *M* stands for *miracle yourself.* And it's a really important part of the method to me. Maybe the most important part."

"'Miracle yourself'? Is that what *you* thought it stood for?" Jasmine mumbles from the side of her mouth, as we wait for more applause.

"No. I thought . . . meditate, maybe?" I whisper back.

"Or massage? Uh-uh, I'm not trying to miracle myself tonight. What kind of culty-ass shit have you gotten me into, girl?"

Claudia, my bestie, turns around and angrily shushes us.

"And to explain why, I want to start with a story tonight. Some of you have heard this already, but I feel so called to share it again, in this moment. Is that okay?" There's an echo of affirmatives, a few cheers, and even a "Yes, Bethany! You tell 'em!" like we're in church or something. Her face glows as she basks in it all.

I expect her to keep standing as she launches into her TED Talk/sales pitch to this adoring audience, but to my surprise, she pulls a chair onto center stage and sits down. She tucks her right leg underneath her and leans in. I think it's supposed to signal intimacy, like she's just having a casual chat with fifty of her closest friends, but there's something rehearsed about it, at least to me. The rest of the room doesn't seem to feel the same, though. They lean in just like her, as if they'll absorb more of her wisdom, her *love*, with proximity.

"So, less than a year ago, I was sitting in an exam room at Beachwood Memorial Hospital. I knew that room well. I had spent a lot of time in that room, finding out I had breast cancer, going through all the tests and surgeries and chemotherapy until it went into remission . . . and then finding out the heartbreaking news that it came back, surprising everyone. Stage four." My stomach twists, thinking of my mom getting this same news, with me, her infant daughter, waiting for her at home. I almost feel guilty—but *no*. This woman uses her experience to make money off of people. She may have done even worse to Cole. I'm *not* going to fall for it.

"But this day was different," she continues. "This day was the *hardest* day I'd ever had in that room by far. Because this day— *this day*—my oncologist had just told me that the clinical trial, the one that took a *miracle* for me to even be let into, the one that was supposed to work a *miracle* on my stage four breast cancer— had failed. I had no other options."

She pauses and looks around the room, as if she's trying to make eye contact with every single woman.

"I felt discouraged. I felt angry. I felt . . . *hopeless*. But then it came to me. If other people's miracles didn't work, I needed to miracle myself."

Mackenzie leans into me. "So inspiring, right?"

"And so I did all the things that as women, as moms, we think it'll take a *miracle* to find time for. I gifted my body movement and sunshine. I ate nourishing, whole foods. I spent time in deep reflection, providing my mind with the stillness it requires to function at its optimal frequency. I went to *so many* sound baths. I did all the things that have now become the foundations of my I LUV ME method—which you'll have immediate access to if you join us tonight."

Of course she still hasn't told us what the rest of that ridiculous acronym stands for—it's behind a paywall.

"I trusted that my body and mind are connected and when you show that you care for one, it gives the other the will to keep fighting. I was patient. I was dedicated. I put care for myself above *everything*. And that allowed me to discover the exact combination of brain and body care I needed to bring about the healing of my *whole self*."

I look around me to see if anyone else is sniffing out this bullshit, but other than Jasmine, who is scrolling on her phone, everyone is nodding like Bethany is saying something profound. But on top of this all being woo-woo nonsense, I *swear* I've heard some of this word-for-word from her before. She's acting like this is all off-the-dome, a special experience for just this audience, but she *must* have a script. Don't they care that this is a script?

It doesn't seem like it. Mackenzie—who as an Absolute Wellness Guru has *definitely* heard this before—looks like one of those women in the late-night Christian music commercials I used to watch during sleepovers as a kid.

"And my miracle came." More applause. A joyful shout in the back. "At my next scan, my oncologist said my cancer was gone. He was astonished, shocked. But I knew." She shakes her head and chuckles softly. "I knew. He had given up on me. '*The clinical trial failed*.'" She says it in a whiny voice that can't possibly be what this doctor sounded like. "But. *But*." A single finger in the air signals that this is the take-home, the finale of her performance. In front of me, I notice Christine taking furious notes, nodding the whole time. "You only fail if you quit, and no matter what he told me, what he believed, I was not going to quit my fight against cancer—or in my mission to empower all women to practice self-care. I will make my own miracles."

Oh my *fucking* god. I already thought this woman was the worst. But did she just *pull yourself up by the bootstraps* CANCER? Is she the *actual devil*?

My wide eyes find Jasmine, and her brow is furrowed, facing her lap. Her phone is now facedown there.

After several minutes of applause, Bethany seamlessly transitions into talk about the structure of her tree-shaped business, where the money moves constantly downstream to nourish everyone. She shares the exciting opportunity everyone in this room has to become part of her quickly growing family of 129 self-care consultants if they just empower themselves to make their own miracles tonight.

One hundred and twenty-nine. This lady gets a cut of 129 consultants' profits. That's a whole lot of money moving *upstream* to her. And she's used curing her own cancer as her hook to lure them all in.

I want to stand up and go all "*I saw Goody Proctor with the Devil*," get this evil woman on the stake where she belongs. I want to stampede through all these chairs and tackle her with the unbridled rage of a Real Housewife who just got told she's been put on pause. I want to burn it all down.

But that's not going to do any good, I know it. These women aren't going to listen to me. I can't stop them from believing her scam, that Bethany has the self-care cure to cancer. I'm an outsider here. But I *can* find out if she had anything to do with Cole's death. I can gather the evidence I need to be sure, to bring justice *there*.

I raise my hand and start talking as soon as Bethany makes eye contact. "I'm curious about your new supplement line. When is that coming out? What, um . . . experts did you collaborate with to create them?"

There's a gasp behind me, and I turn to see Pamela's jaw dropped in horror that I will no longer be fulfilled by my self-guided silent retreat.

"Thank you for that question, *Kim*." Bethany smiles pointedly at my name tag. "I know everyone is buzzing about these and I'll announce *very* soon, but I'm happy to give you all a special little sneak peek." Next to me, Mackenzie claps in excitement. "I've been working for over a year now to develop the exact combination of vitamins, minerals, and botanicals to help you be your best self. This is such a good moment to join our family, because you're going to get in at the ground floor of something truly revolutionary. And actually, can I have my Clover Scouts friends here stand up? Give these women a round of applause, please."

Christine and Claudia don't look as comfortable in the spotlight as Bethany does when all eyes in the room shift to them.

"I'm really excited to share that as part of our philanthropic arm, we're going to offer these supplements to women who are less fortunate, along with discounted Balanced With Bethany beginning consultant memberships. Thank you to Clover Scouts Troop 1207 for generously funding this special project that's going to change so many lives. I love seeing young female entrepreneurs already doing so much good for the world."

What? How is Pearl's troop funding that? Is this with the cookie money Christine's been sending emails about? It was already clear that the girls' vote meant nothing, but what about the parent survey she was passive-aggressively telling us to fill out in her emails? I mean, I didn't actually fill it out yet . . . but was it just a formality, too? I'm not about to be selling those stupid, delicious cookies just so Bethany can get *more* money funneled straight into her pocket.

Her greed really knows no bounds . . . but does that extend into murder? She didn't mention anything about Cole, her former business partner, in that answer.

"Now, I know you probably all have more questions, but I feel like it's better if we get to know each other and our unique self-care journeys in a less formal setting. Why don't we all head over to these beautiful tables Pamela has set up for us in the back? There will be a self-care consultant at each table leading you in making some—yay!—face masks!"

"Well, that was bullshit," Jasmine says when we walk out thirty minutes later with, okay, I'll admit, baby-soft skin from Bethany's special-recipe rose face masks. When it became clear that Bethany was going to avoid our table at all costs, and the self-care consultant we were assigned to—Rebecca—spoke exclusively in Bethany-isms, I gave in and rubbed the stuff on my face.

But I don't feel relaxed at all as we walk back to my car. I feel riled up.

"I know! She's making bank off all these gullible ladies! Did you hear how she told one of her consultants that they just need to *work harder* to sell more self-care? I thought the whole point of this was *less* work. And she's acting like this thing cured her cancer, when it was the doctors! I wonder what they would think about—"

"I don't think they would think anything," Jasmine cuts me off. "Because I don't think they're real."

"Yeah! Wait. What?"

"That breast cancer clinical trial she mentioned. It wasn't at Beachwood Memorial. I know because I helped one of my patients enter it, and I double-checked on their website when she was talking, too. Just in case it changed." I take in Jasmine's furrowed brow again, the expression that's remained firmly in place since Bethany's talk, and realize she's not just skeptical or annoyed—she's pissed. "It didn't. It's at Anders-Bynum. And to my knowledge, Beachwood doesn't even *have* a substantial oncological department, let alone a research center. That's why they usually refer out to Anders-Bynum."

I rush to catch up with her. If that hospital doesn't have a breast cancer clinical trial . . . "What does that mean, then? About everything she was saying?"

"That it's bullshit."

Jasmine must be able to tell the leaps my mind is making, because she quickly adds, "I don't know if this makes her a murderer, but Bethany is definitely a liar. She's lying about her little method curing her cancer, we already knew that. But now? Mavis . . . I'm not convinced she had cancer at all."

SEVENTEEN

I'M LYING ON MY BACK GETTING A SIGNIFICANT AMOUNT of hair ripped out of my face when I finally remember where I recognize Bethany from.

"Holy shit!"

Vicky, the esthetician with severe bangs and sleeves of floral tattoos, tuts and snatches another patch of hair from my unsuspecting follicles with a glob of sugaring paste. "I told you it's better to come more often, before the hair has had a chance to grow back so . . . full. Much less painful."

"No, it's not that." I squint one eye open just in time to catch Vicky's disbelieving eyebrow raise. Her eyebrows are perfectly groomed, unlike the bushy caterpillars I presented her with at the beginning of this appointment.

Bethany. I saw Bethany here, in Vicky's salon. It must have been the last time I was here, which was . . . well, a very long time ago. Over a year, Vicky insisted, when she squeezed me in after a cancellation.

Bethany was walking out when I was coming in. I remember it so clearly now, the same unblinking doll eyes and small frame.

But there were some notable differences, too—no eyebrows, for one. I was confused, probably did a double take, wondering *Is that the new eyebrow trend? I lived through the early 2000s and I refuse to go back!* But then I took in her head covered by a thick beanie in the hot fall temperatures and immediately felt like a terrible person. This woman didn't have eyebrows, have *any hair*, for a reason.

And the same things that made her stand out to me then are what have kept me from placing her familiar face for weeks now.

"Do you have, like . . . patient confidentiality?" I ask tentatively.

"You going to do the lip, too?" Vicky counters.

"Do you think I need to?"

She raises her eyebrow again in response.

"Sure."

"No, I'm not a doctor," she says, narrowing her eyes as she comes up with a plan of attack for the mustache that, yes, I *know* is there. "But I'm thinking of getting my license to be a therapist. Basically do that anyway."

"Can I ask you about one of your clients then?"

"You used a razor here, didn't you?" She touches a spot between my nose and mouth. "Or one of those electric hair remover things? They say they do the same thing but they do not."

"Um . . . maybe?" Of course I did, because, again, *mustache.* "Did you hear me, though? About one of your clients?"

"You had an ingrown hair. Then a dark spot because of hyperpigmentation. And yeah, go ahead."

I decide to skip past analyzing if she's insulting me or not and get down to business. "Bethany Bowman. I'm pretty sure I've seen her here before? What do you, um . . . do for her?"

Vicky is quick, like a spider ambushing a fly. I barely see her move, but the side of my lip stings with the evidence of her work. And I don't know if it's just because I haven't done this in a while, but it felt like there was a little extra fire in that last pull. I wouldn't be surprised if a top layer of my skin went with that hair, too.

"Yes, she used to be one of my sugaring clients. But not anymore." She does the other side, and I blink away tears. Maybe *this* is why I've put this off for so long. Has she always been so aggressive about this? You know what doesn't hurt? A mustache.

"Her eyebrows were going to fall out because of . . . you know." I expect Vicky's hard stare to soften, but it doesn't waver. "So I removed them completely. To keep them even."

"What did they look like? Before, I mean?"

What I'm really asking is: Was her hair already falling out? Do you think she was actually going through chemotherapy, that she had cancer at all? Or was she just faking it to sell her self-care miracle cure-all? But I can't outright say any of that to Vicky—to anyone. Jasmine and I may have our suspicions, but if we're *wrong*? We instantly become the villains here, the lowest of the low.

"They looked fine. Normal," Vicky says, scanning my face with a critical eye as she checks her work. "A little patchy, maybe. I suggested she just microblade, when they kept growing back in, but she liked them . . . even. You should consider microblading, too, for the bald spots in your brows."

"I don't have bald spots."

"Sure, okay." She wipes away the last stray hairs on my face and hands me a small mirror. "Just over-plucking, then, between your annual sessions."

Or the enduring consequences of the early 2000s. I glance at myself in the mirror, but another question hits me. "So she kept coming then? Every four weeks to get her eyebrows removed?"

Wouldn't they stop growing altogether with chemo? But, no.

I don't know that for sure. Everyone's body is different. I feel slimy even asking Vicky about this, and her tight expression as she nods makes it evident she thinks I'm slimy, too.

"What do you . . . think about her?" I'm gonna have to find another eyebrow lady, so I might as well get everything I need.

Vicky's lip curls and I'm sure she's going to tell me off for being so insensitive, for prying into this woman's business. "I don't. Think about her. Because I don't see her anymore. I don't like being used."

Okay, now, *that's* a surprise. Maybe that's why Vicky is being so grumpy . . . or at least more grumpy than she usually is. The top of my lip still feels like it's on fire. And "used"? Is she saying what I think she's saying?

"Also, she never tipped." Vicky raises her eyebrow one more time, and then she whips the black cape off me, making it clear this conversation is done. "I'll see you in *four weeks*."

That's something, I think as I get back home with my mostly hairless and slightly inflamed face. *It has to be something.*

I mean, it's definitely more than I got from scrolling through years of her Instagram posts after the self-care party—all the way back to her time at Agape Essentials, with a brief stint in a collective of spiritual healers, before she founded Balanced With Bethany. Jasmine looked at a lot of it with me, fact-checking the medical jargon and descriptions of the treatment plan, but she couldn't say anything conclusive from that. It could be legit, or it could be googled. There's like an endless amount of blogs and Instagram profiles from women going through the exact same thing, and it's impossible for us to know if Bethany just copied and pasted. She probably was much more careful with her paper trail than with what she shared in person at an event. We weren't going to catch her in a lie that way.

And even if I do prove she faked her cancer, that she's a

grifter moving from MLM to MLM—what does that prove about Cole's murder?

Nothing. Not really.

I close my eyes right now and try to picture it, her crouching over that Capri-Sun, dropping Visine *and* sodium nitrate into the tiny hole, with *no one* noticing. I can't see it. It feels too impossible. But who else would it be? And if she's willing to do something so morally reprehensible as lying about cancer, then it's not too many more steps to think she could murder, too. Right?

God, I need more. I know these hunches and theories are not enough.

I sit down on the couch next to a snoozing Polly and open up her profile again on my phone.

How can I get more? It's not like I can just send her a DM demanding the truth. Or find her at pickup today and casually ask, "Hey girl, so what was going on with your eyebrows?"

But she *has* wanted to talk to me when she thought I was a potential girlboss recruit, so that's my best chance here. I know that lady won't turn down a dollar.

I scroll down to the bottom of her latest post, all about how she's joined the board of the goddamn Beachwood Business Association.

I feel so empowered in my mission and grateful that I'll get to help even more women in my beloved community reach their true self-care potentials. ♡ The Balanced With Bethany family is growing bigger and stronger every day!

Want to join us? Comment "FAMILY" below to schedule one of my extremely limited one-on-one in-person sessions! I can't wait to meet you 🤗

I ignore the sour taste that rises in the back of my throat and comment "family." Seconds later, I get an automated DM with a calendar to sign up for one of the sessions during her office hours at a coffee shop on Flower Street in a few days. If I didn't need this for my own personal benefit, I'd be concerned about her lack of precautions when it comes to internet safety.

"And now we wait."

It takes me a second to realize I heard those words rather than thought them, and then another few seconds to place the voice. Ms. Joyce. Is Ms. Joyce in my house?

No, Polly is still snoring next to me on the couch, and that definitely wouldn't be the case if an old lady (or a baby) snuck in here.

"Now, wait a minute, is this dang red light a good thing or a bad thing?" Ms. Joyce's voice calls out again from the side of the house. Pearl's room. Ah, okay. I've been through this before.

"These things really aren't for kids," I mutter to myself as I find the walkie-talkies under Pearl's bed. She must have turned them back on. I think I might just hide these things in my room for now and hope she forgets about them.

"Why can I only hear myself and not Mavis's little friend?"

Wait—why am I in it? And my little friend? My mouth drops as I start to put it together. I'm across the street, banging on her door, in record time.

I can hear her muttering to herself as she shuffles to the door, and when she opens it, she fixes me with a face that makes me feel like a child looking up at her again, even though I've got almost a foot on her now.

"Baby, now why are you knocking on my door like you the police? Are you trying to send me to an early grave? I mean, really." She sighs. "I'd have a right to haunt you."

I'm about to launch into an apology, but then my eyes catch

on the small black device in her right hand. It has a speaker on the front next to a tiny red light, and there's an antenna extended on the side. It's the reason I could hear her through Pearl's walkie-talkies, the reason I came over here in the first place.

"What's that, Ms. Joyce?" I ask, gesturing to the device with my chin. I *think* I clock a flicker of sheepishness on her face, but it's gone so fast I can't be sure. She crosses her arms and holds her head up high.

"Oh, this?" she says, examining it with an expression of wonder, like it just appeared in her hand at that exact moment. "It's part of the new security system Corey helped me to set up. But he left me to finish this part. Talking 'bout *ethics*. Hmmph." She sucks her teeth and shakes a finger at me. "You need to have a talk with him. Because I didn't appreciate the little high horse speech that man of yours gave me. As if I—*his elder*—would ever do anything unethical."

I shake my head. "Ms. Joyce, you know Corey is not my man. And what do you mean *unethical*?" Though I think I'm starting to have a pretty good idea, with what I overheard in my house . . .

Ms. Joyce waves me away, while simultaneously stepping back to invite me into the entryway.

"They're just some listening devices to go along with the cameras Corey helped me set up—because *those* were okay, apparently. He really moves that line, let me tell you. Probably just wanted to go home, and that's why he left me to set these up on my own." She holds the thing up again and I notice a small dial and a toggle button. "I can't get them to play me anything, even though the dang red light is on. I don't know why they make the instructions so small. Even with my readers, I could hardly make them out."

"Listening devices? Why do you need listening devices?" I

don't know *how* she did it, but she must have somehow turned the signal around, so they were broadcasting instead of listening? Maybe that's how Pearl's walkie-talkies picked her up—they were on the same channel? But if she has the responder, that means there are—what . . . bugs somewhere? Was her voice playing out on those, too? "Where did you set these up? Who were you trying to listen to?"

"I needed listening devices because the audio on those cameras wasn't crisp enough for me. You know my hearing isn't what it once was."

"Okay, but what about my other questions?"

I don't need to wait for her to meander her way around to the answer, though, because Mackenzie walks up the front path in a lime-green sports bra and matching leggings. She's holding up something tiny and black, and I squint as she gets closer. Is that a . . . microphone?

Oh my god.

"Ms. Joyce? Is this yours? I found it on the sill of my kitchen window, and . . . I could hear your voice coming out of it?" She has a tentative smile on her face, as if this is all some misunderstanding and she's happy to be set straight.

"Ms. Joyce! You put that in her kitchen window?!"

Ms. Joyce gives me a look that's the old lady equivalent of "snitches get stitches." But then she purses her lips together and says sweetly to Mackenzie, "Oh, thank you. I must have misplaced that . . ."

"In her *kitchen window*?"

If Ms. Joyce wasn't going to haunt me before, she *definitely* will now.

Mackenzie twirls her ponytail and bounces on her feet nervously. "I also noticed the cameras on your side of the fence.

They kinda, well . . . they feel like they're directed at our house? Did they just get, um, well . . . turned around in the wind?"

She's being incredibly polite. But I guess, like, how *do* you come out and ask your elderly neighbor if she is watching you with security cameras and has also apparently creeped into your backyard and slipped a bug into your back window? All because you installed a Ring camera and asked about a neighborhood HOA once??

Ms. Joyce nods and reaches for the bug. "Yes, they must have, thank you."

Mackenzie bites her lip as she places it in Ms. Joyce's hand. I can see she wants to say more, but doesn't want to be disrespectful. Even with how much Ms. Joyce is, objectively, *wilding out* here. I feel a burst of tenderness for my little friend.

"I'll help her get them all fixed, Mackenzie. And make sure they face her side of the fence." I hear Ms. Joyce make a small sound of protest in the back of her throat.

"Thank you, Mavis," Mackenzie says, relief flushing her face. "And I'm so sorry to bother you, Ms. Joyce. Your scarf is beautiful, by the way."

Ms. Joyce touches her pastel head wrap and nods magnanimously.

"And if you find any more of those things," I say, nodding to the bug in Ms. Joyce's hand, "feel free to bring them to me. I wouldn't want her to somehow misplace any more of them . . . in your house."

The slight upturn of Ms. Joyce's lips as she suddenly becomes fascinated with the toile pattern of her wallpaper lets me know *for sure* there's more.

"Oh yes, of course!" Mackenzie chirps, beaming at us both. How is she so nice? If I found out that my neighbor was spying on me, I wouldn't *bring them back their bugs*! How does that level of nice even exist? But actually, this might work in my favor . . .

She starts to walk away. "Well, I'm going to go for a run—"

"Wait—can I talk to you about something?"

I glance back at Ms. Joyce, who seems to be caught between her natural states of disapproval and nosiness.

"I'll be right back, Ms. Joyce. To . . . help you." I walk down to the end of her path, hopefully out of earshot, and Mackenzie follows.

"I hope it's okay to ask, but I've been thinking so much about Bethany and everything she shared the other night. I was wondering: Were you around when she was going through chemo? When she . . . miracled herself? I've just . . . never heard anything like it."

Mackenzie's blue eyes go wide and awestruck, like they were at the self-care party. "Yes! It was so, so inspiring! I met her after her cancer went into remission the first time and was there when we got the, just, awful and heartbreaking news that it came back. I was already a self-care consultant, but seeing her go through that . . . that's what made me want to commit to this business with everything I have. I *needed* to be there for her. And I needed to help other women find the I LUV ME method, so they can protect themselves." She smiles and reaches forward to touch my arm. "So, you're going to join our team? I think you're going to be so happy—"

"Did you ever go to the doctor with her, though? Or meet any of her care team?"

Mackenzie jerks her hand back like my skin is on fire. Her face is confused, and then angry. With all of Ms. Joyce's antics, I've never seen Mackenzie's eyebrows drop so low, or her frown so deep.

"Mavis. I know what you're getting at," she huffs. Her cheeks are more red than they've ever been from her daily workouts. "And I . . . I'm not—how *dare* you?"

"I'm sorry. I'm not trying to offend you. But you don't think her story is strange? At all?"

"No! This woman has been through so much and all she wants is to help others. She told me this might happen. That people might question her. When you bring so much good into the world, some people get jealous. They want to take down what they *wish* they could do, instead of focusing on their own path and self-care journey. She *told me*, and still—I was shocked when it happened!"

"Wait, wait. So. This has happened before? I'm not the first person to question her?"

"No. I mean—yes." She winces. "But it was just one person. And he was *wrong*. Just like you."

"Who was wrong? Who's 'he'?" But even as I ask, it's already clicked. I know who she's talking about, who it *has* to be. "It was Cole, wasn't it? The person who questioned Bethany?"

Her face looks wild with panic. She takes one step back, and then another. "I—I . . . didn't mean to say that. It was nothing. I need to go."

"What did Cole question her about, Mackenzie? Did he find something out?"

"There's *nothing* to find out. You should be ashamed of yourself, Mavis." And then she takes off running down the block.

This could be the missing piece of evidence I've been looking for. If Cole found out Bethany was lying about her cancer, what would he do with that information? It could take down Bethany's whole moneymaking operation. What would she do to keep him quiet? Would she make sure he stayed quiet . . . forever?

"So she really *isn't* your little friend." Ms. Joyce somehow is right behind me, carried by the same silent feet she used to sneak into Mackenzie's backyard.

"I told you she wasn't." I sigh. "But I think I might have made her my little *enemy* now."

"Hmmm. Well, you really shouldn't be getting involved in these Caucasian problems anyway. If her *real* little friend is faking cancer, and she wants to believe that, that's not any of your business."

I stare hard at the bug from Mackenzie's kitchen that's still in her hand and then throw in a few slow blinks for good measure.

"Yes, let's all stay in our own business then, huh? That sounds good."

🔍 Anders Bynum breast cancer clinical trial

🔍 Balanced With Bethany FTC

🔍 Balanced With Bethany BBB

🔍 Balanced With Bethany scam?

🔍 George Washington wig

🔍 George Washington wig CHEAP

🔍 Listening device in neighbor's house illegal?

🔍 Plausible deniability

EIGHTEEN

I KEPT MYSELF AS OCCUPIED AS I COULD WITH THE REAS-
sembled heart-and-Shrek murder board, adding in every detail
I just learned from Mackenzie. But by midafternoon, the frantic, fizzy energy feels too big to contain in my body, let alone my
house, and I need to talk this through with a human—as op-
posed to a construction paper ogre. Luckily, the school day is
done, so I'm free to pace Jack's office while I wait for Pearl's
theater class to end without being interrupted by pesky children
needing counseling.

"So Mackenzie didn't confirm it then? That Bethany is lying
about her cancer?" he asks, rotating his chair back and forth in
time with my laps around his room.

"I mean, no. But she basically did, right? Because if Cole
sniffed out that she was lying and *he* worked closer with her than
anyone, it seems—well, then something was clearly shady there.
And then there's what Vicky said, too. About the eyebrows."

"Right. But she didn't actually confirm anything either."

"Okay, not with her words, she didn't," I agree. "But she did
with her face!"

"Do you think the detective will accept face evidence . . . or?" He grins at me and I roll my eyes. But a laugh escapes from my chest and pretty soon he's laughing, too. For a second I feel like I've flashed back to last fall, when the two of us were tucked away in his office just like this, talking (and laughing) through our theories—Stabler and Benson.

Of course, it's not the same, though. Solving that mystery may have brought us together, and sure, he's listening to me now. But how he really feels is lurking like a shadow on the edge of my vision. He doesn't approve of me getting involved in this—I know that. He thinks my time would be better spent dealing with my trauma in therapy, or looking for a job that's going to make me feel appreciated and fulfilled. And those are, like, annoyingly normal and admirable things for him to want for me. So as I'm talking to him, I have to simultaneously convey that I'm okay, that I have a totally sane, totally healthy relationship with this mystery. I have to be a lot more careful. And that sucks out a lot of the thrill, the lightness, that was there before, when discussing what Trisha did with the body was really just a pretense for flirting.

But that's all right. The thrill is replaced with the comfort that he's mine, that I don't need a mystery as a pretense to be with him.

I stop my pacing and sit down in the chair across from his desk. His hands are already reaching out, and I weave my fingers through his.

"I know this is bonkers."

"That's okay. I like bonkers."

I narrow my eyes at him, and he smiles back.

"I just feel like I'm getting close to . . . *something*," I say. I let out a long sigh and shake my head. "If he knew she was lying, if he threatened to expose her, that's motive. The most realistic one I've found so far."

His phone lights up on his desk in between us, a notification of a text. It's quick, but I catch the slight tensing of his jaw as he flips the phone over. And then he's talking again before I can decide if it makes me look like a paranoid, jealous girlfriend to ask about it.

"Yeah, but if Cole knew, and Bethany did *that* . . . Mavis, that's even more of a reason to be careful here. What will she do to you? Pass it on to the detectives and let them take the risk."

I know what he wants me to say. "I will."

He raises his eyebrows. Because *he knows* I know it's what he wants me to say.

"Eventually."

His jaw drops in exasperation.

"Soon!" I say in between giggles. "I promise, soon!"

He stands and comes over to my side of the desk, pulling me up into a hug. "I'm fully aware you're humoring me, and I know asking you to give this up entirely is a fool's errand. So I guess I'll just ask you to be safe about it. Don't do anything with this woman alone, and if it starts to get dangerous—actually, before *you* think it starts to get dangerous, let the police handle it." He clears his throat, and the spark of silliness in his eyes is replaced by something more somber. "I was so scared . . . when we didn't know where you were that night. I don't know what I'd do . . . if anything happened to you."

He strokes my cheek with his thumb, holding me tight like I'm a treasure. And it feels so good my brain is momentarily erased of all thoughts except for *Wow, I get this. I deserve this.* And I tell myself *that's* the reason I don't ask who that text just now was from. Or tell him about out my upcoming (alone and maybe dangerous) meeting with Bethany.

We walk to the auditorium together, just in time to catch Anabella warbling, "N-Y-C! Just got here this morning!" and hitting notes that she surely invented herself. Pearl follows close behind her with a truly epic side-eye.

"Derek is very invested in that scandal, too," Jack whispers behind his hand. "It's become our top dinner table topic all week, even more than his predictions for *Celebrity Jeopardy!*"

"Tell him I tried. You know, maybe I can send an anonymous email to all the parents so they know what's going on. Make sure Trisha gets hers that way." I laugh for plausible deniability, but it's not the worst idea . . .

I see the exact moment Jack realizes what I'm realizing, amusement to *oh no*, and that makes me laugh even more.

"Hello, Jack," Pearl says when she reaches us. There's mischievous delight on her face, and then exaggerated embarrassment as she pretends to remember. "Oh, I'm *so sorry*. Forgive me, Mr. *Cohen!*"

She may not be the lead, but baby girl is definitely getting the most out of these acting lessons.

"Hello Ms. Harding," Jack says, in an exaggerated formal tone as he bows. "Permission to escort you to your car?"

"Yeah, sure. Mom, did you bring any snacks?"

We have a surprise waiting for me at my Prius, though. I *knew* I should have done another circle until I found a spot within one hundred feet of the front gate.

"Hey! Hey, Mavis! We need to talk."

This is about to be real bad if I don't even get a yoo-hoo. I look to Jack and there's wariness on his face . . . and maybe even a little disapproval? But I don't have time to analyze that now. I nod my head to the side in question and he nods back.

"Hey, Pearl, Anabella. Do you want to play that imaginary bubble game from class?"

Anabella nods excitedly, oblivious (either because she just is or because that's a defense mechanism you pick up when your mother is the devil). Pearl, though, knows something's up and looks over her shoulder suspiciously as Jack walks them farther down the sidewalk.

"What do you want, Trisha?"

"Oh, don't be coy, now!" she shouts, throwing her hands up. Hopefully the imaginary bubble game is louder. "You weren't coy when you went behind my back to Mr. Smith, trying to get Anabella's role taken away."

"Oh my god, I did *not* try and get her role taken away. If that happened, it's your—"

"You're damn right! Because that didn't happen. I explained to Mr. Smith that this was all just a misunderstanding, and Mr. Forest confirmed." She smiles smugly. "But it *could* have. You really should think about the consequences of your actions and how your little Sherlock hobby affects other people."

I let out a sound that's half shocked laughter, half shriek of fury, and she takes that as a sign to go on. "Because I see what this really is. You *and* that Florence. You like to play the victim so you can get attention and get your kids ahead instead of doing the hard work to make it happen, like me. *Oh, she threatened someone at my kid's party! Oh, she hurt my kid's precious mental health!* She screws her face up into an exaggerated frown, making her voice squeaky and high, and I can't even take a beat to feel offended because I'm trying to catch up with her. Is that supposed to be me . . . and Florence? How did Florence get into this?

"Moms don't want to work anymore. They just want to do everything the easy way. And then they'll go cry on NPR when their little snowflakes don't get into Stanford—when they didn't do what *needed* to be done!"

"Trisha, *what?*" Did she just quote . . . Kim Kardashian? And again—how did *Florence* get into this?

But I don't get a chance to clarify anything, because she's

already marching back over to her minivan, an eerie calm settling over her features. "I hope you've learned your lesson, Mavis. And I'm happy to move on if so. Let's set up a playdate for the girls soon." She beams over at Anabella, who is clapping her hands in front of her face and giggling with Pearl and Jack. "Come on, sweet girl! We need to meet your tennis coach in ten minutes! Thank you for your help, Mr. Cohen!"

I'm still standing there, processing, when Jack and Pearl reach me.

"Mavis, are you—"

"You solved the mystery, didn't you?!" Pearl squeals. Her eyes are bright and her dimple is deep, and that nearly wipes out all the annoyance and anger and what-the-fuck-ness left behind in Trisha's wake.

"I did," I say, and she looks at me like I'm one of the tween girls on Disney Channel. Or Shrek. "It turns out Anabella's mommy did something not so nice to get Anabella the Annie part. But I don't think Anabella knew, so you don't have to be mad at her."

Is it a little immature that I kind of hope she is, though? If only so I don't have to regularly interact with her best friend's mom anymore.

She shrugs. "I'm not mad at Anabella. I just wanted to know why she was Annie 'cause she can't sing."

I don't know, that side-eye from just a short while ago told a different story . . .

"Right, Mommy? You heard she can't sing? When you were sneaking during our rehearsal? Mason told me he saw you hiding in the curtains last week."

My eyes flick to Jack, and yep, there's definitely some disapproval there. Not *a lot*. It's not *a problem*. But I can feel it in the way his eyes don't crinkle and those two parentheses don't appear around his lips. I mean, I guess I *did* just get into a verbal altercation in front of his place of work, which really isn't helping my totally sane, totally healthy argument here. It wasn't my fault! But, still . . .

"You are *so* cool, Mommy."

"Did you hear that?" I elbow Jack, searching for that smile. "I'm cool. I'm a cool mom."

His eyes curve into half-moons and I want to jump up and do a cheer. "You are the coolest mom."

Pearl scoffs, "I wouldn't go *that* far, Jack."

FLORENCE ORGANIZES A SPECIAL SOCCER PRACTICE FOR the Aquamarine Alligators—on Sunday, of course, to avoid another run-in with Dom's band of capture the flag enthusiasts. And I consider asking her how she got tangled up with Trisha, and if it has something to do with Mr. Forest's sketchy casting, too. But as I watch her cheering the kids on to "Be your best selves!" and "Keep your lights shining bright!" while they haphazardly run through the aesthetic burlap flags she brought instead of neon cones, I think better of it. It's only going to get me into some long, drawn-out conversation about Axel's sensitive spirit and how hard it is on her mama heart to gently shepherd him to his one true purpose, and I do not have the energy to keep my face together for that. I already know Trisha is a self-serving asshole who probably did something terrible to get what she wanted for her kid—I don't need additional evidence and mind-numbing small talk to prove that. Also, I already have another, much more important, mystery on my plate, so it's time to move on from that one. Case closed. Cool mom, signing off!

"Good hustle, Alligators!" Hank shouts, cupping his hands into a loud clap. "Finish strong!"

"If that is what your bodies are telling you to do!" Florence chimes in.

"Push yourselves! Your body is going to thank you tomorrow!"

"But it's okay to take a break, too! You are all winners already, just for trying!"

"Winners have discipline! You wanna win? You gotta earn it!"

I feel like I'm getting a part two of their walkie-talkie fight . . . or probably a part two hundred and sixty-five, by the sound of it. It must be *real* bad if the cracks are showing in public, where it could hurt Florence's shiny Instagram image. And again, I should feel guilty at the little spark of satisfaction I get from seeing their flaws, but this is like watching something on Bravo live, and I'm only so mature and evolved.

I look around to see if anyone else is enjoying the show, and that's when I see *another* show happening. I'm stalking over there faster than you can say "I need Andy and a camera."

"So it's been confirmed, one hundred percent, that it was a burner phone?" my dad asks as I walk up, motioning his microphone back to Leon.

"And can you repeat what the texts said again? I'm worried the kids may have contaminated our sound," adds my dad's best friend and podcast partner, Bert. I thought it was weird that Dad brought him along today, but now I know why.

"Keep. Your. Mouth. Shut," Leon says loud and slow, his lips almost touching Dad's mic. "Or. Else. And then there were a few expletives. Are you sure you want me to say those?" He looks around warily at the parents and children nearby.

"Yeah, go ahead," Bert says, adjusting the massive Beats headphones that are sitting on top of his graying fade. "And feel free to really sell—"

"What is going on?" I cut him off. "What texts, Leon?"

"Oh, Irene got an update from the detectives. They found threatening texts on Cole's phone, and they traced it to a burner bought at a CVS in Beachwood."

"What?!" My mind races to catch up. Someone was threatening Cole before he died? That's huge. "You found all that out, and you're telling . . . *them*?"

Leon shrugs. "Well, your dad asked first."

"That's right," Dad hollers, brushing off his shoulder, and Bert does some shuffly TikTok dance that one of his grandkids probably taught him. It would be hilarious if it wasn't so annoying. I look to Leon to see if he's seen the error of his ways after this display of professionalism, but he's just laughing along with them.

Does he . . . think me and my dad are on the same level here? Because *we're not*. Are we? No, we're definitely not. This is more than a silly hobby for me—I am conducting an extensive investigation to find the truth here. I solved a crime just months ago! I basically saved our principal's life! Probably . . . Corinne said she wasn't going to actually kill him—but who knows!

"I'm willing to share my sources, Maves," Dad offers. "You scratch my back, I'll scratch yours. Because Leon also just told me that you and Jasmine found out something about that Bethany woman this week, and I'm the one who got you that lead, technically."

"Bethany?" Bert asks, rubbing his hand over his freckled brown cheek. "This the Avon lady?"

"Leon, when were these texts sent? Did they say anything else?" I bat away my dad's mic that's found its way next to my face. "I do not consent to be recorded, Dad!"

He squints his eyes in mock confusion. "What's that? Can you say that louder?"

"Irene didn't tell me the exact dates, but it seemed like they were pretty recent. The detectives are on it, though. Like I said, they traced the phone, where it was bought. It was that CVS over on Marshall? The person paid cash, but I think they're going through the security footage. Might take a while, but they'll find who did this."

I feel a jolt of excitement with each bit of information he reveals, sparks setting my mind on fire with new what-ifs and maybes. But then it's like a big bucket of water being dumped on me, his clear, underlying message here: *The police are handling this. And you . . . I'm just humoring.*

"So what did you find out with Bethany, Maves? Did she have a reason to threaten him?"

"Or Dom Dwyer? You said he was on her board, too. Right, Elijah?" Bert asks, nudging my dad. "Could it have something to do with that meeting he was supposed to have with the city?"

"Dom? The guy on the big mower?" Leon sucks his teeth. "Man, did you guys find something? Because I can pass it on to Irene . . ."

"Mavis found something! When she broke into his shed!" Dad's eyes are shining with pride, but I can't even enjoy it, because he's blowing up my spot.

Leon's eyes go wide. "Don't get yourself in trouble, now."

"I'm fine. And Dad, how did you even know that?"

"It was on your murder board. On one of those green guys."

"Each one of you has unique gifts to share with the world!" Florence cheers at the kids, and I jump.

Wow, she's way closer than she was a few minutes ago. When did that happen? And is she listening? God, she probably *is* with the scene we're making. No wonder Leon thinks I'm an amateur like my dad. I'm acting like one, letting all my evidence be dragged out into the street. And—ugh. I wouldn't even be surprised if Florence knows Bethany. Their brands of bullshit are adjacent, if not the same. I can't risk any of this getting to her before we have our one-on-one consultation tomorrow—I'm honestly surprised she hasn't canceled it already.

I need to walk away. Right now. Before I mess things up even more.

"I've gotta . . . I need to think about this," I mumble, waving away Dad's protests as I walk farther down the field. I need to distance myself from them. And I need to be alone to think this through, to add these new pieces to the puzzle . . . to, okay, stomp my foot and grunt and throw a little grown-woman tantrum over my dad butting into *my investigation*.

"Are you okay?"

But of course, being alone is a lot to ask for in a park on the weekend during kids' soccer practice.

"I'm fine, Corey."

"Um, all right." He looks down, trying to hide his one-dimpled grin, but I see it. And it makes me feel like flames are lapping at my throat. "I'm not trying to judge," he continues. "Like, you do you. But it's kinda obvious? That you're trying to solve this thing with Coach Cole. Well, you and your dad, too, but he's got Bert for backup." He laughs, but it dies quickly when met with my steely gaze.

"Anyway, I just want to make sure you're not getting yourself into any dangerous situations. You know, like what happened in September. So whatever's up, I'm here for you."

I don't know if it's his unintended echo of what Jack told me yesterday or the falseness of him telling me he's here for me when I know he's already planning his exit—when I know he's about to leave me to deal with the consequences again. But I'm like a thread pulled too tight. I snap.

"Can you stop? All of this!" I twirl my hands in his direction, and I know it looks stupid, which makes me even more mad. "Can you just stop?!"

His full lips frown in confusion. "Did I . . . do something to upset you?"

Of course you did! I want to scream. You've done more things to upset me than anyone else in existence, but *now* you expect me to just let that go? *Now* you want me to trust you, to rely on you, just so I can get my heart broken again?

But I can't say any of that. Not here, with Pearl only yards away on the field. My eyes find her now, and I can see her watching us, biting the side of her cheek as she waits to do another weave through Florence's stupid burlap flags. I smile and wave, hoping she didn't hear me yell. I take a deep, steadying breath, quieting the fire that still wants to escape, so I don't yell again.

"No," I say, and a skeptical brow jumps on Corey's face. "It's—I'm . . . on my period." I'm not. But that's the fail-safe way to get a man to stop talking to you. And then, just in case that doesn't work: "I'm going to go for a walk. You got Pearl?"

He nods, and I catch movement at his side, his thumb circling his pinkie. I've made him nervous. *Good.*

I take off through the grass, with no plan for where I'm going, except away from Corey. Really, that's the extent of my plan. But if you keep walking through Brady Park, past the open fields and the basketball courts, well, eventually you're going to reach the other side. Where the playground and Dom's shed are located. And so . . . that's where I happen to end up. Unintentionally.

Except I want so badly to think about anything else other than Corey, and as annoying as it was, that interview I walked into between Dad, Bert, and Leon gave me some new clues to chase. Plus, it looks like . . . *yep*, Dom's new padlock is just hanging there, undone. That's basically a sign from the universe to come right on in. It can't hurt to take a quick look around and make sure there's not a burner phone in there, just to rule him out for sure. Who knows how long it'll take the detectives to do the same, with all the red tape of warrants and probable cause, and honestly I'm helping Dom, doing this before he has to suffer the embarrassment of all that . . .

I reach for the doorknob, noticing too late the shift of someone else's shadow on the door, next to mine.

"I wouldn't try that again, ma'am."

NINETEEN

I KNOW IT'S DOM BEFORE I EVEN TURN AROUND, SO I TAKE a second to make my face look extra lost and innocent.

"Sorry? Is this the bathroom?"

Dom is tall and broad-shouldered, with dark hair, sun-weathered skin, and a scruffy beard. Wraparound sunglasses sit on top of his battered baseball cap, and he's wearing a tan Beachwood Parks and Rec utility shirt with matching pants. He's got thick, Jack McCoy–level eyebrows, and he raises one of them now at my half-assed bathroom excuse.

"I know why you're here," he says, fists on his hips. "And I know you've been here before."

"I, um . . . don't know what you're talking about. I really was just looking for the bathroom. And yeah, I've . . . gotta go find it now." My hands fall behind me, all on their own.

"I caught you on camera. There are several set up in there." He nods toward the shed.

My body stills and my cheeks burn because he's caught me, clearly, and also—did I just grab my own ass like a toddler who has to go potty? This is not my best work. I need to get it together.

"How do you know it wasn't . . . someone else? You could be confusing me with another Black woman?" I realize that's low, gaslighting him—and also acknowledging that I'm Black at all, because it, pretty reliably, makes most white people take off running. But . . . desperate times. "And there's a lot of Black women here in Beachwood. Not as much as there were, like, five years ago, with all these new people moving in, changing the neighborhood, building Erewhons—"

"You left this," he says, interrupting the lecture I'm apparently giving on gentrification. And there, in his calloused hand, is my Project Window ID card. I took the picture three years ago, but it's unmistakably me. And if there was any confusion, there's my name right there in bold Comic Sans (because Rose thought *that* was a good idea): **Mavis Miller**.

"Huh. Yeah. Well . . . would you look at that." And I don't know what to say, so I just stare at him. And he just stares back. So we end up just standing there, staring, way past the point of awkward, with only the muffled sounds of kids shrieking in delight or distress at the nearby playground.

He's the first one to break. "So. *Why* were you in my office?"

"I mean, it doesn't look like an office. So I wasn't really sure what this place was, and I was just curiously, um . . . seeing the sights—"

His bushy brows jump in disbelief again. "Again, cameras, ma'am. I saw you going through the papers on my desk. Now, can you be honest with me here? Or do I need to bring in someone more official?"

I don't want that. If Detective De La Rosa thinks I'm a nuisance now, that's not going to get any better if he gets more insight into my methods. Also . . . I guess I broke a law? Technically.

"Okay, so I'm kinda looking into what happened to Coach Cole? The soccer coach who died here a few weeks ago," I explain, even though I know *he knows* who I'm talking about. "I'm trying to figure out who actually killed him because at first it sorta seemed like they thought my ex-husband did it? And I'm *so* mad at my ex-husband right now, but that doesn't mean I want him to go to jail, you know? He's a good person. A person who doesn't poison people's Capri-Suns, *for sure*, so even if he makes me *so mad*, I had to, like, look into this."

He holds up a hand, stopping my explanation that is not going as well as I'd hoped. "I'm having trouble following. Are you . . . a cop?"

"No. This is just . . . kinda my thing." Yeah, that sounds *real* legit, Mavis. No wonder Leon's treating my investigation the same as my dad's podcast. "I have experience. Honestly, probably more experience than Detective De La Rosa, at least, because he just got promoted and how many murder cases could there possibly have been in Beachwood since October? Anyway, when they mentioned the sodium nitrate, I think they thought Corey's gardening was suspicious but my mind immediately went to you—no offense. So, I only took a quick peek around your shed—I mean, *office*. But I didn't take anything. Well, just pictures . . ."

Yeah, I'm really not making this any better. Maybe the detectives will be a little nicer to me if I just call them on myself?

Dom's face scrunches up. "No, it wasn't nitrate, it was *nitrite*. Sodium *nitrite*."

"Um, I'm pretty sure it was sodium nitrate. I've googled it about a million times at this point. Sodium *nitrate* is the one used for fertilizer . . . or something like that. Though honestly, a lot of it went over my head—I almost failed high school chemistry. But I swear it was nitra— *Wait.* How do you know that?"

My body tenses, every nerve ending immediately standing at attention. I take one giant step back and collide with the shed door, trapped.

"First of all, I don't use sodium nitrate here at the park. That wouldn't even make any sense. There's just grass—I'm not running a farm."

"Nitrate, nitrite—whatever! Same thing! How did you know that was the murder weapon?" Should I run? I should run. At least there are witnesses nearby, if he does lunge at me. That guy in the Hawaiian shirt and glittery crocs, pushing his daughter on the swings, looks like he'll give a good *Dateline* interview, so at least I have that.

"Well, actually, they're very different, even though only one oxygen atom sets them apart." I'm really about to be the next victim of a *well, actually* guy. How did I let this happen? "Our bodies convert nitrates into nitrites, so sodium nitrate naturally occurs but sodium nitrite is synthetically made. That's why it's used in a lot of cured and processed meats." I feel my eyes involuntarily glazing over just like they did in tenth-grade chem and, oh my god, this is not the time for that! I need to be planning my exit strategy. The fields are just out of eyesight, but if Dom chases me, I'm pretty sure the guy in the glittery crocs would step in and take him down. "Bacon, beef jerky, prosciutto, hot dogs—that's why they're that pink color—" He cuts himself off suddenly as he takes in my deer-in-the-headlights stance. "Wait. No, hold on! I don't know about the sodium nitrite because I *killed* him!"

"Um, okay, well, I think I'm going to go for, just, a little casual jog—"

"I know because the police talked to me, too. Of course they talked to me, too! Probably before even your husband."

"Ex-husband." *Because, yeah, it's important to argue semantics with a possible murderer right now, Mavis.*

"It's common knowledge that I hated Cole. They came and asked me all kinds of questions, and told me about the sodium nitrite on the juice box. Detective De La Rosa and Detective Berry. But I was cleared. I had nothing to do with that man's death."

"You were cleared?"

"Yes. I didn't go anywhere near his drink that day. And it's pretty well-documented in all the videos from angry parents whose kids' games I interrupted." He crosses his arms and narrows his eyes at me. "They came to talk to me *before* I saw you on my security camera—which is damn lucky for you, because I could have shown them the footage then. I still could. *You* are the one who broke a law here, ma'am."

Okay, rude, but I guess he has a right to be a tiny bit irritated with me. I invaded his personal space, went through his things, and for what? I'm *behind* the detectives. Am I even finding out anything new, with all this time I'm wasting? What am I doing?

"I'm sorry," I mumble, and—*to my horror*—my eyes get a little scratchy and slightly moist, all of my feelings fighting to come to the surface in the most embarrassing way possible. Dom's hard expression falters, and instead he seems freaked out. Maybe I should just tell him I'm on my period and run away, too, be done with it. But I'm already here now, possibly making a fool of myself, so I might as well get all my loose ends tied up.

"There's one thing I still don't get. Why were you so angry about capture the flag?"

"Well, first of all," he says, jabbing a finger into his palm, "capture the flag doesn't get the respect it deserves in the athletic community. It's a complex game that requires strategy, agility, speed—" I must be giving him that tenth-grade-chem glazed look again because he pauses and then smiles sheepishly. His face turns softer, and those aggressive eyebrows look almost . . . cuddly, like Jellycat plushies. "It's like you were saying before, Beachwood is changing a lot. People are moving in, making it what they want, and not giving any thought to what was here before. I'm trying to preserve my little corner. I grew up hanging out at Brady with my friends. Some of my best memories are here. Why should Cole get to walk in and claim almost the whole place every Saturday—and charge people for it?"

"*You're* from Beachwood?"

"Yeah, born and raised, right here in this neighborhood. I went to Knoll, Williams Middle—graduated from Beachwood High."

The same schools as me, but I don't recognize him. "What year did you graduate?"

"Two thousand five."

"Okay, so we didn't overlap. But you probably know Ebony then? Ebony Jemison?"

"Yes, I know Ebony! Her mom, Ms. Bernadette, used to keep me some nights in elementary school because my mom worked third shift at the hospital."

"We must have run into each other at some point then. Did you go to her Labor Day block parties?"

"Every year! Including the one where she did the Cha-Cha Slide right into the Johnsons' kiddy pool."

We both crack up at the same time, remembering the "take it back now y'all" that'll live in infamy, and it's like I've blinked and there's a whole new person standing here in front of me. His weirdly aggressive love for capture the flag seems a little less weird now that I know the context. Because it's made me angry, too, how much our neighborhood is changing. It makes sense that he would be angry at Cole for laying claim to Brady Park, another person coming to our city and using their money to gobble up what used to belong to us.

Could that anger be enough to kill someone, though? I don't think so, but I can never rule anyone out completely, right? Not until I know for sure . . . I need to be smart here. I got so laser focused on Trisha last time and ended up missing what was right in front of my face. Am I doing that now? Just because he's from Beachwood and loves it here like me doesn't mean he's not capable of lying to me—of hurting someone in a misguided expression of that love.

But the detectives cleared him. Well, he *says* they cleared him. He could be lying to me. And it's not like I can just call Detective De La Rosa and ask for a quick fact-check, with how terribly that last call went. All I've got is my own read on him, and I feel pretty sure, in my gut, that he's telling the truth. Maybe I can throw one more thing out there, though, to see how it lands . . .

"What about the tetra . . . tetrahi . . . tetrahello . . ."

"Are you okay? Should I call someone?"

"*The Visine?!* What do you know about the Visine?"

He tilts his head to the side at that, and his Jack McCoy / Jellycat eyebrows furrow. "I'm not following." There's also a little bit of wariness there . . . of me? Which I guess makes sense, considering I broke into his office, blabbered on about my murder-solving hobby, and now just yelled the name of some eye drops at him.

But what I don't see is recognition. At all. He doesn't seem to know there was a second poison that killed Cole. And if he's lying to me—well, he's good.

"Never mind. Don't worry about it. Okay, well, I'm going to

go. Sorry about the whole breaking and entering thing. I promise it won't happen again. Um, so, bye—"

"Listen," he says, holding his hands up. "You don't gotta trust me. I get it." I'm not sure how we got to *me* trusting *him*, because, again, the whole breaking and entering thing—but I'll take it. "There's something else I didn't tell the detectives, though."

My stomach drops. Where's the glittery Crocs guy? Is he still in eyesight?

"I know, I know. I should have," Dom rushes to explain. "It's just that Coach Cole was an asshole, and he probably deserved this lady yelling at him. I didn't want to bring trouble her way for something *he* probably started."

"What? A lady? Who?"

"There's this workout group that comes here every Tuesday. Mostly rich white ladies. You know, the ones all moving in here, buying these flipped houses?" Dom gives me a knowing look, and I return it but not just because I know the type—because I know *these specific rich white ladies.*

"Anyway, it was a few weeks before Cole . . . you know." He winces. "I saw him arguing with one of these ladies. After the rest of the group was gone. It got intense. She was getting up in his face, pointing at him, and he was shouting back. I almost stepped in because it was starting to make me real uncomfortable. You just don't talk to women that way. But then she took off, and—"

"What did the woman look like?" I cut him off, needing the answer right this second. But I already know what I'm about to hear.

"Uh, she had short hair, kinda reddish blond? And big eyes." He widens his own to match. "Like, really big."

THE NEXT DAY, I'M SITTING BEHIND A FIDDLE-LEAF FIG TREE
in a coffee shop, spying on that woman with short, kinda reddish-
blond hair and really big eyes as she meets with her next mark.

I was supposed to be that mark. I made an appointment! But
Bethany DMed me the following last night:

> Mavis! I am SO flattered you booked
> a one-on-one self-care consultation
> but after some careful personal
> reflection, I think we are currently on
> very different journeys and I need to
> protect my own mental well-being
> from exposure to busyness culture
> or any other possible toxic influ-
> ences. I wish you health and
> happiness!

I almost felt . . . offended? After all that time pursuing me,
she's really going to give up on me and the whole new market I
can open up for her, just like that? But I guess I can't blame her.
I may have shown my cards a little *too* much at her party, and
who knows what Mackenzie has told her. If Bethany did what
I'm now almost certain she did after talking to Dom, then it
makes sense she's going to avoid me for the foreseeable future.

But, thankfully, the woman didn't change her publicly posted
schedule to meet up with internet strangers (seriously, if she
wasn't a potential murderer, I would make her watch a couple
episodes of *To Catch a Predator*)—so I still knew where she was
going to be and what times, even if she uninvited me. And I've
been watching her meet with a revolving door of women for over

two hours now, waiting for the right moment to do what I need to do, which is get into her bag.

I mean, ideally, I would break into her house, but I have a pretty bad track record with that at this point, and I'm not looking for a third strike. So, her bag is the next best thing.

I know my bag is full of clues of my current existence—receipts from every store I've been to for the past twelve to eighteen months, an unpaid parking ticket, a snack Pearl took one bite out of and then gave back to me because it tasted too healthy—and her big vegan leather tote looks like it could be a gold mine. Maybe there isn't a signed confession letter waiting for me, but there could be a CVS receipt for a burner phone and some Visine? I've gotta get at least a few minutes alone with it to see if there's anything new and substantial I can bring to the detectives.

Except it hasn't left the arm of her chair, and I know I'm not slick enough to casually walk by and grab it. No, I need her to leave it there, but as time passes, it's seeming less and less likely. She's only gotten up once, for like a second, to buy a gluten-free scone, and I don't think I have much time left. There's a crowd of much hipper people than me in boiler suits and baby tees waiting for tables, and the barista has been shooting me some not-so-subtle looks as I've sipped the one oat milk lavender latte I bought. But I can't risk going to the front to buy something else and being seen by Bethany. Also, this thing was eight dollars!

"I'm so happy to have you joining our family, Joanie!" Bethany chirps, and I'm close enough that I don't even have to strain to hear her over the sound of the espresso machine, thanks to the cover of this giant tree and a couple perfectly placed hanging pothos. I peek around them to see Bethany smiling at Joanie, who is wearing a cable-knit sweater tucked into high-waisted jeans, with a bow tying back her dark brown waves. She gently moves a stroller back and forth with her left hand as her right reaches for the Square reader Bethany is passing her.

"Go ahead and tap your debit there, and that'll get you all enrolled." I've heard Bethany give the same instructions by minute twenty-three on the dot in each of these thirty-minute sessions—and they've all given over their bank information just as easily as Joanie is doing now. It would be impressive if it wasn't terrifying. "And you'll get immediate access to our I LUV ME method and all of our other literature, so you can start reaching your self-care potential, and sharing it with others, right now!"

I fight the urge to jump up and grab Joanie's phone so I can read that intro email and finally know what all those goddamn letters stand for. But that mystery will have to wait.

"Oh, and I meant to ask you? About the monthly sales minimums you mentioned to qualify for commission?" Now *that* is a change in the script, and Bethany's face looks like the physical manifestation of a record scratch. Good for you, Joanie. "What happens if I don't sell enough? Because there's only so many people I know who will want personalized self-care plans, and eventually—"

"Don't worry about it! It's no big deal! You'll meet it easily. Especially with our supplements releasing soon." She stands up, her chair screeching on the concrete floor. "I actually have to pop over to the ladies' room real quick. I'll be right back!"

I check my phone, and we're on minute twenty-four. So Bethany definitely isn't planning on answering that question now that she has this woman's debit card and probably Social Security number, too. And I feel bad for Joanie, but also, I want to pump my fist because Bethany has left her bag there, on the back of her chair. There's still a witness present, but this may be my only chance.

I hop up, abandoning the dregs of my latte that tasted like grandma perfume, and I swear I hear the barista let out a dramatic sigh of relief.

"I, um . . . just saw your friend in the bathroom," I say, approaching Joanie with my most nonthreatening, totally-not-a-thief smile. "She asked me to bring her a . . . tampon?" But no, that won't work. I can't go through this thing thoroughly with her watching. "Actually, maybe I'll just bring her whole bag, so she can find it herself?"

Joanie narrows her eyes at me, and my eyes flick to the front door, already making my exit plan. But then there's a squawk followed by a loud wail. The baby is awake—and *pissed*.

"Uh, sure," Joanie says, her attention shifting to soothe her screaming baby in the stroller. I grab Bethany's bag before she can change her mind and take off in the direction of the bathroom, in case she looks up. I walk just past the door, though, to another seating area, with wide sliding doors that lead to a back patio.

I grab a seat at a communal table with a man who is typing furiously and, ignoring his annoyed look, begin to dig through the bag on my lap.

There's a Glossier lip balm, organic green tea mints, a Tesla key fob, and her wallet. I push down the worry that bubbles up when I see that—I'm *not* keeping it, this is not a crime. Underneath that is her phone—a new iPhone, not a burner from the pharmacy—and some plastic bottles. I pull them out and see the teal Balanced With Bethany logo with cutesy labels underneath distinguishing them: *Let's Move! Let's Vibe! Let's Rest!* These must be the samples of her supplements. They're gummies. Of course they're gummies. And . . . that's it. I dig around the bottom of the bag just to be sure, but there's no bottle of Visine or sodium nitrite, no burner phone with her text to Cole still on the screen.

The disappointment feels like a balloon collapsing in my chest. But it makes sense that it wouldn't be that easy. I'm glad I tried.

I hear the creak of the bathroom door opening, and my self-preservation instincts take over. Unfortunately, my instincts have me doing a weird spinny thing out of my chair and behind another fiddle-leaf fig tree (I thought these things were hard to grow, but they got a whole damn forest in here). I wince as my hip screams in protest because I am a thirty-two-year-old woman and not a Spy Kid. Fortunately, only the typing guy gapes at me in shock and concern, and Bethany remains completely unaware. She's looking down at her phone, texting—momentarily distracted. I need to leave this bag behind this tree and run before she goes back to Joanie. It's going to be a scene once she gets over there and realizes all of her things are missing . . . *her things*. Wait. I just looked through all of her things, and there was a phone. I know there was. I dig in the bag again, just to be sure, and my fingers find the iPhone. So what is she texting on right now? She has another phone? I risk a second glance around the tree and see her aggressively pushing buttons on a black flip phone—it looks like the kind I had in middle school. The kind that required you to push a number a few times to get the letter you wanted when texting. Did she have that in her jacket pocket or something? But why—oh my god, is that—?

My own phone vibrates in my crossbody bag, signaling a text. But before I can even pull it out, a call comes in. Which wouldn't be a problem—my phone is always on silent—except that it's the one number I have programmed to always ring: Knoll Elementary.

I grab for it in my bag, clicking the side button to silence it. My pulse pounds in my ears and my hands feel shaky. Was I fast enough? Am I caught? But when I look, Bethany is gone, and it's just the guy with his laptop. He's glancing around like he's about to call the manager, though, so I take this gift from the universe, leave the bag where it is, and sprint out onto the back patio. Without looking back, I unlatch the little gate and run down the sidewalk, not stopping until I'm in my car.

I'm safely three blocks away when my heart slows down enough for me to process the call I missed. Knoll. Why would Pearl's school be calling me? She has theater class after school today, right? Yes, I *know* she does, because we had a whole long talk about not announcing the mystery I solved to the whole cast of *Annie*. So it's not even time for her to be picked up yet. Plus, it's Corey's day, anyway—that's why I made plans with Jack this evening.

My stomach drops as my mind immediately jumps to all of the reasons why they could be calling me, things that could have gone wrong. But my phone starts ringing again, and I pull over, picking it up just before it goes to voice mail again.

"Hello?"

"Hi, Ms. Miller." I recognize Ms. Lilliam's perpetually annoyed voice. "You need to come pick up Pearl."

"Did something happen? Is she okay?"

"Oh yeah, she's fine. But Mr. Forest isn't." Ms. Lilliam makes a noise that I can't identify. If I didn't know better, I would think it was a giggle—but there's no way Ms. Lilliam has ever giggled in her life. "He had to leave early. It was a code brown."

"A code brown? Oh my god!" I don't know what that means, but code anything sounds bad. I need to get there, immediately, and call Corey after. "I'm on my way—"

"He's dropping Yule logs down the chimney, if you know

what I mean." She makes that noise again, and okay, I do know what *that* means . . . but I wish I didn't.

"Ms. Lilliam—"

"He's stocking the lake with the brown trout."

"I—"

"He's birthing a behind baby."

"I'm going to hang up now."

I hear Ms. Lilliam giggling—unmistakably, uncontrollably—before she hangs up on me herself.

I'm about to pull out onto the road again when I remember the text that came through. Was that Lilliam, too? But as I click into my messages, I see it's not from the school, or anyone else I know. The text is from a number I don't recognize, with an area code that's not Beachwood's. My heart speeds up again as I read it.

YOU BETTER STOP—OR ELSE

TWENTY

"IT'S FROM BETHANY. IT HAS TO BE!"

Jack and I are on the couch, eating the sushi takeout he brought over for dinner. But I'm still so keyed up, like I drank one of Cole's energy drinks, that I can't stop to get a full bite. Polly inches closer to claim the rolls for herself each minute I leave them unattended.

"I saw her text someone from a burner phone right then. And it ends the same way as the one Cole got, too, so it basically proves she also sent that one."

"What I'm still not following," Jack says, setting his chopsticks down, while Polly circles around the coffee table to sniff them, "is how you know it was a burner. Maybe she just has an old phone?"

"Because her iPhone was in her purse. It was definitely a burner."

Jack rubs the side of his jaw and squints at me. "Mavis . . . how do you know what was in her purse?"

"Hmm?" I pick up my giant water bottle and take a

convenient, long swig, avoiding Jack's stare. "Anyway, it wasn't even a good threat. It was very vague. Like, how am I supposed to know *what* to stop? She really should have given me more explicit directions."

"Um, let's pause this critique of her threat and go back to the purse? Did she see you? Because—"

"No, I don't think so. But if I hadn't got that call about Mr. Forest getting the runs and had to go pick up Pearl early—"

Jack laughs, despite the concern rippling across his face. "He is not living *that* down in the teachers' lounge anytime soon." He shakes his head. "Okay, but again, the purse. I really feel like we need to go back to the purse."

"If I hadn't gotten the call, if I had read the text right then— I think I could have confronted her. Then I would have proof that she sent it."

Jack laughs again, but it quickly dies when he realizes I'm not joining. "No, Mavis, you wouldn't! Because that isn't safe. You need to tell Detective De La Rosa all of this. Why don't we call him now? You have plenty to pass on."

I'm shaking my head before he even finishes his sentence. "He won't believe me. And she probably has gotten rid of it already—I doubt this was even the same phone she sent Cole a text on. She's a professional, clearly. I need *more*."

"A potential murderer threatened you." He says it like *The first letter in the alphabet is A*, like he's talking to one of his kindergarteners. It makes me bristle.

"Yeah, and I'm only on her radar because of what I've been figuring out—against the detectives' orders. He's going to blow me off—or even worse, do something more official to make sure I stay away. I can't risk that until I have something he can't disregard. I—I *know* what I'm doing here."

I can hear the edge creeping into my voice, the sharp corners that are always sanded down for Jack. But I can't help but get defensive. He's making me feel like I'm unreasonable and rash. And again, I miss the Jack who was right there with me, willing to jump into something irrational and risky. Because so many good things *can* be irrational and risky—like, you know, a new relationship in your thirties after a divorce. But maybe throwing caution to the wind and jumping is only a good thing the first time. And if you *keep* doing it, well . . .

"Hey. What's up?" Jack asks. He reaches his hand for my knee and strokes it reassuringly with his thumb.

"Sometimes I feel as if you're trying to . . . delicately handle me or something. Like I'm one of your students who you're trying to get to stop, I don't know—eating crayons. But you can't just *tell* them to stop eating crayons because then they'll be like, *I love crayons! Crayons are delicious!* So you have to lead them there and make them realize on their own that crayons are not food." I bite my lip and look into his crinkling eyes. "Does that make sense?"

"I think," he says. "So . . . solving mysteries is your . . . eating crayons?"

"Yeah." Though, when he says it like that, I realize this really isn't helping my whole "I'm not crazy" argument.

"I'm sorry it's coming across that way, and I'm trying to be supportive, even if I don't always agree with what you're doing." He sighs and shakes his head. "Or, it's not even that I don't agree—it's that I'm worried about you. I don't want anything to happen to you. And you have to admit it's . . . a lot. This all happening a second time." It's like he's reading my mind, but in the worst way.

"We had so much fun doing this together last time, though." I remember his scared face when he arrived at Corinne's house with my dad, Jasmine, and the police, and I correct myself.

"Well, for most of it. Why can't we just have fun together with it now?"

Why can't we just eat crayons? Burnt sienna is delicious!

"We can. I'm not saying we can't. But that was where we started, and sometimes I . . . want to keep going? What I mean is . . . that's what brought us together, but it didn't even matter what it was. I thought you were so cool and interesting and beautiful that I just wanted to get to know you, whatever it took. You want me to help you prove the PTA president killed my boss? Sure, no problem. If it meant I got to spend time with you." He winces, and I can tell he's trying to choose each word just right, to make sure it lands with me the way he intends. And that makes me feel a rush of affection for him, how careful he is with my heart—but it also, just as quickly, gives me that too-delicate feeling again. "And it still doesn't matter, Mavis. I'm here for whatever you ask of me. The fun and the not fun. But sometimes it feels like, all of this . . . it might be keeping us from moving forward? Because if we're always talking about this, we're not talking about what our future could look like together and the dreams we have for ourselves, for Pearl and Derek. Whether our values and wants and nonnegotiables make sense together, long-term." He sighs and looks at his facedown phone on the coffee table and it reminds me of last week in his office, when I could tell something was bothering him. Another thing I didn't talk about—that I *forgot* about until now, because I was swept up in my own things.

"And even just everything going on with my family right now. My mom—"

"What's going on with your family? Is Derek okay? Wait—your *mom*?"

"It's—I wasn't trying—" He shakes his head. "I don't want to go into all of that this second."

I open my mouth to protest, and he quickly adds, "I will later. But . . . what I'm trying to say is, it just doesn't feel like there's space sometimes. For, you know, the real things. The big things."

"I want to talk about the big things."

Even as I'm saying that, though, the question whispers in my mind: *Do you?* I've been one-track minded, putting all of my focus on Coach Cole's murder, to block out all of the things I don't want to think about: my unemployment and mental health and co-parenting with my ex-husband. Have I blocked out Jack, too?

And his *mom*? Jack and Derek's mom lives in Ojai. He rarely brings her up, and she visits even less—not once since we started dating. Is that who was texting him the other day? God, *why* didn't I ask who was texting him? Or at least ask him what was wrong, instead of jumping right back to Bethany.

Jack's been my comfort, my sounding board, my investigation partner—but I know I want him to be *more* than that. I want him to be my partner, period. Am I letting that happen, though? Is our future just another thing I'm avoiding thinking about by keeping my spotlight firmly trained on this case? Am I giving him what *he* needs? Do I even have the capacity to do that right now?

I try and figure out how to actually say all of that, to be as careful and precise as he is with his words and my feelings. But it takes me too long, because every start feels like it could lead to an ending. And that's the only thing I know for sure—I don't want this to end.

He breaks the silence first. "I think you know what I've been trying to tell you. And it feels like maybe . . ." He lets out a long exhale that I can feel on my cheek. My stomach tightens. "It feels like you don't want me to . . . and I can be okay with that.

For now. I know you've been hurt before. And if you want to keep things here, where they are, I understand that. I don't want to rush anything because of the way I feel about you, I can wait for you to be ready. But—"

"Mommy! Daddy drove into the curb! It sounded like his tire popped!"

I don't get to hear what comes after Jack's *but* because Pearl explodes into the house, followed by Corey, carrying Pearl's backpack and a Target bag. Polly abandons her post at the coffee table to greet them.

"Good golly, Miss Polly! Now why do you have rice all over your face? And Pearl girl, you *just* told me you wouldn't tell her that. For the record, I didn't even ask her not to tell you, because it's my car and—*oh*. Hello."

"Hey Pearl. Hi Corey." Jack stands up from the couch smiling, and I follow suit.

"Hi Jack! I mean, Mr. Cohen. But actually, you're in my house, so that means I can call you whatever I want, I believe."

"You good, Mavis?" Corey is technically talking to me, but his eyes are on Jack, narrowed in suspicion. Pearl picks up on this immediately, and her eyes drift between them, her little forehead creasing. This is exactly what I *don't* want, for her to feel any worry or weirdness, so I shoot daggers at Corey to get it together.

"I'm going to head out," Jack says, with a measured lightness. And I feel sad, because I know we need to talk more, but also relief and gratitude because I know he accepts, without resentment, that it can't happen right now. He leans in to quickly kiss my cheek and I squeeze his hand. "See you tomorrow, Ms. Harding. Hope your tire is okay, Corey."

As soon as he clicks the door shut, I turn to Pearl with the brightest smile I can muster. "Why don't you go find Papa, and he can help you get ready for bed? He has his big headphones on, so he won't hear you coming, which means you can probably scare him."

I know she probably realizes this is code for *Daddy and me need to talk*, but the flicker of worry on her face instantly shifts to a mischievous grin with the prospect of scaring Papa.

She runs off, Polly chasing after her, and I glare at Corey. He opens his mouth to say something, but I hold up a finger. Seconds later, my dad hollers and then they both erupt into laughter. I grab Corey's wrist and pull him to my room. I shut that door, pull him into the closet, flip the light on, and then shut *that* door, too. This is our best chance at not being overheard by a curious Pearl.

"What's your problem? Why were you like that? It'll make her upset!"

Corey sighs. "You're right. I'm sorry. *You* just looked upset. I wanted to make sure he wasn't . . . hurting you."

I scoff. "Of course he wasn't. If anything, I hurt him."

He nods, almost in approval, and I roll my eyes, ready to tell him off. But something in his face makes me stop. His brown eyes look darker and there's a heaviness in his features.

"It's not easy to see you with him. Like that."

It's so outside the realm of anything I expected from him that I feel like my brain is buffering, trying to catch up. "What? Why—why would that even bother you?" I sputter. "That doesn't—what? Corey, it's been years. Since we were . . ."

"I know it's been a long time, but that doesn't mean I'm happy with the way things are. That doesn't mean I don't miss us . . . that I don't want us back."

"You mean . . . you and Pearl together. In the same house." I *know* that's not what he means but I need to give him an out. Because surely, he doesn't want to do this. *I* definitely don't want to do this—I've dealt with enough big conversations for the night—for the year!

"No, I mean . . . us. Me and you."

Okay. So, we're doing this.

He bites his bottom lip and his eyes lock on mine with a steady intensity, like I'm all he sees. My stomach twists, aches, remembering all the years between us when that look was all I needed. But that quickly blooms into a fire because I'm pissed at him for *making* me feel this way. He has no right.

"How can you even say that? When you're already making plans to leave."

"What? What are you talking about?"

He has the nerve to look confused, like this is some minor misunderstanding and not a huge thing that's going to blow up our whole lives. It makes me want to scream—to roar—but our eight-year-old is on the other side of the house, so all I can do is whisper very harshly, which isn't nearly as satisfying.

"Pearl overheard you on the phone a couple weeks ago. Talking about Wembley Stadium? So you can't be too serious about missing us, if you're heading out to London god knows when." I take a step toward him, pressing my finger into his chest, and he lets out a sharp breath. "This is only temporary to you. And I know you don't mean to hurt us, Corey, but it's almost cruel—how you keep being so nice to me, helping us, getting me to rely on you. Because I can't. It's not safe for me to. Because I *know* you won't always be here. I *know* your work will always come first. And this was just, like, a fun little interlude for you, something to make you feel good. So don't come around saying you miss us, that you want us back. Because my heart—it can't . . . it can't handle that."

My voice catches and my eyes are blurry with tears that I *will not* let fall. And I hate being like this in front of him, showing my gooey, weak insides after years of making myself hard and strong. But there's also a release in expelling all of the vulnerability, the sadness and pain. Like after a bad bout of food poisoning, when all of the sickness has finally been purged and you feel wrecked but cleaned out. Maybe we can finally, *firmly*, move on from here.

Except, Corey doesn't look chastened—or even freaked out by my emotion. He looks mad. Which doesn't make sense because I am the one who gets to be mad here, not him.

"Mavis, see, this is always our problem. You hold everything in. You don't tell me how you're feeling. And if you did, then we could have squashed this two weeks ago." He sucks his teeth, blinking furiously. "I *knew* you were mad at me about something, but I didn't know what."

"What do you mean, squashed this?" I ask, irritation rising. "And yeah, I'm mad. I'm still mad. But I needed time to process my feelings about it—and that's my right, Corey."

"Yeah, you'd have a right to be mad if I was hopping on another tour and going to London, but I'm not. Pearl probably overheard me talking to Kyle—you remember my buddy in Silver Lake? My agent came to me about this big six-month contract with this singer, starting at Wembley. But I turned him down—*of course* I turned him down—and I suggested Kyle instead. Which you would know if you actually told me what you were upset about and gave me a chance to fix things before they were too far gone."

He's right that I try to push my feelings down, that I avoid big conversations. And I know that doesn't make things easy in a relationship with me . . . Jack was just telling me something not too far off. But: "Don't act like all of this is my fault." My finger whips between us, signaling all the years we're somehow re-litigating now. "And I think we both know if I had just told you how I was feeling back then, that wouldn't have magically fixed everything. You wanted to be gone. Your work was *everything* to you. How was I supposed to know you were choosing different now?"

He sighs, running his palm over his face, and it's like the fire in his fight goes out. "I know I've made mistakes. I know that my priorities were all out of whack. I've been working through it with my therapist, why I attached so much of my value to my work." His voice is scratchy, almost pleading. "I've been trying to show you that I've changed, though. You don't have to believe me yet—I know I've got a long time to make up for, and it's gonna take a while. But I'm not going anywhere. This is where I belong, and I'm just sorry . . . I'm *so* sorry I didn't realize that sooner. I'm gonna be here for Pearl—from now on, for good." He swallows and I study how his Adam's apple bobs, just to avoid his steady stare. "And for you, too, in whatever way you'll let me be. I meant what I said: I want us back."

I'm suddenly aware of how close we're standing in my little closet, and then he takes another step toward me, making us even closer. He reaches forward and brushes my elbow, just barely, but it sends electricity through my whole body. It's quickly doused, though, with an overwhelming wave of guilt. I step back, knocking a few jackets off their hangers. "I can't do that."

"Yeah, yeah. I understand. I'm sorry. I'll go." His arm bats behind him, looking for the doorknob. And when he opens it, letting in fresh air and the bright light of my room, it feels like we're stumbling out of the rabbit hole, back into reality.

"Oh, I forgot. This is for you." He holds up the Target bag that I first noticed when he walked in. I consider refusing it, as if that'll go back and uncross any lines I may have stumbled over, but that'll just make things even weirder.

I'm confused, though, when I see overnight ultra thin pads in the bag, size five in the brand I like, next to the shiny purple wrappers of my favorite chocolate.

"I remembered that you only buy one pack, and it's never enough. And then I saw these chocolate bars and figured I'd get you a couple because you always would say they were too expensive and never buy them for yourself."

When I keep staring at the bag, giving him absolutely nothing, he clarifies, "Because you said you were on your period."

I want to laugh, but I also want to cry. Because this is like the laundry app and the chain on the door but it doesn't make me mad anymore. It just makes me . . . confused. So the best I can do is mumble "Thank you."

And that's enough for him, for now. He says good night to Pearl, and then I take over for my dad, braiding her hair and flossing her teeth (because she somehow convinced Papa "we don't do that anymore") and reading her bedtime story and checking on her "just one more time." And then after she's finally out, I put away the dishes and fold the towels and clean out the lint trap in the dryer and go through every paper in Pearl's stuffed backpack and send my résumé out to three jobs on ZipRecruiter that I don't want but I should probably just grow up and accept because it's work and no one loves work.

I keep myself so busy that by the time I stagger to bed, bleary-eyed, I'm out before my tears can even hit the pillow.

TWENTY-ONE

"THANK YOU FOR MEETING WITH ME."

Principal Smith's words hit me like rocks to my throbbing skull, and I try to smile politely, but it comes out more like a grimace. I feel like I'm hungover even though I didn't drink anything last night. It's an emotional hangover.

"Sure. Happy to."

I didn't want to say yes when he called me this morning asking me to come in, after how this ended last time. And it's not really safe with me dodging Mrs. Tennison's many emails about that freaking costume. But it's a good distraction from everything with Jack and Corey last night.

I can be okay with that. For now.

And *I want us back.*

Both have been blasting so loudly in my head they've drowned out all the thoughts about the investigation—along with visions of those goddamn overnight ultra thin pads from Corey, dancing and doing high kicks.

I don't think that's what Jack had in mind when he asked me to move on from this case already.

"So, I'm sure you've heard," Principal Smith says, bringing me back. "Mr. Forest went home sick yesterday."

"Yes, I know. Ms. Lilliam called me." And told me a lot more than I asked for, so why are we discussing it again? Does Mr. Forest know they're spreading his butt business around town like this?

Principal Smith glances at the ceiling, like he's thinking something over, and then leans forward with his chin resting on his knuckles, looking me right in the eye. "He thinks . . . someone may have done this to him. *Purposefully*."

"Oh. So, I guess it wasn't just 'interpersonal issues between parents' then?" I was right. I knew I was right, but now he does, too, and maybe Trisha will finally get some more serious consequences this time, because clearly just banning her from the premises isn't enough. And wow, is my headache gone? Trisha getting in trouble may be my cure-all.

But why is he looking at me like that? All . . . squinty. And with his lips pursed. I feel like I'm being studied, like he's a scientist and I'm some poor specimen under a microscope.

"Oh my god! You think it was me?"

Principal Smith's eyebrows jump. "Well, you were upset about Trisha . . ."

"And you think I'd make him sick over that? I didn't blame *him*! I blamed *her*! She was the psychopath who was blackmailing him just so her kid could wear that little red afro! And that's why I told you about it, so you could do something, but you blew me off because you said it wasn't your problem. Except now it looks like it is."

"Yeah, I didn't really think it was you," he mumbles, suddenly interested in shuffling papers on his desk.

I start to stand up. "Okay, well, I'm going to go then—"

"It's just, he's insisting I take action! He says it's my job to protect him!" The papers in his hands scatter as he runs his hands through his thinning brown hair in frustration. He continues to stare at his desk, though, as if he's not even talking to me. "These after-school programs are getting out of control—no, they're past that. These parents want their precious children to have everything: robotics, yoga, fencing! And there's no one to coordinate all of it, so of course it falls on my shoulders. Meanwhile, we've got someone poisoning the theater teacher and chessboards being snapped over people's heads like this is WrestleMania and not an elementary school, all because no one can handle their kid not being the best. And I can't take it anymore!" He makes a sound like a scream trapped in the back of his throat and starts pulling at his hair again. A piece in the back stands straight up. "You know what, I'm just going to shut the whole thing down and lock the gates at three. It'll be better that way. If they want enrichment, then they can get it somewhere else!"

"No, I don't think you should do that." Pearl would be so sad to lose this theater class, and she's already asked me to sign her up for ceramics in the spring. But beyond Pearl, what about all of the families that use the after-school programs for childcare, since school is done hours before most jobs are? Or the ones who can't just go and sign up for the expensive enrichment classes at all these private academies popping up in Beachwood? Why should they be punished because of a few entitled (and *insane*) parents?

"I mean, I don't know about the . . . chess wrestling. But do you even know for certain he was poisoned?" *Poisoned.* My voice trembles slightly saying the word, as my mind jumps to Cole. This wasn't *that*. This was just a couple of hours on the can. "Maybe he just ate a bad corndog from the cafeteria . . . ?"

But Principal Smith is shaking his head before I'm even

finished. "He insists that someone did this to him. He says he does . . . intermittent fasting? And that he only drinks clear beverages until—oh, I don't know. I stopped listening. But he demanded that I look into it and ask Trisha, specifically." He winces. I guess I should be flattered that at least I wasn't his first suspect?

"I'm assuming that didn't go well."

"No," Principal Smith says emphatically, eyes flaring. "She threatened to sue us for harassment. And even before that, I knew it was a long shot. She's banned from campus, and the teachers know to call a code royal blue if she's ever sighted." Wow, they really do have a code for everything around here. "So, unless she paid someone to do it for her . . . and with what I've seen of this woman, I wouldn't put it past her. But I don't know. I just don't think it fits because—"

"Because she already got what she wanted," I finish. I hate to defend Trisha, but it's true. "Why would she make Mr. Forest sick and take the chance that he might quit over the whole thing, if Anabella is already Annie?"

"If it's not her, though, it just reinforces the fact that this is a larger problem at Knoll. It's a real special place y'all have got here, isn't it?" His mustache lifts in a patronizing smile, like the one he gave me last time I was here. Annoyance rushes over me, but then it's gone just as quickly, because there's another thing, right on the edge of that same memory. What did he say when he smiled at me like that? Something about, I wasn't the first parent who came to him pissed about their kid not getting the part they preferred.

"Okay, what about that other parent? Who was mad their kid didn't get a part? Have you talked to them?"

He snaps his fingers and points at me, impressed. "I didn't think of that. But how should I approach her?"

"Well, definitely don't pull her in here and stare at her all weird like you did to me, because *that* was a failure. I would frame it more as . . . you want to hear her concerns more? I think if you give her enough time to talk instead of cutting her off, she'll show you just how mad she is, all on her own."

"That's good. That's actually good." He grabs one of the papers from his desk and clicks a pen, ready to take notes. "Maybe let's . . . role-play this? So I can make sure I get the words right."

I'm about to continue, but the annoyance comes raring back, knocking me over like a bat to the head because I didn't get the message before. What am I doing? Principal Smith is *not* a good guy, and he went out of his way to make me feel small when I came to him with my concerns last time. He did *much* worse to Corinne. Why am I sitting here giving him my labor for free, when he made it extremely clear before that he didn't want it? Yes, I want to make sure that Knoll keeps its after-school programs, but I don't need one more thing on my plate right now. Last night showed me that I have plenty.

"I think you can figure it out." I stand up and take one big step away from my chair so I don't backtrack. "You made it very clear this was your school to run and you didn't want me butting in."

His brow furrows. He opens his mouth as if to say something, but I beat him to it. "And I think you'll find that if you cancel all extracurriculars, you'll have an even bigger fight from the parents. In fact, maybe I should make a post about how you're considering it on the Facebook group right now, so we can see what they have to say?"

With that I stroll out of his office, feeling nice and smug. In my head, I look like an early-aughts pop star, strutting at the end of a music video as flames erupt behind me. If my hair wasn't up in a puff, I would flip it. But that feeling is quickly replaced with icy dread creeping down my neck once I see who's waiting in the front office.

It's Bethany, sitting in one of the two plastic chairs. Her eyes are glossy, and her lips are pulled into a bravely suffering smile that I know she's perfected with practice because it's all over her Instagram feed.

Why is she here? Is she meeting with Principal Smith, too? Oh my god . . . does that mean—is *she* the other parent that complained about Mr. Forest? Could she be responsible for his code brown? *Poison!* Which means this is the same MO. This could be the last piece of evidence I need to convince the detectives she's the one who did this.

But just as fast I realize, no, her Dakota is definitely not in the show. I would have seen her at pickup or when I snuck into the auditorium. I feel deflated with defeat.

Our eyes meet, and the only sign that she's the one who sent me a threatening text is a slight twitch in her jaw. But then the tears that were brimming at her lids spill over in two perfect parallel lines down her cheeks, covering up the evil that I know is lurking underneath.

"Ah, Mrs. Bowman. Welcome." Principal Smith stands at his door behind me. He pulls at his collar, clearly uncomfortable with her display of emotion. "Why don't you come on in? And— not to worry—I can tell you already that Knoll Elementary will be proud to donate to your cause with our Fun Run funds. Let's just discuss the details."

"Thank you. And I'm sorry." She gestures to the tears on her face as she stands up and moves toward his office. "It just means so much to me."

My jaw drops. First the Clover Scouts, and now Knoll? This

greedy woman knows no bounds, and everyone keeps falling for it because, why? She can cry on demand? White-woman tears really are the most powerful thing on this earth.

The door clicks behind them, and almost immediately, Ms. Lilliam heaves out a long sigh. I look at her and she's shaking her head and tutting to herself. It's clear she wants me to ask her about whatever it is, and I'm curious. But I'm also not trying to risk another play-by-play of Mr. Forest's bowel movements.

"Oh, Mavis! Wonderful! I was hoping to run into you," a voice calls from down the hallway that attaches to the main office. My stomach lurches in momentary panic. Oh no. Has Mrs. Tennison finally tracked me down? I ordered a George Washington costume off Amazon, and it'll be here tomorrow. But I'm gonna need at least one more day after that to scuff it up a bit, take out a few stitches, so it looks like I actually made it.

Before I can bolt, though, Mrs. Nelson appears next to me, a smile on her face. And I turn the panic down, just a couple notches.

"I talked to your dad a couple weeks ago for his podcast."

Okay, never mind. Panic back.

"That's, um, great. Listen, I'm running late to a meeting." Hopefully she doesn't ask for any more details, because my brain is definitely too scattered to make them up.

"Oh, then just very quickly," she continues, "I wanted to tell you how much I enjoyed speaking with him. He asked such insightful questions and really . . . helped me to process my feelings? I didn't think I would get so into everything that happened. But he made it such a safe place. He's very good at what he does."

"Wait, my dad's podcast? Are you sure we're talking about the same guy?" Because what she's describing doesn't fit in with the sensationalized interviews I've seen him chasing with his mic.

"I have to admit, I got a little teary-eyed, talking about, well . . ." She clears her throat and nods to Principal Smith's door. I had wondered if they were still doing their thing, now that Mrs. Nelson and her husband are getting divorced, but the look on her face—anger mixed with deep pain—makes it clear they're not. "His questions and . . . his *empathy* helped me to forgive myself, because I feel like I understand more now why I made the choices I did."

Out of the corner of my eye, I notice Ms. Lilliam come down from her perch behind the desk and move closer to us. She starts tidying around the plastic chairs and the table between them, but it's clear she's just trying to eavesdrop.

"That's, um, great." I lower my voice, hoping Mrs. Nelson will notice and follow suit. "Again, though, I need to clarify here. My dad?"

"Uh-huh. He made me realize that all of that nonsense about a twin flame"—she shoots another venomous look to Principal Smith's door—"it was just an easy escape from everything else I didn't want to deal with. And it's part of my pattern, of searching for validation in others when really I can only find it in myself." I feel the need to pull up a picture of him. *You're talking about this guy. Elijah Miller?* "After the interview, he even helped me apply to a fellowship for teacher librarians at the Library of Congress this summer, so I can work on building my own identity outside of my relationships."

"Wow. I didn't realize . . ."

But I guess this does fit in with the man I know, the man who raised me. He's always been kind and generous, with a deep love for his community. *We are each other's business.* That's why his true crime podcast turn was so jarring. Yeah, we like ourselves some *Dateline* and *Law & Order*, but I never expected him to be the one turning people's trauma into content. It looks like . . . he might be doing something different? Helping to heal the same pain he is documenting?

"Anyway, please pass on my thanks to him. And I can't wait to listen to the episode when he releases it."

She waves and walks back down the hallway, and I'm left blinking after her. Could I have misjudged him here? Maybe I should have listened first, asked more questions? But he really *was* wildin' out with that mic everywhere, so it's not totally my fault.

I should talk to him . . . at some point. Eventually, but not now. Now I don't have time to think about any of this. Now I need to deal with Bethany. And Corey and Jack . . . and my unemployment.

But first Bethany.

My eyes dart to Principal Smith's door. I wonder if I'll be able to hear what they're saying if I get a little closer. But, *ugh*—damn it. Lilliam. There's no way she'll let me get away with that, and she's still right here next to me, pretending to clean.

"I think that's the last of the juicy details for the day, if you want to take your lunch."

But Ms. Lilliam ignores my snarky callout and bends down to pick something up off the floor. "That woman has a lot of nerve, dropping these in her eyes like I couldn't see her. Mm-hmm, and then she leaves 'em for me to clean up."

"Who? Are you talking about Mrs. Nel—"

The question dies in my throat, though, when I see what it is she's picked up. From underneath the chair Bethany was crying in, just moments ago.

It's a small plastic bottle, clear with a red label. The letters on it are white, but they might as well be flashing neon. *Visine.*

TWENTY-TWO

"HELLO? DETECTIVE DE LA ROSA?" I SAY, ONCE I'M FINALLY put through to his extension. I told the receptionist that it was an emergency, but after she confirmed that I wasn't in any immediate danger, I was put on a very lengthy hold.

"Ms. Miller." His voice is flat, like he's purposely trying to hide his emotion, but there's no time to analyze that now.

"Hi! Okay, please listen for a second. Don't write me off yet." I can feel my words tumbling over each other as I talk as fast as I can, pacing around the living room just as fast. "I found out something that is going to help your case. Bethany Bowman. Do you know who she is? Actually, you must, because I mentioned her last time we spoke!"

"Yes, you did." I give him a beat, waiting for more, but there are only muffled sounds of his office around him. I guess I should just be happy he hasn't hung up yet.

"Well, hopefully you've already looked into her then, and you know she was in a business deal with Cole. Probably a pretty lucrative one, for these gummy vitamins? So she has a *motive* for him being out of the picture, because it would mean more money for her. Also, I'm pretty sure he was suspicious about her faking cancer, which would, like, blow up her whole self-care MLM, so that's another *motive* right there." I pause again for any sign that I'm swaying him with my use of official detective language, but he seems intent on giving me absolutely nothing. "So, anyway, today, I saw her at Knoll Elementary, and guess what fell out of her bag? A bottle of Visine! Or, you know . . . tetra-tetril—yeah, Visine. I don't know if she has sodium nitrate—sorry, *nitrite*—too, but I'm sure you can get a warrant now and look for that."

It's still silent. And, okay, I admit that might not have been the best delivery. I'm not some TV detective, laying out the facts in a perfectly rehearsed monologue, but still—everything he needs is there. Maybe he's already hung up, racing to the first judge he can find, and he'll call back to thank me later.

He clears his throat: proof of life. "Ms. Miller . . . how did you know about the Visine?"

So apparently he's *not* in any hurry to get that warrant signed.

I sigh, weighing my options here. I don't want to get Irene or Leon in trouble and lose that information source, but I also need to sound legit.

"I have my sources."

He lets out a snort, which is honestly uncalled-for.

"It doesn't matter where I heard about it, because are you listening to me? She carries it around with her and uses it to fake cry! I saw her do it today in the main office, before a meeting with the principal. She was trying to get money from him. And I think she probably has it with her all the time, because I saw her crying suddenly at her party, too! So if it was in her purse that Sat—"

"You went to a party," he says, cutting me off. "With this woman you think is a murderer?"

"Um . . . yeah? But only to get evidence!"

He snorts again. "Why are you doing this, Ms. Miller? I tried to make it as clear as I could last time, we don't think Corey Harding was involved. He is no longer an official suspect." He exhales sharply. "Damn it. I shouldn't even have told you that. But, just—there's no reason for you to be involved in this anymore. You can move on. *Please* move on."

I can feel my pulse rising, and my words speed up to match it. "Except, if I wasn't still looking into this, you wouldn't know this about Bethany. That she carries Visine around in her bag—well, she *used* to, but it fell out today, so Ms. Lilliam in the office has it. You can probably go get it now, though, and test for fingerprints. I tried to take it from her, but she insisted on putting it in the lost and found? Because it's protocol? She doesn't like me very much, but she might be nicer to you."

I'm blabbering again, and I can feel him slipping. My chest feels tight with the urgency. This may be my last second before he hangs up. "She threatened me!"

"Ms. . . . Lilliam?"

"No, Bethany. I got a text yesterday. Telling me, 'You better stop—or else'! She knows I'm onto her, about faking cancer and killing Cole, and she's trying to get me off her trail."

"She sent you this from her personal phone number? Why didn't you start with that?"

"No, a burner! And I know Cole got a threat from a burner, too, so . . ."

"Should I even bother asking how you know that?" Another uncalled-for snort. But maybe he has a cold? Maybe he's gulping down Robitussin and that's why he's not moving with a sense of urgency. "Please send me a screenshot of whatever it is, and we'll look into it."

"A screenshot? Don't you want to go through my phone or something? And get the . . . data?"

"Sure. Feel free to bring it in and leave it for me at the front desk."

His tone is flat again, just like it was when he answered, and I can tell he's placating me. My time is up. "In the meantime, I'm going to ask you again, Ms. Miller, to please allow us to do our jobs here. Any interference is only going to make this harder for us. I'm going to look past all of your . . . excitement, but I can't promise that I'll be able to do the same in the future. Detective Berry definitely won't."

Basically, *Let the people in charge handle things. We know best. And you should be grateful we've let you do the work you have.* As he hangs up, I feel the same misery and building fury that I did with Project Window, with Principal Smith. *What am I doing?*

I drop down to my knees and let out a guttural sound, hoping it'll release my tight chest and steady my speeding heart, but all the feelings remain.

I've been putting so much of my energy into this—instead of looking for a job, instead of paying attention to my boyfriend. Instead of self-caring! And what is it all for? Detective De La Rosa clearly thinks I'm, at best, a joke, and at worst, a liability. Why am I wasting my time? Why am I wasting my time *again*? Why do I keep doing this when literally no one is asking me to?

"It's hit me, man. More than I thought it would."

I jump at the sound of a man's voice, faintly drifting from across the house—a voice that is not my dad's, the only other person in here. But quickly I realize: those goddamn walkie-talkies . . . I need to just trash them at this point, for the heart attacks they keep giving me. I'm enough of a mess on my own.

"It's made me think about my own mortality, what I would leave behind for Jasmine and Langston, what people will say about me."

But no. I recognize that voice. It's Leon. And it's coming from my dad's room. I think I know what this is.

"And also . . . I just really miss my friend. Playing golf on Sunday afternoons, grabbing a beer together afterward while he gives me shit about my bogeys. I keep thinking about how I didn't know it was the last time. And how we're not gonna get the chance to do it again."

I arrive at Dad's door in time to see him click his mouse to make the audio stop and reach his hand up to wipe something from his cheek. It makes me freeze, this display of emotion that I wasn't expecting—from him *or* Leon. It makes me hit pause on my own. But then his smile is in place, like nothing's the matter, when he spins around in his chair.

"Sorry. The sound wasn't right in my headphones, and I needed to see if it was a problem with them, or the audio itself."

"You don't have to say sorry, Dad," I say, taking a few more tentative steps into his room. "I didn't—that was . . . that was different from what I expected. For your podcast. That's your podcast, right?"

He waves me away. "Oh, let's not get into that back-and-forth again. I wasn't trying to scoop you with Leon, and you got the information you needed, now, didn't you? I saw you talking to that park guy after."

"Yeah, I did." I sit down on the small leather couch that's next to his desk setup. "But I'm not trying to complain about your podcast. Or talk about the case." After that call with De La Rosa, and the anxiety I can feel waiting in the wings for its next performance, I kind of want to forget the whole thing exists.

He raises an eyebrow. "Oh yeah?"

"Yeah. I actually talked to Mrs. Nelson earlier, and she

couldn't stop singing your praises. She said you made her feel very understood, and, like, helped her figure out her next steps? She said your podcast was really insightful, and sensitive."

"Well, of course it is!"

Now it's my turn to arch my eyebrow at him.

"Okay, okay," he mutters, palms up in defense. "Maybe I got slightly off track with this second case, but can you blame me? Having the whole thing go down right in front of me? But that's the goal. I want to give people space to process, offer any help I can. The crime is second to the people."

"Why, though? Why are you doing this when you could be watching TV or taking a nap or . . . literally anything else?" It comes out harsher than I intend, but that's probably because I'm talking to myself, too—maybe even more than him.

Dad stands and walks over to his bed, picking up a gold-framed picture from the nightstand. I can see the picture vividly, even before he hands it to me, because I've stared at it for years, memorizing every little detail of my mom. She has deep brown skin like mine, tight curls shaped into a teeny-weeny afro, and well-worn lines around her eyes and mouth, earned from her easy smiles and laughs. I can hear that laugh now, saved in my memory from videos my dad would play, and it makes me want to cry but also laugh along, too. She's holding me in her arms, wrapped in a yellow-striped blanket, and my dad has her in his arms, beaming proudly behind us.

"We used to dream about our second acts," he says, beaming at her picture now. "We promised each other that we wouldn't get all old and boring once we had a chance to wake up every morning and do exactly what we wanted to. Don't get me wrong, she loved being a social worker, and I'm proud of my years in court—but that was also what we had to do, for a paycheck. We wanted to make the years that were just for ourselves count, and do whatever made us feel most alive and happy. She was always joking that she didn't care if we were doing it in diapers and dentures—we were gonna do what we wanted!" He laughs and then clears his throat. "Even when we knew she wasn't going to make it, your mom still talked about her dreams for the future. She was an artist, I've shown you her sketchbooks, and she talked about learning how to sew up all the designs she had in there. She talked about making clothes and selling them, maybe creating a whole wardrobe for her grandbabies one day."

A tear spills out, trickling down over his lips, which are still smiling at her. And my eyes water, too, at the idea of Pearl sporting Nana-made fashion. I always wish she was here for Pearl and for me, but I don't think about it enough, how much it probably pains my dad every day, the loss of her. They had years together to dream up their lives, their futures, and I wonder if every milestone, every phase, without her feels like another loss.

"I wish you both got to live this second act, Dad."

He sniffs. "Me too, Maves. Me too."

"So Mom wanted to design clothes, and your thing was . . . you wanted to make podcasts?" It sounds so stilted it could be read as sarcastic, but luckily he just chuckles softly and pats my shoulder.

"No, I thought I might get back to my baseball roots, find a rec league, maybe do some coaching. But, you know, my knees." He sits back down in his chair, and they pop, emphasizing his point. "It's been fun, though, and surprisingly fulfilling, working on this podcast with Bert. I get to talk to people who have experienced some of their worst moments, but also be there for them as they're figuring out how they're going to live after that. It's interesting. And it makes me feel connected to others . . . which is harder now that I'm not working anymore."

He sucks his teeth and then cracks a smile. "And yeah, I'm nosy—just like you, girl—so it scratches that itch, too. But I'm trying to maneuver in the most respectful, human way possible, doing these interviews." His grin grows. "And Bert, well . . . he's not the best interviewer, but he figured out how to get us up on the—the Spotify? So that's why he gets a co-credit."

"What if . . . what if other people don't understand it?" Again, another question that's more for me than for him, because he's made it very evident no objections are going to stop his project, even his judgy daughter's.

"That doesn't matter, because I do. And your mom, she would understand it, too. She didn't get her chance for her second act, so I better live mine well, instead of watching TV or taking a nap." His eyes are still wet, but his face is playful. "I owe it to her—and to myself—to do what I want to do right now, instead of putting it off."

It makes me think of the goalpost I keep moving for myself, pinning all my hopes on a finish line many years ahead of me. I look at his computer screen, instead of our family picture or him, so I don't start crying again. And the big logo projected there, of him and Bert holding up magnifying glasses with matching deerstalker hats like Sherlock and Watson, does the trick.

I nod to it. "So, a true crime podcast is your second act."

"It is."

"Then I'm glad you're doing it. But maybe just . . . not at Pearl's soccer practice?"

"Ah, hey! No promises," he jokes, but then his face is suddenly serious. "And what about you, Mavis? What would make *you* happy?"

"I am happy." It comes out quickly, a reflex, and Dad fixes me with one of his X-ray looks, instantly seeing through all my fronts and defenses.

Is he asking about my job? My romantic life? The panic attacks? Knowing him, probably all three—plus two more things I haven't thought of yet. But he'll let me get there on my own. The look is just to let me know that he knows . . . whatever it is he knows.

"Well, you deserve a life that makes you happy now. You deserve to *do* what makes you happy. Don't put it off." He taps the picture in my hands. "Why don't you keep that with you while you think about it?"

And I do think about it. As I walk back to my room and shut the door, throwing myself on the bed like a petulant teenager.

What would make me happy? What do I want?

I feel like I ask myself this question all the time and then ignore all the answers until a more convenient time. And *that's* working out great for me . . .

I want to feel calm. I want to feel . . . whatever the opposite of overwhelmed is—*underwhelmed*. I want to be underwhelmed! I want to feel cared for—by myself and others. And really, the others are already doing their job just fine. Jasmine and Dyvia. Jack. And . . . Corey. So, it's me that needs to step up to the plate, finally. I'm not trying to make it my life's work, like Bethany, but it should definitely move up the priority list, *at least* above cutting out hearts and faking a hand-sewn costume for Mrs. Tennison. (Side note: I want to email Mrs. Tennison my two weeks' notice.)

I don't want to push the goalpost anymore. I want it right now. But how? How do I do that when everything else is still the same? I still need a job. I still don't know if I'm cut out for being in a relationship. I still need to give Pearl my everything, always. And there's still this mystery that I can't just forget—Cole deserves justice; whoever did this deserves consequences.

How do I claim everything that I want and choose my own happiness, unapologetically? Like my dad is doing. Like my mom dreamed of. It feels like an impossible equation, and yet I've already given myself the final answer. There's a finite number of variables and operations that'll get me there. I can figure them out if I want to.

Later, after I've gotten through pickup and homework and McDonald's drive-through for dinner, Pearl finds me on my bed, looking at the picture again.

"You're in the blue zone."

"I am."

She crawls on top of the covers and curls into me, her head on my shoulder, her legs tucked into my side, like puzzle pieces clicking into place.

"Because you miss Nana?"

"I do."

"It's okay to be in the blue zone about that. You can stay there for a while, and I'll stay with you."

She kisses my cheek, and I feel something sticky left behind—probably the remains of that hot fudge sundae she had for dessert. I kiss the top of her head and rest there, breathing in the scent of my baby girl.

Mom and I didn't get to be together like this, and that's a loss that'll be with me forever. With all those dreams for the future, she didn't get her second act. But I get to be here for my kid. I get all these moments that are small, but sacred, that require nothing at all from me but to be here—*really* let myself be here. And maybe that's the first step in this impossible equation I'm trying to figure out: being present in each moment. Instead of finding a distraction, instead of trying to follow every decision I make down long and winding paths to inevitable disappointment and failure.

I can allow myself to just be. To breathe. To trust that I'm doing the best I can and I'm good right now, in this moment.

I tell myself that now in my head, repeating it over and over with each breath.

I'm good right now, in this moment. I'm good right now, in this moment.

I hear Pearl breathing deeply along with me. And my chest finally releases fully, my heartbeat is slow and steady, and my body is light like I could float up to the ceiling.

It feels like peace.

It feels like self-care? Oh my god, *am I self-caring?*

"What are you thinking about, Mommy?" Pearl asks.

"I'm thinking . . . this is nice. And it doesn't have to be just for . . . certain moms. I deserve this, too, feeling like this. It's up to me to make it a priority."

"Huh," she murmurs. And I know I'm supposed to make my brain stay right here. I know I'm not supposed to start thinking about the future, because that's when the anxiety creeps in. But I can't help but think about the legacy I can leave for Pearl if I figure out how to treat myself well, to show myself that I am deserving of slowness and peace. Maybe it won't be so hard for her.

"What about you?" I ask. "What are you thinking about?"

"Bees."

"Bees?"

"Yes, bees. They're going to go extinct and I don't know if I can stop it."

"Oh. Okay." It's not quite the heartwarming moment I was hoping for, but it's perfectly Pearl at eight.

"Permission to say a bad word?"

I sigh. "Sure, why not?"

"Bees dying is *shit*."

The word explodes out of her mouth, like she's been holding it in for weeks. And then we explode into giggles together, until we're crying and our tummies hurt, and that feels like self-care, too.

LAST NIGHT, I PUT MY PHONE ON DO NOT DISTURB AND slept better than I have in months, maybe years. And that peace has followed me through drop-off and into my morning walk with Polly, to Brady Park and back.

I know I still need to mend things with Jack, talk to Corey . . . but not in this moment. I'm just walking my puppy on a sunny February day in this moment, while I listen to a meditation on that app—which is actually really useful if you pay attention to what Tanya's saying and also stay awake.

Polly jolts to a stop, nearly pulling me over with her. Unfortunately, *she* didn't get the whole "we're peaceful now" memo and keeps stopping to sniff at every tree and speck on the sidewalk, which makes it a little harder to get into the flow. I tug her along. "Why are you acting like it's your first day in the world? Get with the program, girlfriend."

There's also Bethany. I need to make a decision about what I'm going to do there. Honestly, though? I'm thinking about letting it go, moving on. I don't *want* to, but everything is pointing to it being the right thing to do. Because I like feeling this way, and it's all on me whether or not I get to experience it. If I leave this to the detectives, then I can finally stop moving the goalpost and take what I want right now, like my dad said.

A phone call cuts into Tanya's soliloquy on giving our bodies loving-kindness, and when I take my cell out of my pocket, I see Ms. Joyce's face replacing the tranquil blue of the app.

Okay, I'm still going to take what I want, but . . . right after this. Because if I ignore her, that's only going to cause more problems for my peace down the line.

Polly stops to sniff at something else on the ground and I pull her along, accepting the call.

"Mavis! Mackenzie hit the woman! And then she took her back to her lair!" Her voice is so loud that her mouth must be pressed right up to the receiver. My body tenses. Peace who? I don't know her.

"Ms. Joyce, what?" I must have heard her wrong. Because who would Mackenzie hit? And a *lair*?

"This poor little skinny woman!" she shouts, huffing like she's just run a marathon. "Mackenzie hauled off and punched her in the face! There's blood everywhere and now she's hiding her in her house, probably gonna chop her up like one of those documentaries I've seen on the Netflix, and then—then . . . put her in a workout smoothie or something! They always say they never saw it coming, but for the record, I saw it coming! Asking for an HOA? It's just not right. Things like that tell you who people are."

"Ms. Joyce," I say, trying to keep my voice full of loving-kindness. Tanya would be proud. "I don't understand what you're talking about. Mackenzie is not putting anyone in her workout smoothie."

"T'uh. You don't believe me? Fine. See how you come out on the Netflix documentary. But I got the footage they're gonna want. And I'm 'bout to bust in there and stop her myself!"

"Don't do that. I'm coming, and we'll sort this out." I hate to encourage this, but maybe it'll keep her busy for the two blocks

I need to walk . . . "Don't you have mics in her house? Can't you listen in on those and make sure everything is okay?"

"Oh, my security system doesn't sound so bad now, does it? But no, that was the only one I had in her house. Would've got another one in there if she didn't come home early that day. Nearly broke my hip again coming down from that window. Hmmm—maybe if I go in that way, I can catch her unawares."

"No! Just stay right where you are. Please."

But I can hear her moving around as she mutters, "Don't know why I called you, acting so scared."

I start to speed-walk. Mackenzie might've let the slight breaking and entering and minor stalking go, but accusations of cannibalism could be her breaking point. After only a few steps, though, Polly stops me dead in my tracks again.

I pull on her leash. "Polly, I swear, come on!"

But when I look down to see what fascinating thing she's sniffing at this time, my irritation quickly evaporates and ice runs through my veins.

There are drops of something dark red. Under Polly's nose and in a steady trail up the sidewalk in front of us, as far as I can see.

I lean down, squinting. Is that . . . ? I think it is. Blood. And it's still wet.

I jerk Polly back, and she frowns up at me with disapproval. "That's *not* food."

"Excuse me?" Ms. Joyce asks, still on the line. "I know pepper spray isn't food. I'm old, but I'm not senile."

"No, that's not—" I spin around and see splatters behind us, too. That's what's been making Polly stop. How long have those been there? All the way back at Brady Park? I pick a very bothered Polly up and walk as fast as I can. "Ms. Joyce. There's blood here. On the sidewalk."

"I told you!"

"Who did Mackenzie hit? It had to be really bad for all this blood. And why—put down the pepper spray!"

"I don't know her, but I think it's one of those Caucasian women she works out with. Hmmmm, short hair, wide eyes? Kinda looks like . . . Mia Farrow? Lord, all that woman's gone through with her marriages, and now she's got your little friend trying to blend her up in a smoothie!"

I break into a jog and then a full-out sprint, following the path of blood all the way back to our block.

TWENTY-THREE

"FINALLY!" MS. JOYCE IS STANDING AT THE END OF MAC-kenzie's pathway when I arrive, and she throws her hands up in exasperation. "What, did you take the long way? Go for a nice little stroll?"

She knows from the amount of sweat pouring off my body right now, and the sheer size of the stains under my arms and boobs, that I definitely did *not* stroll. Next to me Polly pants rapidly like *she* had something to do with us getting here so fast.

"Are you *sure* you saw Mackenzie hurt that woman?" I ask Ms. Joyce, ignoring her attitude because we have much more important things to deal with here. "The lady you described, she's dangerous. It's more likely *she* hurt Mackenzie."

"Of course I'm sure," she huffs. "And we don't got any more time to waste." She starts walking up the flagstone path to the Skinners' house, and I follow behind her quietly. Or as quietly as I can with Polly, who has started to whimper. Even the tiny droplets of dried blood that lead right up to the door have lost their novelty to her.

"It's okay, girlfriend," I whisper, reaching down to scratch her ears.

"Don't lie to her now."

We both hesitate when we reach the door. It's a tall mahogany thing, rustic-looking with an iron grille, as if it's been here for a hundred years—though of course the Skinners just installed it recently when they gutted and renovated the house. It looks like the door to a fortress.

"I think I can get us in with a credit card." But I pat the pockets of my jeans and find them empty except for my own keys. "Do you have one? Or I can run home real quick—"

"Step aside, baby," Ms. Joyce nearly growls, her face full of determination. "I've got this."

She backtracks a couple of feet and then lowers herself into a running crouch, or as low as she can go considering she's in her eighties. Oh no. Is she really about to—?

"Ms. Joyce, no!"

"Ahhhhh!" She lets out a battle cry as she runs toward the door, and I instinctively hide my face in my hands. I'm not trying to see her crumple to the ground. But it's only after the door flies open without any resistance that I realize she just pulled down the unlocked handle. The whole busting-the-door-down act was just for me.

"Who's there?" I recognize Bethany's voice immediately. And I feel like jumping up and doing a fist pump because I was right, and then get the overwhelming urge to run away, because *I was right.*

The door opened into an entryway with a wall decal that says, *LIVE every moment, LAUGH every day, LOVE beyond words.* And I would cringe if my whole body wasn't already tense with anticipation and fear. I don't think they can see us yet. We could still get away. But Mackenzie . . .

Ms. Joyce grabs my shoulder and leans in close. Time to talk strategy?

"What is that smell?" She wrinkles her nose disapprovingly at the bag of Polly's poop in my hand, which I'd kind of forgotten was there. But can she blame me with the whole my-neighbor-is-a-serial-killer phone call?

"Does that really matter right now?" I whisper back. She shakes her head at me and plows ahead right into the house. So much for strategy. I scamper after her and almost instantly drop the offending poop bag. Because it *doesn't* matter. Because we can see straight through the living room and into the dining room, where Mackenzie is sitting at the big oak table, her entire body still. Because next to her Bethany is leaning in close with a long orange crystal in her hands, the sharp tip of the obelisk pointed right at Mackenzie's throat.

Except . . . Bethany's face is covered in blood. She's been hurt. Just like Ms. Joyce said. No, that's not right. Bethany is not the victim here. Maybe it was self-defense?

"Did you call them?" Bethany asks Mackenzie, the crystal moving dangerously closer. My stomach tightens in fear, like the crystal is at my neck.

"No—" Mackenzie starts, but Ms. Joyce cuts her off.

"Of course she didn't, because she doesn't want any witnesses. But we're here to bust you out!" Ms. Joyce strides right up to them, oblivious to or unafraid of the crystal shiv. "She didn't start cutting now, did she?"

Bethany's bloodstained lips pull into a small smirk, but Mackenzie's mouth drops open.

"Cutting? You think I did this to her? I didn't do this!" She jerks her thumb at Bethany. "She did!"

And okay, I am firmly Team Mackenzie here. Not because she's my little friend, but because I know Bethany is guilty. That argument isn't looking so great, though, with the blood still dripping from Bethany's nose, spilling onto her Balanced With

Bethany–branded sweatshirt. Is she saying Bethany hurt herself?

Suddenly Mackenzie launches herself out of her chair at Bethany, and Bethany's crystal-wielding hand falls back in surprise.

"Whoa! Whoa!" I yell.

"See! See!" Ms. Joyce hollers back, hopping with excitement and vindication.

But instead of disarming her or scratching out her eyeballs or getting another lick in, Mackenzie goes straight for Bethany's nose, sticking her thumb and pointer finger up one of her nostrils. Is that some secret way to take someone out? Is Mackenzie *actually* a smoothie-making serial killer?

Her fingers come out a second later and they're holding something? Part of Bethany's brain??

Oh my god. Oh my god. Forget Team Mackenzie! I am Team Mavis Makes It Out of Here Alive! I need to split or I'm going to be next. But, wait, I can't just leave Ms. Joyce and Polly . . . Polly is *sleeping*? Are you kidding me? This damn dog is curled up at my feet, snoozing away as a possible serial killer is claiming her next victim right in front of us.

Forget them both! They're on their own!

"I knew it!" Mackenzie yells. And it makes me pause. Because she doesn't sound bloodthirsty or murderous. She sounds . . . triumphant? I know I need to run, but the confusion and curiosity are sending my body mixed signals, blocking out my self-preservation instinct.

"What in the devil is that?" Ms. Joyce asks.

I follow her narrowed gaze, losing precious moments to save my own ass, and . . . it doesn't *look* like brain matter. Not that I've ever seen brain matter. But I don't think something ripped out of someone's nose would come out looking so . . . structured.

And plasticky? The things in Mackenzie's palm seem to be clear capsules, sitting in a puddle of deep scarlet.

And Bethany . . . she looks more annoyed than in pain. That's something I *do* know for sure—if someone just tried to pull out your brain you wouldn't be wrinkling your nose and giving them the side eye.

"You really couldn't just be honest with me. After all I've done for you." Mackenzie's cracked voice sounds pained, pleading.

Bethany crosses her arms, her orange crystal still tightly clutched in her hands, but no longer ready to slice an artery. She pointedly looks away from Mackenzie standing over her.

"Mackenzie, *what* is happening here?" Polly, the worst guard dog ever, lets out a loud snore to punctuate my point.

Mackenzie shakes her head and then meets my eye. Her chin trembles, and then her whole face hardens with resolution. "I didn't believe you, Mavis. I was furious with you for suggesting that she could be lying about something so—so terrible." She shoots a glare at Bethany, who is still committed to avoiding eye contact. "With Cole, I could just brush it off. He complained about the exercise classes to me before. He said he was doing most of the work, so he deserved more of the pay—it didn't matter that her name was on it. When he came to me saying she faked cancer, I thought maybe he was just trying to ruin her reputation, so he could make more money. I thought he was the evil one." Another poisonous look is launched in Bethany's direction. "But with you, Mavis . . . I couldn't let it go. What reason did you have to lie? You didn't even know her. So last week, after I talked to you, I started looking into some of the details she'd given us over the years—the hospitals, the experimental trials, the relapses. And it didn't add up. I wanted it to. But it didn't."

"So you punched her," Ms. Joyce says, and Mackenzie's sad

eyes squint in confusion. "I didn't punch her! I showed you"—she holds up the capsules in her hands—"the blood is fake."

"But Ms. Joyce saw you punch her on her cameras."

I look to Ms. Joyce to explain, but she sucks her lips in and then pops them out. A guilty grin appears. "Now, I didn't say that. I *said* I saw Mackenzie taking the woman with the bloody face back to her lair—house. I assumed—fairly, based on the evidence—that Mackenzie punched her."

Lord. But it's not worth arguing this now, when we're so close to finding out the truth here. "Okay, so you *didn't* punch her. What did you find out then, Mackenzie? What happened when you confronted her—"

"Why do you hate me so much, Ms. Joyce?" Mackenzie's chin is trembling again, and the blood capsules drop from her hand.

"I have never said I hated you."

"But you do. It's obvious you do. The looks and the cameras and the microphones and—"

"It's 'cause you asked her if Beachwood had an HOA!" I interrupt. We really gotta move on here.

"I knew that's what it was!" Mackenzie snaps and points her finger, her blond ponytail bouncing. "I told Todd you were mad at me for asking you that—I was even going to go over and apologize a few weeks later, but he told me I was being too sensitive. That I would look *crazy* if I went and apologized for something you probably long forgot." She snorts and a relieved smile spreads across her face. "I didn't want an HOA. I was making sure there *wasn't* one here because the one back at our condo complex was always on a power trip, sending out tickets January second for the Christmas lights or measuring the doormat to make sure it was the right size. I didn't want to deal with that again."

Ms. Joyce nods, very reasonably, as if this was a simple misunderstanding and not a grudge that's lasted over a year. "All right. My mistake, baby."

I sigh. "Can we get back to—"

Bethany stands up. "I think I'm going to head out—"

"Sit down!" Mackenzie and Ms. Joyce shout together, and Ms. Joyce shuffles over to Mackenzie's side, like she's her backup. Or her new bestie. Bethany slowly lowers herself back into her seat.

"Once I realized what she was doing," Mackenzie continues, "I still didn't want to believe it. So I asked to meet with her at the park. I showed her everything I found, practically begged her to prove me wrong, but she chose to keep lying. She started crying, and she actually told me her cancer was back!" Mackenzie lets out a short, bitter laugh. "Then, out of nowhere, her nose started bleeding—but she wouldn't let me call an ambulance. No, she insisted she just needed to rest at my house, that it would stop soon. And at first I felt bad—my friend is sick and I'm making her life harder. But then right here at this table, I saw her take a fucking selfie of her bloody face. For content! To sell this stupid self-care cure-all to even more vulnerable women like me. And that's when I knew, it's all been a lie. A greedy lie."

"Hmmm." Ms. Joyce shakes her head as she looks down at Bethany. "Well, what do you have to say for yourself?"

Bethany is hunched over in her seat, her arms curled around herself as if she's freezing. Her big eyes look wild, like a wounded animal about to lash out, and I feel another wave of panic. Are we safe here with her? She looks so unassuming, so innocent, but that's intentional—I know what she's actually capable of.

"I *was* sick," she finally says, her voice delicate and small. "What that man did to me *made* me sick. He was trying to take away everything that I've built. Take food off my family's table. He wanted to ruin me. And he—he had *no right!*"

Did she just say that? And the worst part is, she actually seems to believe it.

"Just to clarify . . ." I say, my eyes darting to Mackenzie and Ms. Joyce to make sure they think this is as ridiculous as I do. "You're saying Cole made you sick because he knew you were faking cancer and was going to tell people the truth."

"Yes! And it was my truth to share when I was ready! He was trying to take away my agency!" Her shoulders shake, and her eyes, somehow, get even larger, suddenly glossy. "The anxiety . . . it was overwhelming! Life-encompassing! Never knowing when the shoe was going to drop, when my life would end. I stopped sleeping. I couldn't keep any food down. That's why I've gotten so—so *thin!*"

She lets out a sob, and two tears spill from her eyes, trickling into identical lines down her cheek.

Before I can tell her to stop, Ms. Joyce rushes at Bethany and bats something off her lap, like an angry cat. The crystal falls to the ground with a thud, but there's something else, too—a more hollow clatter. I dip my head under the table and find the culprit at her feet. A bottle of Visine.

My body jolts in understanding. That's where those tears came from! How in the hell is she so quick with that? But it's also a chilling confirmation of something else, something much more evil than faking cancer. She *murdered* the man who figured out her secret, by putting that *poison* in his drink.

Again, I feel conflicted. Are we safe? I want to get all my questions answered, finally get closure for this mystery that has taken over my life. But the more responsible thing to do here would probably be to call the detectives and let them take over.

I know I *don't* want to do that by the resistance that surges through me at just the thought.

Mackenzie and Ms. Joyce are here. Even Polly would probably wake up if someone tried to *kill* me. She can't take all of us, all at once. This won't be like Corinne. I'm not alone this time.

"So you decided to put your little fake tears in his drink. To make sure he kept his mouth shut. Is that what the 'or else' meant in the texts you sent to him?"

I hear a sharp intake of breath from either Mackenzie or Ms. Joyce (or maybe just Polly having a bad dream), but I don't take my eyes off Bethany's face, which instantly shifts from depressed to defensive. "What—*no*. I mean, I did send him some texts, but that was the extent of it. It was just cosmic alignment, or maybe divine timing, that his journey of life ended and he was no longer able to share my personal truths."

I blink at her. Was that a confession?

"I didn't do anything to him!" she rushes to explain, her face stretched into an incredulous smile. "But I can recognize and accept a gift from the universe in my favor. That's what happens when you walk in your true purpose every day and actively repel negative energy." She taps her lips and then murmurs, more to herself, "So someone put Visine in his drink? Huh, I didn't know that could kill you?"

I . . . don't know what to do. If she did do it, she's clearly not going to admit it easily. And she's a good liar. That's how she's made god knows how much scamming all these women. I look at Ms. Joyce and Mackenzie for some direction here, but they're just looking back at me, like I'm the one in charge.

"It doesn't matter if you believe me," Bethany says, interrupting our silent conversation. "Because the police do."

My eyes dart back to her. "*What?*"

"Yeah, they came to see me last night. Detective Berry and

Detective . . . I don't remember. Something ethnic? We can call them right now—"

"No," I cut her off. I definitely don't want to do that now. "Just—what did you tell them?"

"Detective Berry apologized for intruding, right in the middle of Dakota's bedtime, but the other one had all these questions about my business model and the contract I had with Cole for my new supplements. He was implying the same thing as you. That I would kill someone for—for—*money*! It hurt!" She scrunches her features up into a dramatic mask of pain, but it's not as effective with her bottle of Visine out of reach on the floor, so her hands fly up to cover her face. After a few body trembles and heaving sobs, though, she looks between her fingers, like a child peeking out from their hide-and-seek spot.

Ms. Joyce has her hands on her hips with an eyebrow arched, I'm giving her a *really?* glare, and Mackenzie is telegraphing just how over it she is by scrolling on her phone.

Bethany clears her throat and continues. "He asked me where I was when it happened, and I told him Dakota and I went to the health food store to get some green juice and nutritional yeast popcorn—it's her favorite. Yes, I admit, I was trying to avoid Cole, but I just didn't have the emotional bandwidth to deal with any awkwardness." Uh, yeah, awkwardness because he found out you were *faking cancer to scam vulnerable women*? "I showed the detectives the drive logs and dash cam footage on my Tesla. Also, Xena at the store has footage of us, I'm sure of it. She installed security cameras last year after a bad break-in— they took all her krill oil and goldenseal root. It was devastating!"

Drive logs, dash cam footage, security cameras . . . that all sounds pretty ironclad. She could still be lying—she is about her feelings, for sure. If she isn't, though, that means I was all wrong here . . . again.

But: "You sent him threatening texts. You sent *me* one, too."

"Yes, Detective What's-His-Name asked about that. He was *very* accusatory, and it made me *very* uncomfortable. But I'll tell you what I told him: I was practicing radical empathy. Even with all the pain Cole caused me, I was trying to give him a chance to move on from this negative dynamic he had created." She smiles beatifically, a firm believer of her own bullshit. "And you—*you* just wouldn't let it go. Even when it didn't affect you at all, you couldn't travel your own path and focus on your own journey." She shakes her head in smug disapproval. "I was trying to encourage you to move on, too, for your own good. Because you were making very destructive choices."

"Is that why you texted me at the coffee shop? Did you know I was there making 'destructive choices'?"

"No." Realization dawns across her face and then her brow furrows in indignation. "My *purse*. That was *you*. How dare you?" She looks around at Mackenzie and Ms. Joyce for validation, but when it's clear she's not getting it, she doesn't even bother to continue the performance. "I didn't know you were there. I just had a break in my meetings. I was multitasking."

Mackenzie gasps. "But you told us to give ourselves the gift of presence! And reject hustle culture!" As if *that's* the biggest reveal today.

"I know, Mackenzie, but it's hard running this business. Sometimes I have to break the rules a little bit and . . . hustle." She lets out a whimper. "It's why I've been so—so *sick!*"

Ms. Joyce sucks her teeth. "Oh, cut the crap!"

"Why did you bring a weapon then?" I can feel myself grasping at straws as my certainty drains away, but I can't give up yet. "You were threatening Mackenzie!"

"This?" Bethany picks the orange thing up off the ground and waves it around . . . and, okay, it looks a lot less dangerous now that I'm not busting into this house high on adrenaline. "This isn't a weapon. This is carnelian to support my emotional well-being in courageous conversations. Because"—her voice breaks into a whine—"because this is really *hard*."

She doesn't look so dangerous now, either, with her fake tears and emotional support crystal and dried up Spirit Halloween store blood. She looks . . . pathetic. And that's where all of her power lies: in her perpetual victimhood, in the sympathy she manipulates, in the underdog narratives she creates just so she can bravely, inspirationally rise above it—and cash in.

It's some real *we are the witches you could not burn* shit. Like, girl, you're the only one calling yourself a witch, and why do you keep going live on Instagram from that aesthetic stake you made yourself?

My gut is telling me she didn't do this. It would just be too hard for her to do the mental gymnastics, to keep being the victim, if she *murdered* someone. It would honestly be *better* for her brand to be accused by Cole—a bitter man, jealous of everything she's built—and then to rise above that. I want it to be her. I want to have been *right*. But . . . I don't think it's her.

Ms. Joyce lets out a long exhale and then swats the air in Bethany's direction. "Now you better stop with all those alligator tears and walk your little booty right on out of Ms. Mackenzie's house. We'll send you the bill for the cleaners." Bethany is slow to get up. She looks a little dazed that her usual MO isn't working, but Ms. Joyce turns her back on her like she's already gone.

"Baby, you want some tea?" she coos in her sweet-honey voice, smiling at Mackenzie. "Where's your kettle? We've sure had us some excitement today."

"Are you gonna tell anyone?" Bethany asks. The fake emotion is long gone, and all that's left is naked calculation.

"I already did. You might want to check my Instagram," Mackenzie says with a shrug. And then she turns her back, too, on Bethany's gaping mouth and wet eyes that might just be real this time. As Bethany silently shuffles to the door, blinking in disbelief, Mackenzie squeezes Ms. Joyce's arm and beams back at her. "It's in that cabinet next to the sink, but please sit down, Ms. Joyce. I'll make it for you. How does some Relaxing Chamomile sound? Mavis, I'll make you a cup, too."

Knoll Elementary Parents Facebook Group

Leslie Banner

I tried to sign Julian up for the next session of Chess All-Stars, and Ms. Lilliam said enrollment for after-school programs is paused until further notice. Does anyone know what's going on? Julian is going to be so disappointed!

Della Lively

I heard that Principal Smith is planning to cancel all after-school classes for the remainder of the school year after some bad behavior from a few parents.

Trisha Holbrook

This is UNACCEPTABLE! Our kids already have to make do with so much less going to a regular public school, and now he wants to take away their limited enrichment opportunities?? What will the repercussions be for their futures? I encourage everyone to think about how much our school community has suffered since Mr. Smith became principal. Our children deserve better! Knoll deserves better! WE CANNOT LET THIS STAND.

Angela Hart

I agree, Trisha! This is not okay. What can we do? Organize? My cousin runs the Beachwood Breeze, and he'll definitely let us write an op-ed. Parents need to know what's happening!

Charlie Lee

Unrelated, but are there any lawyer mamas in this group? I need some advice on getting out of an MLM contract that I don't want to do anymore, and all these terms and conditions are really making my head spin.

Ruth Gentry

Are you referring to Balanced With Bethany? I'm so sorry you got wrapped up in that! I knew there was something fishy there and I tried to warn whoever I could.

Della Lively

I just saw that on IG! She was faking cancer???

Ruth Gentry

It's people like her who give network marketing a bad name 🙁 But she doesn't represent all of us! @Charlie Lee if you're still interested in working for yourself, I can send you some materials for Agape Essentials. It's a great opportunity!!

Dyvia Mehta

@Ruth Gentry that's your third strike, and unfortunately, I'll need to remove you from the group.

Angela Hart

I think we need a presence at pickup and drop-off to make sure our voices are heard! If everyone wants to send me their sizes, I can get some "Save Knoll After-School Programs!" T-shirts printed by tomorrow.

Good morning Mavis,

I received your email about a "two weeks' notice," and that really isn't necessary. I would be happy to connect you with other experienced room moms who might offer you some support and guidance, so you can fulfill your commitment for the year. Are you part of the parents Facebook group?

And we really must begin our preparations for the Presidents' Day skit in class. Your email didn't mention if the George Washington costume was ready? At this point, I will gladly take it in whatever state it's currently in. I'll stop by your house today during lunch. Please don't forget the wig!

Thank you,
Mrs. Alene Tennison

TWENTY-FOUR

I SIT DOWN AND I DRINK MY TEA AND I TRY NOT TO LOOK like I'm spiraling over the fact that Bethany didn't do it, but I'm totally spiraling over the fact that Bethany didn't do it. So I leave as soon as I can—though Mackenzie and Ms. Joyce hardly notice, the way they're gossiping about everyone in the neighborhood (turns out they have the same favorite afternoon show: the views out their front windows). And when I head back across the street with Polly, I unlock the door and walk into a quiet home—Pearl still at school, Dad probably out with Bert—which is great because I prefer to spiral in silence.

It's like I've been working on a crossword puzzle for weeks, one of those really tough ones in the *New York Times* that geniuses do for fun but I usually give up on after a few frustrating minutes. This time I didn't, though. This time I was convinced I could do it. Except, just when I was about to reach the end, just when I was filling in the last blanks, I realized that I got one across all wrong, and once I erase that, well . . . I have to rethink everything. And then there are holes ripped in the paper from all the erasing and eventually the whole thing is a lost cause, newsprint smeared, totally illegible, and all I'm left with is a feeling of foolishness for thinking I could do this in the first place.

I throw myself down on the couch, and Polly hops up with me, putting her head in my lap.

"What am I gonna do?" I say, absentmindedly stroking her smooth black fur.

I can call Detective De La Rosa again and tell him what I learned. But . . . he probably already knows it. And if there *is* anything new, he'll just make me feel silly and stupid for calling him and then go chase my leads, which he apparently did last night.

No, I'm not doing that to myself again. If there was anything new revealed, someone else—Mackenzie, Ms. Joyce—can bring it to the authorities. It's apparently already all over Instagram.

Instead, I can . . . do nothing. And the world won't end and I'll actually probably feel pretty good. Again, if I let myself. I can just choose my own peace.

Yeah, that sounds nice.

I stretch my body out on the couch, and Polly looks up at me perturbed, but soon adjusts her position so she's curled up next to me. I close my eyes. I take deep breaths. I do nothing. And it is wonderful.

For ten minutes. And then the nothing is interrupted by a loud squawk and voices projected across the house.

"I can't believe you did it again!"

"It's fine. You need to stop being so dramatic. And be quiet. I don't want Marigold to hear us over *Bluey*."

I stand up. I'm throwing those fucking walkie-talkies away.

"I'm dramatic? Flo, I'm being realistic." It's Hank and Florence again, and as juicy as this argument is probably gonna be, I don't want to hear it. I am removing myself from other people's business—officially, starting today.

"I feel like I'm the *only* one living in reality here. I can't believe you would be so reckless, with everything going on!"

"I wasn't reckless!" Florence shouts back as I make my way to Pearl's room. "I was careful. I know the correct amount to use now. And we don't know that Principal Smith knows. That message just said he wanted me to come in and talk about Axel's part. Maybe Mr. Forest realized the error of his ways. Maybe he wants to *apologize*."

That makes my steps slow. So *Florence* was the other parent complaining about her kid's part. I guess that makes sense. She *does* think he is a precious gift to the world. But then . . . does that mean . . .

"I *told* you to stop doing the eye drop thing! You don't know how people will react. It's not always diarrhea. Remember that time with his piano teacher? She was out for a week, Flo!"

"Well, she should have moved Axel on to the next level then! It hurt his spirit, having to stay in the red book when he wanted to move on to the purple book. You know how much he loves purple."

Eye drops. They're talking about eye drops. Like the eye drops that were put in Coach Cole's drink. My heart starts to race as I put together what this could mean. Florence didn't like the part Mr. Forest gave Axel—or, oh my god, *he* could've had the solo that Trisha blackmailed Mr. Forest into giving to Anabella. So Florence . . . gave him diarrhea with eye drops? Did she do the same with Cole?

"And this is why we need to work on our communication, like I said," she continues. My legs feel shaky with anticipation, and I drop down on the floor with the walkie-talkies next to Pearl's bed. "I didn't know you were putting that *stuff* in a Capri-Sun and handing it to him. That was so risky—he never ate the kids' snacks! Which you would *know* if you ever *helped* me with anything."

Stuff in the Capri-Sun? They found sodium nitrite in the Capri-Sun . . .

"See, this is what I'm talking about," Hank snaps back. "You're always trying to make me the bad guy. And I *do* help! I go to every one of these games, just like you—*that's* how I knew to put some in his energy drink, too!"

Florence gasps. "You didn't tell me that. Oh my god, Hank! How much did you give him? And you're blaming *me*?"

"It was just a small amount. That can't be what did it, though. It's just salt, basically. They sell the stuff at Erewhon! I got a few crystals in my mouth when I was tasting that first batch of prosciutto, and it didn't do nothing to me." My arms start shaking now, too. *Sodium nitrite* is used for curing meats—that's about the only thing my chemistry-challenged brain remembers from Google and Dom. And Hank cures meats! They brought those bougie homemade charcuteries boxes as snack for the first game. How did I not think of this before?

"I thought it would only make him a little bloated and like . . . dry him out? I don't know. Just mess him up a little, so I could step in and coach our kid the right way for the day. That guy didn't respect our kid's potential. He treated Axel like he was weak."

"I know," Florence says sweetly, as if that was a totally understandable reason to *put poison in the' soccer coach's drinks*! Who are these people? I don't know them at all.

"I didn't plan to hurt him either. But when he said that thing about Axel being in his own little world—it just made my blood boil! I had to do something. Because how—how . . . how *dare* he! Axel is a gift to this world!" I was mostly joking before but there it is, completely serious. "It was only a few drops. And those energy drinks are probably *way* more toxic than the eye drops! I didn't know he would . . . he would die." Her voice breaks, and she lets out a keening sound. I hear the rustling of fabric. Are they hugging?

"I know, baby. I know. Come here."

And yeah, they are definitely hugging. And kissing, too, it seems from the sharp, wet sound also coming through.

God, I want to throw up. But there's no time for that. They're literally confessing to murder, and through some bonkers twist of fate it's being broadcasted from their 19.564-month-old's baby monitor to my daughter's cursed walkie-talkies. I don't believe in any of that woo-woo shit Bethany was spewing, but the universe *is* doing something for me here and I need to take advantage of it. I'm going to record them so I can show Detective De La Rosa. Otherwise it'll just be my word against theirs.

"*Neither* of us were the bad guy here," Florence says. "It wasn't murder. It was an accident! An honest mistake!"

I reach my shaky hands into my pocket for my phone and open up the camera app.

"Somehow, I don't think the police are going to see it that way," Hank says, with a chilling laugh. "*Sorry, Officer! I didn't realize my wife also put something in his energy drink. Whoops! Next time we'll make sure we do our things on different days, so he doesn't* die."

I start the video with my right hand, holding up the walkie-talkie with my left. But my hands are unsteady, every one of my nerve endings feels like it's pulsing, and I must somehow push a button, because there's a loud, jarring beep.

I let out a grunt of frustration. "This damn thing."

Someone hisses, and then there's a moment of eerie, terrifying silence. Finally Hank whispers, "Did that come from the monitor?"

"It did. Oh my god. It's on."

"Shit. Shit shit shit." I fumble with my phone and the stupid, cursed walkie-talkie, dropping them both in the process—but not before pushing the button again.

"Who was that? I *know* that voice."

I frantically turn the things off, for real this time, and I can barely hear my thoughts over the pounding in my ears. Can they trace me? No, of course they can't! They're fucking walkie-talkies! My chest tightens and the edges of my vision blur. But there's no way they could realize who I am just from that. It's not like I'm known for going around and yelling, "Shit!" I'm good. This is fine. I am fine.

Okay, but what am I going to *do*? I've figured this out and now I need to be smart here. I can't go barreling over to their house to confront them, like I did with Corinne. So I'll do what I should have done then: Call the police. Let them take over. I don't need to be the star here. I just need to make sure Florence and Hank are caught.

When I call the station and ask for Detective De La Rosa, and the operator asks if it's an emergency, I say no. It technically is this time, I guess, but I need to be put through to someone who knows what's going on, who can actually help me. I regret that choice more and more, though, as the minutes on hold tick by, minutes Hank and Florence could be spending figuring out it was my voice they heard.

Finally, the line clicks. "Ms. Miller."

My body freezes. That's not Detective De La Rosa. But I can't be picky.

"Um, hi, Detective Berry! I—I know who did it! It's Hank and Florence Michael—"

"Ms. Miller," she cuts me off, her voice dripping with conde-scension and irritation. "It has come to my attention that you have been harassing Detective De La Rosa."

"Harassing?" Yeah, it is my second call in, like, twenty-four hours, but I'm not harassing him! I've been giving him valuable information—information that they've acted on.

"This is inappropriate and cannot go on. If you continue to call the station with false tips, we will pursue the fullest of consequences. Goodbye."

And then she's gone. My one hope for justice here—for my own protection—is gone. And two murderers could realize at any moment that I'm the only person who knows they did it.

God, what do I do, what do I do, *what do I do*?

I walk the perimeter of the house, checking all the windows and doors, making sure they're locked, just in case. And they are. I'm safe, I'm fine. And I'll call my dad! He knows people at the police department. He'll be able to get them to listen.

There's a low growl, and then the clicking of Polly's nails as she jumps off the couch and breaks into a ferocious bark. My stomach drops with fear, but it's okay, the door is locked, stay calm. No one can get in. I'm safe, I'm fine. And she only barks at old people and babies—Hank and Florence are neither. A delirious giggle bubbles up in my chest at the thought of baby Hank and Florence toddling up to my door. It's not *them*. It's probably Ms. Joyce, already mad at Mackenzie for something new. I'll let her in so I'm not alone. Safety in numbers. We'll call my dad together.

The lock turns and I'm nearly knocked over by a rushing wave of sweet relief. It has to be my dad. I'm safe! I'm fine!

But dread hits me next, followed by overwhelming, paralyzing fear, as Hank and Florence Michaelson walk right in, Marigold strapped into a carrier on Florence's chest. Before I've even taken a step back in retreat, Hank closes and locks the door behind them.

TWENTY-FIVE

"HOW DID YOU GET IN?" AS IF *THAT'S REALLY WHAT'S IM-*portant right now. I would have been better off going with a "Stay back! I'm armed!" Or even just a simple, "Ahhhhh!"

Florence sighs and holds up my keys, with the sparkly-beaded *Mom of the Year* keychain. Marigold's eyes light up as she reaches for them, nearly knocking off Florence's wide-brimmed hat. "These were in the door. You really should be more careful."

"Did you tell anyone?" Hank instantly closes the space between us.

"Yes," I say, trying to keep the fear from creeping onto my face. "I called the detectives. They're on their way now."

Hank mutters a curse and takes off his almost identical hat, running his hands through his greasy brown hair.

"She's lying," Florence snaps. "We need to get her away from the door, Hank. She can't get out. Do you understand that? We'll be ruined. Axel and Marigold will have no one."

"Of course I understand," he says, glaring at her. He turns back to me. "Go to the, um, living room. Sit down. Now."

I follow directions. I'm too scared to do anything else. And

Polly follows at my feet, hopping up on the couch and rolling over onto her back, as if these are just new friends over to rub her belly. For the millionth time, I wonder why I don't have a vicious guard dog. It would be really useful for times like these.

"Puppy!" Marigold says, clapping her hands with delight. I'm pretty sure that's the first word other than "no" I've ever heard her say.

"Are you stupid, Hank? Get that thing out of here!"

Hank rolls his eyes but does what she says. As he grabs Polly by the scruff and gathers her up in his arms, I immediately take back every complaint I've ever made about her. I don't want a vicious guard dog. I just want her unharmed.

"Don't hurt her!" I call after him. Thankfully, I hear the back door slide open and then slam shut without any yelps or whines. It's only once he's back and I know my puppy is safe that I realize I should have made a run for it when Florence didn't have backup.

She starts pacing now, and Marigold glares at her from the carrier. "No puppy! No puppy!"

Florence ignores her. "We have to kill her, Hank. There's no other option."

Hank looks almost embarrassed when he considers me. "You were spying on us," he says, like it's an excuse. "You brought this on yourself."

"I wasn't spying on you. Your voices were being broadcast out of Pearl's walkie-talkies. Who knows—other people could have heard it, too." I need to sow doubt, make sure they know they can't actually get away with this.

But Florence smiles at me. "Oh, we bought her those! She told Axel they were what she always wanted." She raises her eyebrows and her smile changes into a grimace. "*I* personally would be worried that the radio waves might be harmful to a young brain's development, pressed so close to their faces like that, but"—she shrugs—"to each her own."

Is this lady really being judgy about me subjecting my kid to "radio waves," when apparently her baby monitor has the same kind—or no, *when she murdered a man*! Her bitchiness knows no bounds.

"We didn't hear any other voices out of it but yours," Hank says. It sounds like he's trying to convince himself.

"And *I* recognized your voice. You were yelling *that word* at their last game. It made Axel *very* upset—he's never heard such profanity."

So I guess I *am* known for going around and yelling "Shit!" Also, again: What. A. Bitch.

"We weren't trying to kill him, just so you know. It was an accident." Hank's eyes dart to Marigold in the carrier. I don't think she understands much of what is going on, but maybe he feels guilty, doing this in front of her. Can I use that?

"You put poison in his drinks! Marigold, do you hear that? Poi-son! Poi-son! Mommy and Daddy poi—"

"Shut up!" Florence frantically covers Marigold's ears. "Shut up! Shut up!"

"Not enough to kill him, though." Hank rushes to explain, looking between me and Marigold. "Well, it was, all added up. But we didn't do that on purpose. It was just a miscommunication. We're *not* murderers."

Florence scoffs. "Cole wasn't kind to Axel. Were we just supposed to *accept* that? If we're not our child's best advocate, then who will be?"

There's a knock on the door, and I startle in my seat. Is this my chance?

What can they *really* do if I run? Florence is basically out of commission with Marigold, and I could probably get past

Hank. Even if he stops me at the door, it'll be enough of a commotion—

All of my hope rushes out of me when Hank pulls a knife out of his back pocket. It's long and sharp, probably used to cut his goddamn prosciutto. "Don't even think about it," he whispers.

There's more knocking. "Ms. Miller? Are you there? My lunch break is only ten more minutes, and I *really* need that costume today."

Mrs. Tennison. Maybe being a room mom fuckup is my saving grace.

But Hank silently shakes his head in warning.

Florence's eyes bulge, locked on the knife, and her hands are over Marigold's mouth, who is now furiously hitting back.

"Ms. Miller? I know you're home. I asked Pearl, and she said you sit at home all day because you don't have a job."

Wow, rude. But my savage child could have given me my one fighting chance. Could I hit the knife out of Hank's hand? Even if he catches me with it, I might be able to get Mrs. Tennison's attention before I get hurt too much. How bad is a stab wound, really?

But then I hear a loud groan, followed by "Jesus fucking Christ. I'm going to have to go to fucking Spirit Halloween." Before I can make a decision, footsteps recede from the door, and then there's the horrible, soul-crushing sound of a car starting and driving away. My one fighting chance is going back to Knoll.

"Hank, we *cannot* use that on her."

"Well, why not? Just take Marigold to the other room, and I'll take care of it." He glances at me—the *it* in question.

"Because, you idiot, it's going to make a huge mess. Her DNA is going to be all over you and me." She gestures to her gauzy cream dress and light suede Birkenstocks. "It'll get tracked into our house. There's no way to completely get rid of it. That's how people *always* get caught."

Hank rolls his eyes. "Then what's your idea?"

"Poison." The *duh* is unspoken but very loud, and Hank's nostrils flare. "It's the most effective, cleanest way. I'm sure they have bleach." Her eyes dart around the room. "Or maybe anti-freeze, in the garage. That would do the job quickly. Because we *do* have to pick up Axel in a couple hours, and you know how upset he gets if he can't find us at the gate."

What, are they going to force-feed me bleach, all *here comes the airplane?* And how she can be so cold, so soulless, to be thinking about picking up her child from the same school where my kid is right now, all the while plotting the most effective way to kill me. I've always thought Florence was annoying and a lit-tle self-absorbed, but no—she is pure evil.

"Okay, we can put it in her water bottle, then?" He points to the giant metal thing on the table, where I abandoned it days ago, and my first thought is, horrifyingly: *Oh, you're behind on your water goal for the day.*

Florence throws her hands up. "Well, she's not just going to chug it down willingly, now that you've *told* her."

"All right, I'm tired of you talking down to me, Flo. I'm just trying to help here! *You* make the decision then! Clearly I'm in-capable of making the right one."

They start bickering again, and it's definitely not juicy or en-tertaining anymore, now that they're bickering about the best way to kill me.

But the water bottle. My eyes are still there. And my second thought is luckily a lot more helpful than the first. That thing is huge, sturdy. I could probably do some damage if I hit one of them over the head. But then what about the other one? And Marigold—I don't want to hurt her or leave her with some traumatizing memories.

God, what am I talking about? Her parents are trying to kill me! If I make it out of this, I'll pay for her therapy!

There's a heavy pounding on the door, and we all tense, staring at it. Is Mrs. Tennison back?

"Open up! It's the police!"

Hank flings his hand—the one that's not brandishing a knife at me—at the door. "So she *did* call them. Looks like you're not always right."

"Are you kidding me? Really, *that's* what you're gonna do right now?"

"No, no, no!" Marigold shouts as she joins in on the fun, slapping Florence's face.

I know that voice. It's not the police.

It's my beautiful, caring, and not at all annoyingly nosy neighbor Ms. Joyce, and she's given me another fighting chance. I'm not going to waste this one.

I jump up and grab the water bottle. Florence's eyes flash behind Marigold's incessant slaps, but I've already slung it at the back of Hank's skull before she can warn him. He drops the knife, and I kick it away from him into the corner.

Do I get the knife or run? Ms. Joyce is right outside. I decide to run.

The hesitation costs me, though. Hank sinks his grip into my hair right as my fingers brush against the knob, and he yanks me back to him.

"Are you fucking kidding me?!" I scream out in pain—but also in rage, because I cannot believe this motherfucker is touching my hair. I twist and spit and jab him with my elbows, losing all sense of strategy or self-preservation—all I know is I want to hurt him back. I grab behind me, nicking my palm on something sharp—*the knife*—and I scream again.

That's when the pounding starts. One loud thud, and then another. Then a few more. The door shakes with each one, and I fight even harder, with this sign that my salvation is so close.

"Mavis, we're coming!" Ms. Joyce hollers, followed by a sharp crack as the wood splinters.

Is she actually—

A second later the whole thing falls off the hinges and Ms. Joyce and Mackenzie charge through.

Oh, she *did*. I mean, Mackenzie probably gave her more than a little help, with how much she works out—and she uses that same strength now, to punch a shocked Hank in the jaw. He falls back with the force, and Mackenzie lunges toward him, stomping hard on the hand holding the knife. Soon, it's in her hand, pointed at his gut. In the living room, Florence cowers in the corner while Ms. Joyce advances on her.

"Me and your mama are just going to hold hands behind her back while we wait for some more friends to come."

"Hi!" Marigold says cheerfully. "Hi! Hi!"

I fall down to the ground, gasping for air as the sound of sirens gets louder and closer. *I am safe. I am fine.* I repeat it in my head over and over, willing my heart to slow down, my vision to stop swimming.

"Mavis. Mavis!"

"Oh my god, Maves!"

I think maybe I'm passing out, 'cause I'm hearing things. My head spins as I try to stand up on shaky legs, but before I can fall back over, strong arms catch me.

I look up and see dark, downturned eyes I've known for over half of my life.

And then, just behind him, blond hair catching the sun.

"Ms. Joyce called me," Corey says, his voice thick. "And I called your dad . . . and Jack."

"Oh. Okay."

I flash them both a dazed smile and steady myself, gripping the side of the front door. A jolt of pain shoots up my arm from my bloody palm, but it's nothing compared to the tightness in my throat, my chest. Slowly, I stumble past them out the front door.

Sirens are blaring from the cop cars screeching in, drowning out Corey's and Jack's concerned calls. The thundering in my ears is even louder. Two officers in uniform rush past me, yelling warnings at Florence and Hank, but I keep going until I reach our front lawn and drop down to my knees. Right before I face-plant into something resembling child's pose—the only pose other than savasana I kind of remember from all those unfinished yoga videos—I see a gray sedan pull up to the curb. A few moments later, I hear the sound of careful footsteps approaching.

"Ms. Miller, what are you doing?" Detective De La Rosa asks. I don't know if Detective Berry is with him, feeling like shit for ignoring me and risking my life. I don't care.

"I'm doing nothing," I say into the grass. My eyes are closed tight, and if I stay just like this, I can breathe. I'm pretty sure an ant is making its way into my right ear, but I'm not moving for anything.

"Ms. Miller, we need to talk to you right now and figure out what happened here."

"Actually, I don't think anything needs to happen *right now*, because the killers have been apprehended. You're welcome, by the way. So *right now* . . . I'm doing nothing."

"Ms. Miller—"

"Shhhh," I say, and then take a deep, cleansing breath. Just like Tanya from the meditation app, just like in the yoga videos with the lady and her dog. "Nothing."

THREE WEEKS LATER

"WOULD YOU LIKE TO BUY SOME CLOVER SCOUT COOKIES?"

The tiny voice makes me jump, and I immediately feel silly. I'm flanked on either side by Dad and Ms. Joyce. And this eight-year-old in a lavender vest and beret isn't coming for me, at least not in broad daylight in front of the Knoll Elementary auditorium with all these other lined-up parents as witnesses. Still, to my overeager nervous system, she might as well be a knife-wielding attacker. Apparently, once you encounter one of *those*, it becomes the default setting for all future encounters. It's very annoying.

"No, that's all right," Ms. Joyce tells her and then leans in to pat my arm gently. "You're okay, baby."

Ms. Joyce has barely left my side since that afternoon— keeping up with Pearl on her scooter for every pickup and drop-off, mean-mugging the detectives like she's my hired counsel in every follow-up meeting they've asked for, showing up for Pearl's *Annie* debut this afternoon. She even tried to tag along on a date with Jack before I drew the line. But I can't even complain. It's only because she and Mackenzie were drinking their tea and looking for *neighborhood* tea out the window that I . . . well, I don't like to think about what might have happened if she hadn't seen Florence and Hank walk up to my house and called Corey because they didn't look like any friends of mine she'd seen before. (She said it was the silly hats that tipped her off.) If she hadn't been so nosy, so in my business, there could have been a very different outcome, so I'll gladly have her be all up in my business as long as she wants.

"Thank you," I say, linking my arm with hers.

I take a long, deep breath—something I've done so much in the past few weeks it's basically just how I breathe now. And then I start one of the other practices I've picked up from one of my many Google searches to stay present and calm. *List three things you can see.* Crowds of families on either side of us, buzzing with excitement for their star's debut, the giant banner Trisha had made with Anabella in her orange afro wig and red dress . . . this Clover Scout still staring at me for some reason.

"Would you like to buy some Clover Scout cookies?"

"Well, aren't you precious," Ms. Joyce murmurs.

I realize I recognize this little girl with brown pigtails, beaming an aggressively cheerful smile like she wasn't already rejected. It's Harlow, Christine's daughter, so she's in the same troop as Pearl. I vaguely remember now, from one of Christine's long-ass emails, that some of the girls are selling at a booth outside of today's performance of *Annie.*

"Oh, no thank you. We have plenty at home. I'm Pearl's mom." I nod toward the auditorium. "She's in the show."

Harlow maintains her unblinking smile, holding out her wares. "We have Peppermint Patties and Caramel Connies. And they're only eight dollars! That's a deal!"

"Did you hear—um, I already have some." A dining room full of some we have to off-load by the end of the month.

She's still not blinking. Why isn't she blinking? Maybe I was too quick to write off the knife-wielding attacker possibility.

"I have Shortbread Sallies, too." Does this child have eyelids? I feel like I'd remember if she didn't have eyelids. "And I take Square."

"Um, sure." I give in, digging in my bag for some cash. At least I know the money isn't going somewhere terrible. Christine walked back their commitment to donating to Balanced With Bethany real quick, once her scam was revealed. At the pre-cookie-kick-off parent meeting, the moms decided to donate to cancer research and fund a beach cleanup instead. At the girls' cookie kick-off meeting the girls voted to use their money to go to Disneyland. Any of those options are fine, I guess.

"She's got great technique," my dad says as she skips off. He takes the Caramel Connies box out of my hand and expertly pops it open. He's made quite a bit of progress on our dining room cookie situation all on his own.

"Is being creepy a technique?"

"It got you, didn't it?" he says, offering the cookies to Ms. Joyce. She takes three. "Have you seen her numbers? I want Pearl to do some booths with her, see what she can pick up. This is our learning year, but I know Pearl could give her a run for her money next season."

Clover Scouts cookie sales have quickly become my dad's newest obsession. He has a sales tracker up on the living room wall that rivals my heart-and-Shrek murder board, and he's coveting that lavender stuffed platypus you get after selling three hundred boxes even more than Pearl is. I'm not as horrified by his podcast anymore, now that I've listened to a couple of episodes, but I'm also not mad that this is cutting into his recording time.

"Oh, Caramel Connies? Those are my favorites." Corey

strolls up to our place in line with a bouquet of purple flowers wrapped in newspaper tucked under his arm, probably freshly picked from his garden. He grabs a couple of cookies from the package Dad holds out.

"I know," I say, taking a cookie of my own since I paid for the damn things. "Pearl says you've eaten six boxes."

Corey throws his head back in a laugh. "I told her to keep that between us. But yeah, I'm gonna have to pick up some more tonight. My stock is running low."

"I thought this thing started at three," Dad says, twisting his head to look around the small crowd in front of us to the closed door of the auditorium "They're cutting it close, aren't they? I need time to set up my equipment." He pats the bag around his shoulder that's holding a camera and one of his fancy mics.

"Now why is that woman in the front of the line carrying 'reserved' signs?" Ms. Joyce asks. "She can't be putting those down. It's first come, first served."

I follow her steely gaze to Trisha, who does in fact have a stack of neon-pink papers in her hand, with *RESERVED* printed on them in all caps. I don't know how she got her restraining order lifted for this event. Maybe when it comes out that someone else was going around poisoning the music teacher and the soccer coach, it automatically makes you the lesser of two evils.

"You know what, I might go say something to her, because that ain't right."

"You don't need to say something, Ms. Joyce," I insist, tightening my grip on her arm. I honestly don't know who would win in a battle between Trisha and Ms. Joyce, but I don't want to find out today with the entirety of the Knoll Elementary Parents Facebook group here to report the results. "It'll be fine. There's plenty of seats."

"How many do we need?" Corey asks. "Five?"

I can tell by the way his thumb is circling his pinkie at his side what he's really asking. *Is Jack sitting with us?*

"Just four. Jack is helping backstage. Mr. Forest requested some extra assistance." What he really requested was protection, but that feels weird to say out loud when the person he requested protection from, the one who isn't in jail awaiting trial at least, is standing right there with her neon-pink signs.

There's relief on Corey's face, but he tries to disguise it with an easy, one-dimpled smile. They can coexist just fine—they *have* to, for me and Pearl—but I know both Corey and Jack prefer it when there's a little bit more space. Especially when I'm still putting off the big conversations we need to have.

"They shoulda given you special reserved seats," Dad says, closing up the eight-dollar box of cookies that is somehow now empty. "This show wouldn't be happening without you. I mean, we might've lost Mr. Forest like we lost Cole if it wasn't for you."

"Shhhh, Dad, it's okay." I look around to see if anyone is listening, staring. People are talking enough about everything that happened and my involvement in solving it all, *again*—I don't need to give them any more reason to. And I don't like to think about it too much myself either . . .

"You know, I might go on up there and see if they have a separate line for the elderly. I should get in before Little Miss Pink Sign."

"Elderly? Was it an *elderly* woman who had me buying a whole new door recently?"

"I told you to send that bill to Mackenzie."

Dad and Ms. Joyce laugh, and I do my best to join in. But in my mind I also see Hank stalking toward me, feel the slash of his knife on my hand. I hear the pounding on the door before Ms. Joyce and Mackenzie broke it down, when I wasn't sure if I would make it out okay, and Marigold's loud, desperate wails as the police took her from Florence on my lawn. She and Axel were reunited with an aunt in Bakersfield, last I heard, but I still feel that little girl's pain from that day deep in my chest. And that's why I don't like to think about it, even though it had a happy ending. Even though I solved the case, did what the detectives couldn't do. Even though Hank and Florence are locked up and will never be able to get close enough to hurt me again. All the fear, all the danger, that led up to that is still there, as if it's trapped in my cells.

My heart starts to race, and I know I need to anchor myself in the present. *List three things you can see.* The soft petals of the bouquet Corey is holding. The paisley print of Ms. Joyce's blouse. A flash of familiar bright red hair—wait, *what*? I blink rapidly, trying to focus on the owner of that hair, but whoever it was is gone. Vanished. Did I . . . imagine that hair? Is this a brand-new I'm-losing-it symptom? Hallucinating my long-gone former friend? God, the heart palpitations and tight chest were enough . . .

Corey's fingers brush against my back, just barely, and that snaps me back to right here, right now, much faster than the strategy from Google I can never seem to get all the way through. Dad and Ms. Joyce continue their back-and-forth about securing the best seats, so he whispers, just to me, "I forwarded that list of referrals from my therapist. Did you get them?"

"I did. I actually, um, have an appointment. For next week."

I never thought I would be willingly seeing a therapist. Just a couple of months ago, Corey even saying the word *therapist* in my presence would have made me lash out. But once I accepted that it was a panic attack that nearly took me out after a *real* attack . . . well, I finally asked for help. Amateur lawn yoga and Tanya on the meditation app and calming strategies from

Google can only do so much, clearly. Jasmine, Dyvia, and Jack all offered to help me look, but it was Corey who asked if it might be easier for me to open up to a Black therapist specifically. And he got a list of referrals from his own, because a Black therapist was surprisingly hard to find in network. I have my insurance from Project Window for a little while longer, and then . . . that makes my heart race, too. But it's okay. I'll figure it out from there. I *also* need to figure out what it means, Corey helping me like this, making me feel like this, when I'm with someone else. That's something else I can talk to Charlotte Green, LMFT, about next week.

"Oh, they're opening the doors."

"You take the right side, Elijah, and I'll take the left. Whoever finds the best seats, just lie on across them until we regroup. Don't let Little Miss Pink Sign tell you nothing."

I feel a hand on my elbow, and I jump. God, I've got to stop doing that.

"Ms. Miller. I was hoping to talk to you," Principal Smith says, his thick mustache lifting in a smile as I turn around. Okay, so the jump was valid.

"Does it have to be right now?" Or, like, ever? I nod toward the line in front of us, where people are slowly starting to move forward. Miss Joyce is bouncing in place, like she's about to compete in a 100-yard dash.

"I promise I won't take too much of your time," he says, and I want to say no immediately, but I stop myself. A quick chat now is better than another uncomfortable meeting in his office, whatever this is about. I nod that it's okay to Dad, Corey, and Ms. Joyce. She looks like she wants to hang back and fulfill her security detail duties, but her desire to beat Tricia must take over, because a second later she's gone, Corey and Dad struggling to keep up.

"What is it, Principal Smith?" I ask, stepping over to the side.

Maybe he's going to apologize, finally, for even having the nerve to think it was me poisoning Mr. Forest, now that we know for sure it was Florence. Not to mention Trisha blackmailing Mr. Forest and Bethany trying to scam money out of the school. *I'm* not the parent who's a problem.

"You were right." That's a good start. "Word got out that I might be canceling extracurriculars, before I could even put together an official statement myself, and there was a five-hour parent sit-in in the school rose garden—did you hear about that? They chained themselves to the bushes. And I can't prove that it was a Knoll parent, but someone left a burning chessboard on my driveway."

I hold in a laugh. Again, *I'm* not the parent who's a problem.

"So, it seems as if I can't cancel the programs completely, but the fact remains that it's too much for me to handle." He clears his throat. "And that's why I would like to ask—"

I hold up a finger. "I'm gonna stop you right there, Mr. Smith. I have enough on my plate, and I am no longer adding anything else. I'm doing plenty for the school as it is, and I can't continue to get involved in everything just because you guys can't get it together. I need to focus on myself and Pearl, and that's it." I may not have had my first appointment yet, but I don't need therapy to teach me that saying no, setting firm boundaries with all this Knoll Elementary mess, is going to be the first step to a more peaceful, present life.

"I understand," Principal Smith says with a grimace. But I can see his eyes working, that he's going to try and argue his point more. And maybe I should just walk away before he gets a chance to do that. I've worried so much about being polite and likable with everyone at the school, all of the parents, but look where that's gotten me? A couple of solved crimes, yes, but also people trying to kill me and panic attacks and maybe red-hair hallucinations now? It's not worth it. "Of course, I understand, Ms. Miller. We can't keep using your advice and, uh, *expertise* in dealing with Knoll parents for free. But what if I paid you? For a more permanent arrangement?"

My mouth drops open. *Pay me?* Is this what happens when you set boundaries? Could I have been getting *paid* all along?

"I have talked to the district about our issue here at Knoll, and they agree," he continues. "We need someone who can take on this issue full-time. Support our staff, keep parents in line. And most importantly, develop an after-school program that is inclusive and equitable—that reflects the needs and interests of all students at Knoll, not just the ones with the most, uh . . . involved parents. I've seen the great work that you and Dyvia have done with the PTA's DEI program and the wonderful changes it's brought to our school. I'd love to see what you could do for Knoll as the official Director of After-School Programming."

I don't know what to say. Is *this* a hallucination? Because how is this man just offering me everything I've been looking for, but not finding, in my frustrating weeks of job-hunting? A schedule that allows me to be present with Pearl, a chance to be creative and innovative instead of following someone else's orders. Instead of just doing the admin, converting Word docs to PDFs while someone else makes the decisions, I could be making a real difference myself.

"I've heard from your daughter that you're unemployed." Lord, why does this child keep telling the whole world my business? "And we can offer you a competitive salary, great health benefits. We're anxious to have someone start soon, but I can email you the terms, let you think it over."

"Yes . . . I'd need to think it over." I wonder if those benefits include therapy.

"The position is set to go out internally next week . . ." And massages—Jasmine told me she gets fucking *massages* covered with her insurance. That's one self-care thing I haven't tried yet. ". . . but I told the district I'd like to hold it for you if you're interested—"

"I'm interested." I know I shouldn't look so eager. I know I should leave room for negotiation. I've read all the articles on LinkedIn. But my brain is already spinning with ideas. A sliding pay scale to make sure every kid gets to participate. And I could bring in more people from the Beachwood community to be teachers—maybe Dom wants to start a kids' capture the flag league? And, oh, we could do a musical with more flavor next time, *The Wiz* instead of *Annie* . . .

"Wonderful." Principal Smith flashes a smug smile, like this was the outcome he expected, and the excited whir of ideas in my head stops. I've seen that smile before—I *know* who this man is. Do I really want to work with him? Just because he's offering me exactly what I want, what I *need*, as my savings quickly dwindle . . .

As if conjured by my own guilty conscience, right behind him I see that signal flare of red hair in the crowd of families again. My chest tightens.

"I think things will run much more smoothly with you keeping an eye on things, Ms. Miller," Principal Smith says, reaching out for my hand, a done deal. I shake his hand and smile like I'm supposed to, but as he walks away, my eyes are chasing that hair. So, I didn't imagine it before . . .

And it *is* that same red hair. Not Corinne, but her son— River. I haven't seen him or his brother, Mason, since their dad, Ben, pulled them out to be homeschooled for the rest of the year. They still live down the street, but they keep their distance from Knoll and Principal Smith—*of course* they do. I'm surprised they made an exception for *Annie*, of all things. Maybe one of their friends is in it? And does this mean Ben is here? Would it be strange if I said hello? I feel another wave of guilt. Oh god, did he just see me talking to Principal Smith?

River runs into the auditorium, and I realize it's clearing up out here. The show is going to start any minute. I can't think about the Ackermans—or this job, or what it says about me as a person if I take it—in this moment. I'm here to see my baby girl perform in her first musical, and that's it. Be present, be calm. And save all the rest of that for Charlotte Green, LMFT, next week. That lady better be good.

I walk through the double doors and quickly find Ms. Joyce waving for me. She managed to score the second row, just behind Trisha, and I scoot past Dad on the aisle with all of his equipment and sit in the open seat between Ms. Joyce and Corey. Corey's hand is twitching again at his thigh, and he's staring intensely at the burgundy curtains, biting his bottom lip.

"You good?" I ask.

"I'm fine." So *that's* what it looks like to everyone else when I try that lie. I arch my eyebrow.

"It's just . . ." he starts with a sheepish smile. "You know, before that last long note, how she sometimes forgets to take a breath? Do you think they'll let me back there for a sec, to remind her?" He starts to stand up.

"Oh my god, you cannot," I say, swatting him down with a laugh. "When did you become such a stage parent, Corey Harding?"

It started with them just playing around on the keyboard he got Pearl for her birthday, but soon Corey memorized all of her lines from running them with her and signed her up for biweekly vocal and piano lessons at his friend's studio. But they both love it—this new routine, how much time they're spending together. And Corey's actually going to start teaching drum lessons for kids at his friend's studio, too, on Monday and Wednesday evenings, which means he's putting down even more roots. Something I know is good . . . even if so much is still unresolved between us.

"*Okay. I guess* I won't force my way backstage," he says, laughing with me. His hands settle, and he sighs. "I just want her to feel good—proud, and like she belongs up there, you know? I want her to really believe, to know in her heart, that she belongs."

I know exactly what he means. And whatever is happening between us, it's nice to have someone here at a school event, worrying even more than me, after all the ones I did alone. It's nice to not carry it all by myself.

"Your little boo is trying to get your attention." Ms. Joyce pats my arm and then nods to the side of the stage, where Jack is peeking his head out. I feel Corey tense next to me. Thank you, universe, for that reminder of what *else* is unresolved.

Jack and I still haven't talked about the big things—what's next in our relationship, what's going on with his mom. The past few weeks have been so full, with me trying to get better, with helping Pearl through it all . . . it's been easier to just keep putting it off. He said he was willing to wait, that we could keep things right where we are, and I've taken him up on that. But I know this grace is not going to last forever.

Jack holds up a finger and disappears behind the curtain. Seconds later, he's back with Pearl in her orphan costume, a patchwork dress and dirt smudged on her cheeks. She squints around the big room until Jack gently turns her and points in our direction. We make eye contact, and her whole face brightens, like a shining spotlight. I feel lit up inside, too. Jack is smiling and

Corey is smiling, all of us just happy that this little girl is happy. And as the lights dim and the show begins, I try to push down all the unresolved things in my life—my relationships and my job and why the hell I keep finding myself in the middle of crimes I need to investigate—and focus on all that happy.

Pearl is a star. She delivers all of her lines and hits all of her choreography and basically carries "It's the Hard-Knock Life" when Anabella starts doing that whispery cursive singing again and the other orphans get confused.

But her big moment comes during "N.Y.C.," when she steps into the middle of the stage with a new costume: a blue trench coat with a matching hat and a suitcase clutched in her hand. I hear Corey take a sharp breath next to me in anticipation. This is what the two of them have been practicing over and over; this is what has his hands clutched tightly in his lap right now, like he can will everything to go perfectly. The Star-To-Be solo— originally Axel's, then Anabella's, and then finally reassigned to Pearl by Mr. Forest when he saw how hard she'd been working (and those kids' messy parents meant they couldn't have it).

She holds her head up high, but right before she opens her mouth, I see a flicker of uncertainty in her eye. My whole body braces, and my heart starts racing again—god, did it ever stop? It feels like the thing is going to jump out of my chest and into my throat. *You're okay, baby girl.* I try to send the message from my brain to hers. *You've got this.* But my brain is already speeding ahead to the worst-case scenarios: She runs off the stage in tears, she never sings again . . . she grows up into a sad, lonely old woman who hisses anytime she hears the *Annie* soundtrack. I don't even make the decision to grab Corey's hand. It just feels like the only thing I *can* do to keep me tethered right here in the present, to the only person feeling as nervous as me. He squeezes my hand back, then keeps holding it tight.

But she *is* okay. She's more than okay; she's remarkable. Her voice is bright and clear. She remembers to take a breath and hits that last long note better than she ever has before. And she has a presence up there on the stage—not just taking up space, but commanding it. She knows she belongs.

When she sings her last line, I pull my hand back to applaud, even though the song keeps going and Tricia turns to give me a dirty look. My eyes are teary as they follow Pearl's proud strut to the side of the stage, so it takes me an extra moment to blink the blurriness away and see Jack there, a sad smile on his face, his gaze locked on me and Corey.

Which . . . okay. We were holding hands. But it was just two parents watching their kid go through a big moment, helping each other through those feelings. I need to talk to him and explain, so he understands. He *has* to understand.

At intermission, I jump up out of my seat to find him—scooting past Ms. Joyce and Dad, calling over my shoulder for them to tell Pearl I'll be right back if she comes looking for me. And then I'm rushing over to the side of the curtains—this will be a quick, easy conversation. This is nothing.

But before I can get there, someone steps in front of me, blocking my way. I don't recognize Ben Ackerman at first. He looks . . . different. Greasy hair and dark bags under his eyes. His shirt is missing a button at the bottom, revealing an undershirt that's seen better days.

"Hi Ben. Wow. I haven't seen you in so long." My eyes dart behind him as a fifth grader in a bald cap, Daddy Warbucks, walks out from backstage. "Listen, I really want to talk, but can I just—"

"I have something for you, Mavis." He does a quick glance around him and then reaches into the pocket of his baggy jeans. "Here."

Before I can even decide if I *want* anything coming out of those jeans, he's already pressing a folded, slightly sweaty piece of paper into my hand. And by the time I look up to ask him all the questions that are starting to spin in my head, he's gone.

I need to find Jack, but I also need to know what this is—I need to *confirm* if it is what I think it is. Because I don't feel confusion when I unfold the note. Just resignation. It's like I knew this was coming eventually. I knew this couldn't be done.

On the paper is a phone number, and underneath it, in tiny, careful handwriting, is a message for me:

Mavis, please call.

ACKNOWLEDGMENTS

It was a strange experience to write a book about self-care and rest through extreme burnout and one of the worst flare-ups of my autoimmune disease. I needed to laugh so I didn't cry (though I did still cry a lot!)—I think that's why this is my funniest book. And I also needed therapy. My therapist of many years, Shavonne James, has helped me through the roller coaster of publishing five books in five years, which it turns out isn't great for the mental health of an anxious, perfectionist people pleaser. But I'm still here, still writing stories I'm proud of, because of the work we've done together. Shavonne, thank you for helping me to live the lessons I give my characters, and also reminding me to give myself grace when I need to keep learning them again and again because there isn't a finish line or a gold star in therapy (even though I really, really want that gold star in therapy). Thank you for teaching me that I deserve rest and compassion and care—not because I've earned them but because I'm inherently worthy.

My endless gratitude also to everyone else who's helped me to weather my health issues and find some peace and relief this past year: Dr. Noreen Hussaini, Shannon Kennedy, Dr. Mireya Hernandez, Yoga with Adriene, Jeff from the Calm app, Tricia Hersey, and Taylor Swift.

Taylor Haggerty, thank you for continuing to protect me and guide me and make space for the stories I want to tell. I constantly pinch myself at the fact that I'm able to support my family doing something I love so much, my literal childhood dream, and it's because of your brilliance and care that I can. I'm so lucky to work with you. Thank you also to Jasmine Brown, Melanie Figueroa, and everyone else at Root Literary, my perfect publishing home.

Debbie Deuble Hill, thank you for your work to bring my stories to even more audiences. You've made me dream bigger dreams.

Esi Sogah, I'm so grateful that I get to work with you. From the beginning, you understood Mavis and this series I wanted to create, and it's been a joy to continue building this world with you as my thought partner. Thank you to everyone at Berkley for being so good to me, especially Genni Eccles, Loren Jaggers, Kaila Mundell-Hill, Elisha Katz, Kalie Barnes-Young, Amanda Bergeron, Craig Burke, Jeanne-Marie Hudson, and Alicia Ross.

All of my love and thanks and armpit farts to the Yeomans family, especially Henry for naming the murderer during carpool and Ben for letting me watch one of his soccer games.

Thank you to my Girl Scout girls and their moms for showing me grace as I stumbled my way through being a troop leader and for so many good memories (none of which are reflected in this book): Neely and Tara, Marlo and Ryan, Lilou and Lindsey, Clara and Jocelyne, Vera and Vanessa, Liliana and Carly, Tenaya and Lindsey, Lila and Liz, Elodie and Deidre, Leila and Kay, and August and Heather.

Kyle Becker, thank you for creating such a safe space on your stage and making my kids feel so loved and seen. The Kids Theatre Company is at the center of so many of our family's best memories (again, none of which are reflected in this book).

Christina Hammonds Reed, thank you for all the advice and perspective and commiseration. I love that we give each other the pep talks we can't give ourselves. I'm so grateful this career brought me one of my best friends.

And thank you to the community of authors who have shown up for me in big and small ways over the past year, all of whom mean everything to me: Danielle Parker, Karen Strong, Julian Winters, Susan Lee, Brandy Colbert, Myah Hollis, Diane Marie Brown, Jade Adia, Leah Johnson, Tracy Deonn, Kristina Forest, Nikki Payne, Myah Ariel, Etta Easton, Nekesa Afia, Jason June, Megan Bannen, Alicia Thompson, Sarah Henning, Olivia Abtahi, Jamie Pacton, Emily Charlotte, Rebekah Weatherspoon, Ashley Winstead, Alison Wisdom, Anissa Gray, Anne Wynter, Marisa Kanter, Katryn Bury, Kwame Mbalia, Tembi Locke, Emily Henry, Lauren Billings, and Jasmine Guillory.

I love indie booksellers so much. You have been such champions for my work from the very beginning, making me feel like my voice has value and like I belong. Walking around your beautiful spaces continues to be my favorite thing to do. Thank you especially to Jhoanna from Bel Canto Books, Katherine from Grand Gesture Books, Tameka and Jazzi from Reparations Club, Teresa from the Ripped Bodice, and John from Murder by the Book. (Oh my god, John! I hadn't written the epilogue yet when I visited, and you asked a question that set my mind on a little adventure. You are responsible for that cliffhanger. Thank you!!!)

To my family, I don't know how to keep writing in different ways in each of my books how much I love you, but I'll keep trying! Mom, Dad, Bryan, and Rachal (and Eddie and Nora, too!), I love being a McCutchen. I love how we mess with each other and fiercely protect each other and always show up. Our story is threaded through all of these stories I get to tell now.

Mom, you especially are at the heart of this series. You've made me feel so confident I could write mysteries like the ones we love, and your feedback after each draft is my most treasured.

Joe, to be seen and understood and loved by you is one of the greatest gifts of my life. Thank you for letting me be my full self (even the prickly parts) and for meeting all of my wild dreams with just the right amount of caution before the eventual *okay, sure, fuck yeah!* You've never doubted that I could do anything I said I was gonna do, and that's made me feel empowered to take such beautiful, terrifying swings. I love our family and our life, and I love you.

Tallulah, my little editor, thank you for helping me to figure out this plot with your thoughtful questions and suggestions. Coretta, thank you for being the funniest person in the world, so Pearl can be the second funniest. I hope it's not weird when you grow up and read these books and see how much of both of you I've put in here. (The shit Post-it was just too good to not use!) I hope you always feel how much I love you, how starry-eyed and awestruck I am that I get to be your mom. Everything, always, is for you.

And my dear readers, thank you for coming to my events and making me feel a little less panicked about being perceived with your kind, encouraging smiles. Thank you for sharing my books online and checking them out from the library and reading them with your book clubs. Thank you for sending me the nicest messages ever and making me feel less alone in the world. I love writing for you.

THE GAME
IS AFOOT

ELISE
BRYANT

READERS GUIDE

ELISE'S SUMMER READING LIST

Rest Is Resistance: A Manifesto by Tricia Hersey

Mother-Daughter Murder Night by Nina Simon

Glory Be by Danielle Arceneaux

Happy Place by Emily Henry

What You Leave Behind by Wanda M. Morris

Before I Let Go by Kennedy Ryan

The Faculty Lounge by Jennifer Mathieu

Bluebird, Bluebird by Attica Locke

We Solve Murders by Richard Osman

Colored Television by Danzy Senna

1. Mavis asks, "Why is taking care of yourself so much labor?" Do you agree with this? Who gets to participate in the self-care industry?

2. Throughout the book, Mavis talks about constantly moving the goalpost before she can allow herself to rest. Can you relate to this?

3. Mavis gets annoyed and defensive when Jack gives her advice about taking care of her mental health. Why do you think this is? Is she being fair? Is he being overbearing?

4. What are Mavis's motives for trying to solve Coach Cole's murder? Do you think she wants to clear Corey's name, is trying to find a distraction like Jack suggests, or something else? Do you think she's justified in stepping in again? She claims it's helping her feel better—do you think this is true?

5. Mavis acknowledges her anxiety but doesn't take many active steps to manage it and is very resistant to therapy. Why do you think that is? Is therapy prevalent and accepted in some cultures more than others?

6. When talking to Dyvia about her "sabbatical," Mavis thinks, "people take breaks—but not my people." Why does Mavis feel guilty about taking a break from work and allowing herself time to rest? What do you think about Dyvia's advice to her?

7. Corey is trying to show up for Pearl and Mavis now that he lives in Beachwood. Why is Mavis so resentful of his help? Are his efforts enough to positively change their relationship now, considering their past?

8. Why is Mavis so delighted when she hears Florence and Hank arguing? Have you ever had a peek behind the curtain like this with someone in your life?

9. After job searching for the whole book, Mavis is finally offered a seemingly perfect position. Why does she feel conflicted about taking it? What do you think she should do?

10. Mavis gets a message from a mysterious source at the end of the epilogue. What do you think this person wants? Should Mavis respond?

Author photo by Joseph Sebastia Photograph

Elise Bryant is the NAACP Image Award–nominated author of *Happily Ever Afters, One True Loves, Reggie and Delilah's Year of Falling,* and *It's Elementary.* For many years, Elise had the joy of working as a special education teacher, and now she spends her days reading, writing, and eating dessert. She lives with her husband and two daughters in Long Beach, California.

Ready to find
your next great read?

Let us help.

Visit prh.com/nextread

Penguin
Random
House